The Wood Sprite
Second of the Wallowa Lake Thrillers
by James Dobie
Published 10/31/2023

I0678842

Table of Contents

This novel is dedicated to my loving parents, Ruth and Neville Dobie—may they rest in peace—who instilled in me at an early age a burning curiosity and a voracious desire to read and explore exciting new worlds.

Lastly, but certainly not least, my dear sister and Editor-in-Chief, Dianne Dobie. Without her infinite patience and constant encouragement, none of my novels would have ever seen the light of day.

James Dobie, 10/23/2024

Cover Design: SelfPubBookCovers.com/
DesignbyDanielle

Copyright © 2021.

Brief Accolades from Reviewers for "The Wood Sprite":

"Dobie knows how to deliver thrills and chills." Indie Book Rev.*

"Each chapter is a cliffhanger." Indie Book Rev.*

"The Wood Sprite is a wild ride." Audrey Gil, reader

"A compelling read for fans of paranormal mysteries and psychological thrillers, and one I would not hesitate to recommend." Readers Fav.*

'You can't stop reading despite the heart-pounding trepidation." Indie*

"Readers remain riveted to unfolding events and deeply connected to the characters." Literary Titan

"The nerve-wracking suspense kept me on tenterhooks." Readers Fav.*

"Dobie's narrative is refreshingly crisp and direct." Literary Titan*

"A captivating blend of suspense, mystery, and the supernatural." Readers Fav.*

"Promises a lively reading pace with succinct, gripping chapters that beckon you onward." Literary Titan*

"The suspense kept me turning pages as fast as I could." Readers Fav.*

*Quotes are from one reviewer each from: Independent Book Review, Literary Titan, and Audrey Gil, reader. Quotes from Readers Favorite Book Reviews come from three different reviewers. Complete reviews with reviewers' names are available upon request.

Acknowledgments and Dedications:

THIS NOVEL IS DEDICATED to my loving parents, Ruth and Neville Dobie—may they rest in peace—who instilled in me at an early age a burning curiosity and a voracious desire to read and explore exciting new worlds.

Lastly, but certainly not least, my dear sister and editor-in-chief, Dianne Dobie. Without her infinite patience and constant encouragement, none of my novels would have ever seen the light of day.

James Dobie, 9/01/2023

Chapter One – Taos, New Mexico

A brutal fist slammed into the young girl's face, knocking her off her feet. Stunned, she moaned softly, then gingerly picked herself up, inspecting the damage. The elbow she'd landed on was bleeding slightly, but her left eye had received the brunt of the damage and was already swelling from the savage attack.

Mia Chandler was petite, at five-foot-two and about a hundred pounds. She'd just turned sixteen—and she was damn weary of being a punching bag for that mega-bitch, Freda Ferguson. Freda had started hounding Mia in grade school with children's pranks, but soon realized she'd found a perfect victim, one who would not be provoked into retaliation.

Mia was not a fighter. She would've preferred to be invisible. She was a bookworm, kept to herself as much as possible. While other girls took up athletics or band, she escaped into reading books and playing classical guitar.

Close to the same age, Freda was heavier and almost a foot taller than Mia. Freda's petty harassment had grown nastier as they grew up. Now her rage erupted in sudden, vicious physical assaults during and after school, leaving Mia constantly anxious and fearful. She spent most of her energy and mental resources inventing creative ways to avoid Freda's arbitrary "meet-n-beats."

Worse still, this term she and Mia shared gym class during final period. That meant Freda could easily stalk her after class and catch her off-guard. Today, Freda and her two flunkies had hung around outside after school so Freda could attack Mia as she walked out, unobserved by any faculty.

Seeing her upright again, Freda taunted, "Go on and cry, dick face, you know you want to." When Mia was silent, Freda shrugged and turned to join her toady friends, Jessie and Brianna, for a quick toke before the bus ferried them home to the trailer park.

Ignoring them, Mia quickly brushed leaves and dirt from her hair and clothes. Gathering her scattered notes and lessons laying helter-skelter on the ground, she shoved them all hurriedly into her worn backpack. Spotting her math book face-down in a puddle, she cursed quietly. *Shit!* She'd be paying for another one from her meager allowance.

Mia attracted bullies like flies to shit—had, as far back as she could remember—due in part to an unusual birthmark on her right upper cheek. Her mother said it was an "angel kiss," but Mia called it an angel curse. Unfortunately, the port-wine stain's shape resembled a penis. Though it was less than two inches long, she felt "dick face" was etched under it. With no close friends, school was for Mia a hard, lonely place, made bearable only by a few teachers, math, and her music. While her shy, quiet reserve was most likely the reason for her loneliness, not her facial blemish, Mia couldn't see that.

Aside from occasional titters, most of the boys in school merely seemed indifferent. The small cliques of girls who mocked her with sly glances, smirks, and snide remarks as she passed them were more difficult to ignore. Then, of course, there was Freda.

To give herself a few moments of calm before she met her mother, she set the weighty backpack on the ground. With shaking fingers, she smoothed down soft, mahogany curls that framed her heart-shaped face and helped to hide the birthmark—but sadly, not her swollen eye.

Shouldering the backpack, she sighed and trudged across the schoolyard to her mother's car parked nearby. Mia considered most of high school as a training ground for future assholes and sociopaths. Her mother often said sarcastically that Mia was "sixteen going on thirty," but if this was what it felt like to get older, she wanted no part of it.

With a sigh, she opened the car door, tossing her backpack in the back seat. She climbed in front beside her mom, wishing she could duck the coming confrontation, but there was no hiding the dark blue, swollen eye.

Mary Jane—MJ, for short—stared at her face for a long moment with frustrated anger. "Jesus, Mia, what happened this time, sweetie? You can't seem to stay away from trouble. I know you didn't start it, so what's the story?"

Mia turned and glared angrily at her mother. "The same freaking thing that always starts it. I hate this school; they all look at me the same way. I have no friends. The boys stare at me and snicker; don't even get me started on what some of the girls say about me. I despise them all. I hate my life." Tears flooded her cheeks as she turned away, staring out the window as they drove in silence.

They'd had some version of this conversation since the first grade. Before she started school, Mia hadn't noticed her birthmark. The ridicule of her peers had made her hyper-aware of it, so that now, she even avoided mirrors.

"This bullshit has got to stop, Mia," her mother said angrily. "You're going to tell me who did this to you, and I'm going to file charges against them this time. Was it that little Freda bitch again?"

Mia shrugged, turning toward her. "She's anything but 'little,' Mom—and all you'll do is make matters worse. If you do that, the asshole and her gang of half-witted trailer trash will just find some way to make me suffer more. Payback is a bitch. Have you completely forgotten what high school is like?" she asked skeptically.

MJ was flustered. She did, in fact, remember her high school days. It never took much for girls to say or do hateful things to one another, especially when they were part of a clique. They sensed one another's weakness or imperfections like sharks smelled blood in the water. She sighed, shaking her head sadly.

"Yeah, I remember. Teenage girls can be wicked—it's just an unfortunate fact. But I don't know what else to do, Mia. Do I have to wait 'til one of them puts you in the hospital before I call a halt to this crap? What's it gonna take to make it stop? I know you don't want to fight, but at some point, you'll have to defend yourself or end up crippled ... or worse," she finished. She pulled into the driveway of their aging one-story home and parked.

Mia didn't respond, grabbing her backpack out of the car, slamming the door shut. She marched up to the front door, unlocking it with her own keys.

"You'd better put an icepack on that eye, or you won't be able to see out of it tomorrow, Mia Lynn," MJ called out, as Mia disappeared inside.

Slogging to the kitchen, Mia snagged a small, blue, frozen gel pack from the freezer, slamming the door so hard several refrigerator magnets fell off. She rushed to her bedroom, where the poster on the door read, "You can check out anytime you like, but you can never leave." Slamming the door shut, she nearly caught her cat's tail in it as he zipped through the doorway and leaped onto her bed. Frodo wasn't super sociable, but he gave her the essential three C's: comfort, calm, and companionship.

Dropping her backpack on the floor, she flopped down on the bed, bouncing the cat slightly, which fazed him not at all. Slapping the cold pack over her eye, she winced. Gazing at Frodo as he curled up at her feet, she plugged in her earbuds and listened to music until the left side of her face was numb from the cold. Still pissed, she threw the warm ice pack against the far wall, where it slid to the floor with a sad *plop*.

Gary, her dad, would be home soon from the gift shop he owned. Then the fun and games would begin. If he'd been drinking, a coin toss could decide whether he'd be Dr. Jekyll or Mr. Hyde. On the good nights, he mostly ignored her. But on the bad ones ... she might have the white-hot spotlight, center stage.

"Yea, though I walk through the shadow of death, I shall fear no evil." But Mia did. She knew evil came in different shapes and sizes. It might be the smiling pious priest, or the trusted gynecologist; the day-care worker who smilingly took in toddlers to abuse; the fast-food worker who spat on your food.

Then there was her dad. Mia believed evil, like the mythical Pandora's box, patiently lurked, waiting for someone to open its metaphorical lid—say, the cap on a bottle of whiskey. The bottle was harmless as long as it stayed sealed. But when her dad drank, it turned into Russian Roulette. The best she could hope for on those nights was that the hammer fell on an empty chamber.

Mia sighed, resigned that when he saw her swollen eye and face, he'd go ballistic on her ... or not. He always kept MJ and her guessing. She only hoped that he'd had a good day at his store.

GARY CHANDLER WAS HAVING a shitty day—literally. His employee had quit with no notice, he'd caught a kid shoplifting, and now, he was mopping the shop's bathroom. The damn toilet had backed up and overflowed, leaving turds floating in murky water on the floor like small, brown battleships.

"Gary's Gifts and Curios" was his latest—and last—endeavor running a small business. As long as he could remember, the entrepreneur bug had gripped him. Five years earlier, he'd bought this shop from an old man who wanted to retire, and he moved his family from the sweltering summers in Texas to the drier, cooler climate of this high desert community of Taos.

He'd failed with several different businesses in Texas. Having sunk the last of his meager savings into the present shop, he lacked the financial resources to start over again. Business had been mediocre for most of the last year. He was not an adept salesman—and he wouldn't take advice from anyone who *was*. And like many with fragile egos, he could not, would not, take responsibility for his failures, always finding someone or something else to blame.

He needed a way to find and attract buyers from other states to whom he could export his goods. But when Mia had offered to build him a website to sell his goods online, he'd told her to mind her own damn business. What would a sixteen-year-old kid know about creating and running a website, for God's sake?

As he cleaned and mopped the bathroom floor, he cursed the fat jerk who'd left a hefty deposit in his toilet. Finishing, he glanced at the clock on the wall: 5:00 p.m. on the nose. *Fuck it! Gonna close early. After this crappy day, I deserve a fucking drink*, he thought eagerly.

He was putting the mop away when the little bell over the front door chimed. He looked up as an ancient Native American man dressed in an expensive, three-piece suit entered, carrying a wooden figurine about two feet tall. The piece he held was shaped vaguely like a man with small branches for head, arms, and legs ... no, more like a woman, as what could be tiny, pointed breasts also protruded from its surface.

Gary wasn't happy to have anyone show up at the last minute when he was ready to close. "Hi, what can I do ya' for?" he asked peevishly.

The elderly man stared at him a long moment, then sauntered slowly over to where Gary stood, stopping in front of him.

"Afternoon. Actually, it's more like what I can do for you." His voice sounded gravelly, unused.

Now Gary came to attention, as he eyed the figurine in the old man's hands. "Sorry, but I was just closing up for the day. If you could come back tomorrow, I—"

The elderly man cut him off. "Mr. Chandler, have you ever heard of a 'spirit totem?'"

"It's some, uh, Indian thing, right? Something to do with animals, or some shit?" Gary was irritated and becoming uncomfortable under the visitor's intense gaze. *What strange looking eyes he has.* He took an involuntary step back.

The old man seemed to sense his uneasiness, taking a step forward to close the gap between them. "Yes, It's an Indian ... *thing*, as you so eloquently put it."

His eyes cold and glassy as obsidian, he held the odd wooden figurine out to Gary. Reluctantly, Gary took it, scrutinized it, and saw it had a small, beaded necklace where its slender wooden neck would be.

Although the beads were quality turquoise, they seemed to absorb, rather than reflect light.

"Alright, how much?" Gary asked, impatiently.

"How much for what?" The old man seemed confused.

"How much do you want for the ... thing?" Gary snapped.

Leaning forward almost into Gary's face, the old man's face was solemn. "I'm sorry, I have given you the wrong impression—it's not for sale. It is ... a gift," he said.

Gary smiled skeptically, "A gift? What for? I don't even know you, Mister ...?"

"My name is not important. This gift is not for you. It's *meant* for your daughter." A feeble smile showed.

Gary's temper flared. "How the hell would you even know I have a daughter, 'Chief?' Even if I do, why would I give her an ugly piece of wood from a total stranger?"

Ignoring the slur, the visitor leaned in closer to Gary, their faces only inches apart. "Because I asked you to. Nicely," he asserted in his gravelly whisper, as his rheumy, dark eyes seemed to suck the light from the room.

Without warning, Gary had an urgent need to use the toilet; his bowels rumbled and gurgled. He farted loudly.

The old man took a step back, with another mirthless smile. "You go do your business." He nodded toward the back of the store.

Gary didn't argue, rushing to the can, and slamming the door. He hastily pulled his pants down and plopped onto the toilet seat with relief as his bowels exploded.

He was sweating from the strain as he heard the raspy voice through the door. "You know, you really should check for ass-wipe before you sit."

Giving the closed door a nasty look, Gary glanced over at the toilet paper dispenser with disbelief and despair. *Shit!* He'd put a new roll on only that morning. *What the hell?* Then he remembered the earlier overflow. Obviously, that guy had used up all the paper. To prevent theft, Gary didn't keep extra rolls in the restroom. Now he was screwed. Another wave of misery rolled through his bowels and was violently expelled, leaving behind a disgusting smell. He groaned, wishing with hindsight that he'd closed the shop just five minutes earlier. *Damned old Indian!*

Flushing the toilet, he looked around for anything he could use to wipe his butt. Spotting no substitute, he removed his pants and used his briefs. He tossed the dirty underwear in the trash and rinsed his hands, drying them hurriedly on his pants, and left the restroom.

The old man was gone. The wooden figurine lay on the counter by the cash register. Gary rushed over to the cash register. Thank God, his cash was all accounted for. He closed and locked it. Then he noticed the note sitting next to the totem. It read, 'Mr. Chandler, please tell your daughter this will help to protect her from evil. She must give it a name. I'll see you again. Soon. Good day to you.' Nothing more.

Gary shook his head, tossed the note into the trash, snatched the strange piece of wood, and left the shop quickly, locking the door behind him.

MARY JANE CHANDLER was only in her mid-thirties, but the attractive young woman she'd been was buried now under a constant, harried look. She watched as bills piled up while her husband worked less and drank more. When he drank, he vented all his frustration and anger on her and Mia, becoming verbally abusive to both.

She had long since recognized that the man she'd felt compelled by circumstances to marry in haste was not a good husband, provider, or father—not a particularly good man, period. She'd stuck it out only because of Mia. Having never held a job, MJ knew she lacked the skills to earn a decent living for herself and her daughter.

Sighing, she tied her shoulder-length, brunette hair back with a scrunchie and turned to remove a badly overcooked meatloaf from the oven, as her phone chimed with a text from Gary. Grabbing an oven mitt, she set the scorched Pyrex dish on the stove. Wiping her hands on a dish towel, she picked up her phone to read his message, *'MJ, stopping by store. Then will head home. Got a gift for Mia.'*

Fucking great! She frowned. The only "store" Gary ever walked into was the liquor store. That would be the icing on the cake, as far as her day was concerned. She could already picture the approaching storm. *When he sees Mia's face, he'll go ape shit."* MJ walked to her daughter's closed door.

"Mia, your dad's on the way home. FYI, he's stopping by the *store*. You could try some of my makeup base around your eye ... might make it look better, is all I'm saying." Shaking her head, she marched back to the kitchen to stare in disgust at her miserable excuse for a meatloaf, silently cursing Martha Stewart.

Instantly, Mia knew the big "Wheel o' Misfortune" was already spinning—with her name on it. It was only a matter of when and where it stopped. She'd find out soon enough, she supposed.

She took out her earbuds and got up, opened her bedroom door, and nearly tripped over Frodo, as he shot through her legs headed straight for the dining room. Mia sniffed the air and groaned—burned meatloaf again. Her poor mother tried, but she couldn't cook her way out of a wet paper bag.

Mia got some of her mother's makeup and went into the bathroom, staring coldly at the face in the mirror. Although her birthmark was all she saw, she was attractive, with a small, straight nose and a generous mouth. She had big, brown eyes ringed with gold and framed by dark lashes and brows that matched her hair.

The icepack had helped, but her eye and the surrounding cheek were still puffy, with the bruised look of a gathering thunderstorm. Gingerly, she applied the makeup as skillfully as she could. She'd tried using it to cover the birthmark before, with no real benefit. The purple bruising around her eye was now a bit paler, but the swelling was clearly visible.

Shit! He's still gonna see it, she thought, leaving the bathroom. She walked into the kitchen, glanced at the charred hunk of meatloaf on the stove, and immediately lost her appetite. Her mom was busy tossing a salad. *She should just toss it* all *into the garbage,* Mia thought dejectedly, slumping into the living room recliner to await her dad's arrival.

"Mia, I-I think it would be better if we, uh, you didn't tell him about what happened today, unless he presses you on it. No need to stir the hornets' nest, so to speak." Nervously, MJ dropped a cherry tomato on the floor. Frodo instantly pounced on it, swatting it into the living room where it rolled under the couch.

"I used some of your base, but it won't matter. I'm not hungry, Mom. Getting the crap beat out of you tends to do that," Mia said sarcastically.

"You need to eat. No wonder those girls pick on you, you're skinny as a rail," MJ said absently, nearly slicing off the tip of her index finger as she rabidly chopped up a carrot for the salad.

Mia turned and looked at her, shaking her head, "That's not the reason, and you know it. How would you like being called dick face, or worse, every single day of your existence—it's horrible! I hate my face," she cried. Jumping to her feet, she ran back to her room, sobbing.

Safe in her own room, Mia tried to distract herself from the upcoming tumult. She thought back to her childhood, when things had seemed better. She remembered testing as "gifted" early on. Reading Dr. Seuss by age three; at five, she had finished most of the "Harry Potter" series. There'd been no awful stares back then. Music and math were second nature to her, and by eleven, she'd already been proficient in high school math and science. Though she could've easily passed college SAT tests, she was still a high school junior. The school administration had denied permission for her to take advanced placement exams—which angered her mother—but Mia had begged her not to push the issue, so MJ had reluctantly backed off. Mia figured if the ugly whispers, stares, and stress were this bad in high school, it could only be worse in college. She didn't look forward to that.

With a deep sigh, she fell back on her bed to await her father's arrival.

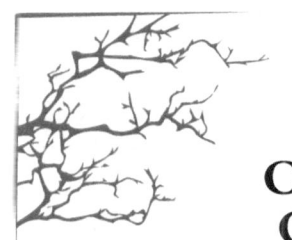

Chapter Two – The Chandlers' Home

Gary pulled into his driveway and glanced into his rearview mirror. His reddish-brown hair was already thinning, and he was only forty. His nose was rosy, as it always got when he'd had a few. He had a florid complexion and even features, but he'd always known he was not truly handsome. In the past, his biggest asset had always been his gift of gab, but it sure hadn't helped him lately.

He parked his twenty-year-old Jeep next to his wife's two-year-old Lexus. *Life just ain't fair,* he grumbled to himself, looking at the Lexus MJ's father had sent to her at Christmas. She'd wanted to reject the expensive—and very unusual—gift, but Gary had persuaded her to keep it so she could run errands, transport Mia to and from school, and he would have his old Jeep to himself. *It's obvious she married down,* he thought sullenly, as he got out of the Jeep, taking another gulp of whiskey before stuffing the more than half-empty pint of "Old Grandad" inside his back pocket.

He'd known Mary Jane came from a wealthy family. Her father was worth millions, CEO and owner of one of the largest cat food manufacturers in the U. S. But she'd never boasted or cared about it, nor was she materialistic. In fact, she deliberately avoided contact with her father, only allowing him to come to see Mia, his only grandchild, for a few hours once a year.

Gary reached into the back seat, hesitating before picking up the odd wooden figurine the creepy old Indian had given him with *instructions* to give it to Mia. *Given, hell!* He'd felt *compelled* to take the damn thing. Something terrible hid behind that old man's cold black eyes that froze the very marrow in Gary's bones. If he never saw those eyes again, it would be too soon.

MJ heard her husband's car door slam and thought bleakly, *let the shit show begin.* Gary always wanted supper to be on the table the minute he walked in. Glancing up as he slammed the front door, she plated the carbonized meatloaf, along with lumpy mashed potatoes and the salad. He held what looked like a piece of driftwood, which he carelessly tossed onto the couch on his way to the table. Quickly, MJ placed a tumbler with ice in front of him as he yanked out a chair and half fell into it.

"Rough day at the store?" she asked, trying not to look as he pulled the half-empty bottle of whiskey from his back pocket and poured a generous shot into the tumbler.

He glared at her. "You wouldn't know a 'rough day' if it bit you in the ass," he snarled, as he downed the shot, slamming the glass down on the table for emphasis. "Yeah, you could say it was a shitty day." He sniffed, "You burn something for dinner again?"

Mary Jane took the insult as she always did, smiling through gritted teeth. "Your favorite: meatloaf *al carbon.* Extra crunchy, just the way you like it, hon." She turned away, rolling her eyes as she brought the ruined meatloaf over, plopping the dish down in front of him.

"Where's Mia? I gotta present for her," he asked, already slurring slightly. "Mia, get your scrawny ass out here. Right now," he yelled down the hallway toward her door.

A muffled shout came from the room. "I'm not hungry, my stomach hurts. You can eat without me."

At his best, Gary was not a patient man. When he drank, his fuse was extra short. He shoved angrily back from the table, marched to her door, and flung it open without knocking. When he opened the door, Mia was changing clothes and only wore a bra and panties. He stared a little too long at her body before averting his eyes and barking, "You'll eat with us, or you won't eat at all, young lady."

Embarrassed and angry, Mia averted her face and grabbed a pillow to cover herself. "Ever hear of knocking? I was just changing clothes, for God's sake."

"This's my house, I come and go wherever, whenever I want. Hurry up, dinner's getting cold. Oh, yeah, I got somethin' for you, it's, ah ...

anyway, you'll get it after you eat your dinner, all of it," he snapped, turning unsteadily to leave.

Mia had no idea what he was talking about. She pulled on an old, oversize Mickey Mouse t-shirt and a pair of shorts, mentally bracing herself for the tsunami once he got a good look at her face. *To hell with it!* she decided, wandering slowly into the kitchen.

The odor of charred meatloaf that hung in the air was even more nauseating than when she'd smelled it earlier. She pulled an old wooden chair out from the table, intentionally scraping it on the old linoleum floor, and sank down to await her dad's reaction to her swollen eye and face. Her mother gave her a warning look, shook her head, and quickly mouthed "no."

Ignoring Mia's arrival, Gary picked up the carving knife and struggled to hack his way through the meatloaf. He dumped a slice on her plate, where it sat like an oversized piece of charcoal.

Yum, Mia despaired, as she helped herself to a couple pieces of limp lettuce and a spoonful of lumpy potatoes. Dumping them on top of the burned meat, she tried to bury it from sight and smell.

Gary slapped a slice on her mother's plate and then his own. Hungrily chowing down, with his first bite, he felt a molar break. *Shit!* Irately, he spat out the meat and the piece of tooth, both landing with a *splat* on the floor.

Frodo was on dropped food in a heartbeat. The cat snagged a quick bite of the lump and swallowed. Looking up unhappily at Gary, he *hurked* it back up—right on top of the breadwinner's shoe. Shaking his head, the cat ran to his water dish, lapping feverishly to get the taste out of his mouth.

"Fuckin' meat! Fuckin' cat!" Gary growled, pushing away from the table, and grabbing his almost empty bottle. "You'd think you coulda learned by now how to cook a simple fuckin' meal just once in your life without burning it, MJ," he ranted.

Muttering, he shoved the nasty mess off his shoe, picked out the piece of broken molar from it, and wobbled over to the sink to wash it off, leaving the rest for his wife to clean up.

"Sorry, Gary, but you knew I couldn't cook for shit when you married me," Mary Jane snapped back. She gave Mia a tight smile, pointing to her plate. "You don't have to eat it, Sweetie, I know it looks and smells like crap."

She nodded when Mia asked quietly if she could be excused. As the teen turned to leave, she spotted the odd-looking wooden object on the couch where her dad had tossed it.

"What's this?" she asked, walking over to examine it.

Momentarily distracted from his tooth, Gary said, "Some ole Indian brought it in as I was closin' up. Said I should bring it 'specially to *you*. He seemed … real pushy about the whole deal. Yeah, called it a 'spirit totem' or some shit, s'posed to protect you from evil. Pretty sure the old guy was crazy, jus' took the crappy piece'a wood to get rid of him," Gary lied. He winced as his tongue probed around and touched the broken molar.

"Did he say why?" Mia asked curiously, looking at the figurine.

Through an alcoholic haze, Gary tried to remember. "Nah, he jus' said you had to give it a fuckin' name, or shome shit. No more ques'ions, take the damn piece'a wood or I'll throw it in the trash. Now I gotta call the damn dentist," he barked irritably, flopping in the recliner to make the call.

Mia picked up the wooden figure and inspected it. It was feminine in shape, with tiny, natural projections where eyes and breasts would be. She examined the petite turquoise necklace encircling its slim neck. The semi-precious stones on it looked highly polished, but they seemed to soak up the light. With the figurine in hand, she walked back to her room and sat on her bed, thankful her eye had escaped her father's notice thus far.

Let's give you a name. "I think I'll call you Wendy. Wendy, the wood sprite. You look more like a sprite or a nymph than a totem." She stood the figure upright on its slightly crooked, wooden legs on her dresser, leaning it against the wall.

As she turned away, she could have sworn the little figurine moved. Shaking her head, she backed quickly away from the wooden effigy, as something brushed up against the back of her leg, startling her.

She whirled around and looked down to see Frodo staring up at her with a look that said, *'Watch it, you almost stepped on me.'* Mia laughed, dismissing her nervous moment. She leaned down and picked up the fat cat, hugging him to her chest.

Frodo did not like to be held. She was the only one he tolerated holding him, and only for a brief cuddle. Looking up at her, he let out a growling mewl, his signal to release him or she'd wish she had. She sat him at the foot of her bed, watching as he curled up into a ball so tight his furry tail completely covered his head. When she heard her parents begin arguing, as they usually did when her father brought home a bottle, she closed her bedroom door. Plugging in her earbuds, she selected some Lady Gaga and cranked up her phone's volume as loud as it would go. Some of their verbal conflicts still bled through, but it was better than nothing.

She'd done most of her homework earlier during study hall, so she opened her current Dean Koontz suspense novel. After she had read for over an hour, she realized the loud voices from outside her room were gone. She put the book down, took the earbuds out, and listened; it was quiet. Strange, since her dad's nasty temper rarely gave out so quickly.

She got up and opened her door slightly to listen, but the living room and kitchen were silent. Nervously, she stepped into the hallway, noticing her parents' bedroom door was open slightly. Normally, after one of their fights, they shut the door and played loud music. Barefoot, Mia walked quietly closer to it. Curious, she reached out and slowly pushed the door ajar a bit more.

The first thing she glimpsed in the dim light was her dad's naked white ass, as he pumped her mom from behind on the bed. *Eeww! They're screwing like rabbits!* Mia was so embarrassed.

I should've known. I will never get that picture out of my head, she cursed to herself, hurrying back to her room, and shutting the door, as she tried to block out the sights and sounds of her parents' lovemaking. Worst, to Mia, was that her mom had seemed to be enjoying it. *How could she, with him? Ugh, adults are so freakin' weird,* she decided. She'd known for years that her parents had sex occasionally, but she certainly had no desire to have these kinds of intimate details. She needed to get that image out of her mind.

Reaching under her mattress, she pulled out a small beat-up tin container and placed it on her bed. She opened one of the small windows in her room, placing a small fan in the window and turning it to face the outside screen. Humming to herself, she sat on the side of the bed nearest the window, opened the small tin and produced a half-smoked joint she'd scored from a geeky-looking goth who sat in the back of her science class.

She lit it with the lighter from the box, inhaled and held the smoke, releasing it out the window in a blue cloud. This was her one, sporadic escape from grim reality, aside from reading. Mia took a couple more puffs, put the remnant back in the tin with the lighter, and shoved it far back under her mattress. She left the fan on to help clear out the funk as she shucked her shorts and T-shirt and climbed under the covers to read before going to sleep. An hour passed ... she pondered why it felt like two. The munchies kicked in, and since she'd had no dinner, she was ravenous. She turned off the fan and closed the window.

She pulled her long T-shirt back on, quietly went to the kitchen and took out some butter, two slices of cheese and bread. She knew how to cook a few things without turning her food to charcoal. She made herself a perfect grilled-cheese sandwich and had a glass of milk to wash it down. With her hunger sated, she made her way back to bed. She laid there, stoned, gazing over at the wood sprite leaning up against the wall. It seemed to stare silently back at her. She sighed, thinking wistfully about her painful lack of friends and the companionship she so badly craved.

"I wish you were real, Wendy," she murmured, as she fell asleep to the soothing sound of Frodo's purr.

A GROUP OF GIRLS LED by Freda Ferguson is chasing her. Freda corners her in the girls' locker room, smirking as she slowly cocks her fist back to punch her in the face. Suddenly a tall girl with jet-black hair steps between them. Motionless, she stands confronting Freda. Her face is not visible.

Freda's fist drops and the smug smile disappears from her face as terror fills it, her eyes bulging in their sockets. Her mouth opens in a silent scream. Her body begins jerking in spasms as her face starts melting like hot, running wax. Her skin dissolves, steaming as it slides viscously off what remains of her face, pooling at her feet in a gruesome pile of gore.

Freda's body slowly collapses in on itself, until only an amalgam of clothing, bloody bone and hair remain on the floor. The black-haired girl slowly begins to turn her head and ...

MIA AWOKE WITH A START, sweating, her heart beating hard. *What a strange, awful dream!* She sat up, squinted at the clock on her dresser. The soft blue glow read 6:30 a.m.

Trembling, she threw off the covers, ran to the bathroom and leaned over the toilet, throwing up the remains of her late supper. She flushed the toilet, rinsed her mouth with water and brushed her teeth vigorously until the nasty taste was gone.

Then she closed the bathroom door, slipped out of her clothes, and turned on the shower until it was steaming. She climbed in, shut the frosted sliding glass door, and let the hot water relax her as she soaped her body. Steam quickly filled the small room. As she was rinsing her hair, a draft of cold air made her look sharply toward the bathroom door. Steam was thick in the air.

"Hello? Who's there? I'm almost through, you can have it in a few minutes," she called out.

Seeing a shadow move by the door, she pulled the sliding glass back enough to peer out. The bathroom door was ajar, but no one answered. Shivering, as colder air poured through the open door, she got out and wrapped herself in a large towel.

Grabbing her clothes, she walked out. When she left the bathroom, the distinct odor of her dad's strong cologne hung in the air. She hurriedly padded to her room and shut the door.

An hour later, "Mia, almost time to leave for school, please come eat something," her mother shouted from the kitchen. Mia didn't "do" breakfast. Her mother didn't make breakfast any better than any of the other meals she tried to cook.

Mia gave a quick glance at the wood sprite as it stood where she'd placed it. It seemed to be smiling at her. *Don't be ridiculous,* she thought, *it doesn't even have a mouth.* Grabbing her backpack, she trudged into the kitchen to make herself a cup of coffee. Her mom's coffee was strong enough to stand up and walk.

Mia gazed disgustedly at the burned eggs sitting in a half-inch of oil in a skillet. Adding lots of milk to her cup, she slurped it down, "mmm, breakfast of champions." She set the cup in the sink. "Let's go."

Her mother shook her head, chiding Mia all the way to the car about her poor eating habits before returning to her main concern.

"Mia, if those girls threaten you in any way, you are to go to the principal's office and tell them what's been going on. Show them your face, and if they don't believe you, have them call me. This crap stops today—or I will by God file charges on that little Ferguson bitch so fast, it'll make her head swim," Mary Jane snarled, pulling to a stop in front of the school.

Mia mumbled, "Sure, Mom, whatever," as she got out, grabbing her backpack. "Thanks for the ride, see you later."

MJ watched anxiously as Mia walked into the building, safe for the moment, at least. Then she drove off to start her own day.

Chapter Three – Taos High School

Mia's first class was advanced physics with Mr. Shepard, and she only had three minutes to be there. She walked to her locker. Pasted on its door was a crudely drawn picture of a girl with a large penis sprouting from her face. Mia couldn't fathom the cruelty and hateful behavior of the kids who never tired of tormenting her. Angrily, she tore the drawing off, wadded it up, and threw it in the nearest trash can, hurrying on so she wouldn't be late.

Turning a corner toward her classroom, she was almost knocked off her feet, colliding with none other than Freda.

"Watch where you're going, you—oh, it's you, dickbreath. You must be a glutton for punishment." Freda had realized it was Mia she'd smashed into. She smiled wickedly, "Hope you liked your new yearbook picture hanging on your locker, bitch. Now get outta my way, or I'll—"

"Is there a problem here, girls?" a deep male voice directly behind Freda asked. Startled, she turned to see Mr. Shepard standing behind her, hands on hips.

Smiling benignly, she said, "Why, no, sir. I was just telling Mia what a great class you teach."

"Really? I don't recall having you in any of my classes."

Freda realized her error. "I-I don't take Physics, sir, math's not really one of my strong subjects."

He just stared at her, having noted the swelling and bruises on Mia's face. "I disagree. From what I hear and see, you excel in utilizing the principles of physics on an almost daily basis," he asserted, glancing at Mia.

Freda flushed with anger. "I don't know what you're talking about, *sir*. She's just clumsy, always running into walls and sh-stuff."

The first period bell rang. Mia looked anxiously at Mr. Shepard—now she and Freda were both officially tardy. He gave Freda a tight smile.

"I believe you're a tad late for your next class, Miss Ferguson. That's cause for detention. Please see me after last period," he told her, motioning for Mia to enter his classroom.

"I—that's not freakin' fair. What about her? She's late, too," Freda protested angrily.

Mr. Shepard gave her a sharp look, "I believe Mia was recently 'detained' by you and your friends. I think that's enough detention for her. I suggest you leave now, or would you like to push for a suspension?" he replied crisply.

Freda rolled her eyes but wisely kept her mouth shut, stalking angrily away.

Before entering class, Mr. Shepard took Mia aside. "Mia, you really need to report that girl to the principal. She's a menace not only to you but to the other students she and her minions harass daily. It only encourages her if no one reports her behavior."

Mia just shook her head. "I appreciate it, Mr. Shepard, but if it wasn't her, it would be someone else like her. Freda and her kind are 'school-roaches,' squash one, another takes its place. I guess I'm just a roach magnet." She pointed to the obvious birthmark on her face, "*This* attracts them."

He winced, nodding. "Still, if you allow them to continue with no consequences for their actions, you're going to end up hurt ... or worse." He motioned her to take a seat. His words echoed those of MJ the previous day.

The rest of that class went by in a blur for Mia. The bell rang, and everyone scurried out into the hallways. Some mingled and texted, others stepped outside to smoke, toke or to make out briefly before the next class.

Mia went to her locker, dialed the lock's combination, and pulled, but it didn't open. She tried again, with similar results. Then she spotted a coating of an opaque substance surrounding the hasp and entryway. *Super glue—shit!* Freda or one of her bitch friends, no doubt.

She gave up, rushed down to the maintenance room by the cafeteria and knocked. A tall, muscular, older man with a face like tanned leather opened the door and looked down resignedly at her.

"Yeah, kid? What is it?"

She smiled at him. "Some ass—I mean, some*one* seems to have super-glued my lock shut, could you please come cut it off so I can get my books for the next class?"

He saw the birthmark and the bruises on her face, shook his head, and grunted. "God, kids are assholes. Used to be one myself—a kid, that is. Let's see if I can help you get your books out."

He turned, rummaging around the back of the cluttered room, and came out holding a pair of red-handled bolt cutters. "This oughta' do it. Show me where your locker's at and we'll get you squared away pronto."

"Thank you, Mr., um ..." Mia hesitated.

"Just call me Sam, everybody does," he smiled.

Mia led him back to her locker. He cut the hasp on the lock and pulled it off the locker.

"There you go, Missy. Easy, peasy." This time he grinned.

"Thank you, uh, Sam, you just made my day." She smiled, opening her locker door.

To her disgust and humiliation, a small avalanche of nasty, used maxi-pads, tampons and rubbers poured out onto the floor. Kids nearby tittered, pointing. Sam was embarrassed for her.

"Fuckin' evil little ass-wipes," he muttered. Grabbing the nearest trash container, he ripped out the bag lining it and helped her scoop up the nasty mess as fast as possible.

Mia's initial discomfort spread; her heartbeat was rapid, she was short of breath, and her eyesight shrank to tunnel vision.

Panic attack—or else, I'm dying, she thought, as she swayed. Sam caught her before she hit the floor. Picking her up, he carried her down the hall shouting, "Clear the way. Move it, you little shits."

He fought through and carried her to the nurse's office. The second period bell rang as they arrived.

He kicked three times on the door, it opened, and he carried Mia into the office, gently laying her on the couch. He stood up, breathing hard, explaining to the nurse what had just transpired.

Emily Tucker was a middle-aged woman with short, dark hair and a kind face. She nodded and listened as he explained the booby-trapped locker and its contents.

Mia had begun breathing a little easier. She sat up, then felt nauseated, as the coffee she'd drunk earlier threatened to revisit her tonsils. Frantically, she pointed to a small waste can. The nurse caught her meaning in time to push it in front of her, as she leaned over and retched loudly, emptying her stomach's meager contents.

The sound of it was enough to make Sam's gag reflex kick in. He hurriedly backed out of the room.

Emily was accustomed to these things, but not immune. She took a deep breath before hurrying to a water cooler in the corner of her office. She filled a plastic cup and gave it to Mia, who took a grateful sip of the ice-cold water.

"Feeling better now?" Nurse Tucker asked.

Mia nodded, "Yes, a little, thank you. Think I'm okay, and I'd like to go on to my class now."

The nurse sighed, "I'm sorry that malicious prank upset you so. If it's any consolation, I'll report this incident to the principal immediately."

Mia shook her head vehemently, "I really wish you wouldn't. You think that will solve the problem, but it won't. The people doing it will just retaliate. As long as I have *this,* I'm always going to be a target." She pointed to her birthmark.

Nurse Tucker smiled compassionately. "You can't let that define who you are, Mia. Please listen to me, if someone doesn't punish these individuals for their actions, their abuse will continue to escalate. Believe me, I know, from personal experience."

With that, she rolled up the sleeve of her blouse—twisting and removing her right arm at the elbow. Mia's eyes widened in surprise at the sight of the prosthetic arm and hand.

Ms. Tucker continued, "I've been in your shoes, and I know all about the callous, vindictive behavior of teenagers." She told Mia briefly about the brutality that had caused her to lose her arm when she was a teen.

"I wish I could tell you it will get better sooner than later, but that would be a lie. What I will say is that you do always have a choice in how *you* respond to others' bad behavior. You can try to ignore it, or you can be proactive, do something positive about it," she finished.

Mia was silent for a moment. "I appreciate your sharing all that with me, and I'll think about it. You have to do what you need to do. But FYI, I'm the one who'll pay for it. I'm so freakin' tired of being a target. Now, may I please leave?" Mia stood.

The nurse smiled and nodded, "Of course. If you ever should feel the need to talk, I encourage you to come and see me. I realize that I'm not one of your Counselors, but as you see, I've lived through what you are experiencing now. You must choose your own path and walk it alone." She re-attached her prosthesis and gave her a permission slip to get into class. Mia thanked her and left her office, feeling bitter.

Sam was waiting for her in the hallway. "I hope the little shits that did this get expelled. Here, I got you a new lock, hopefully you'll have better luck with it," he told her, handing her the lock and its combination.

"Thanks, Sam, I appreciate your help."

She walked back to her locker and added the new lock, memorized the combination, locked it. Then she hurried to her chemistry class and walked in. Everyone was performing experiments with Bunsen burners, heating Pyrex test tubes full of bubbling, colored liquids.

Her usual lab partner was Casey Mitchell, a slightly overweight girl with wire-rimmed glasses and long red hair worn in a curly ponytail. For obvious reasons, everyone called her "Freckles."

Casey looked up from her flask, where whatever she was mixing smelled like burned hair. "You're late. I already started the experiment, but I'm sure you'll catch up." She frowned, as Mia took her seat beside her.

"I had locker issues," Mia said irritably, pulling out her homework. She caught Casey staring at the dark bruise around her eye, which makeup couldn't really cover.

"Looks to me like you've had 'Freda' issues," Casey commented dryly, dragging her attention back to her experiment.

"That, too. Listen, Freckles ... do you think you could trade places with me today for sixth-period gym?" Mia whispered.

"I don't know. Does it involve getting my butt beat or kissing toady-ass?"

"Shouldn't, as long as you don't look like me," Mia snapped back. "Coach Percy never takes a head count, she's too busy flirting with that hot teacher. She won't even notice if I'm there or not," Mia explained.

"Well, if she won't notice, why do you need me to take your place? In that case, just cut class. Besides, my history teacher is very attentive, and I sit up front. No way she'd mistake you for me." Casey rolled her eyes.

Mia saw the logic. *Shit!* There had to be some way to avoid going to her gym class with that Freda bitch. But exactly how, she wasn't sure. She sighed, watching the teacher, Mr. McFry, head her way. "Here's my homework and my hall pass for being tardy, sir."

McFry gave her a concerned look, then took both her homework and pass. "Okay, Mia, but please don't make a habit of being late. It's not fair to the other students if I must interrupt class for one student. You understand?"

"Yes, sir," she replied.

"I still expect your experiment's results by the end of period." He turned and walked briskly back to his desk to grade homework. Mia got busy and completed the assignment with time to spare. She glanced around the room, sensing a strange, oddly disquieting presence.

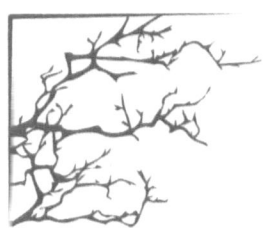

Chapter Four

A tall, lanky girl dressed all in black like a goth, she'd never seen before stared intently at her from a few desks away. She had long, shiny, black hair and the darkest eyes Mia had ever seen. The girl gave her a slight smile, then returned her gaze to her chemistry book.

"Hey, Freckles, who's the new fish?" Mia had already helped Casey to complete the experiment.

Casey sighed, pushed her glasses up on her nose to glance over at the girl, then back at Mia. "Didn't catch her name. I think I was in the can when McFry introduced her. If you're curious, ask *her* after class," Casey said.

McFry called out, "Time's up, all, leave your results or whatever you got finished on my desk; make sure your names are on your paper."

Grabbing her books, Mia stood to leave, gazing around for the new girl, who seemed to have slipped out already. *That's weird, how'd she move so fast?* Mia wondered, placing her results on McFry's desk on her way out. She looked up and down the hall for the tall, dark-haired girl but saw no one resembling her.

She shrugged and went on to her next class, stopping off at her locker. Her cell phone chimed with an incoming text: "U R Dead Meat, Dickface!"

Another pleasant warning from Freda. Mia's stomach churned with fresh nausea as she made her way to her classical guitar class. She was supposed to perform Mozart's "Rondo Alla Turca" for extra credit, and she knew it by heart. Yet when she got up on the small stage to perform, she drew a blank for a second.

Shit. All she could think about was her sixth-period gym class with Freda and her entourage waiting to inflict more misery.

Concentrate, damn it, she told herself. Taking a deep breath and closing her eyes, she heard the music in her mind and her fingers began moving, flying over the frets in fluid motion born of years' practice. She finished, and it was quiet. As she opened her eyes again, her fellow students stood and applauded vigorously. Mrs. Luedecke, her teacher, wore a big grin as Mia stood and made a tiny head bob, with a smile on her face.

"Wonderful, Mia. Perhaps a little bright on the arpeggio of the last progression, last movement, but fine, indeed," she said, as Mia resumed her seat.

She blushed bright red, unused to accepting praise she so seldom got at home. Her stomach growled again, reminding her it was almost lunch time. While two other teens played their pieces, Mia's attention roamed.

She couldn't stop thinking ahead to the day's last period, where she would be most vulnerable to an attack. If Coach "Pussy" would only pry her eyes off that shop class teacher, she might notice the animosity between Freda and Mia. But most of the teachers seemed so bored by their repetitious jobs, they became apathetic.

The bell ringing brought Mia out of her trance. She grabbed her backpack and headed for her locker, dumped her books, then walked to the lunchroom. When she got there, a fairly long line was ahead of her, but it was moving.

"Hey, Mia, thought you'd save me a place in line."

She turned to see Casey next to her. "Sorry, guess I forgot," Mia lied.

I have more important things to think about, she thought. She slid a tray onto the scuffed railing, skipping the "mystery" meat, opting for pizza and fries with a small carton of milk. She paid the cashier with a school-issued debit card and turned to find a seat, preferably as far as possible from the table occupied by Freda and her trolls.

Looking around, she spotted the tall dark-haired girl from her chemistry class sitting alone at a table away from Freda's group. Mia walked over, as the girl busily gnawed a chicken leg, never glancing up as Mia approached.

"Mind if I sit here?" Mia indicated the chair across from her. The girl stopped chewing, gesturing with the chicken leg to sit. Mia sat and took a bite of pizza, laboring to open the stupid milk carton without tearing it to shreds. When it finally ripped open, milk sloshed all over her plate. *Damn, I'm such a klutz.*

Casey walked up just in time to get splashed. "Smooth move, Chandler. That'll teach those milk cartons to mess with you." She wiped the front of her shirt with all the napkins on her tray.

"Sorry, I've had a shitty day, and it's not getting any better," Mia snapped, embarrassed, as she attempted to soak up the milk from her food. The pizza was edible, the fries were a total loss.

"Want some of mine?" The black-haired girl finally looked up, her dark eyes glittering.

For the first time, Mia could study the stranger's face. She appeared to be of Native American descent. Her nose was a bit aquiline in an otherwise beautiful oval face. Her eyes were deep-set pools of black.

"Thanks, appreciate it. My name's Mia Chandler. You're new here, right?" Mia asked, chewing on her slightly soggy pizza.

"I'm Wendy Ravenwood and, yeah ... guess I'm what you'd call 'new' here," she answered huskily, between bites of chicken.

A small shiver ran down her spine, as Mia noticed the girl wore a turquoise necklace encircling her long slender neck. *Something about her ...*

"Hi, I'm Casey Mitchell. Mia and I have Chemistry together," Casey sat down next to Mia.

"Yeah, I noticed," the girl said suggestively, licking the grease from her full lips with a smirk.

Casey turned bright red, making her freckles stand out more. "That's not ... what I—what I meant was, we're just lab partners," she explained, flustered.

Mia added, straight-faced, "Yeah, we're not even friends, really."

Casey elbowed Mia's arm, "I'll remember that the next time you forget your homework and need to copy mine." She was slightly hurt by Mia's actions.

"When can you remember I needed to do that, Freckles?" Mia casually took a fry from Wendy's plate and popped it in her mouth, chewing.

"Just saying, is all. Nice to meet ya,' Wendy. Wouldn't want to take any more of Mia's precious time to chat, see you later." Casey rose, dumped the remainder of her lunch in the trash, and left the lunchroom in a huff.

Mia felt the eyes of other students on Wendy and her as she finished her soggy, tasteless pizza. Wendy seemed unconcerned by Casey's sudden departure.

Then Mia saw Freda get up from her table of toadies, wandering casually toward her table. At the same time, Wendy stood up abruptly, turned, and walked out, leaving Mia alone at the table as Freda approached.

"Chased all your friends away, bitch? Oh, I forgot—you don't have any friends," she sneered, with a bogus smile. Several kids at the next table snickered as she plopped down in the seat across from Mia, staring daggers at her.

"You owe me for the fucking detention, cunt," Freda hissed, pulling a small double-edged switchblade from her pocket, popping its four-inch blade open menacingly. All teeth, she leaned over the table, the knife now underneath, out of sight. Mia was trembling so hard she thought she might wet her jeans.

"See you in sixth period, dick face. I'm gonna fuck you up … real bad. Maybe I'll use 'mama's little helper' and cut that prick off your face. Hell, you wouldn't look any worse," Her fake smile vanished as her arm jerked forward under the table.

Mia felt a sudden burning pain in her leg. Lurching backward in her chair, she let out a muted yelp of pain. Freda was already walking away, the switchblade no longer visible. Mia rubbed her right thigh where it stung—her hand came away with blood on it.

That damn, vicious bitch stabbed me, right in public. I wish she were dead! Mia cursed silently, standing, as kids stared.

Tears flowing, she ran out of the lunchroom, rushed to the girls' bathroom. It seemed empty, all the stall doors ajar. She hurried into the nearest stall, locked the door, and quickly pulled her jeans down to inspect the damage. Just above her knee was a small stab wound. As she watched, blood welled to its surface and ran down her thigh until she staunched it with a wad of toilet paper.

"You should really stand up to that bully, Mia." The husky voice from the stall next to hers echoed in the room.

Mia froze. Looking down, she saw a pair of black shoes and dark pants in the next stall. *But there was no one in here when I sat down, I'm sure of it. And the bathroom door hasn't opened since I came in.*

"W-who are y-you?" she asked. Silence.

Then, "Just ... a friend," was the reply. "Do you really wish Freda dead?" the voice asked soberly.

How did she know that? I only thought it, I never actually said it. Mia was puzzled.

"Thoughts have power, Mia. It's quantum physics, you know that. Some call it 'mind over matter.' You haven't answered my question."

Mia was stunned. *She can hear my thoughts!*

"I'd give anything to be rid of the horrible bitch!" she said sharply. "Nobody seems to give a shit what she does or gets away with. She just freakin' stabbed me!" She was shaking with a mixture of anger and fear.

A moment's hesitation. Then, "I'll need some of your blood. Just a drop will do." A slender hand reached under the stall, palm facing up expectantly.

Mia stared at the hand, skeptical that this surreal conversation was really happening. *But if it could really stop Freda ...* She felt she was having an out-of-body experience, as she watched her hand squeeze the small wound on her thigh, and more blood well up. Catching a drop on her finger, she reached down and pressed it against the cool palm of the extended hand.

She gasped, as a feeling akin to an electric shock passed between her bloodied finger and the other's palm. The droplet of blood disappeared as though drawn into a sponge, and the hand disappeared under the wall.

"W-what happens now?" Mia asked quietly.

There was no response. She heard the toilet next to her flush, the stall door opened, and the bathroom door opened and shut. She continued to sit there for a couple minutes, stunned by the entire experience, thinking she must've dreamed it.

Winding toilet paper around the puncture in her leg, she pulled up her pants and left the stall, all the while wondering, *what have I just done ... and with whom?* She washed the remaining blood from her fingers in the sink.

In the mirror, she saw her face was pale and sweaty, the birthmark on her cheek prominent. Suddenly, she felt nauseous and threw up her lunch in the sink.

The pizza didn't taste much worse coming up than it did going down. Mia thought sourly. She turned on the faucet to rinse her mouth, making a nasty pink soup in the clogged-up sink.

As she stood there, the bathroom door flew open, and Freda's two lesbian toadies, Jessie Gambols and Brianna Moon, entered laughing. Both were "Goth-wannabes," wearing black leather jackets with chains and butch haircuts dyed neon purple and green. The two stopped short when they saw Mia leaning over the mess in the sink.

"What's the matter, Dick Lips, the sight of your ugly puss make you puke?" Jessie sneered.

"She was probably sucking off old Sam and swallowed more than she could handle," Brianna snickered, as they moved to encircle Mia.

Mia wiped her mouth with the back of her hand and snapped, "Fuck off, you ass-lickers, or I-I'll ... I'll ..."

"You'll do what? I'll tell you what you're gonna do. You're gonna' have second helpings, you little bitch," Jessie snarled, pushing Mia's head down toward the sink while Brianna pinned her arms to her side.

Mia struggled to break free, fiercely twisting her head left and right, trying to escape the inevitable. Her screams were cut off when they pushed her face into the vile puke. Her nose was clogged, so she had to open her mouth to breathe. When she did, they forced her face deeper into the disgusting gunk.

Mia panicked. *Oh, God, I'm gonna drown in my own puke!*

Then the bathroom door opened, and the pressure on her neck suddenly vanished.

"What the hell are you two doing to her?" Mrs. Luedecke demanded angrily, seeing Mia's face and hair coated with vomit.

"We were just ... uh, helping her ... something she ate, I guess," Jessie shrugged, with a giggle, as she and Brianna exchanged uneasy glances.

Mrs. Luedecke frowned. "That's not what it looked like to me. Both of you report to the principal's office. Right now, ladies!" she barked, wetting paper towels to help Mia clean up as much of her face and hair as possible.

As they sauntered out the door, the two girls shot daggers at Mia. Still distraught, Mia thanked her teacher repeatedly for coming in when she did.

"I think they were trying to kill me, Mrs. Luedecke. I've never done anything to them. They were trying to drown me in my own puke. They're friends of that ... of Freda Ferguson." Her teacher hugged her and stroked Mia's hair as she began to weep.

"They'll get what they deserve, Mia, I promise you. People like them always do."

Mia described the details of Freda's earlier assault in the lunchroom to her teacher.

Mrs. Luedecke frowned, shaking her head. "They are all headed for serious trouble. You need to report this to Principal Sloan right now, Mia. If you don't, I will. These girls' actions have gone way beyond pranks—this is criminal behavior."

As she began to calm down, Mia groaned. She realized she had to respect her teacher's wishes. Sighing, she followed Mrs. Luedecke down to the principal's office. Mia sat down in a chair in the principal's outer office. She'd never been inside the principal's office before this. She remained scared, but as she thought about it, she became angry because none of this was her fault.

Behind the closed door, she heard raised voices and recognized Jessie and Brianna arguing loudly with Principal Sloan. Mrs. Luedecke knocked twice and went in, shutting the inner door behind her. Mia caught a glimpse of the two bullies crying—trying to appear contrite in front of Principal Sloan.

Crocodile tears, Mia thought sullenly. A few minutes later, the door opened, and the two teens filed out of the office. As they passed Mia, Brianna frowned and shot her the finger while Jessie drew a finger across her throat, pointed to her, and mouthed, "You're dead!" They left, stalking off down the hall.

Mrs. Luedecke motioned to her, and she walked inside nervously to sit in a chair in front of Sloan's desk. Her teacher closed the door.

"Miss Chandler, I'm told that you were physically abused by the two students who were just in my office. They've also implicated another student. From what I've gathered, this harassment has escalated over a long period of time. As you know, we have a zero-tolerance policy on bullying and physical violence. Do you wish to substantiate the allegations your teacher has described?" Principal Sloan inquired, leaning forward in his chair.

Mia was torn between telling him the truth and lying. She wanted the bullying to stop, but realistically, she was aware that even if she confirmed the accusations and charges were filed, these assholes would eventually return. Even if *they* didn't, "school roaches" were everywhere. Eliminate one, and two more took its place. Ratting the trio out was, at best, a temporary fix.

"I'm waiting, Miss Chandler, for your answer. Did these girls force your face into your own vomit, as Mrs. Luedecke has contended?"

She didn't tell him about Freda stabbing me. Mia thought fast, trying to decide how to respond.

"After thinking about it, it's possible th-they might've just been trying to help me after I got sick. I-I think the pizza I had at lunch disagreed with me, sir," Mia prevaricated smoothly. Glancing guiltily at Mrs. Luedecke, she caught the disappointed look in her music teacher's eyes as the lies tumbled out.

Mr. Sloan stared at Mia in uncomfortable silence for a minute before shaking his head.

"Miss Chandler, you do realize that you're not doing yourself—or anyone else these girls are preying on—any favors by not telling the truth? Short of catching them in the act, without your testimony there's little I can do to punish and put a stop to their bullying. I've already given both of these girls detention. But all three of them have a long history of abhorrent behavior. My fear is that their violence will continue to intensify until they seriously injure someone ... or worse."

Mia was ashamed of her cowardice for lying to Mr. Sloan and denying Mrs. Luedecke's testimony. She'd almost decided to "fess up" and tell him about the lunchroom incident with Freda, when agitated knocks pounded on his door.

"Come in," he called. His secretary rushed in, her face ashen, and hurriedly whispered something to him, then walked out briskly.

Principal Sloan frowned, obviously upset. "You'll have to excuse me. I need to address this right away. Please, both of you remain here, I'll return shortly. This conversation is not finished." Grabbing his coat, he rushed out of the room.

Mia looked to Mrs. Luedecke for guidance, but the teacher shrugged and shook her head, confused by Mia's actions, and equally mystified by the sudden disruption. They heard the wail of an approaching siren, then saw the flashing lights of a TPD cruiser that screeched to a halt outside. An ambulance arrived a minute later, as lights strobed off the windows of surrounding vehicles.

Mia suddenly felt an irrational uneasiness worm its way into her as she and her teacher watched the police and EMTs talk briefly and stride quickly into the school. The ambulance crew carried what looked like an over-sized tackle box and a small suitcase, as they hurried inside.

If there was a shooter, the school would've been in lockdown before now, Mia thought anxiously, as the two of them waited for Sloan's return.

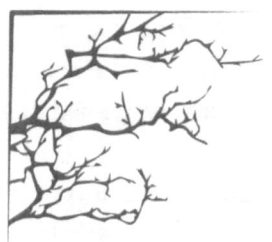

Chapter Five

"**I**s she alive?" Principal Sloan was visibly distressed, waiting just outside the girls' restroom, as paramedics surrounded a young girl's body that lay on the floor in front of the stalls.

"Jesus, what the hell happened to you, honey?" a female paramedic gasped, seeing the condition of the body.

The girl's skin appeared severely burned. The flesh on most of her body seemed to have dissolved, leaving bloody muscle tissue gleaming through the viscous remains. Her face was a rictus of horror. The eyes floated in their sockets like under-cooked egg whites.

"We're gonna need a TOD," the cop on scene told the paramedic.

The medic was obviously shaken, but she did her job. "Call it 1:58 p.m. for now, and get the ME on the phone, tell him we've got a hell of a mess here," the paramedic spoke in a strained voice to her partner.

The cop told dispatch they needed the homicide unit ASAP. Principal Sloan finally caught a glimpse of the body and turned a pale shade of green, as he backed away from the doorway.

"You'll have to declare a lockdown until we can get a handle on this," the cop told him.

"Of course, I-I'll see to it immediately." Sloan turned and marched quickly back to his office. *Hell of a thing to happen,* he thought, still shaken. Back in his outer office, he instructed the assistant principal to send out the "emergency lockdown" text to all students and teachers in the school and simultaneously to their parents.

Sloan got on the PA and ordered everyone to stay in class, informing them that the lockdown was not due to a shooter, but instructing teachers closest to exterior doors to lock them—they all had keys.

As they stared at the text on their phones, Mia and Mrs. Luedecke were both alarmed.

"What's going on? What's happening?" the music teacher implored Sloan, as he re-entered the room, pale and breathless. He gave Mia a queer look, then told them to stay seated.

"Normally, I wouldn't say this in front of a student. But I ... well, a girl's body has been found in the restroom by the cafeteria," he said, staring at Mia.

Mrs. Luedecke's face drained of color. "What on earth happened?"

"They ... don't know yet, but the, uh, body was in really bad shape," Sloan said, nervously toying with a paperclip.

Mia felt her stomach turn to ice at his words. *Do you really wish her dead?* The words echoed silently in her mind. *Maybe it's not Freda. But—what if it is?* a little voice in her brain queried.

"Do you know what color her hair is—was?" Mia questioned quietly.

He cocked his head, looking at her curiously, crossed his arms, and sat back in his chair. "I don't know. There was too much blood to tell. Police did not allow me inside. I only had a glimpse ... and I'll never be able to stop seeing that. She ... it was truly horrific!" he grimaced. "The Medical Examiner will be here shortly, along with a Homicide Squad from TPD. Until they finish their, uh, work, the school must remain on lockdown."

Mrs. Luedecke slowly shook her head, "Mia, you need to tell him what happened really earlier in the cafeteria. I'm sorry, but in light of all this, it could be relevant."

Mia slowly turned to glower at her, feeling betrayed by the teacher she considered a friend and confidant, forgetting that she'd been on the verge of revealing it, herself. *She's no better than the rest, I should've kept my freaking mouth shut!*

"Uh, Freda, s-she had a small knife. She sorta ... poked me in the leg with it during lunch in the cafeteria," Mia said sullenly.

Sloan's eyes widened as he sat forward in his chair.

Again, Mrs. Luedecke shook her head. "Mia told me earlier it was a switchblade—and that she was stabbed, not *poked*, for God's sake!" she corrected, exasperated with the girl.

Sloan simply sat quietly for a moment. "If what you told your teacher is true, that's assault with a deadly weapon, Mia. That rates an expulsion at minimum, possibly criminal charges being filed. By the way, how did you get that shiner?" Sloan inquired.

Before she realized what she was doing, Mia's hand automatically started toward her face. Sloan waited impatiently.

Shit! Lie or tell the truth? Mia weighed the consequences of her answer in her mind for only a second before answering. "I-I fell in the shower at home, slipped on the soap, and hit my head," she calmly lied.

Sloan sighed and sat back in his chair. "Mia, I believe you're lying, thinking you'll keep yourself safe by not naming the person responsible for this. That's just what the bullies of the world want you to think. They rule by intimidation and fear. If you back down now, their cycle of violence will continue. It takes real courage to stop its spread. Think about it," he finished.

Mia stared at her shoes. *He doesn't know what it's like to have* my *face—nobody does,* she thought miserably, a solitary tear running down her cheek.

Sloan turned to Mrs. Luedecke, "Please find out what class Freda Ferguson is in now and escort her to my office immediately. Oh, and get Sam. Tell him to bring his bolt cutters."

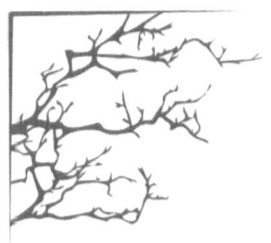

Chapter Six

Freda sat in the very back row and blew a nasty spitball toward the back of her history teacher's head. He was writing on the blackboard, and she missed him by an inch, the soggy missile landing with a *splat* nearby.

Shit, I'm losing my touch, she thought, quickly shoving the ink reservoir back into her pen and pretending to write in her notebook. As laughter erupted, he whirled around looking for the culprit.

Someone knocked loudly on the classroom door and a deadbolt turned before it swung inward. Everyone turned, as Mrs. Luedecke stepped in. She stopped at the other teacher's desk to converse quietly with him. Most of the class turned to stare at Freda. She looked up to see both teachers casting furtive glances in her direction as they spoke.

Fuck! The little pig must have squealed, she deduced, as her teacher broke away from Luedecke. Visibly upset, he called Freda to the front of the class.

Freda rolled her eyes, threw her history book in her backpack, and sauntered up to stand in front of both teachers.

"Miss Ferguson, you're wanted in the principal's office now. Mrs. Luedecke is here to see that you arrive there promptly," he instructed, frowning after her. Mrs. Luedecke led her out into the hall, re-locking the door, and pushed the sixteen-year-old hellion toward Sloan's office.

"What's the beef this time? And why the hell are we in lockdown if there's no shooter?" Freda inquired suspiciously, trying to get a feel for the inevitable inquisition to come.

"Watch your damn language, young lady," Luedecke hissed at her.

"I'm young, but I ain't no 'lady,' ya' old hag," she snapped back, as they approached the outer office doorway.

When she entered, the first person she saw was Mia, who sat in a chair outside Sloan's office, head in her hands, elbows resting on her knees. The second was Sam, who stood beside the principal inside his office, holding large bolt cutters. Freda and the teacher were ushered inside, with the door shut.

"Miss Ferguson? Please empty your pockets and your purse, then dump the contents of your backpack on the floor. Right now," Sloan demanded.

"What's going on, if it's okay to ask?" she challenged, glaring.

"Just do as you're told. You're not here to ask questions," he replied sharply.

Fuckers are looking for the knife, Freda thought uneasily, as she turned out most of the contents of her jean pockets. Her phone, a dollar or so in loose change, a stick of gum, and an unused condom spilled onto the floor at her feet. She upended her purse and her backpack in the same manner. Three class books, a tampon in a wrapper, a red spiral-bound notebook, pens, and assorted junk. But no switchblade.

"That's all of it. What exactly are you looking for ... a bomb, maybe?" she asked with a snarky grin.

The girl's persistent insolence infuriated Mrs. Luedecke. Principal Sloan took the backpack and examined it inside and out.

"We need the combination for your locker," he said, going through the backpack's pockets.

Freda glared at him for a second, then smiled thinly, "I don't have a combination. It's keyed."

Sloan frowned. "We don't allow keyed locks. You're aware of that, Miss Ferguson. Hand over the key."

Reluctantly, Freda pulled a key from a hidden pocket in her jeans and handed it to him. Momentarily mollified, he told her to sit down in his office. She rolled her eyes and slouched down in the chair facing his desk.

"Mrs. Luedecke, would you mind keeping an eye on her for a few minutes while Sam and I check the locker?" he asked, as they gathered the contents of Freda's backpack from the floor and returned them.

"No, sir, I don't mind a bit," she replied smugly, taking his empty chair and engaging in a staring contest with Freda until the girl blinked and looked away.

Mia's phone chimed with an incoming message from her mother: '*R U okay?? Got text from school that U R in lockdown! What's happening? If no shooting, what for? Please let me know U R OK.'* MJ tended to freak out whenever there was a lockdown, which had happened more often in the past year or so.

Mia texted back: *'I'm OK. Something happened to a girl. Don't worry. Am in principal's office, so safe. Will explain later. Gotta go. And no, not in trouble.'*

At least not right now, she thought miserably, wondering if she might've played a part in that girl's death.

Sloan and Sam walked to Freda's locker, where Sloan pushed the key in the lock. It didn't fit. The wretched girl had given him a bogus key. "Okay, Sam, cut it off," Sloan said, standing back as Max applied his cutters to the hasp and removed the lock.

Sloan opened the locker door. Inside, a half-eaten, blackened banana lay on top a couple books, a small unopened box of tampons, and two well-thumbed teen magazines—but no switchblade.

Disappointed, Sloan picked up one of the magazines. As he did, the other one fell onto the floor, and a piece of paper slid from between its pages. He picked up the piece of paper and looked at it. It was a list of three girls' names. Mia Chandler's was at the top, followed by two others. The bottom two names had been crossed out in red. Mia's was circled in black ink.

Sloan sighed and began to shove the magazines back into the locker when something else caught his eye. A piece of plastic hung out from within a thick book at the bottom of the locker. He pulled the book out and opened it, discovering that its center area had been hollowed out to a depth of about an inch and the clear plastic inserted. The opening was two-by-six inches. *Just deep and wide enough to easily conceal a knife,* he thought.

But that was not what lay within the plastic bag inside the cavity. Sam looked over Sloan's shoulder, gawking at the contents of the hollow. Turning away, he vomited on the shiny linoleum floor. Sloan felt his own gorge rise but choked it back. He quickly shut the cover of the book, staring at its title, "The Three-Fingered Ghoul."

He looked over at Sam. "Go find the detectives. They should be here by now. Bring them to my office ASAP."

Wiping his mouth with the back of his hand, Sam hurried down the hall. Sloan clutched the book in a white-knuckled grip.

On the way back to his office, he stopped by the janitorial room to have someone clean up Sam's mess from the floor. Walking back in, he found Mia still sitting on the chair in the outer office, looking like a caged animal.

Don't blame you, kid, this is one fucked-up day, he thought, as he passed her.

Freda and Mrs. Luedecke looked up at the same time when he strode back into his office and sat down. He placed the book squarely in the middle of his desktop with its title facing toward Freda.

Her bravado morphed into uneasy confusion.

"Where did you get this book, Miss Ferguson? You seem to have a propensity for violence in literature, as well as in reality," he queried coldly, watching her closely for any reaction.

Warily, she crossed her arms. "I've never seen that before. What's all this about?" she shot back defensively.

Sloan frowned, "I-that is, we found it in your padlocked locker, yet you're telling me this isn't yours?" he said sarcastically.

Her face grew red with suppressed rage as she fidgeted in her chair, knowing full well they had cut the lock after she'd given him an old key. Freda glowered. "It's not mine. I don't read crap like that," she sneered.

Sloan would bet his granny's false teeth that Freda had never willingly read anything more cerebral than the back of a cereal box. He was stressed—and in hindsight, it probably wasn't his soundest decision—but he reached over and threw open the book to expose what lay within.

When she saw what lay inside the hollowed-out book, Freda did a double take, gasped, and let out a small squeal.

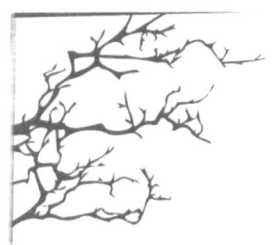

Chapter Seven

Detective Lieutenant Kris Lacey—LT to her men—tucked a loose strand of dark, straight hair under her protective hairnet, as she observed the crime scene before her. She'd recently been promoted to lead the small team that comprised the Taos PD Homicide Unit, having spent the past eight years working her ass off to make detective. To achieve her current position, she'd endured a lot of bullshit, threading her way carefully through the political and personal land mines her career path had taken,

Standing at an even six feet, Kris was taller than many of her male counterparts on the force. She was thirty-two and single, having devoted most of her adult life to police work. Her piercing hazel eyes moved constantly and missed little.

She'd seen a lot in her years on the force, but days like this tested her resolve and faith in humanity. A small amount of blood had coagulated around the small body in the school bathroom, but her gaze was fixed on the body itself.

"Listen up, people—I need this area cleared, anyone who was in the vicinity near the TOD questioned. Someone please tell me there are freaking cameras monitoring this area," she barked, as she moved in for a better angle on the girl's remains.

The crime scene photographer had finished and was leaving the restroom. Lacey was TPD's only Crime Scene Investigator, or CSI, although she was not formally trained in forensics. The police department only employed about twenty-four cops, so each team made do with available staff.

"Who was first on scene?" Lacey asked her middle-aged next-in-command, a sergeant named Hendricks.

"I was, LT," he consulted his notebook. "I got the call and arrived, 2:16 p.m. The vic is ... was a young female, age undetermined. This is how she was found," he pointed to the remains in front of them.

Lacey asked pointedly, "Who discovered the body?"

"That would be ..." Hendricks checked his notes, "a Ms. Serena Gomez, age forty-four, a school custodian. I believe she's in the nurse's office, still in shock, LT," he finished, wishing he could excuse himself and go outside for a smoke.

"The ME should be here any minute. Please see if any video is available for this area." She studied the body lying before her outside the stalls.

At that point, the Medical Examiner, Dr. John Doughty, joined her. Dr. John was a dark-haired man of short stature but wide experience. He strode confidently into the bathroom, ducking under the crime scene tape. He took a lot of ribbing because of his last name, but he was one the best, most skilled MEs in the State.

"Afternoon, Detective, what have we g—*whoa*! What the hell happened to this body?" His voice was muffled behind his protective mask.

"You, tell me. It's apparent she's missing the pinkie and ring fingers from her right hand. The condition of the body and COD, though, that's a whole different ball game. If I had to guess, I'd say it was some type of acid—but how, and why? We found no personal effects on or near the body. Lacking that, the extent of damage suffered makes it impossible to discover her identity right now," Lacey speculated, moving out of his way so he could get a better look at the corpse.

"Well, it's obvious that getting prints is out of the question. The dermis on the fingers appears to have been dissolved, possibly burned off chemically. The fifth finger and ring finger look to have been removed cleanly at the third joint," he said, carefully examining the hand. He adjusted his LED headlamp, moving the light carefully over the body.

"Strange ... the subject's clothing does not appear damaged by whatever process was utilized in COD. The eyes were severely damaged, so vitreous-humor testing for TOD is impossible. Subject appears to be between thirteen and seventeen years of age, hair color indeterminate, worn close-cropped," he continued, speaking in a monotone into his voice recorder.

Opening his medical bag, he removed a small scalpel. Making a small incision in the abdomen, he inserted a thermometer deep into the liver. "Core temperature is stable at 95.4 degrees, best estimate is subject deceased within the past hour," he stated, rising to his full height of five-feet-five inches.

"I'll know more when I get her on the table, but until I've run more tests, I'd be reticent to speculate on the COD." He began bagging up his tools. "I should have some preliminary results by tomorrow. Dental ID could take a bit longer. I'll text you when I'm done, or you can come and observe, your choice."

She gave a grimace. "Think I'll skip the 'grand opening' and wait for your results, thank you very much."

He smirked slightly, picked up his bag, then ducked back under the yellow crime tape and walked out of the building.

"Okay, people, let's run the grid for trace," Lacey declared. "You know the drill—soon as you can, get the young lady bagged and out of here. After you've scoured the place thoroughly, get the cleaners in here ASAP.

"Anybody needs me, I'll be in the nurse's office for a sit-down with the custodian. I need to ask if she saw the vic's purse or phone, as we found neither at the scene," she instructed, pulling off and bagging her protective gear in her tote. She grabbed it, ducking under the CS tape, and almost collided with Sam.

"Excuse me, ma'am, but we need the detective to come to the office immediately," he said nervously.

"That'd be me. I'm Det. Lt. Lacey, I was headed toward there to interview the custodian." She shook his hand.

"I think you'd better talk to Principal Sloan first. We—oh, sorry, I'm Sam, the janitor—we just found something you need to see right away inside a student's locker." Sam led Lacey through the empty hallways to the office.

When they entered the principal's waiting room, Lacey spotted a small, thin girl fidgeting nervously on a chair and glancing toward the inner office.

Mia had heard Freda's small scream earlier; now the sound of sobbing from the other room worried her even more. She looked up to see Sam and a tall lady in a nice suit walk through the door. They stopped in front of

Sloan's closed door. The lady knocked twice, heard "come in," and opened the door. Sam waited in the outer office with Mia. Det. Lacey walked inside where a large girl with a butch haircut was crying and a dark-haired woman who she guessed was a teacher sat beside her, in front of Principal Sloan.

Lacey introduced herself. "I just came from the crime scene. It's being processed as we speak. Uh, Sam asked me to see you right away, said you had something for me."

Sloan stood and introduced Mrs. Luedecke and himself. "Lt. Lacey, this student is Freda Ferguson. She's accused of bullying and assaulting the student, Mia Chandler, who's sitting outside—allegedly stabbing her with a switchblade knife. Sam is our maintenance man. He and I searched Miss Ferguson's belongings and outer clothes for a weapon but found nothing. We then searched her locker and found no knife—but we did find this," he pointed to the book on his desk.

Det. Lacey's eyes took in the title, "The Three-Fingered Ghoul." Sloan flipped open the cover, revealing the grisly contents of the plastic bag hidden inside.

Freda challenged angrily, "That's not my book! I swear I never laid eyes on it before he brought it in here."

Lacey ignored the girl's objection as she opened her CS bag and pulled on a pair of latex gloves. Reaching over, she carefully removed the hidden baggie containing what appeared to be two pale, bloody fingers.

Shit! Somebody's got a sick sense of humor, she thought. Gripping the piece of plastic by its edges, she deposited it and its contents in an evidence container, placing the book inside a larger bag.

"I need to speak to Miss Chandler now, I'll return when I'm finished," she said, leaving his office, closing the door behind her. She sat down in a chair beside Mia.

"Hi there, I'm Det. Lt. Kris Lacey. You're Mia, right?" She smiled at the girl.

Mia gave a weak smile in return, nodding, then studying Lacey. The tall policewoman had straight, brunette hair worn in a short, utilitarian bob that curled behind her ears. She had a square face with a straight nose and a firm, slightly cleft chin. Her generous mouth warmed her otherwise stern appearance.

"Principal Sloan was telling me that you've been bullied recently by the student who's in his office. He told me that she'd assaulted and stabbed you. Is that true?"

When she saw Mia hesitate, Kris said, "Don't worry about her, she's not going to hurt you anymore, I promise, but now I need to record your statement of the facts," she told Mia gently. Pressing a button on her phone, Kris asked, "Can you tell me what exactly led to this assault?" She spotted the dark bruising on Mia's face, despite the heavy makeup covering it.

Mia sighed, deciding to finally unburden herself. "Yes, ma'am, that's true. She's actually made my life miserable since the third grade. Mostly verbal abuse ... but in the last year or two, she's become more physical. It's all because of *this*," she pointed to the birthmark partially hidden by her hair.

Lacey had not yet noticed it, her eyes being immediately drawn to the girl's puffy, bruised eye.

Bitch of a birthmark, poor thing. Compassion for the teen welled in her heart. Kris took the girl's hand, giving it a squeeze.

"Listen, sweetie, you can't let one flaw—no matter how big or little—govern how you live your life. Believe me, if you disregard it, so will most others. Now tell me, how, when, and where did this last assault occur?"

Mia described the lunchroom incident and showed her the small slit in her jeans just above the knee, surrounded by a dried, quarter-sized bloodstain. Then she broke down, sobbing.

"Any witnesses to the attack?" Kris asked.

"No, ma'am, Freda always made sure of that," Mia answered.

Then she told her about the bloody maxi-pads and used rubbers in her locker, the sucker-punch in the face after school the previous day, the pictures and notes left in her locker over the years. She related how Jessie and Brianna had shoved her face into the sink full of vomit, trying to drown her. All the years of fear, anger, and frustration poured out of her like pus from an infected wound.

Kris listened intently to Mia's account, with growing concern. She heard how Freda's hassles and mild pranks early in Mia's life had escalated over the years into bullying and ultimately progressed to physical assaults.

Kris considered herself a tough cop, a professional in all aspects of her job. But she was also compassionate, since as a young teen, she had also been harassed by fellow students. She could empathize with Mia. She was aware how little it took to become a target. So, it had to be tough to have a "bully magnet" on your face. She'd been about Mia's age when she faced similar actions, for different reasons. She'd been able to put an abrupt halt to her own harassment when she sprouted four inches in two years.

Now she put a comforting arm around the sobbing teen and hugged her. "Mia, would you be willing to testify in court that Freda attacked you without provocation?" she asked, handing her a tissue from her CS bag.

Mia thanked her, blowing her nose and wiping her eyes. "I-I suppose so, Lt. Lacey, but I'm afraid it won't change anything. In case you couldn't tell, she has a major anger management problem. All the crap will just start again when she's allowed back in school, and ... I'm really tired of avoiding her and running," Mia protested sullenly.

Kris gave her a tight smile. "We don't have the alleged knife used to attack you yet and with no witnesses, even with your wound as evidence, it would be a case of your word against hers. We do, however, have enough circumstantial evidence to hold her for questioning about the dead girl found in the restroom."

"When we find the missing knife, she won't be bothering you or anyone else for a long time. Okay? So, hang tight and go see the school nurse about that wound. I must interview the custodian, but I'll want to take some pictures of your injury before I leave." She started to get up.

Mia hesitated, then gave her a small hug, thanked her, and headed to the nurse's office for the second time that day.

Kris turned and re-entered Sloan's office, closing the door. She gave Freda a cool stare. "Miss Ferguson, before I ask you anything, I'm going to read you your rights."

Freda's eyes widened with fear and understanding. "Y-you're arresting me—what the hell for? I haven't done anything! This is fuckin' nuts. I-I'd never do anything that horrible!" she shouted belligerently, pointing to the grisly book on Sloan's desk.

Ignoring her complaints, Lt. Lacey Mirandized her. "You have the right to an attorney. If you cannot afford one, one will be appointed to you before any questioning. If you decide to answer my questions now without a lawyer present, you may stop me at any time. If you choose to waive your right to an attorney, anything you say can and will be used against you in a court of law. Do you understand these rights as I've described them to you?" she asked the girl.

Oh Jesus, am I screwed! Freda thought, trying desperately to figure out what to do or say next. "Y-yes, I understand my rights—I-I want an attorney, this is bullshit! What are you charging me with?" she demanded, afraid she might piss her pants when she heard the answer.

"Right now, I'm booking you on suspicion of assault with a deadly weapon and first-degree murder. If you waive your right to an attorney, we can talk right here and now. If not, we'll have to speak down at the station, once you've been appointed council," Lacey told the visibly frightened teen.

"I don't have anything to tell you except I didn't kill anyone! I been in class all day, you can check it out, I ain't lying. Like I told you, I never saw that book before he brought it in here. I-I want a lawyer ... a-and my mother," Freda spoke defiantly, though Lacey could tell the girl was shaking.

"Alright, have it your way," Lacey said, producing a pair of cuffs. "Stand up, please, and turn around, hands behind your back."

Sulkily, Freda slowly got up and placed her hands behind her. Lacey put the cuffs on her.

"Principal Sloan, you can cancel lockdown and dismiss the students for the day. Make sure everyone knows that the restroom where the girl's body was is still off-limits until we finish gathering evidence and get a cleanup crew in there.

"We'll be in touch as soon as we've gotten this young woman a lawyer and had a chance to interrogate her. I'll come back to talk to the custodian as soon as I arrange a ride to the station for Ms. Ferguson," she finished, picking up her CS bag and guiding Freda out of the office with her other hand.

Waiting outside the nurse's office, Mia watched the procession. She released a huge sigh as Freda, in handcuffs, was 'perp-walked' out of the office. The nurse's door opened and the custodian, Serena Gomez, walked out, crying, and still looking shocked.

Nurse Tucker was surprised to see Mia outside her door again. "Well, what brings you back to my humble office, Miss Chandler?"

Mia didn't meet her probing eyes, but she walked into her office and sat down. The nurse closed the door.

"What's going on, Mia, how can I help you?" she said, sitting back down behind her desk.

Trying for detachment, Mia sighed, "Uh, well, Freda Ferguson stabbed me with a knife at lunch. T-the police just took her away in cuffs ... and they might charge her with murder," she shrugged, staring at her shoes.

Emily frowned in concern, "Oh, my goodness. Well, let's see the wound. Where did she cut you, sweetie?"

Hesitantly, Mia unbuttoned her jeans and pulled them down below her knees, pointing to her thigh. Emily came from behind her desk and bent down to get a look at the wound. It had mostly stopped bleeding, but the skin around the small wound was puffy and red. The nurse reached for some disinfectant from a cabinet on the wall, along with a swab, a large band-aid, and triple-antibiotic cream.

"It's not deep, but no telling how dirty the knife was. Does it hurt much?" she asked, gingerly cleaning the wound.

"No, ma'am, not too—*ouch*! That did," Mia exclaimed, as Emily pressed the sore area around the cut.

"You should have a Tetanus booster, but the school requires consent from one of your parents before I can give it to you," she said, applying antibiotic cream gently to the wound, placing the bandage over it.

Mia gave that some thought. *Mama will freak if I ask her. Better to call Dad. He never reads his texts at work, so he won't know about the lockdown.* She wasn't sure how he would react to the news of the attack and her needing a shot.

Emily washed her hands and told her she could pull her jeans back up.

Mia did so, then said, "You can call my dad, he's the least likely to overreact."

Emily nodded and picked up her phone, calling the number Mia gave her.

A gruff voice answered, "Gary's Gifts, how can I help ya'?"

Emily explained who she was and told him briefly about the attack, with few details.

There was a pause before he replied, "Fine, give her the shot. What's it gonna cost me?" he said bluntly.

The nurse was taken aback by his seeming lack of empathy for his daughter. "If you have insurance, it should be covered, Mr. Chandler. Would you like to speak to Mia? She's right he-"

He cut her off, "I can't afford 'Obamacare,' so, how much, out-of-pocket?" he insisted.

"I think it's about fifty dollars, the school will bill you," the nurse responded courteously, biting her tongue. She heard him curse under his breath.

"Sure, they will," he grumbled. "Well, it's gonna come out of her pocket this time, not mine. She's always gettin' hurt. Can't stay out of trouble. Damned if I'll bail her out again. Just give her the damn shot," he hung up.

Overhearing the conversation, Mia's face turned crimson, and she hung her head. Emily felt terrible for her. To have a parent who didn't care enough to ask about his child's welfare after she'd been attacked had to be a bitter pill to swallow.

"Let's get you that shot," she told Mia with a small smile, trying to move past the painful moment. Working quickly, Emily swabbed her arm with alcohol and gave her the injection.

"Thanks, Mrs. Tucker, I—my dad can be a bit snippy sometimes, okay? I mean, he loves me ... in his own way," she explained awkwardly.

"I'm sure he does, Mia, some men just have a hard time showing it. If you need anything else, feel free to come by and visit with me. Be sure to keep that wound clean, put a fresh bandage on when you get home," she said with a smile.

Det. Lacey knocked and entered as Mia was ready to leave.

"Got her patched up?" she asked the nurse, who nodded. "I need a couple pictures, Mia, if you don't mind?" Lacey said.

Mia stood up and reluctantly dropped her jeans again, then gingerly peeled the band-aid back while Kris took several pictures from different angles. She checked them and, satisfied the pics were clear, told Mia she'd be in touch.

"Hang in there, kiddo. If you need anything or just want to talk, give me a call, okay? Otherwise, I'll contact you when we know more," Kris said, handing Mia her business card, with her home number scrawled on the back.

Mia thanked both of them, grabbed her backpack, and walked briskly out of the office. Her phone chimed with an incoming text. Principle Sloan was sending an "all-clear" for the lockdown to end and dismissing classes for the day.

MJ would have also gotten the all-clear text, so Mia texted her mother to come pick her up. MJ texted back that she was already outside, waiting.

Threading her way through the crowded halls, Mia finally made it to her locker. As she was entering the last number on the new lock, she felt a presence behind her. She whirled around to find the enigmatic Wendy Ravenwood standing right behind her, staring at her.

"Heard about Freda—couldn't have happened to a nicer person. Guess she won't be bothering you anymore," she said in her husky voice.

Mia looked at her suspiciously. "How would you know what happened to Freda? Everyone was in lockdown except for her and me."

The tall, dark-haired girl smiled crookedly. "A little birdie told me. See you around, Chandler." She slipped on a pair of dark shades that made her look more mysterious and disappeared into the cross-stream of students rushing out of the building.

Chapter Eight – Outside the School

Waiting in her Lexus, MJ was sneaking a cigarette while waiting for Mia. She'd tried repeatedly over the years to quit, using both gum and the patch. *But both were impossible to keep lit, ha ha,* she thought, tossing the butt out the window when she spotted Mia walking toward the car. She quickly popped a mint in her mouth, knowing it wouldn't completely mask the odor.

Mia opened the back door, tossing her backpack in the back seat. Settling into the front seat, she pointedly sniffed the air a few times and gave her mother a look.

"Don't say *anything*, I've been worried shitless about you for the past hour!" MJ exclaimed, preempting Mia's usual lecture. She started the engine and sped into traffic.

"Why the hell did they lock down the school—wait, what happened to your leg, is that *blood* on your jeans?" she glanced down, even more distressed.

Mia sighed, then briefly summarized her day: the booby-trapped locker, the lunchroom incident and nearly being drowned in her own vomit, ending with her trip to the principal's office, hearing about the dead girl in the restroom, and meeting the nice lady detective.

She did not tell her mom about her strange conversation with the mysterious girl in the bathroom stall or the eerie blood ritual they'd performed. She ended her narrative happily with the police hauling Freda off to jail in cuffs. She said the detective might need her to testify against Freda for assaulting her.

Tears of frustration and rage welled in MJ's eyes. "That girl deserves to go to jail. She's nothing but trailer-trash. She already gave you a black eye;

and this time she could've seriously injured you, Mia. If that detective asks you to testify, you damn well better do it!" she said angrily.

"What if I don't want to? Look, if Freda's responsible for that girl's death, they'll probably charge her with murder. Then they wouldn't need me to testify. I'm pretty sure murder trumps aggravated assault," Mia challenged her mother.

MJ gave her a shrewd glance. "Yeah? Well, what if they don't find enough evidence to prove murder? You'll still need to testify against her for the assault. That girl is a ticking time bomb, Mia. She's a walking, talking psychopath. No telling how many others she's already hurt," she argued heatedly.

Agitated, totally immersed in their contentious exchange, MJ's attention was momentarily distracted from traffic flow—she blew right through a red light. A split second before the impact, Mia glimpsed the truck barreling toward them and tried to scream.

The Lexus was T-boned on her mother's side with enormous force. Mia heard the sickening crunch of metal on metal, as a spray of safety glass exploded inside the car. Flying shrapnel showered Mia's face and body, even as the airbags deployed. Her head was thrust violently back and to the left, as the seatbelt restrained her body. Everything seemed to happen in slow motion.

The Lexus was slammed ten feet sideways before finally coming to a stop. Then there was a deafening silence but for the *tick-tick-tick* of the damaged engine block. The pungent smell of gasoline rapidly permeated the interior of the ruined vehicle. The bright copper smell of blood flooded Mia's nose, as she stared with horror at her mother's broken body crumpled in the driver's seat.

No, no, no! This isn't happening! Mia thought frantically, taking inventory of her own body, aware she had multiple cuts bleeding from the flying glass and her neck hurt a lot, but otherwise seemed relatively undamaged.

That was no comfort. Her mother's head lay limply against the steering wheel, bloodied hair hiding the right side of her face. Apparently, her mother's side airbag had deployed, absorbing some of the impact but also causing its own damage.

What about her left side? Mia thought, with growing terror. The truck's huge grill was wedged *inside* the driver's side of the Lexus; her mother's blood and gore dripped from it. From outside came the mournful wail of a siren, growing in volume.

Dead, she's dead! We were arguing—and now she's dead! The thought kept looping through her addled brain like an unwanted song.

As her vision faded in and out in sync with the painful throbbing in her head, Mia hazily heard a voice. Someone opened her door, hands reached in to unbuckle her seatbelt. She looked up groggily at her rescuer, who seemed vaguely familiar.

Dressed all in black, Wendy Ravenwood stood silently by the open door looking down at her, her dark eyes hidden behind her sunglasses.

"W-Wendy ... what—?" was all Mia managed before her world went dark.

"MIA! MIA, WAKE UP, can you hear me?" the voice sounded distant, echoing as if in a tunnel. It grew more insistent—and annoying. Her eyelids fluttered open briefly, as she tried to focus. Someone stood over her, calling her. She tried to turn her head toward the figure and was rewarded with a lightning bolt of pain that shot through her head and neck.

"Don't try to move, hon," her dad's voice filtered through the cobwebs of consciousness.

"Got that. W-where am I? What h-happened? I'm t-thirsty," she rasped, her mouth dry as desert sand.

"You were in an accident. But you're gonna be okay, the doc said you had some bumps and cuts, nothing serious, nothing broken," Gary tried to reassure, giving her hand a squeeze.

When he leaned down to kiss her cheek, she smelled the whiskey on his breath. He'd been drinking. The smell made her nauseous.

Bits and pieces began coming back —she and her mom arguing, seeing the red light as MJ ran it, the truck smashing into the side of the car in slow motion. Then, her mother's body, looking like a bloody ragdoll propped up by the steering wheel.

"Mama! Mama looked ... is sh-she ...?" she couldn't bring herself to say the word.

Her father's face paled. "She's pretty banged-up, Mia. The doc said she's lo-lost her left arm. Got five broken ribs, a punctured lung, and a ruptured spleen with internal bleeding. She's in surgery right now. Her ... her face—the left cheekbone was shattered. A plastic surgeon's coming if, well ... if she pulls through," he finished in a hushed voice.

"Oh, my God! What about the driver of the truck that hit us?" she asked hoarsely, after he fed her a few ice chips from a cup with a spoon.

His face flushed angrily. "It was some old lady in a big-ass pickup—*she's* fine, just some bruises. The cops said she had a green light, and your mom ran the red. The old woman wore glasses, prob'ly blind as a bat," he grumbled furiously.

Mia noticed his hands clenching into fists. "No, it wasn't the old lady's fault. Mom and I were arguing when it happened, and she was distracted."

Mia didn't know what scared her most. The fear of losing her mother to her injuries was terrible enough. The thought of living without her mother to run interference with her verbally abusive, alcoholic dad was worse, a nightmare. Tears ran down her cheeks at these thoughts. Both scenarios scared her shitless.

She was trying to calm her mind when a tall, dark-haired man in hospital scrubs knocked and strode into her cubicle.

"Hello, good to see you're awake. I'm Dr. Pepper, your mother's surgeon," he said with a quick smile. He shook hands with Gary, then held one of Mia's in his. Mia smiled weakly at his introduction. "I know, I know, I've heard all the jokes."

His smile faded quickly as he took a seat next to Mia's bed. "Seriously, I believe your mother's surgeries were successful. I repaired what I could. Unfortunately, I did have to remove her left arm at the shoulder. It ... well, the blunt force trauma was too severe for us to save it.

"I also had to remove her spleen. Luckily, you can do okay without one. She may be a little more prone to infections after she heals, though. Kinda makes you wonder why nature even bothered to give us those in the first place, right?" He smiled again, as he gave Mia's hand a small squeeze of encouragement. Mia tried to smile back. Gary just looked relieved to hear that MJ would live.

"If no complications arise from the surgeries, Mary Jane's going to be in ICU for about a week or so. Later in her recovery, she'll need physical therapy and possibly some counseling to deal with the lost limb." He stood again.

"I heard through the grapevine that you're going to be released soon, young lady. You can visit your mother as soon as you feel up to it, but only for a few minutes. She's going to need all her strength to recover," he told her with a wink, as he left the cubicle, pulling the curtains closed.

Gary rubbed his face and eyes, shaking his head. "Fucking great—this is all I need! I just lost my employee, some bitch kid stabs my daughter, and then my beautiful but ditzy wife manages to nearly kill you both with her shitty driving. Do you realize how much the damn tow-truck's gonna set me back just to haul off that expensive hunk of junk?" he bitched, self-absorbed as always.

Mia shrank away from his voice and closed her eyes, trying to escape his voice, as his rants grew louder until a nurse stepped in to see if there was a problem.

Gary shook his head and halfway apologized, "Sorry, it's been a shitty day. I'm just leaving anyway, gotta get back and open up my store," he told the nurse.

"Tell your mom I love her, Mia. Call me when they let you out of here and I'll come and get you. Freaking hospital bill's gonna deep-six me," he added a final complaint before he leaned down to kiss her. Repulsed by his breath, she quickly turned her head, stifling a gasp from the pain in her neck.

He pulled back, giving her a strange look, and strode angrily from the room. When he left, she breathed a sigh of relief. *I'll freaking walk home before I call you,* she thought stubbornly, her eyes slowly closing. Mental exhaustion and the pain meds quickly lulled her to sleep.

Chapter Nine – Taos PD Station

Det. Lacey was sweating as she walked out of the small boxy area the TPD liked to call their "Bullshit Extraction" room. The thermostat inside was held at a toasty 85º, keeping both the interrogators and the suspects in sauna-like conditions. It was an uncomfortable but necessary means to extract the truth from suspects while they were interrogated.

She surveyed the small squad room before walking back to her tiny, eight-foot-square office. "Okay, people, listen up. First, whoever ate my freaking jelly donut better 'fess up, or I'm keeping the entire class after school today. Now, get busy." A few officers smiled, shaking their heads, as Sgt. Hendricks rose and knocked on her door before entering.

"LT, the Ferguson girl's lawyer and her mother just left. You have any luck in the BE room?" he asked, standing stiffly by the door. A stain on his tie looked suspiciously like jelly donut.

Lacey gave him a dark look. "Depends on your definition of luck. Did I get a confession? Nope. Luckily for her, we haven't found any weapon ... yet. We're waiting for fingerprint analysis on the bagged evidence to come back. DNA will take forever, as usual. I'll want your written progress report on my desk by end of shift. Get it in gear, Hendricks," she growled at him.

"Yes, ma'am, end of shift," he said sheepishly. He quickly backed out, leaving her behind her scarred, cluttered desk.

He remembered a few years earlier, before she became their superior, when she'd been a genial colleague who would often joke around in the squad room and occasionally have a beer with fellow cops. The combination of her promotion and her recent prickly disposition, as her headaches had grown worse and more frequent, now made all her subordinates wary.

The desk in her office was just large enough for her crappy, ten-year-old PC and printer to perch on, leaving scant room for the small mountain of paperwork she never seemed to put a dent in. The onset of a new migraine throbbed just behind her eyes. Lacey popped a couple aspirin, chasing them with cop coffee strong enough to eat through steel.

Kris had seen her fair share of bodies in bad shape, but this one took the proverbial cake and then some. *What in hell could dissolve flesh like that but not harm the clothing?* she wondered. She knew sulfuric acid could eat flesh, but not that quickly. *Yet the damn clothes were not even discolored.* She sighed, rubbing her forehead to try to relieve the tension in her aching head.

The poor custodian who'd discovered the girl's body had been little help beyond giving them the approximate time she'd opened the restroom door and found the victim. She would likely have nightmares for the foreseeable future.

There were no eyewitnesses to the murder. Just as Lacey had feared, the camera focused on the entrance to the restroom, as the perp had spray-painted the lens with black paint. *Smart, damn it!*

They'd checked the time stamp on the playback from the school's video. The camera captured a couple students moving in both directions past the restroom at 1:45 p.m., then nothing for ten minutes until the victim walked in alone at 1:55 p.m., her back to the camera.

She wore the same kind of clothing as half the students, jeans and t-shirt with sneakers. The grainy video was only black and white, making definition difficult. There was a two-minute window between her entrance and the time the camera went black. So, whoever did the deed had followed her inside, killed her (with ... *what?*), and managed to escape without being taped.

Kris texted Hendricks, "Find out who was missing from classes between 1:45 and 1:55 p.m. Canvas the teachers on the hall where that restroom is located. Odds are, one of the missing kids will probably be our vic. Anyone excused from class in that time frame could also be our perp. Oh, and don't just check for female students, a male could be responsible. The killer wouldn't have given a rat's ass if he or she was caught in the girls' restroom. Also, check on any teachers who were absent from class in that time frame. We can't rule out anyone as potential suspects."

Hendricks read the text and groaned. He texted back, "What about the paperwork you wanted?"

Lacey frowned and texted, "Paperwork can wait. Why are you still here? Go!" She hit "send" and laid her phone down on her desk. Hendricks sighed, pushed up from his comfy chair, and headed out to his patrol car.

FREDA WAS SWEATING bullets, not only from the heat in the police's BE room. She'd been in trouble with the law before. But all her previous pranks had merely received a slap on the wrist compared to what she was facing now.

I was damn smart to have stashed that knife in Jessie's locker as quick as I did. They don't have shit on me. I never touched that book with those disgusting fingers, so it ain't gonna have my prints on it. But still she worried, trying to recall every detail of the day.

She remembered leaving the cafeteria after stabbing "dick face" and walking calmly to Jessie's locker. She'd known the lock combo for over a year without Jessie suspecting, so she'd opened it fast and shoved her switchblade inside one of Jessie's nasty gym sneakers.

She was sure that little bitch, Mia, would rat her out for the stabbing. Thinking back, maybe she shouldn't have stuck the little freak, but she had to make sure Mia feared her. Fear gave her power. Without it, she'd just be another lousy loser like those two muff-munching wannabes, Jessie and Brianna.

Being accused of murder was a whole different ball game, though. For the first time she could remember, she was truly scared. Her lawyer had assured her that the cops had no hard evidence so far, only circumstantial evidence. Therefore, he assured her, they wouldn't have a leg to stand on in court. When the fingerprints for that grisly cache planted in her locker and the forensic DNA results all came back negative, she'd be in the clear.

What if they don't come back negative? she asked herself, playing devil's advocate. Someone could be trying to frame me for murder. Well, now, that's a hearse of a different color, as her old, dead granny used to say. She would be forced to stay in jail.

The cops could potentially hold her for up to three days on suspicion of murder before charging her with a crime. If they didn't charge her, she'd have to be released.

Her court-appointed lawyer had grinned at her. "I know it sucks, but look at this way, the longer you're here, the odds climb in your favor that they haven't found any evidence to charge you with murder."

Yeah, fucking great. That'll just give them more time to build the case against me for stabbing the little bitch. Either way, I'm screwed! she thought angrily. She saw the door into the small, sweltering room opening.

She was handcuffed to a chain that looped around her body, then connected to cuffs around her ankles. A cop built like the Hulk walked in, got her out of the chair, and escorted her out of the room. She shuffled her way through the dimly lit corridor, and he placed her in a grungy, graffiti-covered, six-by-eight cell. She stared bleakly at the filthy, paper-thin mattress covered with stains.

The big cop removed the overly tight cuffs and chains. "Here you go, home sweet home. Enjoy your stay," Hulk gave her a sneer she'd have seen in a mirror, turned, and walked out, shutting the door with a resounding *clang.*

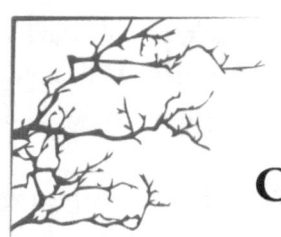

Chapter Ten – Taos Hospital

Beeping sounds from several monitors filled the air as Mia made her way into the ICU to see her mom for the first time. The charge nurse took her past patients in diverse amounts of pain to Bay Four, where her mother lay, intubated. Swelling and dark bruising made MJ's face almost unrecognizable. Mia stared at the bloody bandage covering the small stump where her mother's left arm had been.

As she sat in a chair by the bedside, hot tears fell from Mia's brown eyes. *This is all my fault! If I hadn't been arguing with her about that stinking bitch, Freda, Mom would have seen that damn red light*, she thought guiltily, watching the steady drip of solution flowing into her mother's remaining arm.

"I love you, Mama. If you can hear me, I'm so sorry for what happened," she whispered, giving her mother's hand a squeeze.

She sat solemnly watching her mother's chest slowly rise and fall until a nurse came and gently told her that visiting hours were over. Mia nodded, stood up, and leaned over her mother's shattered face, lightly kissing her right cheek. Reluctantly, she left and walked slowly back to her room to await her own discharge from the hospital.

The right side of her head where she'd hit the passenger side window still throbbed like a rotten tooth, and her neck felt like someone had tried to strangle her. *Yeah, whiplash sucks, but it sure beats the alternative.*

She heard the chime of an incoming text and glanced at her phone on the small table by her bed. The sender was unknown. She opened the text. As she read it, her head began to pound even harder.

It read: *'Sorry about your mother. For every action taken, there are unknown consequences. Remember, blood was given of your own free will. The pact is sealed. You and I are bound as one until you fulfill this portion of your destiny. W. R.*' Mia read the text with growing horror, feeling as if ice water had been poured into her veins. *What the hell have I done?*

GARY CHANDLER NEEDED to piss. Drunkenly, he weaved his car into the strip mall housing his small curio shop. He narrowly missed hitting a kid on a skateboard and wearing earbuds who shot in front of him. The little bastard didn't even look up at the sound of the approaching Jeep.

Gary yelled, "Fuckin' asshole, wassh where you're goin.'"

Swerving as he avoided the kid, he plowed into the rear of a police cruiser parked in front of the barber shop. His forehead bounced off the steering wheel when his airbag failed to deploy as the Jeep rebounded from the cop car's heavy-duty bumper, rolling back a couple of feet, and dying.

He sat, momentarily stunned, and felt his full bladder release. Wet warmth spread through his jeans, as a small crowd gathered to check out the idiot stupid enough to hit a police car.

The officer marched out of the barber shop with a hair apron still draped around his neck and shaving cream on one side of his face. He was not happy. Wiping off the shaving cream, he yanked the apron from his neck, tossed it to a bystander. He approached the driver's side cautiously, his hand lingering over his service weapon.

The cut from the steering wheel over Gary's left eyebrow was bleeding copiously, blurring his vision more than the whiskey already had.

Seeing the blood on Gary's face, the cop queried, "Sir, are you okay?" Leaning in the driver's window, he immediately smelled the whiskey fumes.

"Afternoon, ossifer, sorry 'bout your car. Thish hass been one fucked-up day! My wife wass in a bad wreck earlier—been at the hoshpital all day ... well, mos' all day. My damn kid wass banged-up, too," he slurred, trying to wipe the blood out of his left eye and smearing it.

The cop was not impressed by his sad story. "Sir, I'm going to call for an EMT to come check you over, but first, do you think you can get out of the car and stand up for me?"

Drunkenly, Gary thought it over for a second. "Sure thing, ossifer," he slurred, struggling to release his seatbelt, and open the door. The cop stood back as Gary slowly wobbled to his feet, leaning against the Jeep for support.

The officer noted his wet pants without comment. "Can you stand on one foot and count backwards from one hundred for me, sir?"

Gary nodded okay, but the moment he lifted one leg, he lost his balance. The cop reached out to grab him, sitting him down on a nearby curb while he continued his questions.

"Sir, do you have your license and registration. I need to give you a Breathalyzer test, do you consent to have it done now? If you do not, we'll get a court-ordered warrant for a blood draw and do it at the station. It's your call," the cop said, while they waited for the EMT to show up.

What the fuck choice do I have? Gary thought frantically, as the adrenaline of fear sobered him slightly. He brushed away the blood dripping down his face, wiping his hand on his soggy jeans. He groaned, resigned to almost certain incarceration, and dug out his license and registration.

"Go ahead, do it," he muttered.

The officer had him blow into the device. It registered 0.24—three times the legal limit. *I am so screwed.* Gary thought dejectedly, as the cop read him the results.

"Mr. Chandler, I'm arresting you for DWI." The officer then read him his rights. "Do you understand your rights as I've read them to you, sir?" the cop asked, after running his license plate.

Gary sighed and answered. "Yesshir."

This would be his second offense in two years. He'd gotten into an altercation in a bar the previous year, for which he'd gotten deferred adjudication and some community service.

An ambulance arrived and the EMT checked his vitals. He was okay, except for elevated blood pressure, and the cut on his forehead. They cleaned and bandaged that, clearing him from a trip to the ER. The cop helped him to his feet, handcuffed him, and put him in the back seat of his cruiser.

Gonna need a damn good lawyer before this is over! Gary thought, cursing his crappy luck. He groaned inwardly as he sat with his hands painfully cuffed behind him in the police car.

Anxiety sobered him for a few moments, while he thought about his shop being closed, with no one to run it while he was jailed. *Could he even make his bond?* He wasn't sure he had enough in savings to cover it. It all depended on the judge. Before it was over, this new offense would probably sink him financially.

He pondered his misfortune as they drove to the police station, but he never once thought to ask one of the cops to inform his daughter he was going to jail.

"Whass gonna happen to my Jeep, ossiffer?" he asked, as the policeman helped him out of the police car.

"It'll probably be towed and impounded. Let's go," the cop replied curtly, guiding him into the station to the booking officer. The officer there said the judge would set bail later, but he could call a lawyer now if he wished.

"The judge will probably get around to you late today or early tomorrow, we do it by video now. In the meantime, you'll need to wait in our holding area," he told Gary.

"Holding area, nice term for a stinking jail cell, Gary thought dejectedly, as he was led back to the holding tank to wait.

THE OLD NAVAJO SAT cross-legged in the dirt, staring into the glowing embers of a fire burning in a pit a few feet away. Nothing but the crackling of the burning wood could be heard inside the Hogan. The firelight danced across his black eyes, giving them an illusion of life, but that spark had been extinguished long ago.

"How is the girl?" he asked quietly.

The young-looking, raven-haired woman seated on the ground across from him did not answer right away. Her dark eyes also mirrored the firelight's swirling embers, but the small beaded turquoise necklace around her neck reflected no light.

"She's ... making progress. She's coming to appreciate that her decisions can have unforeseen consequences for others—as well as herself."

The old Navajo gave a small, perceptive nod. As he fed a small branch of wood into the glowing center of the blaze, tongues of yellow-white flame kissed it, engulfing the bone-dry tinder in seconds.

"Did she offer her blood?" he asked softly, stirring the glowing coals in the pit.

The girl hesitated, "Yes ... she did. The pact was made."

He sighed. "The mother lives?" he queried.

"Yes ... but she is no longer whole," she replied hesitantly.

Another protracted silence ensued as he stared into her coal black eyes. "The sacrifice was *not* completed. The blood demands it. This, you know," he hissed.

She shook her head, her raven hair glistening blue-black in the flames' light. "I do ... but must *she* be the one to forfeit her life?" she questioned tentatively.

The grizzled old man gazed impassively into her cold eyes until she was forced to look away.

"We are not the ones to decide who lives or dies. We are merely the facilitators. Blood for blood, so be it. The pact cannot be broken without consequences. Go, '*Nitch'i Asdza*,' and do what must be done," the elder directed her.

She met his eyes with an imperceptible nod, stood, and left the Hogan.

MIA DIDN'T LIVE TOO far from the hospital, but she didn't relish walking home in the dark unless she had to. She really didn't want to be alone right now, but with her mother injured, she had few alternatives for a ride. Thanks to freaking Freda, she didn't have enough cash left in her purse to pay for a Lyft ride home. Her parents couldn't afford to put much into her PayPal account each month, so that was not an option.

Despite her previous resolve not to—and hating like hell to do it—she called her dad. He hadn't spoken to her since leaving the hospital, but he should be home by now. The call went to straight to his voice mail. "You've reached Gary Chandler, leave a message."

She left a brief one, "Please come and take me home," texting the same message to him. The doctor had already discharged her. It was pushing nine p.m., and the hospital staff seemed antsy to have her gone, maybe they needed her bed. She could think of no one else to call.

When her dad still hadn't responded after fifteen minutes, she thought, *to hell with it, I'll walk home.* She gathered all the paperwork she'd signed, stuffing it into her purse, and took an almost-empty elevator that stank of stale coffee to the ground floor. She had just left the building when her phone chimed with a text.

Must be dad, probably got drunk and forgot about me, she thought angrily, as she checked the sender's name. "Unknown," again. Mia stopped in her tracks, staring at her phone, debating whether to open it. Considering the last shocking message from "Unknown," she opted not to.

The evening was chilly. Despite temperatures that could reach ninety degrees during the day, the dry desert air rapidly lost heat due to radiational cooling. She shivered as she began walking the eight or so blocks to her house. The night air was crisp, and stars twinkled overhead, a million pinpricks of light ebbing back and forth in the dark sky.

She pulled out her phone and texted her dad not to bother coming for her, as she was walking home. She'd just crossed the road from the hospital when she faintly heard someone call her name.

"Mia, Mia, over here." The speaker stood in the shadow of a bank building. Mia froze in mid-step. The voice was vaguely familiar, but she didn't place it before the north wind snatched it away.

Abruptly, she was all too aware how vulnerable she was, a teen walking home alone in the dark. Maybe that hadn't been such a smart move on her part. She turned quickly and retreated toward the relative safety of the hospital's sodium vapor lighting.

"Hey, Chandler. You need a ride?" a husky voice called out.

Mia stopped to look back as a dark figure stepped out of the shadows, advancing until Mia finally saw it was Wendy Ravenwood.

Shit! What the hell is she doing here? Mia thought nervously, as the tall girl slowly approached her from the bank's parking lot.

"I heard about the accident. That really sucks! How's your mother doing? Is she going to be alright?" Wendy asked.

For some reason, Mia did not want to answer the girl's questions. *How does she even know about the accident? Unless ...*

"I-I just remembered ... you were there, at the accident. You opened my car door and released my seatbelt right after it happened," Mia recalled.

Wendy crossed her arms with a tight smile. "That isn't possible. I was on the bus heading home from school," she denied flatly.

Mia didn't know if Wendy was lying or if she'd imagined the girl's presence at the accident, possibly as a result of the mild concussion she'd received.

"Where exactly do you live?" Mia asked bluntly.

Wendy's eyes glittered in the dark. "I live with my ... uncle, on the Taos Pueblo north of town," she answered, after a slight hesitation.

Mia thought about that, then asked, "Why did you transfer schools?"

Wendy smiled slightly. "My uncle thought I'd be better off going to a public school. I was home-schooled before I transferred."

Mia was forced to accept her explanation for the moment. But revisiting all their "coincidental" encounters, she had a sudden intuition. *It must have been Wendy who performed the strange blood ritual with me in the restroom stall. She probably sent the "unknown" text I received earlier.*

She couldn't be sure of any of that, but the girl was undeniably strange—and more than a little eerie.

"What are you doing here? And how did you get here, I mean, you don't have a car or anything, right?" Mia asked suspiciously.

Wendy stared at her with those unsettling eyes for a moment. "My uncle thought I should explain to you. The blood pact you took part in earlier today in the restroom binds us together. Blood demands sacrifice. I'm here to protect you—but it can be costly. Your words and actions have consequences, Mia.

"As far as how I got here ... *you* brought me here. I am *'Nitch'i Asdza,'* which translates roughly to 'guardian spirit,'" the girl finished.

Mia's jaw dropped, she felt like she was dreaming again. "Guardian spirit?" Her knees were suddenly wobbly, and she suddenly fainted, collapsing on the sidewalk.

SHE WOKE TO FIND SHE was lying on her own bed. She started to panic when she felt like she couldn't breathe. Her eyes flew open, and she saw the reason. Frodo was sitting on her chest, his furry butt about two inches away from her nose, *yuck!* She pushed him off her and sat up. He gave her an indignant look and jumped off the bed.

How the hell did I get here? she thought anxiously, when she noticed she was still fully dressed except for her shoes. *Wendy! But how ...?*

With trepidation, she glanced over at the little wood sprite leaning against the wall on the dresser. The wood itself seemed darker in appearance than she remembered, or was that merely her imagination?

She got up and, on closer inspection, saw the wood did have more of a reddish tint to it now. The grain of the wood was streaked a dark magenta, reminding her disturbingly of the dark blood that had stained her mother's face and hair right after the accident.

Then she spotted a note sitting on the dresser and read: 'Mia, I know you have questions. Some will be answered in time, others will not. See you later, don't be late to class. W.R.

P. S. If you're wondering how you got here, my uncle and I brought you home last night. I was with him when he carried you inside.'

"But how did you even know where I live?" Mia posed the question aloud, then glanced at her phone for the first time. It was 7:30 a.m. *Shit!* She barely had enough time to change clothes. The ones she wore were covered with spatters of her mother's blood and her own. As she was pulling on clean jeans and a T-shirt, she suddenly stopped as a fresh thought struck her.

Dad! Where is he? I didn't hear him moving around this morning. She finished dressing and rushed down the hall to her parents' bedroom. The door was open, and the bed had not been slept in. Hurriedly, she texted him, then called his phone and got voice mail again. Apparently, he'd never come home last night.

She began to freak out as she tried to think where he could be. She first pictured him lying bloody in a ditch somewhere, his Jeep rolled over on top of him.

"Stop it!" she told herself aloud, "I have to think logically."

She called the hospital to see if he was with her mother in ICU, then checked with the ER. The nurses said he hadn't been in either place. *Crap!* She could think of only one other place he might be. She called the TPD and got a desk sergeant, who looked at his computer.

"Yes, miss, we have a Chandler, Gary W., booked for DWI yesterday. He's currently waiting for the judge to call him up. The judge will set bail and if your father can pay it, he can leave."

Mia was so angry she could've spit nails. She asked how long it would be before he saw the judge, but the cop told her, "Maybe next couple hours, possibly longer." She thanked him and disconnected.

Shaking with anger and worry, she wandered into the living room, opened the front door, and looked out. The sky to the west resembled the purple-black bruising around her eye, with billowing thunderheads building in the distance. She checked her phone: 7:59 a.m. School started at 8:15; she wasn't going to make it.

She was about to call the school to say she'd be late, when her phone chimed, startling her. The caller ID read "Holy Cross Hospital." *Mama!* When she answered, a man asked to speak with Mia Chandler. Her stomach was doing roiling flipflops as she replied anxiously, "This is she."

"Yes, this is Dr. Pepper, we met last night. Regrettably, your mother has taken a turn for the worse. I've been trying to contact your father but have not been able to reach him on his cell. Your mother developed a high fever overnight, and she's still bleeding internally.

"I performed emergency surgery again an hour ago to find the source and stop the bleeding, but I, ah, I ... couldn't find any bleeding around the sutures I'd put in earlier. Yet, she continues to hemorrhage. We've given her four units of plasma, but... I'm afraid she may go into shock at any moment. Can you get to the hospital quickly on your own?" he asked compassionately.

Mia tried to remain calm and think. *I could call Lyft if I had a way to pay for it.* She was racking her stressed-out brain for a fast solution.

As she paused, the doctor offered, "Listen, if you don't have the money right now, I'll pay for the ride. Just come quickly, Miss Chandler."

Tears cascaded down her cheek at the doctor's generosity—while at the same time, she knew he wouldn't have offered if he didn't believe her mother might be dying.

"I'll be there as soon as I can. Thank you so much, Doctor," she told him. Disconnecting, she punched the Lyft app on her cell.

Keep it together, Mia, she's going to be okay, she kept repeating to herself like a talisman, trying to ward off the terror that threatened to engulf her. Her ride was only minutes away. She texted her dad a quick message about where she would be, not knowing when or if he would get it.

She hurriedly filled Frodo's bowl with cat kibble and put fresh water in his dish. He pounced on the food like he was starving. Then she grabbed her purse and stuffed her phone in it. Snagging an umbrella from the key rack by the door, she stepped outside.

As she was locking the door, an old, red Ford Fiesta shuddered to a stop in front of her house. She checked the driver's picture and license plate against the information on the app and they matched. Jumping in the back seat, she told the driver, "Holy Cross Hospital. Please hurry!"

He sped off, leaving a trail of blue smoke in the car's wake and making the trip to the hospital quickly. He pulled to a squealing stop at the entrance.

"Here you are, Miss Chandler. Today, there's no charge for the ride."

Flustered, she thanked him, rushing away. The old Navajo watched her run through the hospital entrance and disappear inside before he slowly drove away.

Chapter Eleven – Taos PD

Detective Lacey felt like shit. She'd suffered worsening migraines for the past six months, and this one was a whopper. Forensics had come back with preliminary results for the bag that had held the fingers. The bag itself held no clear identifying prints, and the fingers were no help, all their ridges eradicated by whatever caustic process had destroyed the deceased girl's skin.

Whoever had done the dirty work had evidently gloved up. The only good news—if you could call it that—was that they'd learned the dead girl's name from dental records. She was a fifteen-year-old named Jessie Gambols.

Hendricks knocked and entered. "LT, a word? I canvassed all the teachers in the two halls connecting to that restroom."

"And found out exactly ... what?" she snapped. "Sorry, bad headache. Please continue your report, Jason," she added hastily.

He nodded, continuing, "All teachers were present. They all did roll counts, with only two discrepancies. A girl fitting the vic's physical description asked to go to the can approximately between 1:50 and 1:55 p.m. Her name's—"

"Jessie Gambols," she finished. "We just got the dental records. ID's a positive match. Nothing from the 'bag-o-fingers'—the perp either used gloves or wiped it before putting it into the Ferguson girl's locker," she told him.

She rubbed her temples trying to ease the migraine pounding in her aching head. "I'm sorry, you said two discrepancies—what was the other?"

Hendricks cleared his throat and said, "The other was also a female, although she was in a different class located on the opposite wing of the school. She left around the same time for the same reason.

"I fast walked the distance from her classroom to that restroom and timed it. If she hurried, it's doable, fits in the time frame. Description: age range, fifteen to seventeen, height around 5'10"- 5'11," weight about one hundred ten, long black hair, dark brown eyes," he paused for breath.

"But get this—her name is Wendy Ravenwood, only the school office doesn't have any record of a Wendy Ravenwood being enrolled there, *and* she seems to have disappeared right after all this happened," he said, securing Lacey's complete attention. "Also, so far, we've been unable to find a knife or any other object that might have been used on either the vic or the Chandler girl," he added dejectedly.

"We have to find this Ravenwood girl and bring her in for questioning, ASAP," Kris said. She popped a couple of useless, over-the-counter pain pills and washed them down with cold cop coffee, grimacing at the taste.

Hendricks told her he was on it and went back to his desk to do more research.

Shit! It was beginning to look like she might have to cut the Ferguson girl loose, if they didn't quickly find something to link her to either the vic or the Chandler girl. She'd have to hope Mia was not too intimidated to testify against the bully.

This "Ravenwood" girl is a wild card, though. Just how does she fit in, and who is she, really? Lacey was thinking, as Hendricks rushed back into her office.

"Just got a report from that collision over on Paseo del Pueblo and Atascosa yesterday—apparently, the Chandler girl's mother was involved. She ran a red and was t-boned by a truck. She was taken to Holy Cross, where she's in ICU. The girl was also in the car but wasn't badly hurt. She's been released," he informed her excitedly. Lacey's eyes widened at this news.

"That's not all, LT, a witness at that scene swears she saw a girl who fits this Ravenwood girl's description there. And last but not least, the Chandler girl's father was arrested yesterday for DWI. He had a fender-bender with one of our cruisers parked in front of Kerby's barber shop. He's in the holding tank waiting to see a judge," he finished, out of breath.

"What the hell is going on with this family?" Lacey groused, as her headache pounded harder. "So, the name Wendy Ravenwood is possibly an alias. Have you Googled her, checked Facebook, Snap-Chat, 'Tweeter,' and all the other crappy social media sites?" she asked, as her elbow knocked over a cup of cold coffee, which spilled on her PC keyboard. *Shit!*

"Ah, it's Twitter, not Tweeter, Boss," Hendricks corrected.

"I know what the hell it is ... what'd I say? Never mind. Put out a 'Be on the Look Out' on Ravenwood or whatever the hell her real name is—find her. I want her ass sitting in my office before the end of shift!" she snarled, as she tried to soak up the spilled coffee from her keyboard.

TERRIFIED, MIA ARRIVED in the ICU waiting room, telling the nurse there who she was, and why she was there. The surgeon was walking out of the ICU when he saw her.

"Miss Chandler, please come with me," he said gently, leading her to a small room off the hall. As she sat down, he pulled the door almost closed and sat, turning a chair so that it faced her.

"Have you been able to contact your father? he asked gravely. "We've been unsuccessful in our attempts to reach him and ... he really needs to be here."

Mia's heart skipped a beat as she struggled with whether to tell him the truth. "Yes, sir, I know where he is—but I haven't spoken to him, either. He's ... been away from home for the past day," she said, giving him a semblance of the truth.

He gave her a tight smile. "Mia—may I call you Mia?" he asked quickly. She nodded. "Mia, as I told you earlier, we haven't been able to determine why or from where your mom continues to hemorrhage. It's like severe hemophilia. We keep giving her blood, but that's not doing the job. She's losing it faster than we can infuse it. She could go into shock at any time and—well, there really is some urgency," he emphasized, standing up.

She looked up at him, vacillating, then said, "Doctor, my father is in jail. H-he got a DWI yesterday, and I don't know when he's getting out. They said he had to see a judge first. I ... found out just before coming here. I-I just don't know what to do, I'm so scared right now." Wrapping her arms around herself, she rocked anxiously slowly back and forth in her chair, tears trickling down her cheeks.

He gazed sympathetically as she began to cry. "Miss—Mia, you'd best go on in and sit with your mother now. If there's anything I can do to—we're doing everything we can to save her, trust me," he smiled shakily, giving her a small pat on the back. Thanking him weakly, she stood up, and together, they walked into the ICU proper. Reaching her mother, she bent over to kiss her lightly on the lips, as tears from her cheeks splashed onto her mother's ashen right cheek. She noticed her mom's breathing was rapid and shallow and was pretty sure that was a bad sign. Taking her mother's pale, soft hand in her own, she squeezed it.

"I'm h-here, Mama, you're going to be okay. You hear me? I love you. P-Please don't leave me!" she implored, voice quavering with emotion.

Her mother's right eye opened, trying to focus on Mia. Her mouth opened as if to speak, then closed again. Her hand gave Mia's a slight squeeze, then went limp. The machines attached to her suddenly shrieked shrill alarms.

GARY CHANDLER WAS, indeed, screwed. He'd posted the $2,500 bond the judge had set, knowing that it would drain his entire savings. But at that moment, he didn't give a shit, he had to get out of that hellhole. He stepped out into the pouring rain of a passing thunderstorm, only then remembering that his Jeep had been impounded.

"*Fuck it*!" he snapped, ducking back under the sheltering eaves of the cop shop. He dug his phone out of his jeans, turning it on for the first time since the previous day. The notifications feature chimed several times.

With growing anxiety, he saw the hospital had left two messages urging him to contact them as soon as possible. Mia had also left a couple.

He read the ones from the hospital first. MJ had apparently suffered some serious complications from the surgery. Urgent that he contact them immediately or come to the ICU, ASAP.

"How the fuck am I s'posed to do that?" he growled to himself. All his credit cards were maxed out. He counted the cash in his wallet and found five one-dollar bills and some lint. Then he recalled that he'd spent his last ten-spot on a bottle of booze yesterday after seeing MJ and Mia in the hospital. Actually, it had been *before* he learned about the accident, but that was just splitting hairs.

Finally, he read Mia's message telling him she was back at the hospital with her mother. *'Please call or text me as soon as you get out.'*

"As soon as you get out." *So, she already knew I'd been arrested and was in the can.* He was trying to think who he could call to get a ride, when an ancient red Ford Fiesta belching smoke from its tailpipe pulled to a stop in front of him. The fogged-up driver's side window cranked halfway down in the pouring rain—revealing the old Navajo who'd brought that wood totem to his shop, staring darkly at him.

"Need a lift?" the old man inquired, pausing to light a pipe and blowing out a cloud of blue smoke that smelled suspiciously like something patently illegal in New Mexico.

Gary considered: either this old man has brass balls to light up in front of the cop shop, or he's fucking nuts ... or both. *But beggars can't be choosers,* he thought grimly, opening the door, and climbing in the back. The old man's dark eyes met his briefly in the rearview mirror.

"Good day, Mr. Chandler. You'll be wanting to see your wife in the hospital. I'll take you there shortly. First, I need to inform you of something important," the old man said, puffing on his pipe and blowing out another cloud of acrid-smelling smoke.

Whatever that is, it ain't weed. And how the hell did this old fart know that I needed to go to the hospital? Gary thought nervously, waiting for the ancient driver to put his pipe down and talk.

The old man saw the concern on Gary's face. "This is not 'pot,' if that is what you're thinking, Mr. Chandler, so relax. I need you to understand that your daughter Mia is an extremely ... *unique* person."

Gary stared back at the cold eyes in the mirror. "I *know* she's special. She's my only daughter. Can you just drive me to the damn hospital?" he replied indignantly. Gary thought he saw a brief glint of something dangerous behind the old man's eyes, before it quickly vanished.

"The girl must be protected—*at all costs*. I cannot emphasize this strongly enough. It is imperative that nothing deflects her from the path she is on. That is why the spirit totem was sent, to watch over her. Until she is ready to become *'Hatalii,'* she must keep it with her always," the elder continued, as he finally pulled out toward the hospital.

GARY COULDN'T BELIEVE this guy. The old Indian had some sort of fixation on his daughter that Gary didn't like one fucking bit.

"Listen... whatever-the-fuck your name is, let's cut through the bullshit, okay? I don't know what you're smoking in that pipe of yours, but you need to stay the hell away from my kid, or I'll have your Indian ass arrested!" Gary snarled belligerently.

The old man glared at him in the rearview, then gruffly said, "You would have me arrested for keeping your daughter safe?"

Gary stared irately back at him, not answering. He felt impotent, pinned under the man's steely gaze.

"I suspect there are mounting legal and ... financial problems looming in your future, Mr. Chandler. Perhaps I can be of some help with that. But above all, you must eliminate the *need* to feed your demons. Indeed, a man of your temperament should embrace sobriety by all means possible," the old Navajo chided, as he pulled into the hospital drive and parked by the entrance. He turned to look at Gary.

"Remember this, Mr. Chandler, we *all* make sacrifices for the ones we love—some are harder than others. Make no mistake, *you* must choose wisely. The futures of your wife and daughter are in peril, as well as your own. No charge for the ride, or the advice. Good day, Mr. Chandler," he finished abruptly, turning back to face the rain pummeling the windshield with a furious racket.

Flummoxed, Gary rushed out of the car without further comment and ran for the sheltering cover of the awning over the front entrance to the hospital.

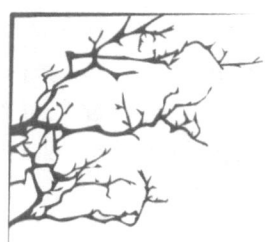

Chapter Twelve

S haking his head with disbelief, Sgt. Hendricks looked over the ME's report. *What the hell?* He printed out a copy and hurried over to Lt. Lacey's office. He'd had no luck so far locating the Ravenwood girl. It was as if she didn't freakin' exist. He had scoured the internet and come up with exactly nothing on her. She had no priors anywhere in the system. The lieutenant was going to be pissed.

Kris was on her phone when she wearily looked up and saw him standing at her door. She motioned him in, pointing to the chair in front of her cluttered desk, as she did her best to end the call.

"Yes, well—we, we appreciate your help, Mrs. Kelly. We will contact you—yes, ma'am, you'll be the first to know if we find—yes, ma'am, I'm aware of your eyesight—and your age," she glanced over at Hendricks, rolling her eyes, then finishing, "Yes, ma'am, we have your number—yes, we'll be in touch. Thank you, have a good day," she added, quickly disconnecting.

"That was the elderly driver from the Chandler accident. She's eighty-eight years old, has macular degeneration, and wears glasses that likely don't help. It's a small wonder she *hasn't* killed anybody ... yet. What have you got for me? And where's the Ravenwood girl, why isn't she sitting in that chair instead of you?" she queried impatiently.

Hendricks explained that the girl's name had gotten no hits in the local or state criminal database. "No one matching her description popped up on any of the social media sites I've checked. I mean, if you're a kid nowadays and don't use one of those, what does that say about you?" He hoped to appease her.

"It says, she's probably smart. Hell, Jason, she can't just disappear into thin air. She's got a home somewhere; someone takes care of her and feeds her. Somebody provides for her, damn it. Find who that someone is, and we'll find her," she growled, irritated that the girl hadn't been located yet.

"LT, the ME just sent the preliminary report on the Gambols girl—you won't believe this shit," he told her, handing her the report.

She took it, slipping on a pair of reading glasses she kept in a desk drawer, frowning as she scanned the results.

His official cause of death was:

"Burns compatible with microwave radiation exposure on over 99.5 percent of the body, epidermal destruction at the cellular level consistent with that. Overall condition of body suggests said exposure likely had a duration of at least two minutes. Fat cells liquefied, blood plasma and water in sub-epidermis essentially boiled away. Loss of bodily fluids along with other contributing factors would have led to shock and ultimately death within minutes of exposure. In conclusion, homicide likely. Method of delivery—indeterminate at this time.

J. Doughty, M. E"

"*Holy crap*! How the hell is that even possible?" Kris was incredulous at the report's findings. "Something very bizarre is happening here. How is it possible that a girl goes to the can and a few minutes later, she's fried like a chicken? There isn't a microwave oven big enough to do that," she pondered out loud.

Hendricks agreed, "I know, it's some crazy shit. But something sure did a number on her."

Kris looked up from the report, scowling at him. "I think we'd better get a handle on this Ravenwood girl, and fast. Didn't one of the descriptions of her mention somewhere she might be of Navajo descent? I know we don't have jurisdiction on the Reservation but see if you can contact the Tribal elders and ask if they might know someone fitting her description. In the meantime, I guess I'm going to be forced to cut Ferguson loose. I just hope the Chandler girl will have the gumption to testify to the assault. If we don't find the weapon, it'll be up to the girl or the DA to press charges." She sighed tiredly.

Hendricks shook his head in disgust and left her office. How the hell do you kill someone with microwaves in a high school restroom? he wondered.

Kris decided to call her friend, Phil Bryan, who was an electrical engineer for the city. Getting his voicemail, she left a text asking him to contact her about the microwave conundrum. She didn't know shit about microwaves, but she was willing to bet he had more than a passing knowledge of how they worked.

She glanced at the clock on the wall: 4:57 p.m. *Thank God this day is almost done.* She rubbed her temples in a circular motion, as if that would take away the sharp pains shooting through her head and down her neck. She finished typing a report that was delayed because of the news Hendricks had delivered. She'd just turned off her PC to leave when her phone chimed.

"Det. Lacey speaking. Oh, hey, Phil, thanks for calling me back so fast." She told him something about the case she was working on.

He informed her there was basically no way microwave radiation so intense could be delivered accurately by someone using a portable device. The military might have a weapon like that, but someone in high school, not a chance.

Crap! She thanked him for his time and info and hung up. As she glanced out the lone window in her office, a shiver ran up her spine. A large, blue-black raven perched on the outside windowsill seemed to be staring at her through the window.

It had probably taken shelter under the eaves to get out of the pouring rain from the recent thunderstorm rumbling across the desert. The bird turned its head left and right, as if studying Kris as she sat there. Unnerved, she got up and quickly closed the blinds. *Shades of Edgar Allen Poe*, she thought, as the bird's daunting visage was shut out.

FREDA WAS TRYING TO stay cool but having a difficult time keeping up the charade. She was in deep shit and knew it. *Even if they don't find the fucking knife, that little dick face is sure to rat me out for sticking her,* she thought, spitting in contempt on the disgusting floor of her cell. She jumped, as the cell door suddenly slid back and opened.

Officer Hulk stood in the doorway, scowling. "Looks like you got a 'get out of jail free' card," he deadpanned.

"I-I'm free to go?" she asked warily, thinking he might be screwing with her.

The big cop sourly informed her to move her ass if she didn't want him to change his mind.

She hurriedly stood and slid by him into the hallway. When he put his hand on her back, she halfway expected him to cop a feel, but he just gave her a little push to move her toward the door.

He unlocked it, and she walked out into the booking area's bright fluorescent lighting, squinting, after sitting in her cell for so long. She saw her mother and her lawyer were having a heated discussion with the lady cop who'd arrested her.

Her mother spotted her and rushed over. "That Lt. Lacey called and tol' me they was releasing you—fer now, anyways. They couldn't find no knife! Lawyer Daggett tol' me there weren't no evidence to hold you on no murder charge, neither. By God, Freda, if you gets in any more trouble, you gonna be the death of me," she hissed, chastising her daughter in front of the cops and her lawyer.

Freda's face flushed, embarrassed both by the attention and her mother. "Please, Mama, can we just leave now? I just wanna go home," she said quietly.

The lady cop came over and stood in front of her, staring intently. "Miss Ferguson, as your mother said, you're free to go ... for now. Your lawyer paid your bail on the assault charge. But even if the Chandler girl doesn't testify, the DA can and most likely *will* prosecute you for assault with a deadly weapon." Freda paled visibly. "So, don't get your hopes up about getting off scot-free," Lacey snapped tersely.

Freda avoided her eyes, grabbing her mother's hand. "Let's get outta here, Mama, I hate this fuckin' place," nearly pulling her mother off her feet in her hurry to leave.

"Better get used to it, kid, I've got a feeling you'll be back sooner than later," Kris muttered, watching them exit the station.

GARY BURST INTO THE ICU waiting room and ran up to the charge nurse's desk. "I got here as fast as I could. How is my wife doing?" he asked.

The middle-aged ICU reception nurse looked up over her reading glasses at him. "Name, please?"

"It's Chandler, Gary—no, I mean, it's Mary Jane Chandler—my wife, that is!"

"Do you have the password?"

"What password? Nobody gave me any fu—freakin' password."

"I'm sorry for that, sir. Then may I please see some identification?"

Gary was ready to blow a gasket, as he dug out his wallet. *Shit! My driver's license! They took it when they arrested me—automatic suspension for the DWI. Fuck a duck!*

"Listen, ma'am, I'm sorry, I have a little problem. I, ah, lost my license, a couple days ago. Would my MasterCard do?" He pleaded with her.

"I'm very sorry, sir, we require a photo ID unless you can produce something with a—"

"Dad!" He turned at the sound of his daughter's voice. She had just come from the ICU. She flew into his arms, weeping. He hugged her to him.

"It's okay, sweetheart, I lost my license, and they won't let me in to see your mother without it."

"Dad, Mama—she was bleeding out ... they couldn't stop it. And s-she's gone! I can't believe she's gone!" she sobbed into his chest, as she held onto him tightly.

He stood in shocked disbelief at her words. *Gone?* He turned angrily to the nurse who'd denied him his last chance to see his wife alive.

"I hope you're fuckin' happy. Because of your little bureaucratic dance, I lost my last chance to be with my wife! No fucking time to say I'm sorry, no chance to say goodbye or anything! So, fuck you very much!" he bellowed, with impotent rage and despair.

The nurse looked mortified by his emotional tirade.

"Can I at least see her *now*?" he asked hotly.

The charge nurse called the triage nurse inside the ICU. They spoke quietly for a few moments. Then she turned back to Gary, her face still flushed from his dressing-down.

"I-I'm so very sorry, Mr. Chandler ... but they've already taken the b—your wife downstairs to the morgue. They ... they'll need to do an autopsy to determine the cause of death."

Gary couldn't believe this had happened so fast. He slumped, crying, into a nearby chair.

He thought of the old Navajo's last words, "We all make sacrifices for the ones we love. Some harder than others!"

You got that fucking right, Chief!

Interlude - Joseph, Oregon, Sixteen Years Earlier

Five-year-old Pete Chandler was playing hide and seek with a neighbor kid. He'd just hidden in his best secret spot behind a myrtle bush when he heard his mother shriek. Giving up the game, Pete rushed up the steps to the partially open front door.

As he started to push it all the way open, he saw his furious mother slap his father's face. Shocked at the sight of such violence, he backed up quietly, pulling the door nearly shut but leaving it ajar so he could still observe and eavesdrop.

"You sorry asshole! How could you do this to me? To us?" Erin Chandler screamed at her husband, tears streaming down her grief-stricken face. She slapped him again, hard.

Gary Chandler stood and took the blows without flinching, the imprints of her palm bright red on his left cheek. He had earned them, and more, dipping his wick where it didn't belong—and this time the young girl was pregnant.

Erin punched him in the chest. "How could you be so fucking stupid and thoughtless? Get out of this house! I never want to see you again, you miserable sack of shit," she wailed between angry sobs.

Gary realized that his marriage was finally over. All because he couldn't keep his damn tool in the toolbox. He knew trying to worm his way out of this cluster-fuck with Erin wouldn't work. Not this time. They'd been down this road too often before.

"All I can say is I'm sorry, Erin. I won't lie and try to tell you it won't ever happen again, but if you could just forgive—"

"No more fuckin' excuses, Gary. I've turned a blind eye to your bullshit for too damn long. Leave. Now! Go back to your slutty pregnant girlfriend. You're not welcome in my house anymore," she screeched, pulling their framed wedding picture off the wall and throwing it at him, missing his head by inches. It shattered on the wall behind him—an apt metaphor for their marriage.

Gary retreated quickly to the front door and opened it, almost stumbling over Pete, who stood still with shock on the other side. His little face was scrunched up as he wept, tears rolling down his face to puddle on the Nike knockoffs Gary had bought to make up for forgetting his fifth birthday.

Pete looked up at his father, his pale blue eyes brimming with tears. "D-daddy, what's w-wrong with Mama? Why'd she hit you? D-Did I d-do somethin' wrong? Are you mad at me?" he asked, grabbing at Gary's pants leg and sobbing.

As he realized the boy must have heard all the harsh accusations his wife had just thrown at him, guilt and embarrassment flashed briefly across Gary's face, then reverted almost instantly to anger at his wife. Eager to flee the awful scene and his own shame, he pushed roughly past the child, ignoring his son's pain.

Pete watched his father climb into his pickup, slamming the door. Gary reversed out of the driveway in a spray of gravel, roaring off with no word to his frightened, confused, five-year-old son. That was the last memory Pete had of his father, Gary Chandler.

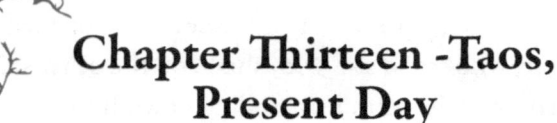

Chapter Thirteen -Taos, Present Day

The Chandler family—what remained of it—left the hospital at 6:00 p.m. in the mood of gloom and despair that horrific day had created. Mia had cried so long and hard before they left the hospital that she now felt like an emotional zombie. Gary wasn't much better.

Still in shock, he'd signed all the needed paperwork; the hospital had then graciously shuttled them back home. MJ's body would not be released to a local funeral home until the autopsy was completed. She'd asked to be cremated, and Gary would honor her wish. It was the last thing he would ever do for her.

Need to call her dad, he thought miserably, inserting the key in the front door. He trudged in, Mia trailing behind him. The room still harbored the burnt aroma of overcooked meat from the previous night's dinner.

Funny, the things we take for granted, Mia thought despairingly. There would be no more of MJ's burned meatloaf.

Frodo appeared as if conjured, mewing pitifully, as if saying, *where have you been? I'm starving.* Woodenly, Mia walked over to the counter and opened a can of "Kozey Kitten" cat food. Thanks to her grandfather, Kurt Koser, who owned the company that made the crap, they had an endless supply.

If we ever run out of food, at least the freaking cat won't starve, Mia thought, a little meanly. Her grandfather, probably a billionaire, was not known for his generosity to his family. He'd told them he was leaving most of his fortune to his seven sphinx cats in his will. Mia shuddered at the idea of hairless cats.

"I've gotta call your granddad and let the crazy old bastard know about MJ. He'll shit a brick and then somehow find a way to blame it all on me, sure as hell," Gary groused, as he settled into his recliner and looked up the number on his cell.

Mia ignored him, spooning the fishy-smelling food into Frodo's bowl. She already missed her mother terribly. *Now, there was no one to run interference between her dad and herself.* She loved him, but his drinking scared her badly. It was as if someone threw a switch within him. After a few drinks, he turned into Mr. Hyde.

Without her mother there to deflect and calm his alcoholic rage, Mia was terrified of what might happen. All that negative attention would now be laser-focused on her. Just the thought suddenly made her queasy and nauseous. She ran to the bathroom and threw up.

She rinsed her mouth and brushed her teeth, feeling a bit better. She could hear part of her dad's conversation with her grandfather from the other room.

"Listen, Kurt, I'd have called you sooner, but I—no, I haven't been drinking. I had ... some problems with my phone."

Yeah, jail problems, Mia thought sourly, listening to his excuses.

"The last two days have been hell! I—of course, I called you first. Listen, everything happened so fast. She ... MJ and Mia were in a bad accident and Mary Jane was bleeding internally. They couldn't—hell, yes, Mia's fine! She's just got a few bumps and bruises, she's okay. No way, Kurt, I'm sorry but MJ will be cremated. She didn't want any memorial service, either. Look, I'm really sorry, but it's what she wanted," he said, agitated by the old man's questions.

"Yes, I'll call you as soon as the autopsy report's in. Yeah, I'll contact the lawyer and have him send you a copy. Anything else? Kurt, I gotta go, Mia needs me for something," he lied and hung up, slumping back in his chair, tired of the old fart's badgering.

Mia crept into her room and closed the door, wishing more than ever that she had a lock on it. Her dad always said if there were a fire, he might not be able to get to her in time, but he'd never installed smoke alarms in the old house. The "no-locks" excuse had been okay when she was younger, but all she wanted and needed now was her privacy.

Depressed, she sat on the bed to insert her earbuds for some music, then she heard the front door open and slam. Curious, she got up and walked into the living room. Her dad's chair was empty.

"Dad? Are you here?" she called out. No answer. She checked the whole house; he was gone.

Shit! Where did he go—and how? She knew his Jeep had been impounded. She opened the front door and looked out. He was nowhere in sight. *He must have found some money and called Lyft, or else walked,* she thought anxiously.

Pacing nervously into the kitchen, she found an empty envelope leaned against the saltshaker on the kitchen table with a note on its back. *'Mia: Went to the store. Back in a while.'*

She read it with a sick feeling in the pit of her stomach. She knew too well that he really meant "liquor store." She'd known this shit would happen. With the stress of losing his wife and the trip to jail, her father would always turn to any escape he could get.

She guessed she should try to eat something. But knowing her dad would come back with a bottle of whiskey dropkicked her appetite out the window.

Her phone pinged with an incoming text from "Unknown" again. She opened it and read, 'Mia, I'm sorry about your mother. We need to talk, in person. Would it be alright if I came over and hung with you for a while, Y or N? W.R.'

Mia thought about her dad's return shortly and shuddered. She did not want to be alone with him when he drank. She texted back, *"Yes, please come on over."* There was no reply. She was about to sit on the couch to wait when the doorbell rang.

Mia looked out the peephole before unlocking the door. The concave image of the raven-haired girl was distorted. She stood on the porch clad, as always, in a black T-shirt and jeans, staring directly back at the peephole, waiting for Mia to open the door, which she did.

Mia greeted her and motioned her in. Wendy smiled tightly and walked into the living room. She looked around, then stood waiting for Mia to tell her where to go. When Mia indicated the couch, Wendy nodded and sat.

"I need to tell you that the police are looking to question me about the ... incident at school yesterday. That will not happen. They won't find me because I don't exist in any of their databases," she spoke huskily.

Mia felt a chill run down her back. "D-did you have something to do with that girl's death?" she asked hesitantly.

Wendy's dark, unreadable eyes glittered as she thought about her response. "Let's just say that you won't be hurt by her ever again. I am here to protect *you*—it's that simple. But the spilled blood of one demands an equal sacrifice. Blood for blood. Your mother's life was taken in exchange for the girl's."

Mia felt the chill in her back turn to ice. "Did you have something to do with our accident yesterday, Wendy? Are you seriously telling me that my mother died because of some stupid fucking blood ritual? If you were responsible for their deaths, you should be in jail!" Mia's eyes flashed with fury. Painfully, she finally accepted that the—girl, "guardian spirit," whatever the hell she was—had likely been culpable in both deaths.

Wendy's countenance didn't change at her accusation. Calmly, she said, "It was necessary. I don't expect you to understand. I am here to protect you from harm—"

"*Harm*? You don't call killing my mother *harm*?" Mia interrupted furiously. "I didn't ask you to kill anyone! Now you're telling me that I'm partially to blame for the deaths of two people, one of them my own mother! No way in hell will you make me believe that a single drop of my blood triggered all this. I don't fucking believe you!" Mia stared at her irately.

Wendy was silent for a moment. "You wished for the bullying to stop. You made your choice in that bathroom stall. These are the consequences of that decision. I am merely the manifestation of your darkest thoughts and desires made corporal. *You* are the facilitator, the orchestrator of this symphony of pain. What has been created is of your own making, Mia Chandler. I am *of* you," Wendy said. Mia was shocked speechless by her words.

"What's done is done, there is no turning back," Wendy continued dispassionately. "I am not here to argue semantics with you. You have an important role to play in the future. You are *becoming*, as we speak. I must do what is necessary to ensure your destiny is fulfilled. Further discussion of why this was necessary will not help you move forward.

"Your father will be coming through the door in approximately two minutes. I will return if there are ... problems," she finished abruptly, standing up. Calmly, she walked to the front door, opened it, and disappeared into the night.

Thirty Minutes Earlier

GARY WAS WOUND TIGHT as a coiled steel spring. He had dug out twenty dollars from MJ's cookie jar and gone to the liquor store with one purpose on his mind—to get drunker than Cooter Brown, whoever the hell *he* was. MJ's father had twisted his gut in a knot with all his ill-concealed sarcasm, insinuating that Gary hadn't done the best he could for MJ under the shitty circumstances. *Bullshit! The rich old fart doesn't give a rat's ass about anybody but himself and those hairless freaks he calls cats. When was the last time the old fuck even called to say hello to his only daughter?*

Gary had reached up on the top shelf of the whiskey aisle to grab a fifth when he glanced at the convex security mirror hanging in the corner of the store. That scary old Navajo was standing right behind him. He whirled around, almost losing his grip on the bottle, and ... no one was there. *Shit!* He was really spooked.

Anxiously, he looked around but saw no one else in the store. He looked back up at the mirror, seeing only himself and the guy behind the register. *That old Indian has got me seeing things*, he thought, shaking his head and walking up to the counter to pay for his whiskey. The short, fat guy behind the counter looked up from his newspaper as Gary approached.

"Hey, Cueball, how they hangin'?" Gary asked, setting the bottle on the counter.

The man's name was Franklin, but he was bald, so ... He folded his paper, placing it below the cash register where he kept a .44 magnum to discourage shoplifters and the occasional robber.

"They're hangin' where she can find 'em, Chandler," he replied gruffly. "That gonna do it tonight?"

"Yeah, that'll do it ... say, you didn't see an old Indian dude in here a couple minutes ago, did you?"

"Nope, just your ugly puss. I'm gonna have to see your ID, Chandler," the clerk replied with a grunt, holding out his hand.

Gary gaped at him like he'd just asked to see his dick. "Say *what*? Since *when*?" he asked indignantly.

"Since New Mexico Regulation and Licensing busted the owner for selling to a minor, is when. Sorry, no ID, no booze. You lose your wallet or something?" he snapped back.

Gary opened his mouth to reply, then shut it. His face grew red as he pushed the bottle toward the man. "Just fuckin' keep it," he snarled, stalking angrily out the door.

MIA DIDN'T KNOW WHAT to expect when exactly two minutes after Wendy left, her father opened the door and walked in. But seeing him carrying what remained of a six-pack of beer in one hand was completely bizarre. He didn't like beer—in fact, he said he hated it.

Irately, muttering something about a cue ball, he yanked open the refrigerator door and tossed the three remaining cans inside. Apparently, he'd downed two between the store and home and was ready to open the third. He slammed the frig door, knocking off a magnet that held an old photograph of MJ. The picture fluttered down, landed in Frodo's half-filled water dish, and sank like a stone.

Gary didn't notice. He popped the top on the can, sucked down a large gulp or two, wincing at the taste. Finally, he realized Mia was watching him carefully from the hall between the kitchen and her bedroom.

"I'm sorry, Mia ... for everything. This has been the two shittiest days of my life. I just don't know what to do now MJ is gone. Who's going to cook my freakin' dinner now? How am I gonna get to my shop? They took my fuckin' license. I can't afford to taxi my ass back and forth to work. Not after paying $2,500 to get out of jail. Hell, without my fuckin' license, I can't even get a cheap bottle of booze at my favorite store. I'm relegated to drinking this piss," he grumbled, draining the can with two more gulps.

Mia couldn't believe how selfish her father was acting. Like *his* life was the only one that had been turned upside down. She was more furious with him than she'd ever been before.

"Maybe if you acted a little more like an adult and less like a selfish teenager, you wouldn't have gotten arrested in the first place," she snapped, the words spilling out before she could stop them. "I miss Mama as much as you do, and I'm scared shitless—or didn't you even notice? Do you even care what I feel? You're not the only one suffering here!" she shrieked, trembling with rage.

For a second, Gary looked like he'd been slapped. Then he got mad, the veins stood out on his forehead.

"I don't need a fuckin' snot-nosed kid telling me how to act. So back the hell off or you're grounded forever, Miss Priss," he snarled, crushing the empty can and throwing it in the general direction of the sink. It bounced off, landing at her feet.

Mia looked up from the can to her dad's glowering visage. "I hate you! You never loved me. You've ignored me and treated me like an embarrassment since I was born. I wish you were *dead!*" she screamed, fresh tears running down her face.

She ran to her bedroom, slamming the door. Suddenly what she'd just said to her father hit home, and an icy dread filled her with terror. She had just wished her father dead!

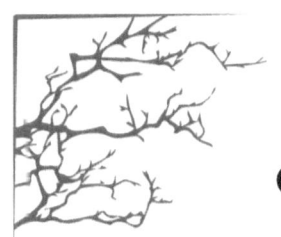

Chapter Fourteen

Freda Ferguson and her mother, Jenny, lived on the edge of town in a small, dilapidated, two-bedroom mobile home that was slowly eroding away. The middle cinder block supports under the structure had crumbled and cracked, so the whole structure sagged like an old dog's spine.

When Freda was five, her mother and she moved here to get away from Jenny's abusive husband. After smoking crack two previous times, he'd raped her mother, but the third time, he'd nearly beat her to death. That time was his last.

The following night, her mother had slipped some Rohypnol into his final beer. When he passed out on the bed, she undressed him, took an ancient glass coke bottle, and shoved it three-quarters of the way up his ass.

Taking a hammer, Jenny had smashed the exposed bottom of the bottle three times—once for each time he'd raped her—shattering it inside him. His unconscious body had shuddered and twitched on the bed as if he were being electrocuted.

She'd quickly grabbed young Freda from her bedroom, taken all the cash from his wallet, stood over his unconscious body, and said, "You always tol' me I wuz a pain in yer ass. You wuz fuckin' right!"

Then she'd taken the keys to his old Ford pickup, and she and Freda had hauled ass from Arkansas as fast as the piece-of-shit truck would go, staying off the main highways whenever possible. They'd arrived in Taos with the gas gauge on empty and about twenty dollars left in Jenny's purse.

An old couple who ran a gas station had taken pity on the fugitives. They had a spare bedroom attached to the back of the station and offered Jenny and Freda a place to stay until Jenny got back on her feet. She'd gotten a job at the Mega-Mart and saved enough over a year—thanks to the old folks generously feeding them two meals a day—to be able to buy the used trailer they still lived in.

Now, her mom's stereo was cranked up loud enough to rattle the windows. It was 10:00 p.m. and Freda couldn't sleep if she'd tried. Her ass and upper thighs still burned from the Mexican quirt her mother had used on her as punishment for her trouble with the law. The raised, bloody welts hurt like a bitch. She wouldn't be wearing shorts any time soon.

All Freda could think about was that dick faced bitch, Mia, and the trouble she'd caused. She lay on her side in bed staring out the tiny widow in her room at the star-filled sky, scheming the best way to deal with the Chandler slut. She had time—she'd been suspended indefinitely, pending the outcome of the charges against her.

Closing her eyes, Freda snarled, "I am *so* going to fuck up your life, bitch!"

MIA LAY ON HER BED, terrified that she could have sealed her father's doom. The old saying, "words will never hurt me," might not apply in Wendy Ravenwood's convoluted world. What Mia had shouted at her father in the heat of the moment could very well come back to haunt her.

She didn't hate her father, and she didn't really wish him dead. She only hated feeling ignored and unloved by him. She knew he'd been hoping for a boy when she was born. When he wasn't drinking, he treated her decently but remained indifferent to her wants and desires. She wished with all her heart that he could love and accept her for who she was. His disappointment in her gender was evident in her earliest memories.

Mia heard a familiar scratching at her door. She got up and cracked it so Frodo could enter. He jumped onto the foot of the bed, curling up to stare at her with his dark green eyes while he purred.

She glanced over at the little wood sprite leaning against the wall. Because of its apparent link to Wendy, she was starting to wish her dad had never brought the thing into their house. It was beginning to creep her out. She went over to pick it up but dropped it again fast. The wooden totem was fiery hot!

She backed away, inspecting her fingers for blisters. Finding none, she left her room and walked quietly into the kitchen. Her father had passed out in his recliner, empty beer cans strewn around him. The lights were still on. She grabbed an oven mitt and ran back to her room to find Frodo standing on the bed with his back arched. Hissing, his fur fluffed out and teeth bared, he glared through slit eyes at the wooden figure.

Now Mia was thoroughly spooked. She put the mitt on her right hand and quickly seized the piece of wood. *That's all it is, just a piece of wood,* she told herself, gathering her courage. Holding the wood sprite at arm's length, she raced to her window and shoved it open. As she prepared to toss the totem outside, she swore she felt it squirm in the mitt like it was alive.

Badly frightened, she threw it out into the dark, slammed the window shut, and locked it. *Good riddance,* she thought. Still shaken, she tossed the mitt on the bed. Frodo's fur was still spiked up, but he began to calm down once he saw the totem was gone.

She walked to the bathroom to pee and brush her teeth, barely recognizing the stranger in the mirror. Her life had become a nightmare, with no end in sight. Sighing, she walked back into her room. And uttered an astonished yelp.

At the sound, Gary jerked awake and sat up, trying to orient himself as the room spun for a moment. Lurching out of the recliner, he stepped barefoot on one of the crushed beer cans scattered around the chair. He let out a screech of his own. Hopping on one leg, he lost his balance, falling face-first into Frodo's litter box.

He jerked back out, sputtering, and spitting cat crap and litter from his mouth. *Rotten fucking cat!* Showing himself up, he rushed to the sink, turned on the faucet, and stuck his mouth under the water spigot 'til the nasty taste was almost gone. As he cut off the water, he heard voices coming from Mia's room.

He dried his face on a dish towel, kicked another crushed can out of his path, and stumbled his way to her room. The door was open, and Mia stood near her bed, talking to someone. Sitting there—holding the little wooden figure he'd brought home—was a strange, dark-haired girl.

Mia had heard him yell and fall, but her attention was fixed on Wendy Ravenwood, as she tried to get over her shock at finding the girl in her bedroom. *How the hell had she gotten in?*

She could smell her dad before she saw him. He stank like a brewery and ... *cat pee?*

"What the hell's going on, Mia? You know you're not s'posed to have people over without our ... my permission," he stammered, half-drunk and still tasting cat shit on the back of his tongue.

"I'm afraid that's my fault, Mr. Chandler. I was going to knock, but the front door wasn't locked when I tried the handle."

That's bullshit! Dad always locks the door before going to bed ... or passing out, Mia thought, smoldering at Wendy's smooth lie.

Wendy continued, undeterred, "I saw the light was still on, so I just decided to come in. You were asleep, and I didn't want to wake you. I didn't mean to frighten anyone, but I needed to see Mia. I'm a ... friend, from school," she said, with a forced smile.

As her dark gaze locked onto his, Gary felt weirdly uncomfortable until he realized why. She had the same cold, black eyes as the old Navajo.

"Listen, I don't care who the hell you are, you can't just walk into someone's house. I know damn well the door was locked before I, ah, fell asleep. Maybe I should just call the cops?" he challenged her, unsure of what to do next.

The dark-haired girl stood up. "That won't be necessary, Mr. Chandler. I was passing by and found this outside, and I knew Mia wouldn't want to lose it, so I just brought it back to her," she told him, pointing to the wood sprite on Mia's bed.

Her dark eyes glittered as they focused on Mia. "You really should take better care of such an exceptional gift. I'm sure whoever gave it to you would want you to keep it ... *safe*," she emphasized the last word looking directly at Mia. "Well, *Nizhonigo haadiilyjh,* that's wishing you a good night in my language." She smiled coolly, walking confidently past the stunned Mia and her muddled dad until she reached the front door.

She paused, then said over her shoulder, "You really should have this lock checked. You never know who might walk in on you while you're sleeping." Then she was gone.

Gary was outraged. "Well, that was fuckin' strange. She gives me the creeps. You need to make sure your 'friend' knows, from now on if she wants to visit, she better damn well call, text, or however the hell you kids talk to each other, so I'll know about it *before* she sets foot back in my house! Is that clear, Mia?" He was irate about the whole encounter.

"Yes, sir. I-I'll tell her," Mia said—knowing full-well that nothing she said to Wendy would keep the girl—or *whatever* she truly was—from coming and going as she pleased.

He tempered his tone of voice. "I'm sorry, sweetheart, it's been a rough couple of days for both of us, losing MJ like that. I'm trying to keep my shit together for both of us," he said apologetically, reaching out to hug her.

Hesitantly, she accepted—wishing with all her heart it was her mother comforting her instead of him. She smelled the beer on his breath as he held her close. When she tried to pull free of the embrace, he tightened his arms.

"I-I'll try to be a better dad, but it's going to take some time to get used to the idea of your mother not being here to help take care of us. I'll do my best, but it won't be easy. You know that, right? I do love you, Mia," he murmured close to her ear.

As he gently stroked her hair, reeking of stale beer, she grew increasingly uncomfortable. He hugged her tightly to him as his tears dripped down onto her ear and cheek. With sudden alarm, through his jeans, she felt him harden against her belly.

Shit! This is not happening! She felt nauseous. Panicking, she shrank back and said shakily, "D-dad, I-I have to go to bed, I missed school today, and I-I have homework to finish that was due yesterday," she lied, trying to push him away.

Finally, he seemed to see that his embrace had been too close for too long, and the effect it had produced on him. Embarrassed, he quickly released Mia and stood away from her.

"I-I'm sorry, Mia, I don't know why I—please forgive me. I ... goodnight," he mumbled, hastily leaving her room.

She felt totally bewildered and lost. The past few days had put her emotions through the wringer. The bullies at school she could usually manage. But the loss of her mother tore at the very core of her being.

Her father's sudden, and obvious, arousal had shocked and upset her badly. She shoved a wooden chair under her doorknob, tilting it to form a sort of doorstop. Then she grabbed the oven mitt off the bed, pulled it over her small hand and warily approached the wooden figure that once more lay seemingly benign on top of her bed.

It's only a stupid piece of wood, she kept telling herself, as she cautiously reached out to pick it up. Holding it at arm's length, she opened the closet door with her left hand and flung it inside, where it tumbled to a stop near a shoe. One wooden arm seemed to point accusingly at her as she firmly closed the closet door. Hearing the latch seat into the keeper with a satisfying *click,* she pulled on the closet doorknob to make sure. It didn't budge. *Good!*

She checked the time, 11:30 p.m. She laid down on top of her bed covers, fully dressed sans shoes, curled up in a fetal position, with Frodo purring at her feet. She reached over, turning off her bedside light. Darkness immediately enveloped the room.

It's just a stupid piece of wood ...

Chapter Fifteen – 5:00 a.m., Chandler Home

*S*omething is burning. Darkness surrounds her. Someone calls her name; it echoes slightly in the cool, crisp air. She gravitates toward the sound. In the middle of a small clearing of trees, a large fire burns brightly with a flickering, orange glow. It draws her toward it as a moth to a candle. A shadowy figure faces her, silhouetted against the glow of the large bonfire, black wood smoke obscuring the face. The voice calls to her again, "Mia! Mia!"

Slowly, she moves closer until she sees the figure of a man. The heat from the fire grows intense. He stands not three feet from the huge pyre, yet the extreme heat doesn't faze him. He should be burning, but he is not.

Opening his mouth, he screams at her to run! She shakes her head, confused. She is suddenly terrified, as the figure transforms into a hideous beast. Out of the smoky darkness, Wendy Ravenwood suddenly appears by Mia's side. She grabs her arm and vigorously shakes it, shouting at her, "Wake up, Mia! Run!"

MIA BOLTED AWAKE, COUGHING and hacking. *Fire! Oh, my God.* She reached for the light, fumbling in the dark until she found the switch. Dark, billowing smoke spread everywhere, making it difficult to breathe. Frodo paced frantically, yowling at the top of his lungs.

Mia quickly scrambled off the bed and shoved open her window. Grabbing Frodo, she tossed him out onto the relative safety of the yard outside. Leaving the window open would feed the flames, so she hurriedly slammed it shut.

Dad! Frantically, she pulled away the chair lodged under the doorknob and felt the door handle. It was warm, but not hot. When she pulled the door open, thick smoke surged into the room. Turning on the hall light, she snatched a hand towel from the bathroom, wetting it and pressing it over her nose and mouth so she could breathe. Squatting low to escape the enveloping noxious smoke, she rushed to her parents' room.

She reached for the doorknob but jerked her hand back. The knob was red hot. If she opened the door, the flames inside would feed on the oxygen, increasing the conflagration there—if she didn't, her father would die!

As she pulled the towel from her face, intending to try to enter the inferno in the bedroom, she heard a moan behind her. Coughing, she turned and moved through the black smoke toward the sound. She could just make out her dad, reclined in his chair, where he'd probably passed out.

Thank you, God! She walked over and shook him hard. "Dad—wake up! We've gotta get out of here!"

He hacked and coughed as she helped him from the chair and pushed him down low. Together, they crouched toward the front door, as thick smoke boiled around them, making the air unbreathable. They both fell on their knees, gasping. Mia tried to share the one damp towel with her dad so he could get a breath, too.

Mia found the front door handle, twisted it, and pulled it. The handle turned but the door didn't open. *Shit! Why won't it open?* She grew more panicky by the second. They were gasping and retching before her oxygen-deprived brain could grasp it. *Dad had engaged the damn deadbolt.*

Both were on the verge of passing out. With fumbling fingers, Mia stretched up to release the deadbolt. Grabbing the handle, she pushed the door open. As they struggled to escape, there was a loud *whoosh* when the fresh air was sucked in, fueling the fire within.

The super-heated air made breathing almost impossible. With strength born of equal parts adrenaline and desperation, Mia managed to drag her dad farther from the inferno that raged inside. Coughing and gagging, they crawled, then rolled out into the front yard, taking in huge gulps of fresh air. Looking back, they watched with helpless horror as tongues of orange and red licked greedily at the eaves, devouring rafters like a ravenous beast.

Their neighbor who lived on the left ran toward them clad only in his underwear, dragging a long garden hose unspooling behind him. Only as he reached them did he realize that in his haste, he'd forgotten to turn on the water. Cursing, he ran to turn it on before rushing back.

"You folks okay? Where's the wife?" he hollered at them over the roar of the fire, while he valiantly but vainly directed the weak flow of water toward the house. His well-intentioned efforts had no real impact on the inferno.

"I called 911, they should be here any minute," he added, approaching sirens growing louder. As they arrived, Mia's world went dark.

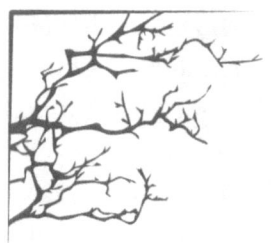

Chapter Sixteen

One Hour Earlier - 4:00 a.m., Taos Trailer Park

Freda's mother had passed out from an overdose of sleeping pills. Freda had liberally spiked her vodka an hour earlier, enough to send her to sand-land for the duration of the night, and then some. She'd lain patiently in her bed until her mother's loud, rhythmic snoring reverberated through the trailer.

Wincing in pain from the welts on the back of her thighs, she quietly got up and walked to her mom's bedroom. With the first part of her scheme completed, minutes later she dug the car keys from her mother's purse and let herself out the front door.

Turning on the tiny LED flashlight she carried, she spotted what she needed. She walked over to the red plastic can sitting beside an old rusted-out lawnmower. Picking up the can, she gently shook it. It felt about half-full. After securing that on the backseat floorboard of their old Buick station wagon, Freda opened the front door and slid behind the wheel. The car had many miles on it, but her mother kept it dependable.

Freda didn't have a license yet, but her mother had taught her how to drive when she was twelve. She started the engine and reversed out of the driveway. Driving the speed limit and obeying the law at all costs—she'd be a "cop magnet" this time of morning—she followed her phone's GPS to the street where the little snitch lived. She only spotted one cop on her way. He had some guy pulled over and never glanced her way when she passed him.

As she cut the headlights and cruised to a stop in front of the house, a shiver of anticipation and excitement shimmied up her spine. Quietly, she opened the car doors, grabbed the red plastic can, and got out, leaving the keys in the ignition. Shading a small penlight with a finger over the lens, she walked up the vacant drive where two vehicles usually sat. At the back of the house, two windows were separated by about twenty feet. She didn't know which room the little rat slept in, but it didn't matter.

Freda unscrewed the cap on the red can and sloshed the gas onto the window frames and side walls, spreading it around. Grinning savagely, she pulled out her lighter. Bye-bye, dick face! The gas lit with a *wummpph!*

She longed to stick around to enjoy the show "up close and personal," but her survival instinct kicked in, and she ran back to the car, cranking the engine. She had about eight minutes to make her escape. She'd read that was the average response time for emergency vehicles nationwide—especially at four a.m. in a town this size.

She never panicked, coolly pulling away from the curb while watching the flames spread in her rearview mirror. At the end of the block, she did stop, taking one last look at her handiwork, before remembering to turn on her headlights. That would be a stupid, dangerous mistake to make at this point.

She took all the back roads, checking her phone as she drove to see how much time had elapsed since she'd started the blaze. Seven minutes passed, and she hadn't seen or heard any cops or sirens.

If pulled over, she had no back-up plan or excuse for being out this late. That was part of the thrill of getting away with murder. As long as she played it cool, the risk of being caught was minimal.

She was a quarter mile from her house when she heard the first sirens wail in the distance through her car's open window. She glanced at the clock on her phone. *Eight and half minutes, right on schedule.* She felt a strong rush of adrenaline, drug-like in its euphoria, almost like the meth she'd smoked with Jessie and Brianna when they'd stolen a neighbor's car and gone joyriding.

They'd been caught—but only because Jessie had bragged about it to a friend whose dad happened to be a cop. Freda wasn't telling Jessie about this.

When she turned onto the loose gravel of the trailer's driveway, her headlights swung briefly across the dilapidated front steps. A dark figure sitting on the top step was momentarily illuminated. Freda slammed on the brakes hard. The almost-empty gas can she'd tossed on the passenger seat tumbled to the floorboard as the Buick slid on the gravel.

The car came to an abrupt halt a few feet from the unwelcome visitor, raising a dust cloud that swirled in the headlights' beam. An icicle of dread formed in Freda's stomach, as she recognized the figure as the strange girl she'd seen with Mia in the lunchroom. *What the fuck is she doing here?*

MIA FELT SOMETHING wet and warm licking her face. She came to with the muzzle of her neighbor's black lab inches from her face. The dog seemed to grin at her, pink tongue dripping and panting. Its chocolate brown eyes glanced anxiously between Mia and its master, who had abandoned his garden hose and—still in his underwear—stood talking nervously to some police officers.

The firemen had arrived a few minutes earlier and were hosing torrents of water onto the remnants of her home. She watched a stocky EMT checking her dad's vitals and giving him oxygen. A brawny EMT squatted beside her to place a mask over her nose and mouth, forcing pure oxygen into her deprived lungs, making her cough.

"Easy does it, young lady, just breathe regularly, you'll be okay," he told her calmly, taking her vitals.

Then he gently moved her onto a gurney like the one her dad was on. After receiving the pure O2 for a few minutes, she watched, while they loaded him into a waiting ambulance. She was feeling a bit better. Longingly, she gazed with an aching heart at the blackening hulk that had been home for the past five years. Enduring so much misery and loss in such a brief time was threatening to overwhelm and devastate her emotionally.

As they wheeled her toward another waiting ambulance, she saw the lady detective she'd talked with in school two days earlier, speaking animatedly to two of the emergency personnel. When she was loaded into the ambulance, Mia lost sight of her.

"Code 3, Charlie, let's roll, now." The burly EMT got in with her, pulling the outer doors closed. Both ambulances pulled away with lights and sirens blaring, heading for the ER.

The EMT called in Mia's physical description and approximate age, along with her vitals, reporting that she had some mild burns and was suffering from smoke inhalation.

Mia was thinking about what could have started the fire. That was useless, though. It would probably be days before the fire department could determine the cause. *More imperative was, where would she and her dad live now?*

She'd lost her mother, and she and her father now had no transportation and no home to return to. If she had any tears left, she might cry, but now she was just plain scared.

They arrived at the hospital, where the husky EMT, with another's help, offloaded her, wheeling her into the ER. A nurse met them, and Mia was moved into the triage area. *Where's Dad?* she thought frantically, as a nurse inserted a needle in her arm. The room swam briefly, and her world went fuzzy.

THE COLD DESERT WIND had increased, blowing in gusts strong enough to rock the old station wagon on its rusty suspension. Freda's alarming visitor didn't seem bothered by the blowing dust and sand. She strode down the steps and slowly walked over to the driver's side of the car, where she was hidden from the headlights.

Freda cracked the window a couple inches and shouted with more bravado than she felt, "Whatever you want, bitch, you just screwed up, big time. Get the fuck off my property now—or I'm gonna fuck you up bad!" she growled menacingly, reaching under the front seat where she hid her spare switchblade.

The tall girl stood quietly in vague silhouette against the trailer's dirty white background, as the blowing dust obscured her features. Her silence frightened Freda more—and when she was scared, she covered it with anger and bravado.

"Gonna cut you up and feed you to the buzzards!" she snarled, flicking open the six-inch blade where it was visible.

She pulled on the door handle, shoving the door halfway open—before it was violently slammed shut. Every door lock in the car suddenly snapped down into the locked position. Freda gasped with fear, frantically reaching over to pull her door lock up. It wouldn't budge. She tried the passenger side lock, with the same result.

"What the fuck do you want from me, you crazy fucking bitch?" she shrieked, as terror superseded anger.

The figure standing outside the car took three steps closer to the window, leaning down until her face was level with the partially open window.

"I simply need you to die," she calmly replied in her husky voice, her dark eyes glittering coldly in the reflected light of the dashboard.

She stood up and backed away from the car.

Freda pissed her jeans. Never had she been this frightened. She didn't like being on the receiving end of fear—doling it out had always been her forte.

Suddenly her right hand holding the knife twitched, lurching up involuntarily. Her arm was yanked sharply upward, bringing the blade's tip up close to her face. She no longer had any control over its movement.

Screaming and cursing, she grabbed her right wrist with her sweaty left hand, grimacing with terror as she desperately tried to push the deadly piece of steel away as it inched relentlessly toward her face.

Her traitorous right arm would not obey her. She thrashed her head to the left and right trying to pull away from the razor-sharp tip edging inexorably closer despite all efforts to stop it.

Abruptly then, her head snapped forward as if shoved from behind. The entire six-inch blade impaled itself through her right eye, thrusting deep into her brain. The hand holding the blade gave it one final, vicious twist. Freda's body jittered twice, then slumped forward onto the steering wheel. A mixture of terror and surprise contorted her face as she died.

Chapter Seventeen – Taos General Hospital

P recisely at noon on the following day, a shiny, black Cadillac Escalade pulled up to the hospital entrance curb. Max Stryker, the driver, got out and stretched. He stood six foot eight at 250 pounds and was built like a linebacker. He was chauffeur/bodyguard and silent partner to his boss, Kurt Kozer, the owner and CEO of the "Kozey Kitten" Cat Food company. Max was a man of few words.

He reached over and opened the back door. Kurt stepped from the car, straightening his tie, and smoothing possible wrinkles from his expensive *Brioni* suit. He was a lean six foot-two and had recently turned sixty-five. His silver-gray hair was cut short, military style. Mentally, he still felt like he was in his early forties. His body begged to differ.

"I've seen better days, Max. Let's find my granddaughter and sort this crazy mess out," he directed, pressing both hands against his stiff back, with a relieved sigh.

Max nodded, and they strode inside the brightly lit hospital. After inquiring at the front desk where to find Mia Chandler, they followed the color-coded strips on the walls to the ER.

Several nurses glanced at the approaching pair as they walked into the busy triage area. The nearest one looked directly up at Max, before swiftly averting her eyes.

"I'm looking for my granddaughter ... and her father. I was informed that they were being treated here," Kurt told the nurse.

She glanced back up from her PC screen. "What are their names, sir?" Attempting not to look again at the larger man's face, she kept her gaze down..

"Chandler. First name, Mia ... father's name, Gary," Kurt added, with a grimace.

The nurse's gaze reverted to Max, who grinned at her, reminding her why she hated horror flicks. Gazing down, she pointed. "Miss Chandler is in room four, the father is in six, just around the corner."

What the staff called "rooms" were actually partitioned cubicles. Kurt gave her a tight smile, and he and Max walked to cubicle four. Kurt opened the curtain.

Mia lay asleep on a hospital bed with an IV in her right arm, saline solution dripping slowly down the small tube into her arm. An oxygen mask covered her nose and mouth. The skin on her arms and face was bright red, as if she'd gotten a bad sunburn.

Seeing them stop outside that unit, a slim, attractive woman in a white lab coat approached. "May I help you? I'm Dr. Kelsey." Smiling, she walked over with her right hand extended.

Kurt looked at the outstretched hand with aversion. "I apologize, but I don't shake hands. I suffer from Mysophobia, and I'm rather OCD about it." He jammed his right hand into his pants pocket.

Withdrawing her hand, she grinned. "Boy, did you come to the wrong place," she kidded. Her smile slipped as she glanced up at Max, who stared down at her with almost frightening intensity.

The big man looked like his face had caught fire and someone had tried to extinguish it with a shovel. Dr. Kelsey instantly recognized the disfiguration as *acne conglobate*—a rare, unusually severe form of acne that no one would wish on his worst enemy.

Max spoke in a deep, gravelly voice, "We're here for Miss Chandler."

The doctor was reminded of the character of Lurch from the "Addams Family. Warily, she addressed them both again. "Are you family?"

"I am Kurt Kozer, Mia's maternal grandfather," Kurt offered crisply.

Turning toward him, the doctor spoke tersely. "Your granddaughter suffered first-degree burns on her face and arms, along with smoke inhalation. The father is—"

"I'm not concerned about the father at the moment, only my granddaughter." He stopped her, coldly. "I've come to take her back home with me as soon as it's medically advisable. Now, how soon will she be able to travel?" he asked.

Dr. Kelsey had met his type before—rich, entitled, authoritative—in other words, a real asshole. She cocked a brow, picking up the chart at the end of the bed and examining it closely.

"Well, if she continues on the O2 at four liters for another hour and her blood oxygen stays in the mid-nineties, she should be able to travel. Her burns are superficial, but you will need to keep her well-hydrated for the next twenty-four hours, Gatorade or the like will do," she told him, as she checked Mia's vitals.

Max glanced at Kurt, who merely shrugged. "We'll be waiting in my car out front. Please text me when she's released, the sooner the better." Kurt passed her his business card, careful that their hands didn't touch.

The two had turned to leave when the doctor called out, "Wait, don't you want to know the father's condition?"

Koser and his companion ignored her, turning the corner and walking out.

Chapter Eighteen – Taos PD

The Previous Day

When the call came about a house fire on Madison Street, Kris had been on shift for only an hour or so. Remembering that Mia Chandler's house was on that street, after the events of the past couple days involving the Chandler family, she went with her gut and asked Sgt. Hendricks the exact location of the fire.

He found the address and excitedly hollered, "Hey, LT, you ain't gonna believe this shit! The fire is at—"

"The Chandler home," she finished for him. "I sort of figured. What is it with these people, are they freaking cursed? I'm guessing you haven't located the Ravenwood girl yet, either?" She barked at Hendricks, choking down a sip of coffee that had probably been brewed three days earlier.

"I checked with the Tribal Council, who claimed they knew of no one fitting the girl's description. And she hasn't shown up in any class since the homicide was reported. We'll find her, LT, it's just a matter of time." He was hoping to placate his boss.

"Yeah, well, I'll bet my last paycheck she's involved in all this. I don't care if you have to scour the whole city, I want that Ravenwood girl in my office for questioning. This is total BS. She hasn't just disappeared into thin air. Let's get rolling before I'm forced to drink any more of this crap," she said, throwing the Styrofoam cup in the trash on her way out the door.

Hendricks hurried after her, and they piled into the Crown Vic parked in her regular spot. The early morning temperature outside hovered around fifty degrees. She cranked up the heat, knowing they'd be there before it produced any warmth.

As they turned onto Madison a few minutes later, they saw the orange glow of the fire in the early morning sky. Two fire trucks were parked in front of the burning house. Two ambulances stood at the curb with lights flashing, doors open.

They parked and walked over to where firemen continued to direct forceful streams of water into what was left of the Chandler home. One of them told Kris the fire had started at the back of the house and spread quickly, likely with the help of an accelerant, and said the two residents had been lucky to get out alive.

Kris watched as EMTs attended to the girl and her father before wheeling them into separate ambulances. She felt the girl's gaze focus on her as she was loaded into the waiting ambulance.

Who would want you or your dad dead, Mia? And why? Another migraine was looming behind Kris' eyes.

At that moment, one of the firemen was startled by a blur of fur racing out of the dark straight at him. Freaked by the blaze, Frodo had sheltered under the neighbor's car as the excitement unfolded around him. He had watched them take away his human, along with the unfriendly one who lived with her. Finally, he'd deemed it safe to come out, and he zipped across the yard, running over the fireman's shoes, surprising him.

The skittish cat came to a screeching halt when he came face to face with the neighbor's black lab. The dog merely turned its head to the side, scrutinizing him curiously. Frodo did a neat cat back-flip mid-air, puffed up like a blowfish, raced straight for the closest open door of a fire truck, and leaped inside.

Det. Lacey watched all of that happen in the space of a couple of seconds and had to chuckle, despite her headache.

"I'll bet that cat belongs to the girl. Hendricks, please secure the cat, put it in the back seat of our car. We'll take it to the vet and see if it's been microchipped. I'll need to talk to the girl and her father ASAP. All this centers on the Chandler girl and that Ravenwood kid."

Cautiously, Hendricks tried to coax Frodo close enough that he could grab him, finally managing to seize him by the scruff of the neck, the way a mother cat holds its kits. Kris opened the back door of the cruiser and

Hendricks sat Frodo down carefully on the back seat, talking to him in a soothing voice.

"There you go, kitty ... good kitty ... nice—*fucking cat*!" he screeched, yanking his hand away, as Frodo nipped his thumb.

"You making new friends there, Sgt.? I think he likes you, Jason," Kris teased, as he backed away, shaking his hand and cursing. She hurriedly shut the car door, watched the cat pace nervously around the back seat. The safety partition between the front and back seats would keep him from joining them upfront.

"You can never trust a cat—all nice and purring one second, next thing you know they're sinking their freaking teeth in you," Hendricks whined, inspecting his thumb for damage. Seeing no blood, he quit complaining and settled back in the passenger seat to organize his report on this latest incident.

Lacey walked the scene of the fire for a good while, talking to the last of the firemen and taking notes, as the rising sun blazed over the eastern horizon, chasing shadows in the cold desert morning. She returned to the cruiser and was ready to leave the scene for arson investigators when dispatch called.

"LT, we have report of a possible DB. See the manager at the Taos Trailer Park, be advised subject is female, age unknown. Subject reportedly in a 1989 Buick Sky Master, proceed code two."

"Copy, code two," she replied, turning on the emergency lights and speeding away toward the trailer park, accompanied by Frodo's loud yowls from the back seat.

KRIS PULLED THE CROWN Vic into the Taos Trailer Park entrance and past a leaning row of rusted mailboxes just inside the park. Swinging in the wind, a small sign outside the front door of the largest mobile home proclaimed "Manager's Residence" in black stenciled lettering.

Kris parked in front of the trailer, zipping up her jacket as she and Hendricks got out and walked up the small set of stairs. She rapped three times on the aluminum door, shaking it in its frame.

"Hello, police. Hello, this is TPD," she said loudly at the door. There was no answer.

She was raising her fist to knock again when a woman's voice yelled cut over the gusting wind, "Over here."

They turned to see an elderly woman ambling toward them, holding a leash attached to a dog small enough to fit in a small purse.

They hustled over to meet her, as she stopped in the middle of the gravel road while the little dog squatted and took a dump. As usual, Lacey reached her first.

The little woman was almost breathless and shaking. "Look at that, scared the crap right out of him, it did. Lordy! What a thing to find on such a beautiful morning. I'm Lou-Ann Crumley, I manage the place. Been running this park for over twenty years, never seen nothing like this!" She bent down to pick up the tiny turds with a gloved hand and deposit them into a plastic bag.

"You reported seeing a deceased person in a vehicle, is that correct, ma'am?" Lacey asked the woman. "

"Yep, she's over yonder in that shitty excuse fer a car. Just a-sittin' there. Horrible! I was walking Pepe here to do his business, like I always do 'bout this time of day. I was walking past it, noticed the engine's running and the headlights on. So, I walk over to say hello to Miz Ferguson. Her car, and she's usually gone by this time, she works at the Mega-Mart." Lou-Ann pointed at the car.

Kris's eyes grew alert. "Ferguson? Does she have a young daughter named Freda?" she asked the woman.

Lou-Ann snorted, "Sure as hell does, or did. If you'll just let me finish … anyway, I get to the driver's side and look in, and it-it's just awful. I-I think it's that young hellion of hers still a-sittin' behind the wheel. Looks like someone kilt her dead," Lou-Ann finished.

Kris thanked her and told her to go inside and get warm, they'd handle it.

The woman stopped on the steps, turned, and said, "Best check on Miz Ferguson while you're here, not like her to miss work. What a mess," she clucked her tongue and half-dragged Pepe up the steps and into her trailer.

Chapter Nineteen – Taos Hospital

Once more, Mia woke up in the ER, from the mild sedative they'd given her earlier. As her eyes began to focus again, she saw a hazy figure sitting by her bed.

The dark-haired figure leaned forward. "It's time for you to leave," she said abruptly. "Your father will live. Your grandfather is here, he will take you to stay with him ... temporarily. Listen to me carefully. The one responsible for the burning of your home has paid the price for that treachery and will hurt no one again." Wendy spoke calmly, as if discussing the weather rather than someone's death.

Mia's eyes widened at the news, but she was numb beyond caring. An alien from outer space could have walked in now, and it wouldn't have fazed her.

"Did you kill Freda?" Mia asked quietly.

"I killed no one. She took her own life. It was ... self-termination," she said coolly, dark eyes glittering.

Mia snarled, "Why are you here? I don't want anyone else harmed because of me. Don't you get it? If you hadn't insinuated yourself into my life, my mother might still be alive."

Wendy was quiet for a moment. "What has occurred would have happened regardless of what I did or did not do. Only the circumstances, the manner, might have differed. I am here to ensure that *you* survive to fulfill your destiny," she replied, standing up.

"You're telling me that *my* freaking *future* is so important, three people had to die because of it—my mother included? You're insane." Mia erupted angrily at her.

The strange girl stared at Mia as she pulled an object from a bag on the floor. It was a turquoise necklace, identical to the one she wore.

"Your destiny is playing out as we speak. Lean forward so I may place this around your neck," Wendy commanded.

Frightened, Mia eyed the necklace suspiciously. "W-Why should I wear that thing? It-it looks like the one on that creepy wood sprite," she asked.

Wendy replied impatiently, "It is a gift. The totem, or 'wood sprite' as you call it, was simply a talisman, nothing more. *This* will be our connection to each other—this, and the blood pact."

She fastened the necklace securely around Mia's neck. It felt warm to the touch, as if it were alive. "Do not take it off for anything or anyone," Wendy said ominously.

"Or what? It's only a freaking necklace," Mia snapped.

"Or I might not be able to protect you," Wendy replied icily.

"Protect me from whom? I was managing alright until you showed up in my life," Mia shot back angrily, ignoring all the problems she'd struggled with before Wendy's arrival. "This is such *bullshit*! I had a beautiful mother who loved me. Now s-she's gone! Along with my home and my poor Frodo," she began to weep.

Wendy shook her head. "The journey ahead of you will be perilous. You must always be vigilant, wary; not only your life but those of others are also at stake. That is all I can say now. Heed my warning, Mia. Protect the necklace, and it will protect *you*." For once, she sounded almost human. Then she turned and walked out of the curtained room.

Mia reached up, yanked the necklace from her neck and threw it in the wastebasket by the bed. *Screw you, Wendy!*

CAUTIOUSLY, LACEY APPROACHED the car idling in front of a dilapidated trailer, Hendricks close behind her, his hand resting nervously on his weapon. Nearing the driver's side, they bent down to peer at the bloody figure of Freda Ferguson, her head lying against the steering wheel. The black handle was the only visible part of her switchblade; the blade itself was buried to the hilt where her right eye had been.

Maybe we've just found our lost knife, Kris thought grimly. Seeing one glazed, green eye staring back at him, Hendricks quickly turned away from the window. Freda's pale face was frozen in a rictus of terror. Kris was not surprised this girl had met a violent end. She'd been a troubled young woman in life.

Kris spied the spout of the red gas can on the passenger side floorboard of the vehicle and quickly put two and two together. After setting the fire, the girl had probably taken all the back roads to evade the cops and emergency crews. *So, who was waiting for you when you got home?* She wondered.

Kris's adrenaline rose as she pulled her weapon, motioning Hendricks to follow her. They climbed the trailer's steps, and she tried the door. It wasn't locked. Her loud knock echoed on the aluminum door, *bam-bam-bam.*

"Hello, Mrs. Ferguson, this is the police. We're coming inside," she announced. She pulled the door open, holding her weapon in one hand and beckoning Hendricks to follow with the other. Slowly, she entered the trailer's drab interior in a crouch, swiveling fast left and right as she moved farther inside.

"It's clear," she confirmed, as Hendricks squeezed in behind her, glancing around the small living room.

A ratty couch stood against one wall, an ancient TV with rabbit ears sat on a couple plastic milk crates. Empty soda cans littered the floor, and cigarette butts overflowed an ashtray fashioned in the shape of a great white shark's cavernous mouth. "Jaws" feeding on butts instead of people.

"Mrs. Ferguson, I need you to come out, now!" Kris yelled toward the back of the decrepit home.

No answer. *Shit, not good.* They cautiously slid past a small, messy bedroom, which was empty. The door to the other bedroom was ajar. Warily, Kris pushed it open with her right foot, keeping both arms extended, her Glock 19 leading the way.

Jenny Ferguson was dead. She lay naked, face-down on her bed. Kris did a double take—it looked like the woman had grown a tail. On closer inspection, the tail appeared to be a bloody, leather quirt, its handle shoved deep into the woman's ass. Only the numerous leather straps used as a whip were visible, explaining the illusion. Bloody welts covered her buttocks and thighs in a crisscross pattern. *What in hell happened here?*

Kris keyed her shoulder mike, "Dispatch, this is Lacey. I need homicide out here, ASAP. Notify the ME there are two DBs on site." As she spoke, Kris motioned Hendricks to back carefully out of the small bedroom.

"We need to get out of here; we've already contaminated the crime scene," she said, as they exited the trailer to await the homicide crew.

Did Freda kill her mother? Or was the murderer someone else? If so, had the killer first slain the mother, then lain in wait for the girl to return and killed her, too? *Shit!* Kris groaned, as her migraine intensified.

Loud yowling from the back of her cruiser reminded Lacey of the frightened, pissed-off cat imprisoned there.

"Hendricks, when the crew gets here, have them go over everything in detail—twice. I'm going to take that cat to the vet and see if it's microchipped," she told him, as she opened the car door.

"What if it isn't, LT?" he asked, eyebrows raised.

"Then you'll canvass the neighborhood 'til we find the owner. Come on, Jason, use your head. I'll be back soon. Hey, you want a breakfast sandwich from 'Bozo Burgers?' I'm gonna grab something on the way back."

"Yeah, get me the 'Imperial'—it's the one with extra cheese and bacon on it," he said.

Kris rolled her eyes. "That's just what you need, a heart attack on a bun," she chided only half in jest, as she started the cruiser. Frodo wasn't happy, yowling and pacing the back seat anxiously, as she backed up and headed into town in search of a vet.

Chapter Twenty – Taos Hospital

Gary told himself he was lucky to be alive. If Mia hadn't awakened when she did and been able to drag him out of the fire, his ass would have been toast. As the pure oxygen poured into his lungs, he was feeling almost normal.

A pretty, female doctor walked in to look at his chart. "I see you're alert now, Mr. Chandler. Good. Your vitals have improved in the last hour. How do you feel?" Dr. Kelsey inquired.

Gary sat up, took a couple of deep breaths after taking the O2 mask off. "I think I can breathe okay now. Where's my freaking daughter?" he asked brusquely.

Kelsey raised an eyebrow but said nothing as she punched some buttons on the machine that stood by his bed.

"Your *freaking* daughter is doing fine. She's in the next bay over." She quickly pulled the IV from his arm, making him yelp. "Your father-in-law and another very large fellow arrived about an hour ago. He's waiting for you and your daughter to be released. Not a very pleasant man, if you ask me, but it's really none of my business," she replied, ripping the EKG electrodes off his chest, taking hair and possibly some skin, as well.

"Ouch! Could you be more careful? That freaking hurt." He rubbed his chest where the sticky pads had been. "They aren't pleasant people. Kurt Kozer is a rich snob. Thinks he knows what's best for everybody. Him and Max are fuckbuddies, from what I hear. I bet ol' Kurt has to take a handful of those little blue pills just to get it up. Max got a face that would scare the stink off a skunk. But I'd never say that to his face—if he had one," Gary snickered.

As she finished unplugging Gary from all the equipment, Kelsey tried to ignore his lack of empathy for the disfigured man she'd met briefly.

She handed him release forms to sign for himself and Mia. He took the proffered pen and scribbled their names at the bottom of the forms, giving them back to her.

"Are we officially checked out now?" He sat up.

She nodded once and left the cubicle to check on another patient. He slipped on his shoes and walked over to the next bay, where he found Mia sitting on a chair beside the bed, chin in hands, staring at her shoes.

"I need to talk with you, Mia, before we leave here. Your granddad is outside waiting."

Mia's head came up at this news. "Did he come to Taos just for Mama, or for us, too?" she asked him.

"Both, I expect. Listen, I'm gonna be staying here in town. You're gonna go stay with your grandfather in Boulder 'til we figure out what to do next. Your granddad and I talked about this late last night. With me working all the time, I can't really take care of you like your mom did. I can't abide staying with your mama's old man, he looks at me like I'm a piece of dog shit stuck to the bottom of his shoe. In his eyes, I was never good enough for your mother when she was alive. That sure as hell ain't gonna change now she's gone," he told her solemnly.

"But ... where will you stay? You're not abandoning me for good, are you, Dad?" Mia was suddenly frightened that she would have to live with her granddad and that guy, Max, whoever he was, forever.

Gary gave her a tight smile. "I'll camp out at the store, got a cot in the back to sleep on. Better than nothing. It won't be for too long. I'll figure something out soon. I can't leave the store, it's the only source of income we've got now. You understand?" He shrugged, shuffling his feet.

"Yes, I *understand*. I understand that you never gave a crap about anybody but yourself. You only married Mama 'cause her daddy's rich. I don't believe you've ever loved anything except money and whiskey. Where does that leave room for me?" Mia spat out. She had no more tears. She'd cried them all out in the last two days.

Gary stood there with his mouth open, for once failing to come up with a defense against her brutal honesty.

"You're pathetic. Goodbye, Dad." She walked numbly past him, leaving the hospital. Her granddad's car was waiting to whisk her away to a world about which she knew nothing.

Max was standing by the car as Mia approached the Cadillac. She nodded to him, meeting his gaze. His ice-blue eyes were islands surrounded by a sea of cruelly cratered flesh.

"Miss Mia, your granddad's expecting you. Please get in." His voice was a deep baritone.

He opened the door, and she hesitantly climbed into the backseat. It smelled of expensive leather and fruity aftershave. Max shut the door, walked around to the driver's door, and tucked his large frame in behind the wheel. Her grandfather sat in the vehicle's spacious backseat, reading the business page of a newspaper.

"Mia, how are you, child?" He never looked up from the paper.

"I'm ... scared I guess, considering all the shit that's happened in the last couple days," she told him honestly.

He glanced over at her impassively, scrutinizing her as if appraising an expensive bauble. "Your father has agreed to let you come stay with me for a while. We think it's for the best, right now. You need a change of scenery after losing Mary Jane and your home in such a short span of time. I think we'll be able to find room for you, right, Max?"

"Yes, sir." The big man agreed, as he started the engine.

At that moment, Mia felt more alone than she ever had in her life. *In the space of two days, I've lost everything I love,* she thought with despair. Max had started to pull away from the curb when a police cruiser's flashing lights appeared in his rearview mirror. The car pulled up beside him and stopped, blocking him from moving.

"What the devil do they want?" Kurt groused from the passenger seat. "We are up to date on our registration, are we not?" He frowned.

Max answered, "Yes, sir."

Mia watched a lady get out of the cruiser and approach the driver's side window, then realized it was the detective she'd talked to at school. Max lowered his darkly tinted window.

"Good morning, are you Mr. Kozer, sir?" Lt. Lacey inquired, addressing Max.

"No, ma'am, is there a problem, Officer?" Max asked pleasantly.

"It's Lt. Detective Lacey. I was informed that this vehicle belongs to Mr. Kurt Kozer, Mia Chandler's grandfather. Is that correct?" she asked, leaning down and spotting Mia in the back seat.

"I'm Mr. Kozer, Detective, what can I do to expedite matters? I'm in a bit of a rush as I have a teleconference scheduled, and I need to get my granddaughter settled in." Kurt attempted to placate Lacey and move her along.

"Well, first of all, I have something that belongs to Miss Chandler," Kris said, turning back to open the cruiser's back door. She pulled out a cat carrier with Frodo inside, still wailing his displeasure at being caged and hauled around.

Seeing her beloved pet again touched Mia's heart. "Oh, you found Frodo. Thank God, he's okay." Eagerly, she shoved open the door so Kris could place his carrier inside.

"What's this? I wasn't told you had a cat, Mia. What did you say its name is?" Kurt's voice warmed slightly.

"His name is Frodo. You know, from the 'Lord of the Rings.' It's one of my all-time favorite books," she replied, helping Kris situate the carrier on the back seat next to her. When he saw Mia, Frodo stopped howling and began to purr inside his cage.

Mia wasn't fooled by that. She knew that cats also purr when in distress, and Frodo was still not a happy camper. "He's still freaked out by all that's happened," she said, petting his head through the cage bars.

"Well, we'll see how well he gets along with my brood when we get to my residence. Are we free to travel now, Detective?" Kurt queried Lacey.

"One more thing—I need to speak privately with Miss Chandler for a minute before you leave," she told him.

"Is this really necessary, Detective?" His smile faded. "We've traveled a long way and I'm sure Mia is quite fatigued from all the ... unfortunate events of these past few days."

"Police business, sir. I'm sorry for the inconvenience and the delay. I barely caught you before you left town. Now if you don't mind?" She motioned Mia to step out, and Mia complied. They walked to the rear of the car.

"First, I want you to know how sorry I am for your loss," Kris said quietly. Mia couldn't think of a response, so she only stared out at the snow-capped mountains to the west. Kris took a deep breath and said, "Second, I wanted to tell you that Freda Ferguson is dead."

Carefully, she watched Mia's reaction to this. Mia didn't visibly flinch. But she cut her eyes away from the view to look directly at Kris.

"Dead? Do you think she was responsible for the fire that almost killed my dad and me?" Mia asked.

Kris hesitated. "It's too soon to be positive, but she was found with an empty gas can in her vehicle. The amount of time between when the fire was started and her death makes it likely that she was responsible."

Mia wasn't surprised.

"Mia, have you been in contact recently with Wendy Ravenwood, or whoever she claims to be?" Lacey asked, watching her closely for any 'tells.'

"She ... she came to visit me in the ER today. She said she was sorry about what had happened to Mama and the house," Mia told her truthfully, only omitting any details.

"Do you know where we can find her? That young woman is somehow implicated in all this mess. Did you know that no one by that name is registered in your school? And she hasn't reported to any class since this all started. She isn't in any state database. No one knows where she lives. Even if she were homeless, we would have found her by now. It's imperative that I find and question her. Help me out here, Mia, please," Kris implored, hoping for some clue to the mysterious girl's whereabouts.

Mia pushed a wisp of curly brown hair out of her face, deciding to stick to the truth. "If I knew how to find her, I'd tell you. But I honestly don't know her well. She just ... tends to show up out of the blue. I don't know where she lives, Lt. Lacey."

Kris studied her for a moment, as the desert sun infused Mia's face in a golden hue of honey-colored light. "Okay. I believe you. But FYI ... I suspect you know more than you're saying," she said, raising an eyebrow. Mia watched, as Lacey moved toward her cruiser.

"I'll be in touch. I have your grandfather's number." Kris paused before getting in the car, turned and gave Mia a last, thoughtful look. "Stay safe,

Mia Chandler," she said solemnly. Then she climbed into her cruiser and sped away.

PART TWO
Chapter Twenty-One -
Wallowa Lake, Oregon

Ranger-in-training Pete Chandler was finally about to graduate from his probation to become a Ranger in the State Park Service. No longer would he be low man on the totem pole, so to speak. An affable twenty-one-year-old who stood five-foot-eight, he'd worked off any excess weight he'd carried before his training began, replacing it with lean muscle by working out every day after his training schedule.

Now, his grey eyes were fixed on the pretty, auburn-headed woman with curly hair who was piloting the fourteen-foot V-hull Jon boat effortlessly across choppy Lake Wallowa. The lake was situated south of the small town of Joseph, Oregon, and was surrounded by the beautiful Wallowa Mountain Range. The woman was his boss and good friend, Chief Ranger Missy (Melissa) Anderson. She was primarily responsible for policing the Wallowa State Park, where she lived and worked. She was an attractive, vivacious woman with a strong personality and a quick mind that readily handled difficult situations.

They were out on the lake today to gather water samples. Missy eased back on the throttle, and the bow settled gently on the deep blue water's surface, slowing to a stop in the middle of the lake. She briefly checked the GPS coordinates, handing off the actual sampling of the water to Pete.

"Your turn to scoop up some nice algae and lake muck for the guys back at Water Quality to 'ooh' and 'ahh' over with their digital analyzers and microscopes." She grinned, slipping her Ray-Bans over her large, emerald-green eyes.

Pete grinned as he lowered the sampling tube into the depths. "Thanks a lot, boss. You know, we could be catching some nice rainbows while we're out here if *somebody* would just bring a damn fishing pole along. We are in a freaking boat, after all," he teased amiably, watching the depth of the sampling tube climb to almost one hundred sixty feet on the small digital depth meter before it hit the lakebed.

"If someone *I* know would learn to bait their own hook, I might consider it. You're a grown man, for God's sake. You act like the damn worm is going to come back to haunt you or something," she laughed. "Anyway, there's no fishing when we're on the clock, Bud."

Pete pretended to ignore her. He was squeamish when it came to fishing using live bait, and he'd taken a lot of ribbing for it. He mostly stuck to artificial lures. He didn't catch as many fish, but he didn't suffer a guilty conscious, either.

"I just don't want one of God's creatures impaled on a hook in order to satisfy my craving for fish, is all," he said, as he started hauling the sample up from the depths.

Missy pulled her sunglasses halfway down her nose with an index finger to stare at him as if he were from another planet. "What makes you think that they feel anything at all? You ever ask a worm if it hurts when you stick it on a hook?" she goaded him.

Pete cringed inwardly at her imagery. "No, ma'am, but it seems to me said worm doesn't get much of a say in the matter. I suspect if it had a choice and could talk, it would tell you where you could stick your hook," he replied.

"Ouch! Okay, enough philosophical fish talk. We need to get this done and get off the lake. There's a front moving in and we sure as hell don't want to be caught out here when it hits." She looked anxiously toward the ominous-looking thunderheads building quickly to the west of the Wallow Mountains.

Glancing up at them, Pete began reeling in his sample faster. Abruptly, the thin eighth-inch steel cable he was retrieving went taut and stopped as if a giant hand deep under the water had grabbed it. He pulled hard but it wouldn't budge. *Shit*! It was caught on something.

"Missy, I can't get the damn thing up," Pete announced.

"Sounds like a personal problem, try Viagra," she smirked.

He blushed, embarrassed. "It's probably hung up on some brush or rocks down there." He yanked hard on the cable. Whatever held it wasn't letting go.

She frowned. "Huh, never had a problem with it getting stuck in this area before. Guess there's always a first time. Let me shift the boat around, Pete. Maybe that'll dislodge it." She started the old twenty-five-horse Evinrude with her second yank of the starter cord. Blue smoke and bilge water billowed out of the exhaust port as the engine coughed to life.

She steered the craft slowly in a tight circle, as they worked to dislodge the sample container from whatever obstruction had snagged it below. The cable was wound around a large reel mounted on a portable A-frame housing that sat on the boat's flooring. As they circled, the tension on the cable grew, and the boat began leaning precariously toward the water.

Alarmed, Pete yelled at Missy to cut the engine. She killed it just as the edge of the boat tilted over to meet the waterline. Water rushed into the vessel before it slowly stabilized, pulling it closer to where the snagged cable disappeared into the depths.

She kept a bailing bucket handy for times like this. She tossed it to Pete. "You get the honors this time, Pete. Best be quick, those storms are heading this way."

She glanced toward the west again, deciding at that moment to cut the cable—the water sampler be damned. She couldn't risk another minute trying to get the uncooperative cable unstuck. They were sitting ducks on the open lake, obvious targets for a lightning strike.

She bent down and opened her tackle box, digging out a pair of wire-cutters from its bottom. As she stood up, a blustery downdraft from the storm's leading edge had reached the western edge of the lake, whipping the water into chop that pushed rapidly toward them.

"Ah, Pete, forget the bailing. Just cut the damn cable. Now. We've gotta get off the lake, ASAP!" she spoke urgently.

As Pete grabbed the cutters from her and bent over the side to cut the cable, the first heavy waves slammed the boat like a watery hammer knocking him off-balance. With a startled yelp, he fell overboard, quickly going under. He came up sputtering and gasping for air—dropping their only pair of cutters, which quickly sank—in his haste to grab onto the side of the wildly rocking boat.

"Grab my hand, Pete," Missy had to shout to be heard over the gusting wind. To keep from being tossed into the angrily churning water herself, she'd quickly wrapped a rope anchored to an eyelet on the bow around her waist. She extended her hand, which Pete grabbed and held onto tightly, pulling himself back on board.

"I-I lost the fucking cutters, I-I'm sorry, Missy," he stammered, catching his breath.

"Screw the cutters, I was afraid I'd lost you to the 'Lady of the Lake,' Bud. She seems a bit pissed right now," she replied tightly. "Help me shove this damn thing overboard before it sinks us!" She grabbed one side of the cable spool's A-frame while Pete grabbed the other. They fought for balance on the violently rocking craft. Together, they managed to heave the heavy spool over the side, watching it disappear as hefty waves pushed more water into the boat by the second.

The skies overhead darkened rapidly. Brilliant strokes of lightning flashed overhead, the sharp cracks of thunder making them flinch. Rain began falling in dense sheets as Missy jerked the starter cord on the old engine. On the third pull, it finally coughed to life. Pete settled in the bow, looking—and feeling—half-drowned, while Missy twisted the throttle, and the boat began gaining speed.

She had to angle the boat's nose into the roiling whitecaps, as its bow bounced roughly over the waves. According to the GPS, they were about a half mile from her dock. The rain was blinding, and she was forced to reduce speed as waves continually pounded the craft's left side. Water was accumulating inside—if they didn't bail it out fast, the boat would swamp and sink.

"Bail like your life depended on it, Pete," Missy screamed over the roar of wind and thunder.

They had both donned orange life jackets before leaving the dock. She hoped like hell they wouldn't have to use them. Pete bailed like mad, scooping buckets of water out as fast as possible, but between the heavy rain and tall waves crashing ceaselessly over the Jon boat's sides, it was a losing battle.

With growing terror, Missy watched a small but powerful waterspout form about fifty yards away and move straight for them. She barely had time to scream for Pete to hold on, before the outer edge of its ferocious winds picked up their boat like a child's toy, flipping it and dumping them both into the icy whitecaps.

Missy surfaced, coughing and sputtering. Looking wildly around, she spotted Pete bobbing face-down about ten feet away. Fighting to keep him in sight as the waves bounced her up and down, she breast-stroked through the choppy water to his side. His head was bleeding from a nasty cut. She turned him over and he coughed up what felt to him like half the lake.

Out of the corner of her eye, she saw the 'no-wake' buoy bobbing around some ten yards away. That should indicate that they were close to her dock and in relatively shallow water.

"Pete, think you can swim?" she grunted between waves, clutching him and trying to keep both their heads above water.

"T-think so. H-head hurts, though," he complained.

"There's a buoy over there, we'll swim for it," she sputtered, as waves crashed over them. They swam through the choppy water, reaching the buoy—only to find that it had nothing to grab onto. *Shit*!

"Okay, my dock is only about fifty yards away ... think you can make it?" she asked, knowing he was injured and might not have the stamina to battle the waves and reach it.

"Remind me—never—get on—'nother boat—'kay?" He coughed out, gasping for breath.

Pushing off the buoy, he swam desperately toward the dock. Missy followed suit, cutting strokes through the frigid water. When they'd left the buoy, they had been almost parallel to the dock, but wind and waves constantly shoved them away from the dock's safety. She knew if they couldn't overcome that drift, they'd be pushed into the cove, where the cliff sides were too steep to climb, and they would likely drown.

"Gotta swim harder," she urged him. "Come on, Pete, you can do it, Ranger," she encouraged, as they were forced to intensify their efforts battling the relentless wind and waves.

Already exhausted, Pete began to get a cramp in his right shoulder, making it painfully difficult to fully rotate that arm to swim. Missy had almost made it to her dock when she glanced back and saw him struggling.

"I-I can't—make it, Missy—my shoulder," Pete yelled, in misery, as his shoulder muscle knotted up.

"Hang on, Pete, I'm gonna get you some help!"

She had finally reached the ladder attached to the dock for exiting swimmers. She pulled herself up the ladder, her own muscles shivering and twitching from exertion and the cold water. She climbed wearily up onto the dock, paused a second to catch her breath, and hurriedly spotted what she needed.

Grabbing the end of a length of rope coiled by a piling, she quickly tossed it out to Pete, still floundering in the waves. It was barely long enough to reach him. Urgently, he paddled with his left arm and scissored his legs with his last surge of energy to snag the end of the rope just before it disappeared beneath the rough water.

"Hang on tight, don't let go, and I'll pull you in," Missy hollered. Wrapping her end of the rope around a piling on the opposite side of the dock to use as a fulcrum, she started tediously pulling him in. By the time Pete made it to the ladder, her arm muscles were like Jell-O.

"You've gotta help me pull you up, Pete. You'll have to use your legs to push yourself up the ladder. I'll keep tension on the rope and take up the slack as you move up," she instructed, gritting her teeth.

With the rope around his left hand, Pete used his right to hold on to the ladder rungs and pushed himself up until she could grab his left arm. She pulled him the rest of the way onto the dock, where they both collapsed, exhausted.

As the storm moved fully over the lake, the rain intensified, enshrouding the area in a veil of torrential water. Missy stood, helping Pete to his feet, as a brilliant flash of lightning arced out of the sky, striking the buoy where they'd rested only minutes before.

The immediate blast of thunder tapped reserve adrenaline neither thought existed. They scrambled off the dock and up the small flight of stairs to reach the old ranger's cabin now used only occasionally.

Chapter Twenty-Two –
Wallowa State Park

S haking with fatigue, Missy fumbled with the clip holding her keys to her pants, then quickly unlocked the cabin door, and they stumbled inside. She reached over and flipped on a light switch, then turned on the small space heater. Although she seldom used the tiny cabin since she got married, she still kept it fully stocked with essentials.

She grabbed some large towels out of the small bathroom. Tossing one to Pete, she inspected the small bloody gash on the back of his head.

"I'm n-not going to the f-freaking ER. *Ouch*! that s-smarts," he grunted, shivering in his wet clothes, as she parted his hair to get a better look at it.

"It doesn't look like it needs stitches," she told him, shining a small flashlight on the injury. "Quit your bitching, you'll be fine. Keep pressure on it," she ordered.

She grabbed some peroxide and a butterfly bandage from the bathroom cabinet, adding some small scissors and a razor. Then she instructed Pete to sit on the cabin's one wooden chair.

"I'm gonna have to take some hair off around the wound to make this work, Bud. I'll try to be careful," she squeezed his shoulder.

"Do what you gotta do—argh, *shit* ... that s-stings." He hissed through clenched teeth as the peroxide hit his wound. His thick, dark blond hair, once worn touching his shoulders, was now trimmed short to Ranger standards.

Carefully, Missy clipped the hair close to the scalp perpendicular to the wound, blotting up leaking blood as she worked. With the razor, she shaved his scalp close around the injury.

"This is gonna hurt, you ready?" She was poised to apply the bandage.

"Just d-do it," he growled.

She pulled the edges of the wound together and quickly put the bandage over it. "There, that wasn't so bad," she said, appraising her work.

"Yeah, w-well, y-you w-weren't on the receiving end," Pete grumbled, touching the bandage gingerly, as he shook with cold.

"I'm going to catch hell for losing that boat and all the equipment on board. I knew there was a front coming in. Bad judgment call." She was pissed at herself.

"I've got to call Jake, he's probably shitting bricks by now," she told Pete. Then she remembered her phone had been sitting next to her on the boat seat and was now at the bottom of the lake. *Shit*! Fortunately, she did have a spare—at home.

"Pete, do you still have your phone?" she asked, as she grabbed some dry clothes from a small dresser, heading into the bathroom to change.

"Yes, m-ma'am, but its p-pretty well d-drowned, d-don't know if it'll w-work or not." He dug it out of his cold, dripping pants and tried turning it on, but the phone was dead. "D-don't think it s-survived the lake. We could d-dry it with your h-hairdryer. B-but by the time it was dry, you c-could have driven home," he replied logically.

"Good point. I'll be out in a minute." She closed the bathroom door.

As she toweled off, she caught a brief look at herself in the small bathroom mirror. Her oval face was pale with exhaustion, making her large emerald eyes stand out against her dainty nose and her full lips. Those eyes were extremely expressive. When she rolled them, it might mean anything from "good grief" to, with one brow raised, "bullshit!" She was expert at shooting nasty looks—particularly at her husband, Jake—who dreaded getting the "stink eye," which often meant, "you're sleeping on the couch tonight!"

Unconcerned with her looks, she usually couldn't be bothered with makeup, except for a touch of lipstick. Her shoulder-length, wet hair curled wildly around her face without her usual hair clip controlling it. Quickly, she dressed in the spare clothes she kept there, and turned the hairdryer on her curls.

While he waited for her, Pete used his towel to dry himself off as best he could while still wearing his sodden clothes.

Suddenly Missy flew out of the bathroom like she'd been shot out of a cannon. "Eww, there's a big-ass roach in there ... I think it flew into my freakin' hair—get it out, get it out," she screeched, eyes wide, while she frantically swatted at her damp hair, making it even wilder.

Pete watched her dance wildly around, shaking her head as if she could remove the offending roach from her hair by centrifugal force. He had to snicker quietly.

Missy was the bravest person he'd ever known. She could outshoot most men he knew, and she was tough as a seasoned drill-instructor when it came to enforcing Park rules. So, to see her cavorting around like a crazy woman, slapping at her hair tickled him.

"I don't think it's there anymore, boss. You'd surely have flushed it out by now. It's probably behind the toilet, hiding for its life," he said, still grinning.

"I freakin' hate roaches—especially roaches that fly. They're not supposed to fly, right? Somebody up there messed up by giving 'em wings." She shook her head once more, angrily. Finally, she gave up trying to flush the bug out and regained some of her composure. She found one of her old scrunchies and pulled most of her curls back into it.

"Let's get out of here, I need to see and hold my baby," she said.

"Which one? Belinda or Jake?" Pete teased.

"That's not funny. What's *funny* is a certain cadet I know who's going to be cited for insubordination if he doesn't get his skinny ass out of this cabin ASAP. Go home and get some rest. You're going to need it," she growled, grabbing an umbrella off a hook by the door.

Pete's smile wilted as they neared the door, "You know it's still pouring out there, right?" He opened the front door hesitantly and glanced out.

Missy stopped and cocked a brow at him. "What? You gonna complain about a little rain after nearly drowning in the freaking lake? Sorry, but I only have one umbrella." She popped it open.

Pete shook his head and dashed out through the deluge to his Honda CRV. Muttering something about feeling sorry for the roach, he climbed in and drove off to his home in nearby Joseph.

Missy locked the cabin door behind them. Trying to avoid the largest puddles, she sloshed to her classic VW minibus. She'd had it restored twice—the last time over a year ago, shortly after she and her husband, Jake Anderson, had first met. On that occasion, the bus had ended up full of mud and water in a ditch after they'd used it to escape from a fiend bent on killing Jake.

Recalling that and the subsequent events, Missy shivered, as the outside temperature plummeted with the front's passage. She slowly drove down the gravel lane, careful to avoid the water-filled potholes peppering the road like moon craters. Taking a right onto the highway, she drove the mile that separated the cabin from her home with Jake, turning onto the narrow lane bordered by tall stands of pinon pines and aspens. The house sat two hundred yards from the highway in the middle of a large clearing in the surrounding forest.

Missy and Jake had married; they and their three-month-old daughter, Belinda, now lived in Jake's boyhood home. The rain had nearly abated by the time she pulled to a stop beside Jake's old pickup. She got out and walked up to the front door, half-expecting Jake to be waiting anxiously for her and slightly disappointed that he wasn't.

Walking inside, she was greeted by a high-pitched howl. She peeked into the spare bedroom to find Jake bent over a crib that held their very unhappy daughter.

Belinda looked and sounded like a tiny, angry prisoner. She kicked at the bars of the crib, screeching her irritation at being awake and unhappy. Missy crossed her arms in the doorway, smiling at Jake, who helplessly attempted to calm his daughter with cooing and clucking sounds, sounding like a wounded duck.

"She wants to be held, Jake. Just pick her up, you know she won't break," she said, startling him. With Belinda's loud cries, he hadn't heard Missy enter. He whipped his six-foot frame around, as seeing her safe sent a surge of relief through him.

Jake had a craggy, almost handsome, face framed by long, raven-black hair. Full, dark lashes and brows made his ice blue eyes more dramatic. He'd been a loner for years before he met Missy. He earned a decent living, writing novels that had so far sold well.

"*Shit*! She just woke up crying; she doesn't usually do that. I think she's either hungry or she pooped her diaper, or both." He took Missy in his arms and kissed her hard. "Did you just get in? I was worried, with the storm and all."

She wrapped her arms around him and squeezed him tight. As she thought of how close she'd come to never seeing them again, tears formed and ran down her cheeks to wet his chest.

Concerned, Jake gently pushed her away to look at her. "What's wrong, Babe? You're shaking. Why are you dressed in street clothes?" He'd just noticed she wasn't in her uniform.

"I had to change clothes at the cabin. Pete and I were taking water samples out in the middle of the lake. The damn sampler got hung up on the bottom just as the storm broke. Then a freaking waterspout came out of nowhere and sank the boat. Pete and I were thrown clear, then had to swim our way to the dock. Something hit Pete on the head, he nearly drowned, and we narrowly missed being hit by lightning." She explained calmly.

Jake's temper exploded. "Dammit, Missy, don't tell me you didn't know that a front was coming? You of all people know not to be anywhere on that lake with storms rolling in. I—we could have lost you forever!" He scolded her while holding her tighter.

"Preaching to the choir, Bud. I knew it was coming, all right? Made a bad judgment call, okay?" She was embarrassed. Pushing him away, she gently plucked Belinda up from her crib.

Belinda's cries ceased instantly, as her mother snuggled her to her shoulder. She grinned, drooling on the diaper Missy had placed on her shoulder.

Jake felt his heart swell at the sight, and his anger drained away as he grinned back at his beautiful baby girl.

"What about Pete? Is he okay?" he asked, realizing he'd momentarily forgotten about him.

"Yeah, he's fine. I had to fish his butt out of the lake. He got a nasty little cut on his head. I would've been here sooner if I hadn't had to take time to clean and bandage it."

They walked into the living room to get comfy on the sofa but encountered a big obstacle, literally. Jinx, Jake's twenty-five-pound, semi-tame bobcat, lay sprawled out on it.

"You'll have to take up residence someplace else, fur-face," Jake told the big, spoiled cat.

Jinx glanced at him through half-lidded eyes, giving him his best *screw you, I was here first* look. Jake reached down and rolled the large cat off the couch, getting a nasty look for his trouble. Hissing his displeasure, Jinx skulked off to their bedroom, no doubt to piss on Jake's pillow.

Missy sat down and handed Belinda to Jake. Pulling up her shirt and releasing her breast, she took Belinda back, cradling her closer. Greedily, Belinda attached to her mother's nipple like a small remora to a shark.

"Hungry little bugger. Speaking of ... what say we go get something to eat after she has her dinner? I'm starving. Fishing half-drowned men out of the lake burns a lot of calories." Missy yawned hugely. Jake nodded his agreement.

"Let's go to the R&R in town. I'm craving a burger and sweet potato tots, maybe a shake. Then we'll go by Pete's and check on him. He got a pretty big bump on his head out there today." She smiled, as Belinda relinquished her breast and fell asleep in her arms.

Missy leaned down to place a soft kiss on her daughter's pink forehead, inhaling the clean baby smell so peculiar to infants and puppies. *I'm so blessed to have you both,* she thought, looking at Jake.

Chapter Twenty-Three – Pete's House, Joseph, Oregon

The rain had slacked off when Pete arrived home to find a tall, raven-haired girl sitting on his front porch swing. She wore a black top and jeans, appeared to be in her teens, and was casually rocking back and forth.

What the hell? He got out of the car and warily climbed the steps.

"Can I help you with something ... er, miss?"

She stopped rocking, as her dark eyes fastened on him. "You are Pete Chandler." It was not a question.

Pete stood for a moment with his mouth slightly open, wondering if he'd ever seen the girl before. "That's me. Sorry ... do I know you?" he asked. The girl's cool, serene stare made him uncomfortable.

She got up and walked over to where he stood. She was taller than him and exuded a quiet, mature presence. Her silent composure caused him to take a step back.

Finally, the stranger spoke again. "Did you know that you have a half-sister, Pete?" she asked in a husky contralto.

Pete frowned, "I have a—w-what?" He was incredulous. His head suddenly throbbed with pain unlike the twinges from his injury.

The corner of her mouth curled slightly. "You have a younger sister living in Taos, New Mexico. She recently lost her mother in a car accident and her home was set afire, burned to the ground. Presently she is in her grandfather's custody. He's taking her to live with him in Boulder, Colorado, for a while."

As she recounted what had led to her presence here on his front porch, Pete's grey eyes were locked on hers.

145

"What about my father ... is he still alive?" he asked hesitantly.

"When I last saw him, he was. Pete, you must listen carefully to me. Your sister's name is Mia. She will need your help very soon. As you will need hers," the mysterious girl finished.

Pete slowly shook his head. "Listen, I don't know who you are or why you're telling me all this, but I haven't seen or heard from my old man since my Ma kicked him out of the house when I was just a kid for getting some girl pregnant. And he sure never told me that I had a half-sister," he said heatedly. "Just who the hell are you and what business is it of yours? Are you a friend of my 'half-sister's' or something?"

She almost smiled, her cold dark eyes glittering, "I am ... 'something like' a friend of hers, yes."

Abruptly, he realized what it was about her that made him so uncomfortable. During their entire conversation, he'd never seen her blink. As he got that, he was even more unnerved. She stepped closer and he instinctively retreated, catching himself at the edge of the steps.

"She is part of your destiny, Pete—blood of your blood. You cannot deny blood. You *will* help her. You are her brother," she asserted, her face now solemn.

Pete sensed a veiled threat behind her words. "I would really appreciate it if you would just leave. I—"

She stepped nearer, close enough for him to smell an earthy fragrance, akin to mushrooms and pine resin, with hints of freshly turned earth. Before he could back away, she reached out to gently touch the bandaged wound on the back of his head.

"Whoa, back off. What do you think you're do—?" Then, his scalp tingled as a sudden warmth flowed outward from the injury, momentarily suffusing his entire head. The pain from the wound was gone. *What the hell had just happened?*

Pete backed awkwardly down the steps to get some distance from the strange girl. His hand shot up to the wound, feeling that the bandage Missy had applied was missing.

"Looking for this?" she extended her palm, displaying the remains of the dressing. "You won't need it any longer. I will see you again, Pete Chandler. When the time comes, you will do the right thing. You fought bravely with your friends against that malevolent creature last year. You persevered and survived. Your actions proved your mettle then, but your fortitude will be tested again—soon!" she told the astonished Pete.

He stood there, pondering how she could possibly know about that hellish night a year earlier, when she suddenly breezed past him without another word.

Where the sidewalk met the street, she stopped as an old "rice-burner" car pulled to a halt in front of her. She held Pete's gaze briefly before climbing into the passenger seat, closing the door. He watched, bemused, as the ancient red Ford Fiesta drove off, belching a blue cloud of smoke in its wake.

Just who or what the hell was she? She didn't talk or act like any teenager he'd ever met.

"Wait, who the hell are you?" Rousing from his muse, he yelled at the car as it sped away.

Pete shook his head, confounded by what he'd just experienced. Turning, he walked back up the steps to his front door. Unlocking it, he stepped wearily inside and flipped on the light. He was startled to see a strange little wooden figure sitting on his couch. *What the hell now?* The hair on the back of his neck stood straight up. Moving closer, he noticed the piece of wood was shaped vaguely like a person. A plain white envelope was attached to one of its legs. Printed on the front was his name.

With shaking fingers, he pulled it off, opened it, and read it: 'Please accept this spirit totem as a gift. I know you have questions. Some will be answered, others will not. In the meantime, stay well, Pete Chandler.' The note contained no clue to the girl's name, only the initials, W. R.

Feeling a little queasy, he let the note fall onto the couch, next to the little wooden figure. A shiver unrelated to his wet clothes ran up his spine. How could she have gotten inside with the door locked?

After showering and changing into dry clothes, he was going to the kitchen to make himself a snack when a loud knock at the door stopped him. He went over and opened it, after looking through his peephole. Missy and Jake stood there, with little Belinda cradled in her mother's arms. In his, Jake cradled a bag of food from the R&R.

"Hey, Pete, we brought you supper ... maybe breakfast, too." With a grin, Jake handed the grease-stained bag to him. He thanked him and waved them in.

"We were just in the neighborhood. Thought you might be hungry after all the exercise you got earlier. We wanted to stop by and see how your head was feeling. Pretty big bump you took out on the lake, Bud," Missy said anxiously, as she tried to keep Belinda from gumming the top button on her blouse off. When Pete didn't answer, beckoning them in, she frowned.

As they stepped into the living room, Jake spotted the little wooden figure propped up against the couch cushion.

"What's this?" He gave Pete a curious glance, walking closer to check it out.

Moving the "spirit totem" to a table nearby, Pete told them sit on the couch as he pulled up an extra chair to face them. He began by describing the strange girl who'd been waiting on his front porch when he got home. Then he told them how she'd revealed he had a half-sister named Mia, saying cryptically that Mia would soon need his help, and he, hers. Finally, he related how she'd touched the wound on his head, he'd felt the sudden warmth, and the pain had instantly disappeared.

Missy arched a brow. "Let me see the wound, Pete," she insisted. Rising, she handed Belinda to Jake and walked around Pete to inspect the wound she'd bandaged earlier.

She couldn't find it. The butterfly bandage was gone, as Pete had described—but there was no vestige of an injury. Either the hair she'd shaved on his scalp had completely grown back, or she was hallucinating. *What the hell?* She looked more closely, running her fingers through his hair for any evidence of the gash. She found nothing.

Perturbed, she asked Pete to continue his narrative. When he revealed the stranger's casual mention of the beast they'd fought together, she stopped him.

"Exactly what did she say about it?"

Pete shrugged. "She just said she knew that I ... that we had defeated it, and that my courage would be put to the test again soon, something like that. The whole exchange was bizarre. She looked like a teenager, but she talked like someone a lot older. I don't know how else to describe it."

"*Shit*! I never did find out her name," he groused, twisting his hands nervously.

He finished by telling them how, after the girl took off, he'd come inside and found the little wooden figure with the note attached. He handed the note to Missy. Jake stood and leaned over to read it with her. Pete watched for their reactions.

Jake said, "So, she must have been inside before you got home. You maybe leave your door unlocked?"

Pete shook his head. "No freakin' way. It was locked up tight when I left this morning and when I unlocked it after she left."

"Maybe she had a lock-pick set with her," Missy said, taking Belinda back from Jake, leaving a trail of baby drool on his shoulder.

Pete thought about it. "Possibly. I never checked the windows to make sure they were locked," he replied.

He hurried into the bedrooms and inspected the windows, but all were locked. Back in the living room, he checked the two facing the porch swing. Locked tight.

"They're all locked, none broken either," he told them, opening the front door and examining the front door latch keeper for scratches. Nothing. *Crap!*

"Well, if she could heal that cut in your scalp, maybe she came in *without* a key. It still doesn't make any sense. Why not just give you the 'totem' when she met you out front instead of going to the trouble to break in and leave it for you to find later?" Missy queried, handing Belinda back to Jake so she could stretch a bit.

Pete shrugged and shook his head. Jake belched, and the smell of hamburger and onions filled the air. Missy made a face and waved a hand to fan the odor away.

Jake flushed with embarrassment. "Sorry, think I ate a little more than I should've." He tried to change the subject. "Pete, do you think she could've had a key?"

Pete shook his head. "Gee, I hope not, but I suppose anything's possible. The whole encounter was damn creepy," he continued, pacing back and forth on his hardwood floor.

Jake was feeling uncomfortable holding the baby. Belinda had woken from a brief nap and was grinning at him. She often did that when she'd pooped her diaper or thrown up on him, sometimes both.

"Uh, Missy, can you take her, I think she needs to have her diaper changed," he said, handing the baby to her carefully, as if he held a live grenade. *What a delightful smell,* he thought, wrinkling his nose as the odor of baby poop settled over the couch where they sat.

Missy took Belinda, giving Jake a look that said, *thanks a lot, Bud.* "Pete, unless you have a spare pair of Pampers laying around, we've gotta go. I forgot to pack a spare when we left the house. Enjoy the burger and tots.

"I don't know what to tell you about that creepy chick. If she comes back, try to find out what the 'W R' in the note stands for. Oh, but don't piss her off. You don't know her from Adam, and she could be dangerous. See you in the morning, Ranger." She gathered up her daughter, giving Jake the full "stink eye" as they walked out to his truck.

From his front door, Pete watched them go. The sun was settling behind the mountaintops to the west, waning rays of daylight hidden by the remnants of storm clouds. He sighed and closed the door, snagging the bag of food off the table. The queer wooden figure lay supine, staring up at him.

"What the hell are you, really?" he asked out loud, half-expecting it to answer. *Of course, it can't. It's just a piece of wood.*

He shook his head, taking the food out of the bag and placing it on a paper plate. He put it in the microwave, set the timer, and sat down to wait at his small dining room table, his eyes drooping tiredly, when the microwave *dinged.*

As he was taking the plate from the oven, a sudden clattering noise from the living room caused him to whirl around. His eyes grew wide with alarm, he dropped his plate—and shrieked.

Chapter Twenty-Four - Kozer Estate, Boulder, Colorado

Mia woke to the sound of tires crunching through ice and snow as the large Cadillac lumbered slowly up the winding, aspen-lined driveway. Some of the cold, wet stuff had recently been plowed, mounds of it piled on either side of the narrow lane.

Passing through massive double gates, the car stopped in front of a rambling, two-story mansion with Gothic, fifteenth-century-style arches overhanging the entryway. Mia gazed at a huge pair of hideous-looking gargoyles guarding either side of the heavy mahogany entry door. Their heads were a weird amalgam of cat and wolf, with open jaws displaying wicked-looking teeth. The bodies were like a misshapen creature from an H.P. Lovecraft novel. She shivered, although the car's vents were blasting out heat.

Max got out and stretched, opened Kurt's door, then came to open Mia's door, leaning his large frame over its top. "We're here, Miss Mia. I'll take your cat. Please follow your grandfather inside." His smile only emphasized his ravaged features.

Mia felt pity for the man. *If anyone knows what it feels like to be different, surely, he does,* she thought as she felt the gusting, snow-laden air swirling in tight eddies. Her grandfather had already gotten out of the car's relative warmth into the biting flurries of snow and ice pellets. He frowned, as he walked around to her side of the car.

"Come on, girl, I need to get out of this shitty weather. I could catch pneumonia out here. Let's go, you're letting snow inside the vehicle." He extended a gloved hand out to help her out. Mia took his hand and scooted out of the car.

"This is where you live? It's much bigger than I imagined," she said, trying to be polite. *And much uglier,* she thought, as they walked between the horrid-looking sentinels guarding either side of the massive door. She'd never been to her grandfather's residence before. He had always visited them briefly, and never overnight.

As Mia grew closer, she noticed the gargoyles' eyes radiated a reddish glow from their stone sockets. *Creepy as hell,* she thought.

Kurt saw where she was looking, nodding proudly. "They're rubies. Eleven and a half carats each, mined from Myanmar. Very lifelike, don't you agree?" he smiled proudly, as Max punched in a code on a keypad mounted outside the front door. Mia nodded uneasily, watching the keypad LED turn green. Max opened the massive door, and they walked inside, greeted by eighty-five-degree air. Kurt kept it warmer in the winter for his hairless cats.

"Well, what do you think? It's a large place, so I keep filling it with things to occupy the empty spaces," Kurt boasted.

Mia thought his definition of "things" was entirely different from her own. Expensive-looking art filled almost every inch of the huge foyer's walls. A huge crystal chandelier hung over an exotic-looking marble floor. To her right, a staircase spiraled up to the second floor. The banister rail looked like some expensive wood. Everything in the estate reeked of monied excess. She'd bet even the hairless cats' litter box cost a gazillion bucks.

"It's really nice, Grandfather. I just need to call Dad and let him know we arri—*shit*! My phone. I forgot that I lost it when the fire started," she exclaimed dejectedly.

Her grandfather shook his head. "You young kids today seem to be attached at the hip to the fu-, uh, freaking things. Don't worry, I still have a landline, though it doesn't always work when the lines get iced. The internet also seems to come and go at will," he growled, guiding her into the house proper.

He led her to the kitchen area, which was humongous. *You could fit most of our house inside this,* she thought, taking in the stainless-steel sub-zero freezer next to an eight-burner stove with an oven probably large enough to hold a small person. *What made me think of that*? she wondered.

"There's fresh fruit in the refrigerator and sandwich material if you're hungry. Otherwise, lunch is served promptly at noon and dinner is at six," Kurt told her, opening the cavernous refrigerator to display what, to Mia, seemed pitifully meager contents. *Crap! No real food.* Everything inside looked healthy.

Then Frodo let out a pathetic yowl from his cage. "I need to feed him, I doubt he's eaten since yesterday," Mia said.

Kurt smiled tightly. "Might as well let him out to see how he gets along with the others. Ah, he has been neutered, correct?" he asked sternly.

"Of course, he's a rescue cat." She rolled her eyes.

Kurt's smile disappeared. "You don't have to be a wise-ass, young lady. It's a perfectly relevant question. All my cats are female and haven't yet been spayed. I can't have some alley cat with his balls intact anywhere near them," he said bluntly.

Mia was startled by his tone of voice. "I-I'm sorry, Granddad, I didn't mean to be flippant. It's just been the longest, shittiest couple of days in my life ... and I miss my m-mom." Her voice quivered and twin tears coursing down her cheeks.

Kurt turned to Max, muttering something she couldn't hear. Max gave a slight nod and left the room. She heard the front door open and shut.

She walked over to Frodo's cage and opened it. Cautiously, Frodo stepped out, looking warily at the unfamiliar surroundings. Sensing no immediate danger, he wound himself around Mia's ankles, rubbing his head against her legs and purring.

Kurt came to stand beside Mia. "I'm sorry about your mother, Mia. I miss her badly, too. But she's in a better place now. Believe me, if she were here, she would tell you not to worry about circumstances you have no control over," he told her.

She heard the front door open and shut. Max walked in, carrying a gold-plated urn, a multifaceted crystal stopper capping it. Mia's eyes grew wide when she realized what he was carrying.

"Is that ... Mama in there?" she asked hesitantly.

"Yes, it is. Your father's insurance wouldn't have been sufficient to cover the cost of cremation and a proper urn to preserve her remains." Max set it down on the counter.

Mia walked over to inspect it. The fancy inscription on it read: Mary Janet Kozer, 1986-2019, Loving Mother, Precious Daughter Taken Too Soon.

Nothing about "devoted wife," not even her married name, she noted cynically. A hissing growl brought her attention back to Frodo. His back arched and his fur stood on end, as two of Kurt's hairless cats had come to investigate the newcomer. Frodo didn't know what to make of the odd-looking cats in front of him. He growled loudly, while the other two merely sat, staring at him. He glanced up at Mia as if asking, *what the heck are those?* Then he turned and raced back into his carrier, cowering in its back corner. Mia smiled for the first time that day—she knew if he could've shut the door behind him, he would've.

"I think he's a little freaked-out. Your cats don't seem to be afraid of him. He's like me, I guess. New surroundings take time to adjust to. Do you think I could feed him now? He has to be hungry and thirsty," she told Kurt.

He walked over to a large pantry and opened the door. It was stocked floor to ceiling with "Kozey Kitten" cat food, naturally.

"The cats will certainly never go hungry. Pick whatever is to your liking. Max will provide some water for Frogo," he started to turn away.

She scowled. "Thank you. And it's *Frodo*, not Frogo," she corrected. Max smirked.

"Yes, well, whatever its name, feed it. I'm retiring for a short power nap before my teleconference," Kurt said curtly, leaving her alone with Max.

He opened the can of cat food she'd chosen, dumped the contents into a plastic dish, and set it and a bowl of water on the floor in front of the open cage door. Hunger and thirst overcame Frodo's fear of the weird cats. Hesitantly, he emerged to attack the food with gusto. The resident cats had already lost interest in the newcomer, wandering off elsewhere in the cavernous mansion.

Mia leaned against the marble countertop and watched Frodo eat. Max was observing her watch the cat. "How long have you had him?" Max's deep baritone reverberated in the spacious kitchen.

"About five years. Listen, Mr. ..."

"It's Maxwell. But you can call me Max," he interrupted, smiling.

Mia nodded. "Okay, Max. If it's alright with you, I'd like to call my father now and let him know I'm here. Grandfather mentioned you have a landline?"

"We do. Like Kurt said, it works when it works. I've got a cell you can borrow if there's any problem with the landline. Looks like your cat's about finished. I'll show you to your room and fetch him a litter box," he told her, scooping Frodo up and handing him to her.

"All of Kurt's cats keep mainly to their own rooms," he explained. "You'll need to keep him in your room with you until he and the others get better acquainted." He picked up the carrier and led her to the staircase in the foyer.

She clutched Frodo tightly to her chest, fearing he might try to leap away at a moment's notice. She knew he didn't like to be held, and now, he began the ominous low growling that meant, *put me the hell down, now.* Luckily, her room was the first one to the right at the top of the stairs.

Sensing the cat was agitated, Max quickly opened the door. Frodo sprang from Mia's arms, running directly underneath the enormous, king-size, four-poster bed that occupied a third of the large room. Silky, pale blue curtains with tassels were tied back at both head and footboard.

"This is beautiful," she exclaimed breathlessly. An antique armoire stood next to a huge full-length mirror, to Mia's dismay. "Is there maybe another room available without a large mirror?" she asked hopefully.

Max recognized the reason for her discomfort. "Afraid not. All the rooms have them. I'm sorry," he said. He turned to leave, then stopped. "Tell you the truth, I hate 'em, myself. Make yourself comfortable, Mia, dinner is at six sharp. Don't be late; Kurt does not abide tardiness," he warned, as he walked out of her room.

With a relieved sigh, Mia closed the door behind him, moved to the bed, and sat down to test its firmness. The mattress practically molded itself to her butt. *Must be memory foam.* It was the most comfortable bed she'd ever sat on.

She picked up the landline phone near the bed to dial her dad's cell, then remembered his had also perished in the fire. Instead, she called his store. It rang five times before voice mail kicked in. She had to leave a brief message telling him they had arrived safely and asking him to call her soon.

She glanced at the ornate grandfather clock standing against the wall. It was five-fifteen in the afternoon. *Where else would he be? The shop doesn't close until 6:00.*

As she set the phone back down on its base, she noticed an envelope on the table beside the phone. Written in elegant cursive was Mia. She picked it up and opened it, and was stunned to read:

'Dear granddaughter, Due to the recent unfortunate circumstances, I feel you should be informed that you have a half-brother about five years older than you. His name is Peter Chandler, and, to my knowledge, he still resides in the small town of Joseph, Oregon. I doubt that either of your parents told you of his existence. Your mother would not speak of it. She was quirky that way, rest her soul, but then, she had a right to be.

Your father was already married when he had an affair with your mother and got her pregnant. You were the result. When his wife found out, she threw him out of the house like a proverbial hot potato, leaving her to raise your brother, Pete, alone. I regret if all this comes as a shock, but in case anything should befall your father or me, you need to be aware that you are not alone.

I will not discuss this with you further, as I have an aversion to emotional displays. With affection, Kurt'

When she finished reading the letter, Mia still had her mouth hanging open. *Shock*, yeah, that was a good word for what she felt. Kurt was right, she could at least understand why her mother had never mentioned she had a half-sibling.

"My *brother*," she said out loud, tasting a word she'd never thought to utter. Various emotions coursed through her, each vying for attention—surprise, anger, and foremost, curiosity. She felt a profound sense of loss, of time squandered.

Her grandfather also knew enough about her dad to predict that he wouldn't have told Mia about his son. She could readily picture her father abandoning his wife and small son without remorse, walking away to start fresh with her mother. It was precisely what he'd always done with his failing business ventures—place the blame elsewhere and walk away. The thought infuriated her. At that moment, she didn't care if she ever spoke to him again. *What an asshole!*

Chapter Twenty-Five – Taos PD

Sgt. Hendricks' throat was roiling with acid. *Gotta quit drinking coffee on an empty stomach,* he thought miserably. He stood, waiting for the ten-year-old, piece-of-shit office printer to spit out the medical examiner's reports. The LT was eagerly awaiting the autopsy reports on the Fergusons' deaths.

With much whirring and shaking, the decrepit beast slowly printed out the ME's documents. Hendricks had scoured the town and had gotten no useful information from the Reservation, so he *still* hadn't located the Ravenwood girl. His ass would go from the frying pan into the fire when he gave the boss that message. He took a deep breath and walked both reports to her doorway, knocking twice.

"Come in, Sgt. I hope you have some good news for me?" Lacey was finishing typing a report.

Hendricks cleared his throat, "No, ma'am, I wish I could say that we have a lead on the girl, but she's ghosted. Hell, LT, we've turned over every rock and come up with zip. No disrespect, but are you sure this girl really exists? We've run aliases and nothing matches her profile."

Lacey sighed and massaged her forehead in a useless effort to forestall another migraine. "I'm assuming that's the ME's reports in your hand. Let's see 'em," she said sharply.

He handed her the reports along with his own progress summary on the case. According to the ME, the Ferguson girl had died of a self-inflicted injury to the brain. No fingerprints other than her own were found on the knife; no defensive wounds to indicate someone else had done the deed. The doors of the vehicle had been locked, suggesting that she wanted no interference in her plan to kill herself. Suicide, plain and simple.

Yeah, right. Or, maybe someone did her, wiped the knife handle clean, and pressed the girl's prints on the handle to make it look *like suicide. Then all they had to do was lock the doors and walk away,* Kris thought, visualizing the crime scene. She took a sip of cold coffee, managing to spill some on her keyboard. *Shit! It's a wonder the damn thing still works.*

But why would she kill herself? her inner dialogue continued. Freda hadn't seemed like someone who would intentionally harm herself—others, sure, but not herself.

Kris continued scanning the reports. The mother's cause of death was ruled an overdose of barbiturates. The autopsy revealed internal hemorrhaging caused by ten inches of a quirt being shoved violently up her rectum.

But most of the bleeding had occurred postmortem, meaning she was dead before it was shoved up her ass. Which implied someone was very *pissed at her. Insult added to injury, meant to humiliate her even after death.* The approximate TOD for the mother was 4:30 a.m. The daughter's death had occurred close to the same time, around 4:45 a.m. No way to know if the mother had overdosed on purpose or by accident. Freda could have killed her mother. She certainly had motive, as established by the pictures of bloody welts on her legs. She'd also had time to do it before killing herself.

Killing... herself. Those two words just didn't jibe with what Lacey knew of the Ferguson girl. She'd had some small brushes with the law, but nothing of a serious nature—until a few days ago.

Mia Chandler. Mary Jane Chandler. Freda Ferguson. Jessie Gambols. Wendy Ravenwood. Three of the five were dead. Mia was with her grandfather. Only Ravenwood remained unaccounted for. Damn!

Her migraine was worsening fast. She dug a bottle from her purse, swallowed a Naratriptan, washing it down with some water. The pills made her drowsy, so she tried not to take them while at work. But if she didn't nip the headache in the bud, she'd soon be in a world of hurt.

Frowning, she looked at Hendricks, "Anything at all from forensics? Fingerprints, hair, blood? There has to be something. There always is, if we look hard enough," she said, exasperated at their lack of leads in the case.

Hendricks shrugged. "They're still processing evidence from inside the trailer, but frankly, Boss, it doesn't look promising at this point."

Kris suddenly stood. "I don't want to hear any more negativity, Sgt., I want results. If I can't get 'em from you, I'll find someone else. I suggest you start thinking outside the box. Do I make myself clear?" she snapped.

Hendricks paled. "Yes, ma'am. I'll do my best to get you some tangible results, I promise." He turned and left her office.

Maybe he's right. Maybe Ravenwood is a ghost. She groaned. She hadn't taken the pill soon enough, now the migraine threatened to make her sick.

GARY CHANDLER HAD A roaring hangover. After leaving the ER, he'd borrowed some cash from Joe the barber, whose shop was next to his, and bought a bottle from a small liquor store in the strip center. Joe had reluctantly lent him ten bucks, knowing full well what he would buy with it.

Gary's savings account was tapped out. Paying that thieving lawyer to spring him from jail had drained most of it. Then there was the little matter of getting his Jeep back from the damn towing company. When all was said and done, he was flat-out broke. If he didn't make a sale today, he wouldn't eat. Simple as that. Not one customer had walked through the door since he'd opened, and it was pushing closing time. His stomach rumbled, reminding him he hadn't eaten anything since leaving the hospital.

He noticed the red light on his answering machine blinking and pushed the button. The message was from Mia. She must have called when he went to get the whiskey. She said they'd made it to her grandfather's okay. He had never been there himself, never been invited. The old skinflint always came to see them, never the other way around. He and the rich old asshole had never hit it off and never would. Mia had asked him to call, but he didn't feel like talking to her now. His head felt like it might come off any minute.

He shrugged. "I'll call her later," he mumbled to himself. The old man could take better care of her than he could, anyway. His bowels suddenly grumbled. Rushing to the bathroom, he sat on the toilet, hoping it was only gas. Nope, the whiskey had given him the runs. Drinking on an empty stomach had been stupid. He heard the front doorbell chime.

Crap! Whoever it is has lousy timing.

"Be right with you. Hang on a sec," he hollered through the closed door. Frantically, he wiped his ass and left the restroom. Opening the hinged drawbridge to get behind the front counter, he recognized his visitor. The dark-haired girl who'd been in his house, *uninvited*, was browsing the counters.

"Can I help you with anything? Uh, sorry, I forgot your name." He forced a smile.

She looked up from the display of polished turquoise. "It's Wendy, Mr. Chandler."

She moved toward the counter where he stood. The girl was tall, he remembered that from her visit. She had the darkest eyes of anyone he could recall meeting—except, maybe, the old Navajo. Both of them gave him the creeps.

"Yes, could I please see that silver turquoise bracelet over there? The one with the little pyramid shapes on it?" She pointed.

"Of course, uh, Wendy. Let me get it for you." He stepped over to the counter she'd indicated. He extracted the bracelet, taking it back to the register and placing it in front of her for an appraisal.

"It's beautiful. The detail is very nicely done. How much?" she asked, holding the bracelet up to inspect it in the light.

"Ah, it's quite expensive, Wendy, $600." He figured the girl probably couldn't afford it. She stared at him in silence for a moment, then nodded as if she'd expected that.

"I'll take it. Could you box it up for me, please?" She dug a small wallet from her purse and counted out six hundred-dollar bills, laying them on the counter, as his jaw dropped open in disbelief.

Where would this kid get that kind of cash? She didn't look old enough to work. But Gary never looked a gift horse in the mouth. Recovering his composure, he grabbed the cash and rang up the sale, putting the bills inside the register's money tray and closing it.

"I'll have to get a box out of storage, be right back," he told her. *Yes! Finally, something's going right.* He smiled as he walked quickly into the small storage room in the back of the store. *Now I can afford to get something to eat—and maybe another bottle for later,* he was thinking. He found a small empty box on a shelf and laid the bracelet inside. Satisfied, he turned and walked back to the girl.

"Here you go, uh, Wendy. I hope you enjoy the bracelet and come back soon." He placed the box in a small paper sack and handed it to her.

She gazed at him for a few seconds. "Best hold on tight to that money, Mr. Chandler—it has a nasty habit of vanishing when you need it most." She turned to leave but stopped at the door. "By the way, you might want to close your 'barn door' before anything ... escapes. Just saying." She smirked.

He'd opened his mouth to reply when comprehension of her words finally dawned. His face flushed red with embarrassment as he glanced down, realizing he'd forgotten to re-zip his fly before leaving the restroom. *Shit!* Quickly, he turned around and eased the zipper up.

By the time he faced the counter again, the girl was gone. *Good riddance,* Gary thought. He glanced at the clock on the wall. Almost 6:00 p.m., time to close. He locked the door and flipped the sign to "closed."

When he opened the register, he got an extremely nasty surprise—a deadly Bark scorpion sat on top of the stack of hundred-dollar bills Wendy had given him. Indigenous to the area, it was the most venomous scorpion in North America.

Its wicked stinger wavered back and forth, while beady black eyes stared up at him as it postured with its claws.

What the fuck? Sweat broke out on Gary's forehead. *I almost put my hand right on the damn thing.* He backed slowly away and rushed to the storeroom for something that would kill it.

Spotting a can of hornet spray on a shelf, he snatched it and ran back to the open register. The venomous creature hadn't budged. He depressed the trigger on the canister, and a blast of noxious spray covered the fearsome arachnid—along with everything else in the drawer. The angry scorpion writhed in circles, its stinger stabbing madly until it impaled its own carapace several times, killing itself. Poking it with a pencil to make sure it was dead, he grabbed several tissues and carefully picked the scorpion up, dropping it in the waste can behind the counter.

How the hell did that thing get inside there? He shook his head. He turned back to the open register, but when he tried to pick up the spray-soaked bills, they disintegrated into green goo in his hands. He spotted a small, soggy note on the bottom of the money tray where the bills had been. He snatched it out and read: *No more booze, Mr. Chandler.*

That Wendy bitch had ripped him off. Obviously, she'd paid him with fake money. Angrily, he kicked the waste basket containing the dead scorpion. An empty whiskey bottle flew out, shattering on the concrete floor. Empty and broken—perfect metaphors for his life just now.

Chapter Twenty-Six – Pete's House, Joseph, Oregon

Pete stared in horror—the wooden totem no longer lay on the table by the couch. It stood on the floor, facing him. There was a scratching sound as it took an impossible step toward him. He couldn't believe what he was seeing.

He ran behind the dining table, looking wildly for something to use as a weapon. Grabbing a large butcher knife from the magnetic rack on the wall, he whirled around to face the thing. Skritch ... skritch ... skritch, it crept nearer.

"Stay the hell away. What the hell are you?" he yelled at the figure, as it scraped closer to him.

Two feet away, the totem came to a halt. The air around it shimmered unsteadily, like a heat wave or mirage, and then the strange girl from the porch stood in its place.

Pete held the knife out aggressively. "W-who are you? What are you? W-what do you want?" he stammered, as his knife hand shook with fright.

The mysterious girl stared at him, dark eyes glittering in the light like the black orbs of a spider. She advanced two swift steps closer, all but impaling herself with the knife he held out defensively.

Pete shrieked and recoiled, losing his sweaty grip on the knife, dropping it. He stumbled back against the sink. She glanced down at the weapon between them. Smiling, she bent down and picked it up. She set the knife on the kitchen table and closed the distance between them in one step, her face only inches from his.

She leaned in close to his ear. "Darkness is coming for you, Pete. Will you be ready?" Her icy breath chilled him to the bone ...

As his body nearly slid out of his chair, Pete jolted awake, gasping! He'd fallen asleep at the kitchen table. His R&R burger and fries sat, now cold and hard, in the microwave where he'd put them. Apparently, exhausted by his struggles swimming for his life and damn-near drowning this afternoon, he'd crashed. *What a freaking nightmare.* Anxiously, he glanced at the couch, where the little wooden figure lay exactly as he'd placed it earlier. He released a big sigh of relief. *Only a bad dream!*

Then he spotted the large butcher knife that still sat on the table beside him.

MIA MEANDERED DOWN the mansion's spiral staircase and into the kitchen at precisely six that evening. Her grandfather was already seated at the head of a long table that could likely seat twenty people. To her surprise, all seven of his Sphinx cats were crouched atop its highly polished surface, each eating some variety of "*Kozey Kitten*" that had been served them on fine china.

The whole scene was bizarre to Mia. *He's just one of those eccentric cat people,* she figured. She pulled out a chair on her grandfather's right and plopped down.

"I read your letter. I appreciate your telling me about Pete, though it seems like Dad should have let me know about him long before now. It really pisses me that he didn't have the guts to tell me himself." She toyed absently with a sterling silver butter knife carefully arranged next to a china butter dish.

Kurt raised a brow at her language, then resumed ignoring her as he continued reading the paper's financial section.

The mouth-watering aroma of cooked fish filled the air. Wearing a chef's apron, Max had just pulled a steaming casserole dish from the oven and set it on a hot pad on the table.

"Chilean sea bass with a cranberry compote," he said proudly, plating the fish. "Fresh asparagus tips with homemade Hollandaise sauce and potatoes au gratin." He gave his semblance of a smile to Mia. "What would you like to drink with dinner?" he asked, placing plates in front of Kurt and her.

"What have you got, besides water?" she asked.

"I believe we have some sparkling Perrier, apple juice, or OJ." He waited for her to choose.

Crap! It figures. She recalled the healthy contents in the refrigerator she'd glimpsed earlier. "Some plain ice water will be fine," she told him.

He got the water and placed it on a fancy coaster near her silverware. When he turned to leave, Mia asked him if he was joining them. He glanced quickly at Kurt, who'd finally put down his paper to concentrate on eating.

Max shook his head. "I'll take my dinner in my quarters tonight. Enjoy your meal; for dessert there's Banana Foster. *Bon appetit.*" He returned to the kitchen, leaving them to eat.

Between bites of the delicious sea bass, Mia asked Kurt, "I don't suppose there's any way I could get a change of clothes tonight, is there?"

He gave her an exasperated look. "I *could* have Max drive back into town and peruse the aisles of the Mega-Mart for something in your size. But I wouldn't want him on the road at night with the current weather conditions. Best wait 'til tomorrow. The storm should have passed by then," he replied.

Mia frowned. "It's just ... I've been wearing the same, grungy clothes for almost two days. I stink, I smell like a barbecue. I want to take a shower, but I have no other clothes," she complained, finishing the last bite of potato on her plate.

Her grandfather sighed, put down his fork, and finished chewing. "The best I can do tonight is have Max toss them into the wash. They'll be done by the time you're ready for bed. He will provide you with a robe to wear in the meantime. Does they meet with your satisfaction?" he asked icily.

Mia nodded. "Yes, sir. Thank you, I really appreciate it."

They finished their meal in silence. Max appeared again to scoop up their plates, placing them in a large dishwasher. Her grandfather gave him instructions to see to her clothing needs after they'd finished their dessert.

Max placed huge bowls of the dessert in front of them both and turned to Mia, "Whenever you're ready, I'll bring you a robe. You can leave your clothes outside your room. I'll knock when they're finished."

With her mouth full of the delicious confection, she nodded. She was sure she couldn't finish all of it. Feeling a little bloated, she asked, "May I save the rest of this for later?"

Her grandfather's spoon froze midway to his mouth, as a queer expression crossed his face. He lowered the spoon, seeming confused for a few seconds, then he glowered at her.

"We eat everything on our plates, or we do not *get* dessert. There will be no leftovers in this house. No late-night snacking, either. Do I make myself clear, young lady?" he scolded.

Mia said, "Yes, sir." *What a hard ass*! She forced down the last few bites. He continued to stare at her coldly until she pushed the bowl away.

"I appreciate the delicious meal, really. Now, may I be excused?" she told him, feeling slightly queasy from all the rich food.

"You'll feel better once you get used to the rules of this house," he relented a bit. "I suppose you'll want a new phone. Max can take you shopping tomorrow if the snow and ice don't keep the roads impassable." He gave her a tight smile.

Mia stood, then paused. "I was wondering, do you have any books to read? Since I don't have my phone, and it doesn't seem you have a television, I-I'd like something to distract me from everything that keeps running through my head," she said hopefully.

"Follow me," Kurt said shortly, folding his napkin and rising from the table.

She followed him out of the dining room and down a long hall. They passed a big, open room with animal heads trophies mounted on the walls, gazing down with creepy, accusatory glass eyes. Other rooms seemed to be closed off.

Finally, they came to another door, which Kurt unlocked and opened. This one was spacious and filled wall-to-wall with shelves of books. Some were historical; all the literary greats and some more modern fiction seemed mixed with many other kinds of books in his large collection.

"Help yourself to anything you wish. I only require you to be extremely careful with them. The rare, signed first editions, which are under glass, are, of course, off limits for general reading. No food or drink around them, either. Other than that, have a pleasant evening. I have an early meeting tc attend tomorrow morning, so I'll bid you goodnight." He turned and left the room, closing the door.

Mia perused row after row of fiction until she found a familiar author. Taking a book she'd chosen from the shelf, she turned to leave, but stopped. Curious about the editions he'd mentioned that were kept under glass, she walked over to check out some of the glass-encased cases scattered throughout the room.

Most were ancient-looking tomes, placed on beds of blue velvet in their respective cases. She recognized a few of the books—H.P. Lovecraft's "The Necronomicon," the Marquis de Sade's "Justine," Dante's "Inferno," among them.

The last case stopped her cold. Inside lay a book whose name and author were in some foreign language. The cover was what had captivated her. Looking up from the dust jacket was her mirror image.

The girl or woman in the picture even had a birthmark just like hers, barely visible beneath her curly bangs. Her hairstyle was old fashioned, but that was the only difference. The book looked old, its binding was cracked, and the material used for its cover hadn't weathered well.

Could this be my grandmother? Mia wondered, leaning closer to the glass to get a better look. She'd never seen a photo of her and had only been told that she'd died when Mia was a baby. MJ had never shared a picture of her mother or spoken about her. Mia had always wondered why.

As she was studying the odd book, suddenly the room went dark as death. *Shit!* Alarmed, she dropped the book she'd been holding. As she bent down to pick it up, something brushed against her hand. Mia screamed and jerked away, losing her balance in the inky black, and stumbling back against one of the glass cases. When her elbow hit it, the glass made an ominous *crack*.

Then she heard a low growl in the darkness to her right, and terror flooded through her. She let out another cry. The door to the room was flung open and light flooded in from the hallway.

"Mia, are you alright?" Max asked breathlessly. He punched something on a wall panel, and the room's lights were restored. Now she saw what had frightened her so badly.

One of her grandfather's cats crouched on the floor near her, like a small tiger ready to pounce. Its Caribbean-blue eyes were narrowed to slits as it growled again and hissed at her. Seeing the door open, it raced from the room, much to Mia's relief.

"Yeah, I-I'm okay. The freakin' lights went out. The cat must've been trapped in here when Grandfather closed the door. In the dark, it brushed up against me and scared the crap out of me." She tried to calm herself as she spoke.

Max smiled his terrible smile. "The lights are on a timer. When anyone enters, they only have ten minutes before it shuts off automatically. Kurt doesn't like to waste electricity." He merely shrugged.

She thanked him for coming to her rescue and decided that first thing in the morning, she needed to learn *all* of her grandfather's rules. She retrieved the novel she'd dropped from the floor.

"I guess I'll go read awhile. Looks like my dad isn't going to call me back tonight, go figure," she said sullenly. "But I'll take my shower first, Max, if you don't mind finding me a robe."

He said he'd bring one up right away and left. She went upstairs to her room to wait for him. He appeared moments later, a large robe in hand.

"I'll change and leave my clothes outside the door. Just be a moment." She took the robe and closed the door. She reached for the lock—but the freaking door didn't have one. *What kind of rich-bitch mansion doesn't have any locks on its bedroom doors?* She shook her head.

Someone could walk in on her at any time, dressed or undressed, day or night. The idea made her extremely nervous. Now she walked over to check the bathroom door—no lock there, either. *Crap!* She looked around, but there wasn't even a chair in the room she could use as a doorstop.

She went into the bathroom and searched the cabinets, finding one bar of some off-brand soap and a single towel hanging on a rack by the tub. *Shit*! She'd have to make do with that. She closed the door and stripped off her clothes, except for her bra and panties. She washed those in the sink with the soap, then rinsed and draped them over an empty rack to dry. Having a stranger wash your clothes was one thing. The thought of Max handling her undergarments before tossing them in the wash was too weird. Wrapping the robe around her, she gathered up the rest of her clothing, including her socks, setting it all out in the basket Max had left in the hall.

She ducked back into the restroom and, with a great deal of trepidation, removed the oversized robe. She noticed that the shower doors were completely transparent.

If someone should come in ... surely, they would knock first. She hoped.

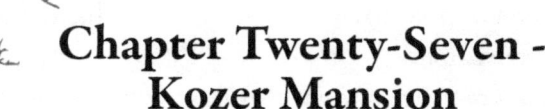

Chapter Twenty-Seven -
Kozer Mansion

He sat motionless in front the flat-screen seventy-inch TV mounted on his study wall. A small bead of sweat rolled down his forehead to drip down onto the head of his tumescent member. He gently stroked it up and down while intently watching the screen. She was so beautiful. It was remarkable—they looked so much alike. Same hair, same eyes, and body.

He groaned as the naked figure on the big screen bent over, exposing herself further, to his delight. The resolution on the large screen was excellent. He could see into every crevice in minute detail. It was almost as good as being in the same room with her ... *almost.*

His eyes devoured every inch of exposed ivory skin, while his hand intensified its stroking motion. His breathing turned ragged, as he climaxed into a silk handkerchief he'd provided for the moment. Gasping for breath, he moaned the name over and over, "Lily, Lily, my lovely Lily ..."

Joseph, Oregon

PETE AWOKE, STARTLED. The alarm on his phone was blaring the late, great Warren Zevon's anthem, "Werewolves of London" from its tiny speaker. Reaching over to shut it off, he climbed out of bed, showered, and dressed for work. He ate a quick, tasteless, microwavable breakfast sandwich. The dang things never tasted half as good as they looked in the ads and the pictures on the box.

The wooden figure remained where he'd placed it last night, on the end table by the couch. Which made him think about the mysterious girl's visit. Did she really intend that he should keep the thing? The little totem weirded him out.

A horn sounded outside, interrupting his thoughts. Missy was waiting impatiently for him to get his ass in gear. He turned off the lights and locked both the top and bottom locks behind him. He hopped into her car and started relating the strange dream he'd had the night before while she drove.

"So, are you asking me what I think the dream was about? Or do you just want my professional opinion?" she asked, half in jest, as she swerved to avoid a large vulture enjoying a meal in the middle of the highway.

"Well, I don't know much about symbolism in dreams, but it really freaked me. It all seemed so real," he said uneasily.

"You're probably over-thinking it. You just need to get laid, Bud," she teased. "Still seeing that girl, uh, what's-her-name?"

Pete blushed. "You mean Sheena? I haven't had much time to spend with her like I did when I was working at the Pizza Palace. Besides, I think she's been dating Dan the Man since he made manager there," he told her.

Missy listened and nodded as she drove them to Ranger headquarters. Arriving there, they exited the cruiser, Missy unlocked the front door of a cabin about the same size as hers, and they entered the tidy, two-room office. They sat down on opposite sides of a scarred wooden table almost buried by stacks of paperwork. An older laptop and printer sat in the table's only clear spots.

"You going to call your new-found sister? Or just wait around for her to call you? From what you've told me, it sounded like she's had a shitty week, is all I'm saying," she chatted, bringing the laptop out of sleep mode.

"All I was told was that she's staying with her grandfather somewhere in Boulder, Colorado. I don't know if she's even aware I exist." Pete glanced at the screen, waiting for the Park's website to come up.

Missy dreaded having to report the loss of the Park's boat and water sampling equipment to her superiors. She knew that she was responsible for it and that she'd used poor judgment. She'd gambled they could beat the approaching storm—and lost. It could've cost them their lives. It had been foolish, and she must now deal with the consequences. She typed out the report and reluctantly sent the email.

"Well, that's done. Hope I still have a job after today," she said, frowning.

Pete was staring out the cabin window, lost in thought. "I don't even know her grandfather's name. So, I have no way to find her right now. Guess I'll have to wait for Mia to contact me. That mysterious girl was pretty stingy with her information." He wasn't really listening to Missy.

She stared at him, shaking her head. "Hello? Did you not hear me? I might not have a job tomorrow, and here you are, worrying about something you have no control over, whatso-effin'-ever. We need to roll, Pete." She turned off the laptop and printer and marched out the front door in a huff, as Pete scrambled to follow her.

"Let's go catch some rule breakers. I'm in the mood to chew some ass today," she almost growled.

They drove slowly through the park in search of an unlucky camper or hiker committing an offense. They helped an elderly couple set up a tent. They thought they'd struck gold a little farther into the park when they caught a man taking a dump behind some sparse brush, as a portable toilet sat a mere twenty yards away.

Missy stopped, and they both got out of the cruiser. "Hey, mister, what do you think you're doing?" she yelled, startling him as he was wiping his butt.

"What's it look like, lady?" he shouted back, hurriedly yanking his pants up.

"You're aware there's a port-a-can about fifty feet away, right?" she said sternly, her arms crossed.

The man looked at her like she was an idiot. "Yeah, I *see* it fine. The fucker's been locked up tight ever since I got here yesterday. They only lock from the *inside,* so either somebody's taking the world's longest dump, or they fell in. Sorry, but when you gotta go—" he shrugged apologetically, turning away.

Missy frowned. "Pete, you have any idea how to get one of those things open from the outside? I've never known anyone to lock themselves inside and not be able to get out."

Pete scratched his head. "I've never even thought about it. You think someone could actually be trapped inside?" he asked.

"Only one way to find out," she replied, without much enthusiasm. "Look in the trunk and find something to pry the freaking door open," she told Pete.

He rummaged around in the trunk for a minute, finally walking back with a tire iron in his hand.

"This is all I could find." He handed it to her.

They headed toward the restroom, coming to a quick halt when they were about five feet away. The horrible odor was overwhelming, raw sewage layered with the unmistakable stench of death.

They looked at each other, then back at the putrid portable with something akin to loathing. The little red panel on the door was turned to "Occupied." *Yeah, but with who—or what inside?* Missy thought uneasily. She took a deep breath and stepped over to it to try the handle. Sure enough, it was locked.

"Hello? Anybody in there?" she hollered, knowing she'd get no reply. Inserting the pointed end of the tool into the tiny gap between the fiberglass door and frame, she pushed hard, putting pressure against the lock. The door didn't budge.

"Hey, Pete, make yourself useful, come lend some muscle to this thing," she told him, as she took in a lungful of the putrid air that shrouded the port-a-can. Reluctantly, Pete obeyed, and together, they shoved against the door. Suddenly, the lock gave way, the tip of the tool popped out, and they fell forward against the toilet. When they jarred it, a nasty, sloshing sound came from inside. The door swung slightly ajar before a spring inside snapped it shut again. The fetid stench of decomposition settled over them like a noxious cloud, and they both turned away fast to puke up their breakfast.

"Holy shit, that's bad," Pete sputtered, trying to clear his mouth of the taste. Missy nodded agreement.

"Well, I'd better have a look," she said grimly.

"Y-you think maybe we ought to notify the Sheriff first?" he asked hopefully.

Missy shook her head. "It's on State Park land—our jurisdiction, Bud."

Steeled herself, she opened the door all the way. A massive cloud of blowflies swarmed out of the toilet, startling her. When she hurriedly peered inside, the blood drained from her face.

She shrieked, "No! Noo!" Then her world went dark.

Chapter Twenty-Eight – Kozer Mansion, Boulder

Mia woke, staring around the unfamiliar bedroom, as someone knocked on her door. She needed a few seconds to remember where she was.

"Mia, breakfast will be served in five minutes. Please try to be prompt, your grandfather is waiting." Max announced from the hall.

"Be there shortly," she shouted, irritated by receiving such short notice. Frodo was still asleep, curled up at the foot of the bed. She crawled out from the covers, realizing that she was practically naked. *Crap!* She retrieved her underwear and the clean shirt, jeans, and socks that Max had returned to her the previous night, dressing quickly. Sleepy-eyed, she glanced at the clock: 5:59 a.m.

She scurried down the stairs to the table, where her grandfather was already seated, reading the financial page of the paper.

"Good morning. Please have a seat," he said, without looking up at her as she sat. "I assume you slept well?" he asked.

"Yes, sir. The mattress is so soft. I, ah, noticed that there weren't locks on any of the doors in my room. Any particular reason?" she asked, as casually as possible. The smell of bacon and eggs cooking caused her stomach to rumble hungrily.

He finally glanced at her coldly. "It's for your own safety. This house is quite old, and it's never been brought it up to code. Fire sprinkler systems were not available when it was built. The cost to install one now would be exorbitant. I assume you don't smoke?"

She shook her head. "No, I don't." *If I had some ganja, I might,* she thought wistfully, thinking of her small stash that had been destroyed in the fire.

Kurt nodded. "Well, then, that resolves the matter. Now I'd like to inquire why the glass is cracked on one of my manuscript displays in the library?" He stared accusingly at her.

Mia gulped and looked around at Max for help. Either he didn't hear Kurt's question or chose not to get involved, while he plated their breakfast.

"I-I wasn't aware the lights were on a timer, and when they suddenly went off, I was disoriented. I didn't know that one of your cats was in the room with me. In the dark, it frightened me, and I lost my balance and ... I-I'm sorry, Grandfather." She was on the verge of tears.

"Did I not ask you to be careful? Those books are priceless," he reproached her, then abruptly changed the subject. "Well, I have to attend a meeting in the city in an hour. When he comes back, Max will take you to the Mega-Mart for new clothes and other needed sundries."

Max placed the steaming plates of food in front of them. Mia ate hers in silence.

After breakfast, Max drove Kurt to his meeting in Boulder, dropping him off there. When he returned to the estate, he found the front door partially open. *Shit, the fucking cats!* He jumped out of the car, nearly slipping on a small patch of sleet and snow. *I'm positive I closed it behind me when we left,* he thought, as he rushed up the sidewalk to the open door.

He didn't see any of the hairless fucks wandering around outside; he didn't really expect to. The strange-looking cats detested any temperature below eighty degrees. Still, the thought of one of them escaping and freezing to death on his watch made his balls shrivel. Kurt would have his ass for dinner.

But why is the door open? Mia? He didn't see any fresh footprints in the snow. He went in and shut the door, the eighty-five-degree air smacking him in the face.

"You here, Mia?" he shouted up at the staircase. No one answered. He didn't like that. *Better check to see that all the frigging cats are accounted for.* He climbed the staircase. He stopped at Mia's door and knocked. Silence. He opened the door and looked in. Empty, except for her cat, curled atop the feather pillow.

Where the hell is the girl? Tendrils of anxiety enveloped him. He backed out of her bedroom, closing the door. He walked to each room and checked. All had pet doors installed so the cats could come and go as they pleased. The cats were all accounted for.

Now, where is the girl? He could think of only one other place she'd been. He ran down the stairs, glancing at the kitchen, which was empty. His shoes echoed in the silence of the huge house. He stopped at the door to the library.

Opening it, he called out, "Mia? You in here?" He stepped inside, walking past several aisles of books, but found no one. *Shit! Mia, where are you?* He left the room hurriedly. He was walking by Kurt's study when he noticed light shining under the closed door. He knew Kurt never left a light on. Slowly, he opened the door—he'd found her, all right!

She sat in front of the large TV screen, staring in shock at the video playing on it. A naked female was showering and bathing herself. Max watched from the door, transfixed by the big screen, as the girl's face appeared.

Thirty Minutes Earlier

MIA WENT DOWNSTAIRS to wait for Max's to return after he dropped her grandfather downtown. Max hadn't locked the front door when he left, the panel was blinking green. She opened the door to see how much snow had accumulated overnight and stepped outside, the cold air making her breath visible. Everything was coated with white except for the driveway, which she figured must be somehow heated to keep ice and snow melted.

She turned and stepped back inside, thinking that she'd closed the door behind her. Bored, she wandered into the library, thinking she'd take a quick look at the strange manuscript she'd seen the night before. She eased open the lid on the case with the cracked glass, gently picked up the manuscript, and shut the lid. Looking around for somewhere she could sit and read, she saw no chairs or benches anywhere in the library. She thought that was weird.

She walked out, carrying the book carefully, seeking a place to sit while she examined it. She decided to check out the other rooms in that hall. The first two doors she tried were locked.

She knew she'd be in trouble if Kurt came back and caught her with the forbidden book, but she wanted a closer look at that cover.

The third door was not locked. It opened into a spacious room covered in what looked like priceless carpets. An elegant, polished oak desk faced a huge TV screen mounted on the wall. She assumed this was her grandfather's study. A comfy looking leather recliner sat near the television. As she flipped on the light switch, recessed lighting came up, illuminating the room.

She closed the door and parked herself in the recliner to examine the strange book with the picture of a woman whose face so closely mirrored her own. The resemblance was uncanny. She opened the cover and saw that the dedication, at least, was in English:

To my darling Kurt,

You will always be the love of my life. I thank God that I found you.

Love always, Lily

Lily? So, who is Lily and why do she and I look so much alike, down to the same unusual birthmark? Mia wondered. The rest of the book was written in a strange language she'd never seen before.

As she delicately turned the page, her elbow knocked the TV remote off the arm of the chair. Picking it up, she somehow pressed a button that turned it on.

The frozen image of a naked, wet, female body filled the screen. Repulsed, but curious, she pressed the "play" button and watched as the girl soaped her body in the shower. As the girl's face appeared, with shocked horror, Mia realized who it was. Her hand froze on the remote.

She felt a scream build that she couldn't give voice to. She sat perfectly still, so stunned, her vocal cords had locked up.

Minutes Later

HASTILY, MAX TURNED the lights up full and rushed over to Mia. He pried the remote away from her clenched fingers, immediately deleting the video, and turning off the TV. A shame that he couldn't as easily delete those images from Mia's head—they'd been burned into her psyche.

Mia was finally able to move. "W-what the freaking hell is going on here?" she demanded of Max, as she stood unsteadily. She shook with rage and humiliation at the thought of her grandfather sitting here, doing God knows what ... while he watched her on a hidden camera, like some sleazy perv.

"What kind of sick asshole does that? *Oh, shit*! I'm gonna puke!" She jumped up, trying to push Max out of the way. She made it to the desk before vomiting all over Kurt's expensive Persian rug.

Max whipped out a monogrammed, silk handkerchief, handing it to her. Unsteadily, she wiped her mouth. Then, to his dismay, she handed it back.

"I'm sorry you had to see that, Mia. My mistake. I had fully intended to erase it. In my haste to get Kurt to his appointment on time, I forgot to lock this door. It's unfortunate ... for *you*, I'm sorry to say." He moved closer until he towered over her.

Mia's rage changed instantly to icy fear. *What does he mean by "unfortunate for me?" Omigod! He's going to kill me.* She still clutched the brittle manuscript. Gripping it in one hand, she flipped open its cover, grabbing several pages in a threatening manner with the other.

"Stay away from me. If you come any closer, I'll rip these to shreds," she snarled, backing slowly away from him. She saw alarm in his eyes at the prospect of Kurt's precious book being destroyed.

"Stop, stop! Mia, let me explain. I'm not gonna hurt you, okay?" He attempted to placate her.

Mia was shaking with fear. "If you take another step toward me, I-I'll do it, I swear to God."

Wisely, Max took a slow step backward. "I'm really sorry about this, Mia. I had no idea Kurt had a hidden camera in the bathroom. Please believe me. I discovered the video this morning when I came in to clean the study. It shocked me, too, when I saw it," he said soothingly, motioning towards the large dark screen.

"I'm sure you noticed the resemblance between yourself and the photograph." He pointed at the book. "Her name was Lily. She was your grandmother, and you're a dead ringer for her. She was everything to him. He ... Kurt lost her before you were born. When she died, well, it broke something in him.

"When he saw your school picture this year, he said it was like seeing a ghost. He's not a monster. He sees her in you, Mia. The man is delusional and lonely. I'm guessing he's mentally unstable ... but that doesn't excuse his actions," he finished smoothly, doing his best to calm her.

Mia didn't know if she could believe him. She sure as hell didn't trust him. "H-he should go to jail for what he's done. He's a freakin' pervert. I'm his granddaughter, for God's sake. I've just lost my mother and my home, and now I'm staying here with a ...You call my dad! Right now! I'm not staying here a minute longer than I have to," she demanded.

Max stared anxiously at the book in her shaking hands. "Mia, give me the book. Give it to me and I'll make the call. Fair enough?" He took a careful step toward her.

"No way! Get him on the phone. After I talk to him, maybe I'll give it to you," she told him, knowing the book was her only leverage. Once he had it in his hands, all bets were off.

"Mia, please give me the book before it's damaged. Now that I've erased the recording, you have no evidence. It would be your word against ours if the police got involved. We don't need to do that. I promise I won't hurt you." He took another tentative step forward.

Mia hesitated. *What if he's lying? Can I trust him?* She made her decision. "Call my dad, get him on the phone first, then you can have the book," she insisted warily.

Max took out his cell and punched in a number from his contact list. She heard the cell ringing, as Max held it out to her. She reached out, taking one hand off the manuscript pages to grab the phone, as it was answered.

"I'm in the middle of something—what is it?"

Panicked, not really listening, she pleaded, "Dad, it's Mia, I need you to come get me right now. I—"

While she was distracted, Max had carefully pried the manuscript out of her other hand. Too late, she recognized the voice on the cell.

"Mia? Why are you bothering me? What's going on there?" It was her grandfather's voice.

Max grinned, as the blood drained from her face. She couldn't believe she'd been so gullible. He took the phone back from her.

"Hey, it's me. Everything's under control. Mia unfortunately made a little discovery in your study," he said. Silence on the other end for a few seconds.

"Come get me at once," Kurt snapped.

"What about the girl?"

"Don't be obtuse—you know what to do. Handle it." He disconnected.

Mia's heart was racing. She turned, ran, and almost made it to the front door before Max grabbed her. He picked her up easily and slung her over his shoulder like a sack of potatoes. Mia screamed and struggled wildly, striking ineffective blows to his back, and kicking him, as he carried her to the kitchen.

With one hand, he opened a door at the back of the room and flipped on a light switch. He carried her down some steep stairs and dumped her on a filthy-looking mattress. Looking around, she realized she was in some sort of basement.

Defiantly, she spat out, "You lied! Y-you promised you wouldn't h-hurt me," she cried in terror.

Max smiled horribly. "Oh, I won't—but *he* will!"

Chapter Twenty-Nine - Taos

Gary couldn't believe that creepy, black-haired bitch had conned him out of an expensive bracelet and left that deadly, six-legged surprise in his cash register drawer along with the halfway-threatening note. That freaking girl had ripped him off, but good. The incident had cured him of his urge to drink ... for the moment, at least.

He hadn't heard anything back from Mia since her first message. He'd called the number she'd left a few times, leaving her messages, but had gotten no reply. He was becoming worried—about himself. *How can I afford to eat?* he wondered, as he checked his wallet, half-expecting a proverbial moth to fly out. *Two dollars. Shit!* That wouldn't even buy him a burger at the Burger Barn, four doors down from his shop.

Depressed, he was about to close the wallet when he noticed the corner of a forgotten lotto ticket wedged between some old business cards. Curious, he pulled out the ticket and noted it was for the previous day's drawing.

I don't remember buying this. What the hell? Shaking his head, he shoved the ticket back into his wallet. *Must have bought it when I was sloshed.* His stomach growled.

He'd had no customers since he'd opened, except for that frigging bitch. *Fuck this!* He opened the front door and marched out, locking the shop.

He drove down to the local Stop-n-Rob and parked. Walking inside, he instantly caught the delicious aroma of hot dogs cooking in a glassed rotisserie behind the counter. He began salivating like one of Pavlov's dogs.

Walking up to the counter, he asked, "Yo, how much for one of your dogs?"

The young kid behind the counter had his back to Gary while he stocked cigarettes, wearing earbuds, and humming something off-key.

Impatiently, Gary grabbed a Slim-Jim from a box on the counter and tossed it at him to get his attention.

Startled, the kid turned around and took out an ear bud. "My bad, can I help you?" he apologized.

"How much for one of those dogs?" Gary pointed.

"Three bucks, my man. You can get two for five," he added enthusiastically.

Shit! A day late and a dollar short, go figure, Gary grumbled inwardly. Pretending to check his wallet for the extra dollar that didn't exist, in desperation, he pulled out the ticket and handed it to the clerk.

"Maybe I'll get lucky and win my two dollars back." He hungrily eyed the hot dogs.

The clerk took the ticket, scanning it, and the machine made a tinny *"ta-da"* sound.

The kid's eyes were bright with excitement. "*Holy Shit*! Hey, mister, you ain't gonna believe this—you just won a million fucking dollars!" The clerk gave the ticket back to him, awed.

Gary's eyes widened in amazement, as he confirmed that his quick pick had indeed matched all six numbers! He immediately fainted.

Chapter Thirty - Wallowa State Park

As Pete's hand slapped lightly against her cheek, Missy woke. He had barely been able to catch her when she fainted. Now she remembered why she had. Sluggishly, she sat up, feeling as though someone had ripped her heart out and shredded her soul. *Mama! Oh, dear God, Mama!*

Missy retched, but nothing was left in her stomach. Pete helped her to her feet, quickly leading her away from the horrific image inside the toilet. Pete had only caught a brief glimpse before the door swung closed again—and he was grateful that it had. The naked, mutilated corpse of an elderly woman was sprawled inside, gutted like a deer. Missy sobbed so hard she shook Pete, who was holding onto her.

"M-Mama, w-who the hell did this to y-you? W-why would anybody... oh, s-shit, Pete, I-I've g-gotta s-sit down. Help me t-to the car," she moaned, breathless from the shock of so abruptly finding her poor mother's, butchered body.

She leaned against Pete, who led her to the cruiser and eased her into the front passenger seat. Looking in the trunk, he found an already-opened roll of yellow Crime Scene tape.

He stuck his head inside the driver's window, "Hang on, Missy, I'll be right back. I've gotta cordon the area off, then we'll try to figure out what the hell happened. Okay?"

She nodded tearfully, blowing her nose in a tissue. Now, dammit, she had the hiccups. Numbly, she watched Pete wrap the tape around the toilet to secure its door, then around a large area surrounding it. He trotted back and saw Mr. Shits-in-the-Woods staring wide-eyed at them.

"Hey, mister, stay away from this john. Don't let anyone come near it until we get back. You got that?" Pete ordered.

"What if I have to, you know, go again?" the guy asked hesitantly.

"Crap in your tent if you have to," Pete snarled. He climbed back into the cruiser, giving Missy a grimace, "We need to call the Sheriff's office and get them out here."

Missy was still trembling with shock, but she nodded her approval. "Call Sheriff F-Frank. G-get him out here. Tell him ... *oh, God* ... tell him to get out here ASAP and have him notify the M-medical Examiner," she added.

Pete stepped back away from the vehicle, then called 911, explaining briefly where they were and what they'd discovered after he'd moved away from Missy.

The officer said, "Sheriff Blackstone is at lunch, but I'll patch you through, hang on."

There was an audible *click,* and crappy music played in the background while Pete waited impatiently for the Sheriff to pick up.

"This is Blackstone. Who the hell is this? I'm in the middle of my lun—"

Pete cut in. "Sheriff, this is Cadet Pete Chandler with the State Park Service. W-we've found a body, sir. It appears to be Mis- ... uh, Ranger Morning-Sta—that is, Ranger Anderson's mother, sir."

There was a brief silence. "You that Chandler boy from the Pizza Palace in town?" he asked, still chewing loudly over the phone.

"Ah, yes, sir, I'm training to be a Ranger now. Listen, Sheriff, this body's ... it's in real bad shape. S-she appears to have been eviscerated. And Mis—uh, Ms. Anderson is the one who found the body, so a medic needs to check her out as soon as possible. I-I'm pretty sure she's in shock," Pete said grimly, glancing back at Missy.

Another silence. Then, "Roger that. I'll be there pronto, son. I'll notify EMS and inform the ME we've got a DB." He sighed deeply, disconnecting.

Pete cringed at the 'DB' abbreviation as the call was disconnected. But if Missy had heard any of the call, she gave no indication. She continued staring, stunned, at the tape-wrapped port-a-john, shaking in disbelief and rage as Pete joined her.

"How could s-someone do that to her, Pete? Why? For the love of God, she never hurt a fly. S-she was doing so well at the rehab place with the therapy for her injuries from the fire. What kind of fucking, low-life scum would do that to a poor, defenseless, old woman?" she asked him hotly.

"Missy, we won't know anything until the Sheriff and the ME process the scene. I'm calling Jake, you need to talk to him, tell him what's going on," he punched in Jake's number and handed her his phone. Numbly, she took it from him.

Jake answered on the third ring. "Hey, Pete, what's up? You and Missy coming by for lunch?"

Missy clutched the phone in a death grip, "J-Jake, i-it's me. I ... Ma ... Mama's been murdered, Jake. S-she was butchered, and ... then the m-motherfucker dumped her body in ... in a fucking p-portable toilet here in the park!" she sobbed uncontrollably.

Pete took the phone back. "Jake, it's bad. Obviously, we won't make lunch."

Jake was silent for a moment. "*Shit*! Listen, Pete, try to keep her calm. Have you called the Sheriff? What about EMS for Missy?" he asked anxiously.

"Already done. Just waiting for them to get here," Pete informed him.

With every heartbeat, Jake wished that he could be there to hold and comfort her. But he couldn't leave Belinda or take her to a crime scene.

"Pete, you know I'm freaking stuck here with the baby. Tell her I'm so sorry, that I love her with all my soul. We'll get through this."

Pete told Jake that she'd heard him. From the baby's room came the piercing screech of their daughter waking from her nap.

"Keep me informed. Bring her home soon as you can, Pete. I've gotta go, Belinda's up." Jake finished. Pete said he would and hung up.

Sheriff Frank Blackstone's relatively good mood had been shot to hell by Pete's phone call. He'd left half of his lunch uneaten. Arriving at the scene, he parked his vehicle behind Missy's cruiser. He was a big man, tall and brawny, with and long, sad face and dark eyes that had seen too much. Both the EMTs and the ME were already there, and an EMT was taking Missy's vitals again.

She had calmed down slightly after they'd given her a shot of something to quiet her. She and Pete told Blackstone how they'd found her mother's body.

"You'd better catch the fucker who did this before I do, Frank. I find him first, he's gonna lose his balls, and that's just for starters!" Missy snarled angrily, as she sat sideways in the passenger seat with her feet out.

As the drug kicked in, she felt mellower by the second. She fought to stay angry, but it was impossible. Pete stood by as the Sheriff lifted the crime-scene tape from around the toilet.

Blackstone opened the door with a rush of *déjà vu*, flashing back to a year earlier. While hunting down a creature he hadn't believed even existed, he'd found one of his officers killed, gutted, and mostly eaten. *Now it seems to be happening again. Shit!* He almost lost his half-eaten lunch from the toilet's stench. After a quick look, he coughed, gagged, and quickly re-closed the door against the awful sight and smell.

The ME was a small, older man of about sixty. He wore booties over his shoes and had gloved up to protect the crime scene. Smiling, he offered Blackstone some Vicks to smear under his nose. Grateful, Frank took it, coating his upper lip with the stuff. It was a little too late, but better than nothing.

"Get me the TOD, Doc. I need to know how long she's been dead. I think I can be reasonably sure *what* the COD was," he said, thinking back to his officer's ravaged body. A shiver of dread coursed through him at the idea that another creature lived and had begun slaughtering innocents.

By the time the ME finished, forensics had arrived. There was some debate about how the door had been locked from the inside. Obviously, the victim hadn't locked herself in. She'd been killed elsewhere, then placed inside. There was little blood inside the chemical toilet. But how the hell had the killer managed to lock the door from the inside and escape? Clearly, there was no way to lock it from the outside.

The ME told Blackstone the time of death was twelve to twenty-four hours earlier. "I'll know more after the autopsy but, Frank, it's definitely homicide. Nasty bit of work. I'll contact you as soon as I know more." He turned to leave.

The body was photographed inside the toilet from every conceivable angle. The EMTs then bagged and tagged Missy's mother, finally moving her body to the waiting vehicle. Several hours passed before the forensics people had finished walking a grid around the portable, satisfied that they had seized all the evidence they were likely to find.

Pete had been keeping his eye on the investigation, as well as watching over Missy, who had almost passed out in the cruiser from the shot they had given her. While the Sheriff was busy talking with the EMTs, Pete got out and walked back over to the foul-smelling toilet.

How did the fucker lock the door from the inside without being trapped himself? The mystery confounded him, but the answer had to be logical. Once again donning latex gloves, he took a deep breath and stepped inside. Pulling a small flashlight from his pocket, he carefully scanned the edges of the four walls. Nothing but some ancient graffiti of crudely drawn female genitalia.

Shining the light up at the ceiling, he perceived daylight filtering in from a slit in the fiberglass that ran around all the walls. He spotted something caught between the top of the enclosure and the back wall. Cautiously, he stepped up onto the plastic seat, crouching and balancing, with one hand against the grungy wall for support. There was little headroom. He reached up and pushed hard against the roof of the toilet. After some initial resistance, the entire roof popped free. It had been cut. That explained how the murderer had been able to lock the toilet from the inside and escape.

The fiberglass panel clattered to the ground outside, attracting the Sheriff's immediate attention. The freed piece of foreign material luckily fell onto Pete's shoulder, where it hung, as he climbed carefully down off the seat, then grabbed it to examine closely. Holding it gently, he quickly stepped back out of the toilet and showed it to Frank. It appeared to be a tuft of animal fur with blood on it. The two exchanged knowing looks of alarm—*It* was back!

Chapter Thirty-One - Kozer Estate, Boulder

Mia sat still, feeling blinded and completely terrified. After climbing back upstairs, Max had turned off the light and locked her in this dark place. Two small windows had been painted black to keep light out and nosy folks from looking in, but one of them, which was above her head, did admit a little sunlight. Scattered scratches in the paint allowed a minuscule amount of light to penetrate the basement's inky blackness.

Feels more like a freaking prison than a basement, she thought, as her eyes adjusted to the dark. Moving cautiously toward that window, she examined the scratch marks closely. It looked like someone's fingernails had gouged away small slivers of paint. *Not good!* That meant someone before her had been her grandfather's "guest" down here.

Where the hell is Wendy when I really need her? If Mia could believe anything Max had said, her grandfather was mentally unstable. She had to get out before Max could bring him back from his meeting. She could barely see a hand in front of her face. The only way out was through that window, but it was a good foot over her head. *Crap!* She needed something she could stand on to reach it. Raising her arms in front of her, she crept forward in a kind of shuffle, toward a workbench she'd glimpsed before Max had cut off the light. Her left shoe brushed against something on the floor, and she reached down, hoping she'd found a weapon. Instead, something bit her finger, hard.

"A rat!" she shrieked, stumbling backward until she tripped over a nasty-smelling mattress, landing on her ass. She shook the bitten finger and felt blood well up from it. The little bastard had drawn blood. *Do rats carry rabies? Shit! Shit!*

High-pitched squeaking erupted within the dark room. Brer Rat had company. The smell of dripping blood and the lack of light seemed to have made them bold. Sitting on the mattress, Mia frantically groped around for a weapon to protect herself from the unseen vermin. She felt something move against her left leg and screeched when another furry body scampered over her right. The squeaking intensified as more rats detected the blood. Wildly, she flailed at the awful creatures, but they kept coming. One leaped up on her shoulder and became tangled in her curly hair. Shrieking with revulsion, she swatted at it and was rewarded by another nasty bite. She howled in pain. Beyond terror now, she was praying for an end to this nightmare.

Unconcerned now if she fell and was injured, Mia stood and stumbled toward the stairway. The rat snared in her hair sank its sharp incisors into the meat of her left ear, but Mia barely felt it, as she slammed her shin sharply against the lower riser of the stairway. Losing her balance, she face-planted onto the cement stairs, bashing her nose and dislodging the rat in her hair. White hot pain exploded through her head. Blood gushed from her nose, spurting down her face.

She crawled to the top of the stairs, shrieking at the top of her lungs, "Max, Max, let me out. Please, Max. They're trying to eat me!"

She hammered her bloody fists against the metal door, while the high-pitched squealing grew louder. She shrieked and beat on the door until she'd almost lost her voice. Suddenly, the door opened, and the light came on, searing her dark-adjusted retinas. Five or six of the hairless cats leaped through the opening, racing past her down the stairs. The rats squealed a shrill equivalent of "retreat," scattering like roaches at the double intrusions of light and cats.

Mia squinted up at the figure standing in the doorway. "P-please, I-I'll d-do whatever you want ... I-I never saw any v-video. J-just p-please, please ... l-let me out of here," she pleaded, sobbing, gagging as blood ran down the back of her throat.

"Afraid it's a little late for that—can't put the old toothpaste back in the tube. I see you've gotten acquainted with my pets," Kurt sneered, nodding toward the basement. "You're going to have to learn not to be so nosy. Remember, curiosity killed the cat. Max, please help my dear 'Lily' to her feet ... and get her cleaned up. You know how I hate the sight of blood," he said brusquely.

He stared coldly at Mia's bloodied face. "When she is ... presentable, bring her to the room." He turned to leave the kitchen.

Max reached down, pulling her to her feet. He grabbed a handful of paper towels and pushed her roughly in one of the kitchen chairs. Wetting the towels, he handed them to her. "Try to clean yourself up. You don't want to piss him off more than you already have. Believe me," he warned.

She took the towels, first, pressing them gently to her distended, bleeding nose. She made plugs from bits of them, gingerly pushing them into her nostrils, as sharp, shooting pains made her gasp. She wiped the blood from her face as best she could with no mirror, cleaning the rat bites last. When she'd finished, the towels were soaked with blood. She couldn't fix her bloody clothes. She'd never gotten to the Mega-Mart—now she was sure she never would. Max lurked, watching, as she wiped her arms and legs with the bloody towels and handed them to him.

"Max, p-please let me go. I-I promise I won't tell anyone about any of this. No one will ever know," She tried desperately to reason with him.

He shook his head, "I'm sorry, Mia, what you saw can't be unseen. You could send him to prison for the rest of his life. That's not an option."

Mia recognized that she was in deep shit. *Think, damn it*! But her intellect wasn't exactly firing on all cylinders. *If I don't do something, they're going to fucking kill me.* A sudden burst of adrenaline made her frantic.

Max briefly turned his back on her to wash her blood from his hands. Urgently, she looked around for any object she could use as a weapon. The freaking knives were on the counter right next to him. No help. The only thing she spotted was a small fire extinguisher sitting on the counter by the big-ass stove.

She needed to create a distraction. "I-I'm g-gonna be sick," she told Max, making a gagging sound.

Scowling, Max turned from drying his hands. He growled, "Aw, hell. Hang on, let me get a fucking pan."

The second he turned to open a cabinet, she leaped from the chair, grabbing the extinguisher. Shakily, she pulled the safety pin and whipped around, aiming it at his face—just as he realized he'd been duped.

Mia didn't hesitate. She squeezed the trigger, and a stream of white chemical retardant flew into his mouth and eyes. He screamed in agony as the powder blinded him.

"You fucking little bitch," he roared, spitting and sputtering, as he stumbled toward her. He grabbed for her, but she ducked and side-stepped him. Then she swung the extinguisher with all her might, hammering him hard against his right temple. He groaned and fell to his knees.

She struck him again, this time hearing a sickening *crunch* as the heavy device connected with the back of his head. The big man fell like a sack of bricks. She thought she might have killed him. Right now, she didn't care a shit. Dropping her weapon, she went through his pockets, grabbing his cell and his key ring.

Gotta get the hell out of here. Grab Frodo and haul ass. She stuffed the phone in one pocket, keys in the other. Then she ran as quickly and quietly as possible up the stairs. Flinging open the door to her room, she shrieked. Her poor cat gently swayed back and forth from a ligature cinched tightly around his broken neck, the other end attached to the canopy above. His glazed eyes bulged in death. Mia was horrified beyond words. *What kind of monster would do this?*

She jumped as a voice behind her spoke. "I told you curiosity killed the cat," Kurt hissed evilly. She whirled around to face him.

Growling ferociously, she attacked. She'd taken two steps toward him when he raised his right arm and pressed something cold against her neck. Her world went black.

Chapter Thirty-Two - Albuquerque, New Mexico

Gary Chandler marched out of the lottery headquarters in Albuquerque feeling like—well, like "a million dollars." The transaction had gone smoothly enough, once he'd gotten a copy of his damn birth certificate and provided an old driver's license to prove his identity.

Shit! He still couldn't believe he really had one million dollars sitting in his checking account right now. *Fuckin' A!* He laughed, shaking his head at how his bad luck had disappeared in the blink of an eye.

He'd tried to call Mia at Kozer's number three times today. Each time it had gone straight to voice mail. It wasn't like her to be out of contact this long. *Did I piss her off? What if something's happened?* He didn't really know Kurt that well. All these years, the stingy fuck had never once invited the family to visit his estate, and Mary Jane had avoided the issue whenever Gary brought it up. The old dude was markedly peculiar. *Asshole wouldn't even shake hands, for God's sake.* Gary never trusted anyone who wouldn't shake hands.

With that thought, he decided he would pay Daddy-fucking-Warbucks a visit. *Can't look down your nose at me anymore, you pompous old prick.*

Gary climbed into his Jeep, stopping first at the nearest ATM to withdraw the limit of six hundred dollars cash before he started the two-and-a-half-hour drive back to his shop in Taos.

During the trip back, he pondered the best way to keep all that loot protected. He decided to stop at his Taos bank before his trip to Boulder and put most of his winnings into a rented safety deposit box. It would be safer there, and he could always transfer money into his checking as he needed it.

Reaching Taos, after visiting his bank, he arrived back at his shop. The first thing Gary did was go next door and pay the barber back the ten he'd loaned to him, with forty more, for his friendship. He opened his store, grabbing a few things he stuffed into a paper bag. Resetting the alarm, he walked out, locking the door behind him, and drove off heading north, taking Highway One-Sixty to Highway Twenty-Five. As he left Taos, he glanced at his watch. It was close to 1:00 p.m.

He figured he'd get to Boulder proper in about five hours, give or take. Mia would shit a brick when she found out her old man finally had some serious coin. He had to be careful to drive at the speed limit. If he got pulled over with a suspended license, he'd be in deep shit; a judge would probably throw the book at him.

He got as far as Pueblo before his luck seemed headed south. Stopped at a light, he saw a police cruiser right behind him in the rearview. Gary felt a cold sweat break on his face at the sight. *Just gotta be cool, I'm not doing anything wrong.*

The light turned green, but he was still distracted, eyeing the cop. When he didn't hit the gas, the cop honked his horn. *Crap! Pay attention, dumb ass,* Gary told himself. Anxiously, he hit the accelerator harder than he'd intended, his tires squealed. He'd gone about a block when the cop flashed his lights and hit his siren. Gary's heart lurched with the icy feeling of dread most folk experience when pulled over by a cop, only magnified. *Motherfucker, I'm screwed!* He pulled over to the curb and stopped. The copy of his recently suspended license was in his wallet. All the cops had to do was run it and—suddenly, the police car blew past him at a high rate of speed.

Gary's heart thumped in his chest like that of a trapped hummingbird. *Thank God.* He took a couple deep breaths to calm himself before carefully rejoining the traffic, making it through Pueblo uneventfully. Now, he was only an hour or so away from Boulder.

Later on, he was navigating a steep mountain curve when his back left tire blew with a loud *bang.* Freaking out, Gary over-corrected, swerving directly into oncoming traffic.

The driver of an approaching eighteen-wheeler slammed on its brakes seeing the Jeep's sudden intrusion in his lane, but too late to stop the impact. The semi plowed into Gary's vehicle doing better than fifty mph. The collision shoved the Jeep—and the horrified Gary—through the guard rail, flipping it over the side of the sheer drop-off. The Jeep plunged to the valley floor five hundred feet below. It seemed to Gary that the vehicle dropped in slow motion toward the jagged boulders far below.

One last, wretched thought ran through his mind before the Jeep impacted—*I never got to spend any of my fucking money!*

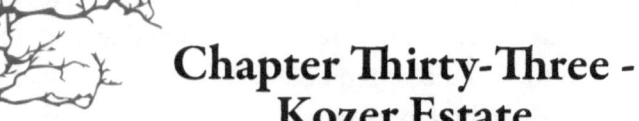

Chapter Thirty-Three -
Kozer Estate

Mia came to slowly, lying on a bed in a mostly darkened room, her brain still fuzzy from the electric shock she'd received from Kurt's stun gun. A solitary lamp by the bed gave enough illumination for her to see that she was alone in the chamber.

Her head hurt like hell. Reaching up with her left hand to rub it, she was jerked to a stop by a shiny metal bracelet encircling her wrist. *Handcuffs—seriously?* Another set of cuffs was locked tightly around her right. Both were tethered to the headboard posts. She looked down, relieved to see that at least she was not naked. *Shit!* She realized she was wearing a freaking dress. She couldn't remember the last time she'd worn one. *What happened to my clothes?* The dress smelled musty, as if it had been stored away for years. *Did this belong to my grandmother? Why would—*

With a small *click*, the door opened, and Kurt stepped in, closing it. He punched in a code on a keypad by the door, she heard a *thunk,* as a deadbolt slid int. Anger and humiliation at the thought of her grandfather, or even Max, undressing her and clothing her in her grandmother's attire sickened her. *He really is bat-shit crazy.* Mia strained desperately against the cuffs, but all that did was painfully abrade the skin around her wrists.

"I see you're awake, Lily. Good—you had such a nasty fall. It's been too long since I've seen you. But I knew you'd come back to me." He walked over to the side of the bed, gazing down at her manacled hands, his cold, mad eyes hidden in shadow.

She was badly frightened but determined not to panic. *I'll have to play along with his delusion for now.* "Why are you doing this to me, Gra ... Kurt?" she asked, forcing herself to remain calm.

"It's for your own good, Darling. I couldn't risk you running away from me again," he said softly.

"Why would I leave you? Did you do something that would make me want to run?" She glanced warily at him.

He sat on the bed beside her and reached out to stroke the sweat-matted hair away from her frightened eyes, smiling insanely at her.

"Lily, Lily, we don't want to go down that road again. No, that's what got you killed the first time—your damn, incessant curiosity. You seem to have managed to dispatch Max. You'll have to pay for that, I'm afraid." He calmly stroked her face.

Mia shivered disgustedly at his touch. *I've gotta get him to release me,* she thought, desperate to free herself from this crazy person masquerading as her husband.

"I-I'll do whatever you want, Kurt, but you need to uncuff me first." She tried to smile at him.

He smiled cruelly, "Lily, darling, I don't think you quite understand. You'll *do* whatever I want whether I release you or not. I won't underestimate you again. You left me no choice but to bring you here. This is where you belong, Lily—and this is where you'll stay," he said firmly. Then he leaned in closer to kiss her.

Mia snapped her head to the right, away from his intended target. At the sight of her bloody, rat-chewed ear, he pulled away, repulsed by the still-oozing blood. He fairly leaped off the bed, backing angrily away.

"I told Max to clean you up! No matter. I'll have to release you long enough for you to clean yourself up. Just don't try any tricks, or you'll get more of this." He triggered the stun gun. Fifty thousand volts crackled and arced menacingly between its electrodes. Mia got the message and nodded. Cautiously, he unlocked both cuffs, then stood back from the bed and pointed toward the bathroom.

Gingerly, she sat up in bed, gently rubbing her chafed wrists. "Are there more hidden cameras in there?" she asked suspiciously.

Kurt smiled crookedly. "Well, if there were, you'd never see them .. would you?" Impatiently, he gestured for her to hurry.

Mia walked slowly toward the bathroom, furtively scanning the bedroom for a weapon but finding nothing. The area was completely devoid of any loose objects. *Shit!* There had to be something she could use.

As she walked warily through the bathroom door, lights came on. Motion detectors, she guessed.

To her surprised relief, she saw that *this* door did have a lock. She shut and locked it quickly, scanning the bathroom for a possible weapon. The only loose item was a disposable plastic toothbrush by the sink. Not much of a weapon—*what could I do with it, brush him to death?*

Anxiously, she glanced up in the corners of the room, looking for small, tell-tale holes that might hide a camera. She didn't spot any, but that did not mean they weren't there. She found a bar of soap, a single towel, and … Surprise! an actual hairdryer inside a cabinet. No shampoo. Gently, she removed the small pieces of paper towel she'd pushed up her nostrils, seeing the bleeding had finally stopped. Warily, she pulled off her clothing and shoes and got into the steaming shower.

The hot water felt wonderful on her bite wounds, deceptively soothing. But its comfort could also lull her into a false sense of wellbeing. As she scrubbed the blood out of her hair, her anger grew. *There must be something I can use,* she thought, rinsing herself and turning off the shower. She toweled off and hurriedly donned the musty smelling dress and her own shoes again. *The hairdryer, if it still worked*—she suddenly remembered a video on the internet where someone used a hairdryer to heat the handle of a toothbrush until it was soft. Once malleable, they had shaped it into a sharpened point to use as a "shiv." She unwrapped the toothbrush and aimed the dryer toward it on its highest setting.

She was determined to make this work. *It's gotta work. My life might very well depend on it.*

Chapter Thirty-Four - Wallowa State Park, Oregon

Pete drove Missy away from the dreadful crime scene as fast as he could, safely. On the way, he briefed her about the roof of the toilet being cut, which explained how the bastard had gotten out, leaving the outhouse locked. Then he described the bloody piece of fur he'd found caught inside, explaining how Frank and he had speculated that it could be the work of a copy-cat killer—or something worse.

"No way! Frank killed that bastard over a year ago," Missy spat out angrily. As they left the Park, her rage at what had been done to her mother quickly overcame the calming effects from the shot she'd received at the crime scene.

"Yeah, I know, but maybe there's more of the damn things out there. All we know for sure is that she was killed someplace else, then her body was dumped there, figuring you'd probably be the first to find it." Pete shrugged.

Missy agreed with that. "Whoever did this is going to wish they'd never been born," she snarled, trembling with anger.

Pete silently agreed, lost in thought, as he turned onto the Anderson's graveled drive. He pulled up, parking the cruiser beside Jake's old pickup.

"The sheriff will come by after he's through at the crime scene. Shall I wait for him out here?" Pete was trying to give her some alone time with Jake and the baby.

She gave him a tight smile. "Thanks, Pete, I appreciate your consideration. You don't mind hanging out here and watching for Frank?"

"No worries. I'll text you when he gets here," he said.

She thanked him, as Jake appeared by Missy's car door as if conjured. He had it open before she could remove her seatbelt.

Sighing heavily, Pete watched them embrace, walking arm-in-arm into the house, closing the door behind them. He envied them a little. Having another person to hold, to give you comfort, must be nice. Wistfully, he thought about his ex-girlfriend, Sheena, who was now living with his old boss from the Pizza Palace. *Guess that's just the way the ol' cookie crumbles ... for me, anyway.*

Tires crunching on gravel pulled him out of his reverie. The Sheriff pulled up beside Missy's cruiser and climbed out as the sun set behind the distant mountain peaks to the west. Greeting him, Pete sent a quick text to Missy, informing her of Frank's arrival. He joined the Sheriff on the front doorstep, as Jake opened the door and motioned them inside.

"Come on in, Missy's putting Belinda down for a nap. She'll be out in a few. Have a seat at the table. Can I get you anything to drink?" he asked, shooing Jinx out from under it. The big cat turned with an indignant look that meant, *you'll pay for that later.*

Pete answered, "Just water for me, thanks," and sat.

Frank eyed the coffee pot. "I wouldn't mind a cup of joe. Gotta be better than the sludge that passes for coffee at the office." He pulled out a chair.

Jake gave them their drinks, grabbed a diet soda for himself. They sat, talking, while they waited for Missy to finish with Belinda. Moments later, she entered the kitchen, still pale and drawn, joining them at the table.

"So, you think this is the work of someone with a grudge against my mother or me? The only person I can think of who'd have a grudge against her is my sister, and you know that she's dead. I need some damn answers, Frank," she snarled.

The Sheriff met her eyes, waiting for her to calm down. "Missy, I know you're angry. Hell, I stay pissed-off most of the time. It's part of the job description. Whoever did this, we'll find 'em. They will pay for what they did, believe it," Frank said, his black eyes never wavering from hers. Jake and Pete nodded in agreement.

"Anyone seen any new faces around lately?" He looked at each of them.

Pete glanced at Jake and Missy, knowing they were all thinking about the same incident. So, he told Frank about finding the mysterious girl sitting on his porch swing, and the little wooden totem and note she'd left him. He added that she'd told him that he had a half-sister named Mia and described how the strange girl had miraculously healed the cut on his head. He showed Frank the back of his head where the boat had gashed him. The scalp wound was healed; the hair had grown back. No evidence of the injury remained.

"Let me get this straight. You're saying she simply touched you and it 'magically' healed?" Frank snorted incredulously.

Pete shrugged and nodded.

Frank sat there, frowning. "Did you get her name?" he asked.

"Nope. Only the initials 'W. R.' on the note," Pete was abashed to admit.

Frank stroked his chin in thought. "What about a car? You get a make or model?" He looked at Pete hopefully.

Pete thought about it for a second. "It was an older model Ford, but she wasn't driving. Someone pulled up and stopped, she got in, and they took off. I didn't think to get the license plate."

Frank took a sip of coffee, the acid causing his stomach to churn. "Well, if she shows up again or you see her, let me know ASAP," he said sternly. "Folks, she could be connected to all this. A stranger appears out of nowhere, and now we have a freaking murder on our hands," he added caustically.

His phone chirped, and he glanced at the text. His eyes widened at the photo on his screen. He hissed, "*Holy shit*! Not another one!"

Chapter Thirty-Five-Kozer Estate

K urt was growing impatient. Mia had been running the damn hair dryer for almost fifteen minutes. He walked over and tried the door handle. Locked, of course. He knocked loudly on the door.

"Lily, unlock the door and come out. Now! If I am forced to break down the door, it won't be pleasant for you." He shouted, to be heard over the whine of the dryer.

Inside, Mia was silently cursing every "how-to" video she'd ever watched online. Either they'd used super-hot hair dryers, or that entire video was bullshit. It showed the toothbrush handle softening in a couple minutes. She'd been at it for close to fifteen. The handle was quite warm, but not nearly hot enough to be shaped into a weapon.

She jumped when her grandfather started pounding on the door, shouting for her to come out. *Shit*! She was starting to panic.

"I-I'll be out in a minute. Almost through," she lied, trying to buy a little more time.

The hair dryer she'd left running on the counter finally stopped, as a circuit-breaker had tripped, and the ensuing silence was unnerving. Kurt pounded on the door again. With time running out, Mia studied the toilet, which looked old. Opening the lid on the tank, she looked inside. The guts of the thing had an old-fashioned float suspended on a foot-long rod that threaded into the fill valve. Frantically, she gripped the float and started twisting counterclockwise.

"I-I'm coming. I-I have to use the toilet, give me a minute," she shouted, while she worked feverishly to disconnect the rod from the valve. She unscrewed the float, leaving her with the long brass rod. Not much of a weapon, but it was all she had. She slid the make-shift weapon into one of the deep pockets in the dress, flushing the toilet to cover the noise as she replaced the lid. She unlocked and opened the door.

Her grandfather was sitting on the bed when she emerged. "A good thing you finally decided to come out. I'm afraid you'll have to be punished, Lily," he said, standing up.

Mia's right hand closed tightly around the metal rod in her pocket.

"You don't think I've been punished enough already? Well, then fuck you!" She snapped, her hand clutching her make-shirt weapon.

He charged her, brandishing the stun gun. She swiftly side-stepped it, ramming the tip of the brass rod up into his throat with all her might in the same breath.

Kurt was staggered by the blow. His eyes bulged in shock, and he dropped the stun gun. The rod hadn't penetrated deep into his neck, but, unfortunately for him, it had nicked a carotid artery. Falling to his knees, he gasped like a fish out of water.

He clutched at her homemade "shiv," pulling it free from his neck and dropping it on the floor. Blood spurted from the wound with every beat of his racing heart. Still, he grinned madly at her.

"You always were a treacherous bitch, Lily. You need a lesson in humility." He reached out to grab the taser, which was on the floor between them. Mia was quicker. She stepped forward, ramming her knee into his face as he bent to grab it. She heard a satisfying *crunch,* as her knee connected with his nose, breaking it.

Screaming in agony, he collapsed on the floor, one hand clasped over the slowing spray of blood from his neck, the other cradling his busted nose.

Mia was shaking with fear and rage. Snatching up the stun gun, she ran to the door, then stopped short. *Shit! The freakin' keypad*—she didn't know the code. She whirled around and barked, "What's the code? Give it to me!"

At that point, Kurt was more than a couple of quarts low on the dipstick, as bright, red blood continued to collect around his head. With his last few gasps of breath, he cackled weakly at her.

"You—can—check out—any—time, but—you—can—never leave—bitch!" His chest heaved twice and was still.

Mia's anger instantly changed to pure terror. *How could I be so damn stupid? He's dead, I killed him and Max, too! I'll never get out of here without the freakin' code.* From the floor, Kurt's dead eyes stared up at her. She was losing it. She faced the harsh reality that if she didn't figure out how to open that door, she could starve to death. She knew she could live two or three weeks without food, but only a few days without water, but she had water.

What happens when you get so desperately hungry... she glanced at her grandfather's bloody corpse. A shudder of revulsion rippled through her. The thought of having to chow down on his bloated, rotting arm or leg to stay alive was disgusting. *Fuck that!*

Mia took some deep breaths to calm herself. She had to think, keep her wits about her. She began punching in random numbers on the nine-digit keypad, but the little LED continued to glow red. *Think! What would he use as his pass code?*

She tried numerous combinations with no luck before it came to her. She punched in 5-4-5-9, the numeric equivalent of the letters, L-I-L-Y. The LED turned green and with a *snap*, the deadbolt slid back.

She was free. She opened the bedroom door ... and shrieked!

Chapter Thirty-Six - Taos, NM, Eight Hours Earlier

Kris Lacey's headaches were growing progressively worse and more frequent. She had difficulty concentrating, and if she couldn't stay focused, she couldn't perform her job. Between the migraines and the pills to mitigate them, she didn't know which was the worst. The migraines made her physically ill; the pills made her lethargic and slow—dangerous, in her line of work.

Her shift had been over for an hour. Glancing down at the file she'd just opened, she sighed, closed it and her computer for the day. She gathered her purse and briefcase and locked her office, saying goodnight to the desk sergeant on her way out.

The desert's cold night air felt soothing to her head for a few seconds, but it quickly sucked the heat from her body. She hit a button on her key fob to unlock her civilian vehicle. Opening the car door, she sank inside its relative warmth, gratefully. She was eager to get home and soak in a hot bath for, like, a year. As she started the engine, she glanced in the rearview and gasped—from the back seat, a pair of cool, black eyes returned her stare. Adrenaline flooded Kris's brain. She snatched her weapon from her holster and whipped open the car door, leaping out.

The dome light came on, illuminating the interior. Kris's gun hand was shaking as she held it in a two-handed grip, pointing it at—*no one*? The back seat was empty. *Shit! Where the hell had the intruder gone?* She quickly circled the car, seeing nothing. *Damn pills are making me hallucinate. That's what I get for taking that extra half a Naratriptan.* She walked back to her open door, angry at herself for being so jumpy. Climbing back in, she slammed the door, and the dome light went out.

She was fastening her seat belt when a hand touched the back of her neck. Kris let out a stifled scream, as cool fingers encircled her neck. In the same moment, she felt something like a mild shock, and her headache disappeared completely.

Her entire body went slack. She couldn't move her arms or legs, they were paralyzed. *What the fuck just happened?* She was almost hyperventilating with panic. She glanced anxiously in the rearview and saw the same dark eyes glittering back at her. Observing the black hair framing the girl's face, Kris realized this must be ... *Wendy Ravenwood?*

"Who the hell are you? Or should I say, what the hell are you? No normal human could have gotten in and out of here without me seeing. You damn-near got your ass shot off—and what the hell did you do to me?" Fear made Kris ramble.

"Sorry for the fright, Detective. I am Wendy. You've been looking for me. Well, here I am," the girl said, with a slight smile. "How's the migraine? Feeling better now?" Wendy asked, ignoring Kris's questions.

How the hell did she know that I had a migraine? Kris was confounded.

"I know a lot of things, Lieutenant. I know that you haven't had much sleep lately. I also know you are a smart and caring person. A good cop. It's unfortunate, though ..." The girl left that hanging.

Kris held her eyes in the mirror. "What's unfortunate? I don't know what you're talking about. Look, I need some freaking answers. First off, where the hell do you live? I mean, as far as the state and federal agencies are concerned, you don't even exist. What's the story with—"

Wendy stopped her. "You have a tumor." she spat the awful word out bluntly.

Kris felt like she'd been punched in the gut. "W-what? H-how would you know I—what the hell are you? You're not a freaking doctor," Kris sputtered.

"It's treatable. I can take away the physical pain, but only for a short period of time. I am primarily... a healer of the spirit, not the body," Wendy replied, never blinking. "I came here to tell you that Mia Chandler's life is in great peril." She sat back.

"How do you ... but she's with her grandfather. Surely, she's safe enough there for now," Kris asserted.

"Her grandfather is a monster in human disguise. Even as we speak, she is fighting for her life." Wendy looked at Kris with no emotion.

"How the hell could you know that? You're the only common denominator in this mess involving the Chandlers, so tell me what the hell is going on." Kris was trying to manage the adrenaline coursing through her veins.

Wendy suddenly leaned forward until her lips were alongside Kris's right ear and spoke softly. "I am *Nitch'i asdza*. That is all I can tell you. I gave you a gift, Det. Lacey. I didn't have to take the pain away or inform you of your malignancy. Go to Boulder. Mia needs your help. Now." The dome light came on as she opened the back door.

As abruptly as it had left, the feeling returned to Kris's arms and legs. She turned to glance in the outside mirror. The girl was gone. The whole exchange between them had lasted only a couple minutes, but it had felt like an eternity. All of it felt surreal.

Kris sighed deeply, as her gut told her she had a long night and day ahead of her. Not questioning Wendy's words or her own actions, she keyed the mic on her radio and asked dispatch to give her Mia's grandfather's address and phone number in Colorado.

She called Hendricks and told him she'd be out of pocket for a day or so. Then she pulled out of the police station and gassed up her cruiser at the local 'Stop n Rob' convenience store. Grabbing one of the dry, pre-made sandwiches and some bottled water for the trip, she called the grandfather's number twice, getting voice mail each time. Frustrated, she hung up and fed the address of the Kozer estate into her cruiser's GPS. With a squeal of tires, she pulled out onto the highway.

This had better not be some wild goose chase, Ravenwood, or your ass is grass, Kris thought sullenly, cranking up the heat in the cruiser as the car flew down the highway toward Boulder, Colorado.

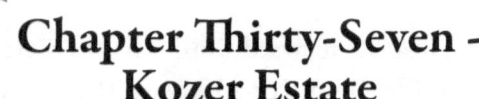

Chapter Thirty-Seven - Kozer Estate

Towering in the hall, Max blocked her exit from the bedroom door she'd just opened, his face a twisted mask of rage and blood. So, she hadn't killed him.

"Fucking little bitch—you're going to wish I'd left you to those rats before I'm through," he roared, grabbing the stun gun out of her hand, and shoving her backwards. She stumbled over her grandfather's cooling corpse, slipped in the pool of blood, and fell onto the tiled floor. Only then did Max notice that his employer and partner lay dead on the floor.

"Omigod, you've killed him. Now you're a murderous fucking little bitch!" He began moving toward her. He shoved the stunner against her bare leg and pulled the trigger, but nothing happened. Cursing, he pulled the trigger again, with the same result.

Mia didn't wait for a third time. Max was straddling her right leg, so she kicked out viciously with her left, striking him squarely in a man's most vulnerable spot. Instantly, he jack-knifed, groaning, and dropped the forgotten stun gun on the floor. His only concern was his wounded balls.

She scrambled to get up and away from him, slipping in Kurt's blood in her haste. With Max moaning in agony, she snatched up the stun gun. Then she spotted her bloody clothes draped over a chair. *Max's car keys and phone were in my pants pockets.* She ran over to them, praying both were still there. The keys were inside the pocket, but no phone. *Shit!* Either it had fallen out, or her grandfather had found and confiscated it. *Can't worry about it now.* She raced past the moaning Max and down the hall, heading for the front entrance. At the front door, she slid to a stop, turning the handle, but it, too, was locked. The bastards had sealed her inside.

Quaking with fear, she shakily punched in 5-4-5-9 again, hoping all the doors were keyed to the same code. Nothing happened. The LED continued to glow red. *Shit!* She heard Max's heavy, uneven steps approaching down the hall. Despite his looming presence, she forced herself to take her time and carefully enter the code again. *Please, please work!* The LED finally turned green, and the deadbolt snapped open. She ran out to the Cadillac parked out front, pushing on the key fob to unlock the doors.

Close behind her, Max bellowed like a wounded bull. "You're not getting away that easy, bitch," he snarled, reaching out to grab her.

Mia had opened the driver's door and climbed halfway inside, but he yanked her back out by her hair.

"Let go of me, you freakin' asshole," she screeched, pain radiating through her scalp. She stretched back with the stun gun. Finding bare flesh, she depressed the trigger. Still, nothing happened. Panic set in—she knew Max would likely kill her if he got her back inside.

On the side of the stunner, she felt a switch. Was that a safety? She flipped it, swinging it again desperately at his huge arm. Triggering the device, she heard the familiar crackling *zzzttt.*

Max grunted, releasing his death-grip on her hair, and fell to the pavement, twitching; Mia herself received a slight shock before his hand fell. Cursing, she quickly got to her feet and jumped inside the car, slamming the door. Pushing buttons wildly, she found the door-lock switch and locked all the doors. She had never driven a car so fancy and had no idea how to start it. Her frustration mounted, she stared at the unfamiliar electronic display in front of her. She pushed buttons on the key fob until the engine finally purred smoothly to life.

She was adjusting the electric seat so she could reach the pedals when the driver's window suddenly imploded, showering her with glass.

"No! Leave me the hell alone!" she screamed, as Max's enormous hand reached in. He grabbed her by her neck, slamming her head against the steering wheel hard enough to make her see stars.

"How does that feel, you murderous bitch?" He reached in to open the door.

Where's the damn stun gun? she thought dazedly. Then she realized, in her rush to get away, she'd dropped it on the pavement. *Shit!*

Max pulled her roughly from the car. Mia barely saw his huge fist before it struck her jaw, and the lights went out.

SHE AWOKE TO COMPLETE darkness, lying on something hard and cold, with a throbbing headache. Her face was swollen and aching from the punch she taken. *Where the hell has he put me?* She groaned, trying to get her bearings. She hoped she wasn't back in the black, rat-infested basement. She couldn't feel her body, it had grown numb from lying there, inert.

As feeling began to return, with a shock, she realized that she was naked. *Oh, crap! Not good!* Moving a hand over, she reached between her thighs and shuddered with relief. At least he hadn't raped her ... yet. She could feel no ties or straps, which didn't bode well. Wherever she was, he wasn't worried about her escaping—that terrified her. Attempting to sit up, she immediately banged her head against something solid. Carefully, she turned her arms so that she could raise her palms, and touched a cool, smooth surface that was about six inches above her body.

Panicking, she pushed her hands out toward the sides and found the same material restricting them only a few inches away. "No, no, no," she shouted, feeling claustrophobia closing in. She continued to yell, beating her fists furiously against the unyielding walls and ceiling.

The bastard had sealed her inside some sort of cold box. If there was nc oxygen, she would slowly suffocate and die.

Chapter Thirty-Eight –
Near Joseph, Oregon

Sheriff Blackstone's cruiser screeched to a stop at the bottom of the handicap ramp that led to the home of Ben Dover. Inwardly, he shrank from what he was already certain he would find inside. One of his deputies was already there. Standing on the front porch of the house, Ned Jenkins looked like he'd rather be anywhere else.

Frank couldn't blame him. He climbed out of his cruiser and solemnly approached him. "What have we got here, Ned?"

The deputy was visibly shaken. "What we've got here is a sick fucking mess, Sheriff. Better see for yourself," he replied, looking a little green.

Frank sighed as he climbed the ramp to the open door. A curious, whimpering sound came from within. Taking a deep breath, he stepped inside. Ben Dover, naked and quite dead, sat hunched over in his wheelchair. Blood splattered everything in a ten-foot radius of his body. He'd been butchered like a hog. A golden retriever lay on the floor nearby, whining and occasionally licking its master's bare, bloody feet. It turned soulful, brown eyes up briefly toward Frank, and he believed he saw tears in the poor dog's eyes.

"Who called this in, Ned? I'm guessing it wasn't the pooch." Frank spoke sarcastically, to cover his own distress.

Ned winced at his boss's tone. "Anonymous tip, Sheriff. 911 operator called the number back, but it was out of service. Obviously, a burner," Ned informed him.

Shit! "Well, I assume you've called the ME?"

Ned nodded, "Yes, sir. He's on the way."

"By the look of things, he's got a hell of a busy night ahead of him," Frank observed, staring at Ben's ruined remains slumped over in the chair.

What kind of person could do this to a cripple? A fucking monster. Carefully, he backtracked out of the house to avoid further contaminating the scene.

"CSI unit should be here any time now, Sheriff. Who the hell would kill a man like that, Sheriff?" Ned asked, glancing nervously around, as if the evildoer might still lurk in the bushes surrounding the house.

Not a who, but a what, Frank thought grimly, grisly images of Missy's mother's horribly ravaged body flashing through his mind. "One sick fuck, that's for sure," Frank said.

The ME soon arrived, joining them on the porch. "He's inside, Doc." Frank motioned with his thumb. "I need to know if he died in the same manner as the old woman," he instructed. The medical examiner nodded and trudged in to begin his grisly work once more.

Shit! What a day! Frank thought miserably. His phone vibrated in his pocket. He took it out and saw Missy was calling. *Just fucking great!* He hadn't told her where he was bound when he got the initial call at her house. Now he'd be forced to inform her that her old boss and close friend was the day's second brutal atrocity.

He broke it to her as gently as he knew how. As he'd expected, she took the news hard. He held the phone away as her invective-filled cries of anger and grief flooded out of it.

He tried to pacify her. "Missy, I'll be—no, you can't come here. It won't do any good for—listen to me, dammit! He wouldn't want you to see him like this. Do you understand? It—yes, it looks like the same—no, ma'am—now, Missy, you know that that's physically impossible to do to oneself. I—yes, ma'am, I—I'll let you know as soon as we know anything, I promise." Wearily, he ended the call.

His feet hurt like hell. He had arthritis in one and bone spurs in the other. "Getting too old for this shit," he muttered to himself.

He heard a car approaching. His CSI people were arriving. He walked down the ramp to meet them. Two techs got out, opened the trunk, and retrieved their equipment while he filled them in on what they'd be dealing with inside.

"Sheriff, I think you need to see this," the ME called out urgently from the doorway.

"*Shit*! That doesn't sound good," he growled. The tech guys followed him up the ramp and onto the porch, where they paused to put booties over their shoes to protect the crime scene as much as possible.

Since he'd already been inside and probably contaminated the scene, Frank thought that a waste of time on his part. On entering, one of the techs, Davis, turned white as a sheet. Harris, the other guy, didn't flinch, as they surveyed the carnage to Ben's body.

"What in holy hell is that?" Frank asked, horrified, shining his light as the doctor lifted Ben's head. His cheeks bulged out grotesquely.

The killer had stuffed Ben's castrated penis and testicles halfway down his throat. His bloody ball sack protruded from his mouth.

"He most likely died quickly, from blood loss and shock. Once the pudendal artery was severed, he'd have bled out quickly," the doctor noted, shining his light on the ragged, bloody hole where Ben's genitals had previously resided.

"For his sake, let's hope so." Frank shook his head. The doctor moved the light upward, revealing a huge split from Ben's scrotum to the top of his stomach. All his organs were missing.

JAKE WAS ATTEMPTING—AND failing miserably—to console Missy. He'd never seen her so upset. Ever since Frank had called with the news about Ben, she'd been almost manic. One minute, she paced the floor weeping sadly; the next, she was cursing like a mad woman. Between her grief and Belinda's distressed cries from her crib, he felt he must be doing a lousy job as comforter-in-chief.

He tried to placate her. "Missy, please try to calm down, you're upsetting Belinda. I know all this sucks, but Frank is right. You can't do anything right now for Ben or your mom."

She stopped mid-stride, did an about-face. "You're wrong, Bud. There is something I can do. Find his fucking killer and rip him a new asshole," she snapped, unconsciously clenching her hands into fists.

Treading warily, Jake shook his head. "You know that's not your job, Missy. Let the Sheriff do his. He'll find whoever did this."

She gave him a look of disbelief, tears of frustration welling. "I lost my mother and a good friend today. You seriously think I'm going to just sit on my ass and twiddle my thumbs, knowing this whack-job is out there, methodically slaughtering people I care about?" She sounded bitter.

Jake was startled by her tone. "Missy, I want to catch whoever is responsible for this just as much as you, but what are you suggesting we do? Nothing they've found so far proves the two murders are even related. All I overheard Frank say was that Ben had been murdered and that you needed to stay away," he told her.

Missy cocked a brow and crossed her arms. "Someone is targeting the people close to me, Jake. So, I'm supposed to wait around and do nothing until the next body is found? It could be Pete next, even you or, God forbid, Belinda. No. Fucking. Way!"

Jake opened his mouth to say something, then quickly closed it. Sighing, he nodded. "Okay, suppose someone is targeting you. First, you need to figure out the 'who' and the 'why'. Frank will fill us in on the 'how.' Next, what's the motive? What do they stand to gain by hurting you? Sex, money, power? Those are the three main reasons people kill." His description was logical.

"You know this for a fact? Or did you get all your info from 'CSI Miami,' Bud?"

Jake shook his head sheepishly. "Okay, guilty. But I did research it for a book I was writing, and that's pretty much the rule." He walked over to get them both diet sodas from the refrigerator.

She flopped down on the sofa, instantly disrupting Jinx's cat coma. "What about revenge? What if this is all about revenge?" she asked.

He looked at her oddly. "Revenge? Why would you say that?" Reaching down, he lightly stroked Jinx, risking being bitten for his trouble.

She was quiet for a moment. "I don't know, but I think these murders *are* somehow connected. I don't believe in coincidence. First my mother, then Ben. Who suffers most from their loss? Me. Mama had no other living relatives. Ben was single for as long as I've known him, he didn't have many friends." She paused to take a sip of her soda.

Jake thought she was jumping the gun a bit. "Why would someone want to hurt you? You haven't harmed anyone that I'm aware of. I can't think of one person who'd want to do you any—*ouch,*" he hissed, yanking his hand back, as Jinx nipped his thumb. Cursing, he shook his hand. He could almost swear the big cat grinned at him before jumping off the couch and slinking into their bedroom.

Missy sighed, returning to her argument. "Maybe someone has some sort of vendetta against me. I've probably pissed off a lot of people. You don't patrol a state park, handing out citations, without making enemies, Bud. People carry grudges. It's human nature." She twisted a curl of her hair around one finger, a clear sign she was distressed.

"You can speculate all you want, Hon, but we have no way to know—" Jake was interrupted by her phone.

She stood and answered immediately, seeing it was Frank. She didn't place it on speaker, so Jake only heard her side of the conversation.

"Yes, Frank, I'm okay. Please tell me he wasn't killed the same way as—oh, dear God, no!" As the Sheriff gave her a brief account, she deflated, sinking back onto the couch. He told her it did appear to be the work of the same individual but spared her the gory details of Ben's castration.

Missy was sobbing again, shaking her head. "Listen, all I know is some crazy person is killing the people I care about, Frank. Who the hell is next? Pete? Jake? Belinda? No, sir, I am not exaggerating the circumstances. I won't stand around with my thumb up my ass. You need to find this bastard, Frank. I believe we're all in danger until you do. I've got to call Pete and warn him!" She hung up and called Pete.

PETE HAD LEFT JAKE'S and Missy's place shortly after the sheriff was called away. He was stepping out of the shower when his cell chimed. *Shit!* Grabbing a towel, he wrapped it around him, hurrying to his bedroom. He dug the phone out of his pants and answered.

"Hey, Missy, can you hold for a minute, I'm dripping all over the floor." He set his cell down, quickly toweling off and pulling on a pair of sweats.

"Yo, Missy, I'm back. What's up?" he asked, drying his hair one-handed with the damp towel.

She told him about Frank's call informing her of Ben's murder, adding, "It looks like the person responsible for these murders is targeting people who are close to me. You need to stay aware of your surroundings. Lock your doors and make damn sure all your windows are locked. I am not losing anybody else to this fucking maniac. Got that?" she demanded.

Pete glanced anxiously out his bedroom windows into the dark night. "Uh, yes, ma'am, I got it. You think I'll need a gun? All I have for protection is a butcher knife and a bat," he said, checking the windows.

He heard Jake say something in the background. "Jake's asking if you have any 'Bear-B-Gone' handy?" Missy asked. Pete thought about it, walking hastily into the living room to double-check the doors and windows. "Yeah, I do, but ... *crap*! It's out in my freaking car. In the dark." He mentally kicked himself for not having brought it inside earlier.

"Well, it's not gonna do you any good sitting in the car, is it, Bud? I'll call Frank and see if he can stop by to check on you before the end of his shift. Maybe he can grab the bear spray for you while he's there. Okay?" she offered, knowing Pete was likely freaking out.

Pete finally seemed calmer, and Missy disconnected the call. Now he felt like a wuss. But better safe than sorry. He turned on the outside light and peeked through the living room curtains, wondering if someone could be out there, hidden in the shadows of the night.

FROM THE COVER OF DARKNESS, he watched Pete pull the curtain aside, nervously scanning the porch and front yard for anything suspicious. He wasn't concerned about being discovered. The inky black night camouflaged him perfectly.

This man had locked his front door only moments before, thwarting his plans to enter the house quietly and kill him. He growled with frustration at having been denied a golden opportunity. He could sense the man's anxiety through the thin panes of glass separating them—the difference between life and death. He could almost smell the fear oozing from the man's pores. It would have been the perfect trifecta of carnage.

He would butcher all those responsible for the deaths of his mother and father. The Ranger's mother and the man in the wheelchair were only the beginning. He'd make sure she suffered the depths of hell before he finally took her life.

Chapter Thirty-Nine - Highway Thirty-Six, South of Boulder

D et. Kris Lacey stomped hard on her cruiser's brakes, as northbound traffic on Highway Thirty-Six abruptly came to a standstill. She noticed the absence of southbound traffic, as well. She cursed, banging her hand impatiently on the steering wheel in frustration. *Shit!* There must be a fender-bender up ahead.

Earlier, she'd radioed the Boulder PD to request back-up at the Kozer address, telling dispatch that possible child endangerment was involved. She was asked to wait—then shocked when the Chief of Police himself took the call. She was told in no uncertain terms that Mr. Kurt Kozer must be handled with kid gloves, as he was a large benefactor of both the Mayor and the Boulder PD. She was essentially ordered to radio their dispatch and wait for backup before attempting to enter or retrieve the child. That had pissed Kris off royally.

The line of cars ahead of her stretched around a dangerous-looking curve, where traffic converged down to two lanes at its narrowest point. She kept expecting her migraine to come raging back any moment, but she'd felt no pain since her encounter with Ravenwood. *A fucking tumor?* She shuddered at the thought of traitorous, malignant cells in her brain, replicating, out of control. Ravenwood had said her pain would return. Kris just hoped it would hold off long enough for her to find Mia and check on her.

Cars were slowly moving up ahead. *Probably a bunch of gawkers,* she thought, as the cruiser crept slowly forward in the bumper-to-bumper traffic. Finally, she came to the apex of the curve, where she saw flashing emergency lights ahead.

A helicopter hovered over an area of damaged guard-rail on the southbound side where an eighteen-wheeler sat, jackknifed in the middle of the road. Drivers on her side had slowed to gape, hoping to catch sight of a mangled car or a bloody body. Kris shook her head in disgust—human nature at its worst. If a body was involved, it was not visible. Highway patrol was on the scene. Passing the crippled eighteen-wheeler, traffic sped up again. Having spotted no gruesome roadkill, most motorists soon returned to their usual distracted driving.

Kris had to slam on the brakes again, as she almost missed the turn-off to the Kozer property. The guy tailgating her in a Mercedes almost plowed into the back of her cruiser. Leaning on his horn, he flipped her off as she made a fast U-turn.

She followed the winding, aspen-lined drive for a quarter of a mile until she was blocked by a forbidding, eight-foot-tall, wrought-iron, locked gate barring her entrance. *Shit on a stick!* How the hell was she going to get past that? An ugly, four-foot-high metal sculpture of a cat sat prominently on the left side of the gate, a recessed keypad embedded in the pad of its raised metallic paw. She spotted a call button inside the hideous cat creature's open mouth. No way was she pushing that and alerting Kozer. If possible, she didn't want to announce her presence.

She surveyed the imposing wall, studded with spikes, continued as far as the eye could see in both directions. Then she spotted the security camera mounted on the top of gate. It sat, watching her like a one-eyed vulture eyeing its dinner. *Fucking great, so much for stealth!*

She studied the gate hinges, noting that they only opened inward. *It might work!* Slowly, she accelerated until the heavy-duty push-bar mounted on the front of her cruiser contacted the gate. She gave it more gas, the front tires spinning and smoking, as the cruiser pushed hard against the well-built gates. Finally, the lock gave way, and her vehicle was able to push them open. *Maybe some safety feature installed in case someone accidentally left the car in gear and it crashed into the gate,* Kris thought. *Probably cost a gazillion bucks to replace. Tough shit!*

She drove up the snow-lined drive, parking the cruiser behind an expensive looking Cadillac with its driver's door hanging open. Her dashboard clock read seven-fifteen a.m. She'd made good time, considering the delay on the highway from that accident and the brief nap she'd stopped to take about halfway there.

She knew she should radio the Boulder PD Chief to alert him she'd arrived. First, though, she tried calling Kozer's landline and once again, got voice mail. *Crap*! She sighed, prepared to key her mike, when she noticed that the mansion's front door stood partially open. To Lacey, that looked like an invitation. *Yeah, said the spider to the fly.* Obviously, something hinky was happening within. She called the Chief's private number and gave him her location. When she described her method of entering the property, he was not happy.

"Damn it, Lieutenant, what part of 'handling this with kid gloves' did you not understand?" he growled angrily. "Stay where you are, wait for backup. I'll be there personally in fifteen minutes."

The open door still beckoned. She got out and approached the mansion with gun drawn.

Chapter Forty – Kozer Estate, One Hour Earlier

Mia had fallen asleep, exhausted. She'd screamed and beaten on the walls and top of her cage until she was hoarse, and her fists bloodied. A loud noise woke her, and panic flooded her with adrenaline. *There must be air holes somewhere, or I'd have suffocated by now,* she thought logically. Earlier, she'd felt around blindly with fingers and toes to find any opening. Unfortunately, the walls of her enclosure felt smooth, cold, and quite solid.

Suddenly, her sensitized eyes were shocked by a bright light that brought her surroundings up in stark relief. Squinting through tears, she realized that she was in some sort of large, clear container. Max stood not six feet away, staring at her icily. She squealed and tried to cover her nakedness, as Max grinned wickedly.

"You're in for a treat." He limped closer to loom right over her glass prison. "I want you to meet some little friends of mine." He pointed to a glass box about eight inches square sitting directly above her on top of her cage. Nothing within the box moved. Mia didn't have a clue what it contained, but she was terrifyingly sure she was about to find out.

"Let me introduce you to *Aenictini* of the genus *Neivamyrmex.*" Reaching down, he shook the small box. What had seemed solid became masses of agitated living things.

She saw with growing horror what looked to be thousands of legs crawling frenziedly around inside the container. "W-what the hell are those? Please let me out of here, Max, I—I swear I won't say anything to anyone. You'll never see or hear from me again, I promise," she pleaded.

Max sneered. "You're right about that. No one will ever see *or* hear from you again, bitch. These are imported African army ants, the piranhas of the ant kingdom. They'll strip the flesh from your body and devour you even as they flay you to the bone." He smiled maliciously.

Mia watched as the huge ants' serrated mandibles opened and closed hungrily in search of fresh meat. They looked like something out of a horror movie—with her in the starring role. If she couldn't convince him to release her from this hellhole, she would be eaten alive.

Desperately, she begged him. "P-please Max, let me out. I-I'll do anything you want. I-I mean, anything." She uncovered her small breasts to make her point.

Max howled with weird laughter. "Nice try. Sorry—I'm gay. Kurt was my partner. You should have minded your own fucking business, you skinny little skank. He planned to take you away from your shitty loser of a father and groom you, put you in charge of his company. But no, you had to go sniffing around where you didn't belong." His mood grew bleaker. "Then you fucking killed him. You don't deserve to live," he snarled, tears of rage and sorrow flowing.

He picked up the box of ants and shook it to anger them, replacing it on top of her cage. Turning back to a small table behind him, he put on a pair of heavy-duty welding gloves that lay there.

Mia knew she was running out of time. With all her might, she pushed up with her arms and feet against the lid of the cage. It moved. Not a lot, but enough so she could see that it was hinged on its far side. *Makes sense. He had to open it to put me in here.*

Max turned and walked back over to the tank, with a nasty smile. He bent over, reaching for the box.

It's now or never! she thought grimly. "Fuck you, pizza face!" she screeched, shoving with every bit of her strength at the top of her make-shift coffin. It didn't fly open as she'd wanted—but her push was enough to fling the horrible container of ants off the cage lid and right into Max's shocked face. It struck him in the forehead and fell to the floor, where it splintered, shattering bits of glass and ants all around his feet.

Max shrieked, "Nooo!" and backed up hurriedly from the vicious, hungry horde.

Retreating in terror, he collided with the table behind him, which knocked him off balance, and he fell on his ass. The voracious ants were on him in a heartbeat, quickly overrunning him as he thrashed around, bellowing in horror. Their hungry mandibles began tearing into every inch of exposed flesh.

As much as Mia wanted out of the tank, she realized it would be death to leave it now. The ants were everywhere. *This is friggin' great—I've trapped myself!* she thought miserably. Suddenly, she felt something crawling on her right foot. One scout ant clamped down on her little toe, causing her to thrash her foot wildly against the side of tank. She crushed the ant, but in the process, badly bruised the bone in her little toe. It took a full second for the excruciating pain to reach her brain, then she sobbed, cursing Max.

She'd read that if you squashed an ant, it released "attack" pheromones into the air, alerting the whole colony to come to its rescue. Basically, it sent out a chemical SOS. Sure enough, a swarm of huge soldier ants began frantically trying to scale the slick glass sides of the tank to assist their brother.

For the moment, Mia was safe. It appeared the slick material of the tank kept them from scaling it, but it didn't stop them from trying. *But then, how did the first one get in?* she wondered. Painfully, she bent her left foot, using it to slowly feel along the confining chamber walls and ceiling. *There it was.* Bending her foot, she felt three holes close together near the Plexiglas lid with her big toe. Those must be the source of her oxygen—and of the rogue army ant.

Turning her head, she watched with morbid fascination as a mass of ants covered Max's face. His last, high-pitched scream filled the room as the ants clogged his open mouth and nose, shutting off the terrible sound.

If any of the other ants make it to the top and find the holes ... Mia shuddered with revulsion, as she transferred her sight to the voracious little eating machines mere inches away from her face. And as she had that thought, the ants began climbing on top of one another, making a ladder of their bodies. They were already four or five inches up the wall of the tank, which was about two feet deep.

Shit! The little buggers are going to find those holes. Mia shook her head, pushing the negative thoughts away, as she tried desperately to think of a solution. Glancing over, she saw they were almost halfway up the tank. She thought she might be able to shove the lid up enough to squeeze herself out. But even if she could get out, the floor was covered with angry ants and pieces of broken glass from their former container. She'd cut her feet to shreds on the glass, and the ants would cover her if she fell. *But they'll get me if I stay, too,* she told herself.

She couldn't think of another plan, and she had run out of time. *To hell with it—I'd rather die fighting.* She thrust upward with all her power and managed to lift the plexiglass lid up enough to slide her right arm out, scraping some skin off. Then, she used the cage wall as a fulcrum and pushing up with her head, she pulled her body halfway out of the glass box—as the last of her strength gave out.

The weight of the lid pinned her, half-in and half-out, like a rat in a trap. *Shit, shit, shit*! The heavy lid squeezed her diaphragm, making her hyperventilate and start to panic. With mounting terror, she saw that the uppermost ants had reached the top of the cage on the other side. They'd be on her in seconds!

Screeching with rage and fear, Mia struggled wildly to force the top of her prison up and away from her. With adrenalin she hadn't thought she had, she pulled her bare ass over the lip of the tank, abrading more skin as she yanked her right leg up and over the side. A couple of the lead ants made it to her bloodied hands before she could wrench the rest of her torso free from her cage.

She fell to her knees with ants swarming greedily toward her. Ignoring the agony of their fiery bites and the shards of glass digging into her knees, she stood up and limped away as fast as she could. She scurried past Max's ant-enshrouded corpse. She was beyond being shocked or repulsed by that sight, as she hobbled on bleeding feet toward the door. Swatting wildly at the ants biting her, she jerked it open, but froze for a second, confused. *Where the hell did Max take me?* He'd moved her to a part of the mansion she had never seen or been in. *Shit! Which way do I go now?* A long, dim hall ran in both directions. Several vicious new bites reminded her she still had unwelcome company. She swatted what she hoped were the last of the voracious ants from her feet, legs, and butt.

At that moment, it didn't matter which direction she chose, as long as it was far from that wretched room. She started off, shambling along as fast as she could, the glass in her feet digging deeper with every stumbling step she took. The corridor seemed to extend for miles. When she believed she was a safe distance from the terrible insects, she stopped for a couple minutes to pull out the largest slivers of glass she could spot from each foot. Then she shuffled on, still treading on smaller pieces of embedded glass and painful ant bites.

Expensive-looking paintings hung on both walls. The blood oozing from her feet made walking difficult on the slick tile floors. She blundered against what looked like a Van Gogh, knocking it to the floor with a crash. *Tough shit!* Her concentration was on the throbbing agony in her wounded feet. As she progressed, the hallway turned, until Mia was beginning to think she might be walking in circles. Her bloody, right foot slipped, and she fell hard on the floor.

Gasping with pain, she clutched at a large painting nearby to help her stand again. Once she was upright, she stared absently at the bloody hand prints she'd inadvertently left on the canvas.

Staring, she realized that the face in the painting was ... *her*? No, not her. It had to be her grandmother. She noted again how similar they were, right down to their birthmarks. *I can't think about that now,* she thought feverishly. *Just get the hell out of this horror-show!*

She rounded a corner—in the dimly lit hall, a dark figure stood facing her, blocking her way.

A large pistol was pointed at her, and a woman's voice commanded, "Freeze! Hands where I can see 'em."

Mia sobbed with relief. "Help me, please." Her wobbly legs gave way, and she fell to the cold tile.

Lt. Lacey was appalled, recognizing the small, bloody figure trembling with terror in front of her. "Ohmigod ... Mia? What the hell has happened to you?" She holstered her weapon to kneel down beside the bleeding girl.

Mia moaned. "Please get m-me outta here. M-my g-grandfather's dead. I-I had to kill him, he took video—I-I tried to get away, but ... but Kurt—the rats! I couldn't—Max is d-dead, too—ants g-got h-him," she rambled hysterically.

Kris didn't interrupt or ask questions. Reaching down, she carefully wrapped the girl in the jacket she'd taken off in the overly warm mansion.

She picked Mia up in her arms, murmuring soothingly. "It's gonna be okay, sweetie, let's get you out of here."

Chapter Forty-One – Pete's House, Late Friday Night

Pete woke with a start. He'd fallen asleep on the couch after Frank had come by to check on him. Frank had come in and revealed his suspicions regarding Ben's murder.

"We won't know for certain until forensics finishes up at the scene. But it looks like it's the same person that murdered Missy's mom." Frank had curiously eyed the little wooden figure on the end table. "Ah, Missy mentioned something about you needing some Bear-B-Gone spray," he said, handing Pete a can of the stuff.

Embarrassed, Pete shrugged and took the can. "I, uh, don't have a gun. If someone tries to break in, all I've got is an old bat and a kitchen knife," he said, by way of explanation.

Frank gave him a tight smile. "Probably won't need it. 'Course, if a bear did break in, your best bet would be to go out a window. You spray 'em in here, all you'd do is piss 'em off. Not recommended in close quarters."

Pete thanked him for stopping by. Frank nodded, glancing again uneasily at the wood sprite. "Something about that thing gives me creeps," he muttered, on his way out.

Pete had given the wooden figure a quick glance as a shiver ran up his spine. Frank had said goodnight and driven away. Pete hadn't felt at all reassured when the Sheriff had told him he'd send a deputy to patrol his neighborhood "just in case."

Pete had locked the door and racked out on the couch. A strange noise had woken him as he was drifting off to sleep. He sat up, listening intently, nervously scanning the room for its source.

Skritch ... skritch ... skritch. His head snapped toward the front porch window. The abrasive sound was coming from outside the front door. *Skritch ... skritch ... skritch.* A sudden feeling of dread caused his sphincter to tighten. He grabbed the can of bear spray from the floor where he'd left it.

"Who the fuck is out there?" he yelled, getting up from the couch. No answer.

Skritch ... skritch ... skritch. He walked over to the window drapes. As he pulled them aside to peer out, the porch light suddenly went dark. Pete went rigid with fear. No frickin' way was he about to open that door. A low growl rumbled from the other side of the old wood door. That was enough for Pete. He turned, ran to his bedroom, slammed and locked the door.

MISSY RUBBED A SORE nipple, where Belinda had gummed her hard during her three-a.m. feeding. Jake hadn't helped it any earlier, as their lovemaking had been a little rough. She lay back beside him, listening to him snore noisily in his sleep. *Must be nice,* she thought enviously. Some nights it was like lying next to a wounded bear.

She'd almost drifted back to sleep when her cell on the nightstand chimed with an incoming call. She glanced at the clock: it was four-forty a.m. Nobody called this late unless it was bad news. She fumbled the phone, dropped it, picked it up, and saw Pete was calling. Sighing, she got up to take the call in the bathroom.

"Pete, what's going on? It's four-fucking-thirty in the morning," she whispered caustically. "Don't tell me you had another nightmare?"

Pete sounded out of breath. "Missy, someone or some-*thing* is trying to get in my front door," he hissed anxiously.

He had Missy's full attention. "Can you see who it is? I mean, your porch light is on, right?" she asked, while she sat and peed.

He told her about the porchlight going out when he tried to peer out the curtains. "Missy, all I've got for protection is the fucking bear spray Frank brought me. I-I don't know what else I can do. I'm in my bedroom. I called the Sheriff's office. The cop said he'd send someone to check on it. But nobody ever showed."

Missy frowned. "Pete, calm down. Do you have a flashlight?"

"Yeah, but I—*ah, crap*! It's in my fucking car—along with the bear spray. Thankfully, the Sheriff had an extra can of that shit." He paced the room while talking.

She yawned hugely. "What about the flashlight on your phone?"

"I thought of that, but it's not bright enough to penetrate outside. The light just bounces off the window, blinding me." he groused. "Missy, I have to tell you I'm a wee bit paranoid. After that thing—" He cut off.

"Pete, are you there? Hello?" Missy was now alarmed, as well. Nothing but silence from his end. "Pete, if you can hear me, stay where you are. I'm coming over as soon as I can get some clothes on. Be there in a few. Try to stay calm." She pulled her rambunctious hair back into a quick ponytail and disconnected.

Crap! She'd have to wake Jake and tell him she was leaving. She left the bathroom to slip on a pair of jeans along with a flannel shirt.

"What's up? Is there a problem?" Jake's voice startled her.

"It's Pete. Says he has an unwelcome guest at his front door. He's called the Sheriff's Office, but I'll bet the deputy on call has his ass planted in the all-night donut shop. I'll be back soon," she leaned down to kiss him.

He gently cradled her face in both hands while holding her gaze. "Be careful, Missy. Remember, you're not a cop. Go check on Pete—and call me when you get there, okay? I'll never get back to sleep, anyway," he yawned. Tenderly, he kissed her again.

She sighed, grabbing her holstered .40 caliber Glock 27, attaching it to her belt. Before leaving, she checked on Belinda, who was sleeping soundly. Missy put on her jacket, locked the front door behind her, and got in her cruiser. The early morning air was crisp. Starting the engine, she shivered, turning the heat on high, though warm air would be minutes away. She accelerated down the drive to the highway, thinking grimly about Pete and his "unwelcome guest." She only prayed that it was human.

PETE'S PHONE HAD DIED. After their horrendous experience in the park and Missy's warning call, he'd forgotten to charge it. *Shit!* He didn't hear Missy's last words before the call dropped. And of course, the damn USB charging cable was in his car—along with everything else he needed now. He didn't own a personal computer. Frustrated, he threw the useless piece of crap on the bed.

Skritch ... skritch ... skritch, Pete froze at the recurring sound. He whirled around to face his bedroom window. The unknown being that lurked outside had him paralyzed with fear. Anger and humiliation swept over him at being forced to retreat and hide in his own bedroom like a five-year-old. Shame, in turn, made him irate.

"Fuck you, asshole! The cops are on their way. You better haul ass while you can," he bellowed toward the window. Shaking now with anger more than fear, he gathered his courage, reached over to pull the blinds up, and leaned close to the window.

Holy shit! From the dark, a face stared back at him. Pete jumped back from the window like a scalded cat. Stumbling, he fell back on his bed as a brilliant light dazzled him from outside.

"Pete, it's Missy. Can you hear me in there? Open the freaking door, I'm freezing my ass off out here, Bud." Her voice was muffled.

At the sound, Pete uttered a huge sigh. "I-I'm coming, hang on," he yelled back.

He ran to open the front door for her. Strangely, the porch light was working again. Missy walked quickly inside, as Pete shut and locked the door behind them.

"I thought you said the porch light went out. It's working now, but no one was anywhere near the porch when I pulled up. Are you certain someone was here?" she probed, now plainly irritated.

"Missy, I'm damn sure I didn't imagine that noise," he said resentfully. He went and unlocked the front door. Opening it and walking onto the porch, he yelled, "Check this out!" Missy joined him. "Don't believe I imagined *this*," he snapped, pointing to the outside surface of the door. Two sets of grooved claw marks about a foot long and a quarter inch deep had been gouged into the wood.

Missy frowned uneasily. "Maybe whoever did that took off when the deputy's cruiser pulled up in front of the house ... but then, where's the deputy?" she questioned.

Confused, Pete looked at her, shaking his head. "What deputy? I told you I called, but I didn't think anyone ever showed up."

A finger of unease wove up Missy's spine. "His car was parked out front when I arrived. I figured he was either in here with you or maybe checking out back." Missy pointed out toward the street.

Squinting, Pete could barely make out the sheriff's logo on a cruiser parked by the curb. Exchanging anxious glances, they walked out and warily approached the cruiser.

When Missy shined her light inside, they witnessed the deputy's body slumped over the steering wheel, blood spattered everywhere. Apparently, his throat had been savagely torn out!

Chapter Forty-Two -
Boulder Medical Center

Mia awoke with a panicked gasp, expecting Max to be leering at her with his ant-covered face. Instead, she saw Lt. Lacey from the Taos PD sitting by her bed and thumbing through a magazine. Kris laid that down when she saw Mia was awake.

"About time you woke up," she smiled, taking one of Mia's bound hands gently in her own.

Mia was totally disoriented. "Det. Lacey? W-where am I?" she asked groggily.

"You're in a hospital in Boulder. I found you in your grandfather's residence, injured and dehydrated. The doctors had to dig a lot of broken glass out of your feet," Kris grimly informed her.

Mia peered under the blanket. Both feet were bound in bandages. She teared up, remembering her recent ordeals: Her crazy grandfather, Max and the cage, the broken glass on the floor, the man-eating ants.

"Thank you, Det. Lacey, for getting me the hell out of there. But h-how in the world did you know where to find me?" She was still woozy from the pain meds she'd been given.

"Well, it wasn't easy. Actually, your friend, Wendy Ravenwood pointed me in your direction."

Mia avoided her eyes at the mention of Wendy's name. "She's no friend of mine. What kind of 'friend' abandons you when you most need them?" Mia said angrily, forgetting that Wendy had sent Kris to help her.

Kris squeezed her hand, changing the subject. "Mia, I need you to explain what happened in that place. Boulder PD found both your grandfather and his bodyguard dead inside. When I found you, you were rambling about rats, ants, and your grandfather." Kris waited patiently for an answer.

Mia sighed and reluctantly told her about all of it:

How she'd found the recorded video of her in the shower in Kurt's study, then, Max finding her watching it and imprisoning her in the dark basement full of hungry rats. How she'd slammed Max in the head with the fire extinguisher to try to escape—only to find that Kurt had strangled her cat. How he'd then stunned her and handcuffed her to a bed.

She went on, explaining with little emotion that, fearing for her life, she'd rigged the toilet rod to protect herself from Kurt. She explained that he'd become deranged, believing she was his dead wife, Lily, and that he'd told her he was going to kill her. Finally, she tried to describe being trapped in the plexi-glass cage and Max's ferocious ants.

By the time she finished, she was weeping wearily. Kris felt sorry for the girl, but she still had a lot of unanswered questions.

"Mia, tell me about this Ravenwood girl. How long have you known her?"

Mia didn't feel she had a reason to protect Wendy, whatever she actually was, any longer. *Bitch left me to die,* she thought bitterly.

"I-I met her in school. She showed up in one of my classes a few days ago. This all began after Freda stabbed me in the leg during lunch. I went to the girls' bathroom to check out my leg. She, Wendy, was in the adjoining stall." At this point, Mia hesitated in her narrative.

"Take your time, tell me what happened." Kris asked softly.

Mia closed her eyes and continued. "I-I was pissed, so damn angry. At that moment, I wished Freda was dead—and somehow, Wendy heard my thoughts. She talked to me then, from inside the next stall. I didn't know who it was. She told me she just needed a drop of my ... my blood, then she said something weird—about 'blood for blood.'

"I didn't think much about it, I was so upset and mad. I never believed she could really change anything. I—I thought it was some sort of weird game we were playing. Anyway, that same day, that toady friend of Freda's, Jessie Gambols, turned up dead in that restroom. After that, my world fell apart—my mother died from that awful car wreck, then a fire destroyed our house and almost killed Dad and me.

"Wendy kept showing up out of nowhere. She ... she claimed she's a Navajo 'Guardian Spirit' sent to protect me. She's a freaking liar—that's all bullshit! She didn't stop my crazy, perverted grandfather from bringing me up here and trying to rape me. Then his boyfriend Max turned out to be a batshit psycho. They both tried to kill me. I never wanted to hurt anyone. I just wanted to get away ..." She paused angrily, as a strange cop with bulging forearms stepped into the doorway.

"Excuse me, Lt. Lacey." He motioned for Kris to step out of the room. Nodding, she went to join him. Mia watched him telling Lacey something in hushed tones, as she stiffened visibly at his words. The burly cop glanced briefly at Mia, turned, and left. Kris took a deep breath, shaking her head. Turning slowly, she walked back to Mia's bed and sat down beside her.

"Mia, I appreciate the hell you've been through these past few days. I'm afraid I have more bad news." She hesitated when Mia's face grew alarmed. "Boulder PD has confirmed that your father was involved in a fatal accident. It appears he was on the way to Boulder when it happened. An eighteen-wheeler was involved. Your dad's vehicle went through a guardrail and over a steep cliff. I'm so sorry, but ... he didn't survive," Kris told her quietly. Strangely, she'd seen the accident's aftermath on her way to find Mia. *Shit! This poor kid can't catch a break,* Kris thought sympathetically.

Mia was shocked beyond speech for a few seconds. "He ... didn't ... survive?" She moaned. "No, no, no! This can't be happening." Tears came then.

Trying to comfort her, Kris took her bandaged hand in her own. Her migraine was returning with a vengeance. "Mia, you must listen to me now. A detective from Boulder PD will be here shortly. They're going to want you to give them a statement. They have two dead bodies at your grandfather's estate—well, three, including your cat. They're going to need answers. Do you understand what I'm saying? I think you may want to 'lawyer up' before you talk to them," she instructed her.

Mia looked like she might throw up. "Why? I've just told you everything that happened. I was held against my will, tortured, almost killed. I was lucky to get out of there with my life. If you hadn't gotten there when you did, I probably wouldn't have," she disputed miserably.

Kris knew that as far as the police were concerned, the deaths would be viewed as suspicious. A wealthy grandfather takes in his only granddaughter—who has everything to gain by killing the rich old bastard. Kris believed in her gut that the girl had told her the truth. The problem was that the story was one-sided; the dead couldn't defend themselves.

"Mia, the police may see this as a possible double homicide. There's no evidence to prove that your grandfather took that video of you if it's been erased," Kris told her.

Mia shook her head vehemently. "Max may've thought he deleted it, but they can still recover it from the SD card. It's all on there, believe me. Everything he thought he deleted can be retrieved. They should also find the camera hidden in my bathroom. That should be enough proof."

Kris realized what she'd said was correct, wondering why she hadn't remembered that detail. Probably because the damnable migraine was taking control of her brain.

"Well, that should help to substantiate your account. But that, in and by itself, won't get you out of the woods." Kris was chewing on her lower lip. "It still leaves money as a motive. Your grandfather was worth a ton of money. And who else might stand to profit from his death, aside from his partner? You. You're his only living relative, am I right?" Kris rubbed her throbbing temples.

Mia started to agree but paused to think for a second. "Kurt told me I have an older half-brother. His name is Pete Chandler. My ... D-dad's son from a previous marriage. I don't know if he'd legally be entitled to inherit anything or not," Mia informed her. Kris shook her head doubtfully. "Could you please try and contact him for me? He's the only living relative I have left. I think he lives in Joseph, Oregon. God, this is all so screwed up. I don't think he knows about me. I need to tell him who and where I am," Mia pleaded.

A sharply dressed woman with brunette hair worn in a short bob interrupted then, knocking on the door and entering. She introduced herself, "Hello, I'm Lt. Det. Dianne Flowers, Boulder PD. And you are?" she asked Kris, extending her hand.

Kris responded, "I'm Lt. Det. Kris Lacey, Taos PD. This is Mia Chandler," she responded.

Lt. Flowers stepped closer to Mia's bedside. "Miss Chandler, I have some questions for you. Do you want a lawyer to be present before we go any further?" she asked coolly, cocking her brows inquisitively.

Mia glanced nervously over at Kris, who held her gaze, nodding imperceptibly. "Uh, am I under arrest?" the girl asked.

Flowers paused for a beat. "No, not at this time. Two deceased people were found at your grandfather's estate. Your grandfather, Kurt Kozer, was found stabbed in the neck, with a bloody metal rod laying nearby. The remains of his partner's body were found covered with some sort of large, vicious ants. You appear to be the only survivor, Miss Chandler. I need some answers," the detective replied.

Flowers watched the girl's face carefully for any tics or tells she might be lying. She also saw Kris shake her head slowly and silently mouth, "lawyer" to Mia.

"I-I don't have anything to hide. My dad sent me to stay with my grandfather, Kurt Kozer, and this guy Max after our house in Taos burned down. Then, I accidentally stumbled on a video he'd made of me. He'd installed a tiny camera in the bathroom of the room where I was staying and recorded me taking a shower. They were going to kill me to cover up the fact that my grandfather was a psychotic pervert.

"Max caught me watching the video. He erased it and locked me in a dark basement full of hungry rats. I managed to convince my grandfather to let me out. Then, I tried to escape by hitting Max with a fire extinguisher, but Kurt shocked me with a stun gun and tied me to a bed."

Mia repeated everything she'd told Kris earlier, only adding as she finished, "They were both insane. Kurt believed I was his dead wife. I think he was obsessed with her. I saw a painting hanging in a hallway that I think must've been my grandmother. We could have been twins. I—I don't believe I would have made it out alive, if Lt. Lacey hadn't found me when she did." Showing Flowers her bruised hands, Mia threw back the sheet to reveal the bites on her legs and her bandaged feet.

Lt. Flowers was silent for a moment, appalled by the girl's horrific story. Her instincts told her the teenager was probably telling the truth. That, or she was the best bullshitter Flowers had ever met. Her BS meter hadn't set off any alarms. Still ...

"Even if all that's true, your grandfather was the wealthy owner of a cat food empire. There's the little matter of who stands to benefit most if something happened to him. He must have been worth a ton of money. You are his only grandchild, right?" she inquired. Her steely blue eyes were riveted on Mia's own.

Mia answered, "Well, my grandfather wrote me a letter telling me that I also have a half-brother, Pete Chandler, who I never knew about. I think he lives in Joseph, Oregon. At least, he did. I don't even know why my grandfather told me about him. Someone should try to contact Pete to tell him about me. I guess he's my only living kin now."

At this point Kris interrupted, "I think you should pull the SD card from that camera and retrieve the information on it. If that video is on there, the evidence should speak for itself, Lt. Flowers. Seems like a clear-cut case of self-defense to me."

Flowers' eyes cut from Mia's wrapped feet to the rat bites on her ear and arms and ant bites all over her. "Possibly. That will be all for now." She turned to leave, but pivoted back. "Don't plan on leaving town anytime soon, Miss Chandler. I'll be in touch when we know more." She strode out of the hospital room.

Kris could tell Mia was visibly relieved at her departure. "Well, I'll be staying until this fiasco is straightened out. If they can find corroborative evidence on the SD card, I don't think you have anything to worry about.

"You're going to need help with your father's, um, arrangements. I'll try to contact your half-brother. When all this is over, you'll need a place to live." She handed Mia her card. "Call me when the hospital releases you, and I'll come pick you up. In the meantime, get some rest. You're going to need it." She gave the girl's arm a light squeeze, and walked out, closing the door behind her.

Mia sighed, closing her eyes, and silently prayed, *Please God, let her find Pete!*

Chapter Forty-Three - Joseph, Saturday, 5:00 a.m.

Sheriff Blackstone was beginning to feel that he really should retire soon. The relentless pressure of his position was slowly eating into his soul. Burnout was inevitable. He'd known good cops who'd either drowned in a bottle or eaten their guns to deal with the stress. He didn't plan on joining them.

Sadly, he stared into the window of his now-deceased deputy's cruiser, still parked in front of Pete's house. The surviving five deputies who stood nearby looked pale and frightened. *As well they should,* Frank thought grimly, while they waited for the ME to finish his latest grisly task.

"Listen up, guys, there's an extremely dangerous individual running loose out here. Until we catch the crazy sonofabitch that's doing this, no one rides alone. Everyone will buddy-up, understood?" he announced gruffly. The deputies replied as one, "Yes, sir."

"Roberts, you're odd man out, you'll ride with me." Deputy Roberts nodded nervously, climbing into the passenger seat of his boss's vehicle. "Whoever did this could still be bloody. They're probably on foot. They should be considered armed and dangerous," Frank finished. The men glanced anxiously from Pete's scarred front door to the empty cruiser nearby and immediately took his meaning.

Missy came down from the porch and pulled the sheriff aside. "Frank, you know in your gut whoever did this won't stop until he's caught or killed. He's hunting us down one by one," she hissed softly.

Frank seemed not to have heard her, still staring at the empty cruiser. "He was just doing his job. He died in the line of duty. On my watch," Frank mumbled and spat into the dark.

"Listen, Frank," Missy touched his arm, "I'm taking Pete back to stay with us. He's in danger here. Safety in numbers, right?" she said tersely.

Frank nodded. "He could be killing randomly, you know. Your mother and Ben might have only been a coincidence," he pointed out.

"Bullshit! I don't believe in coincidence. This piece of shit isn't going to stop until he's killed everyone I care about. Obviously, he blames me for something he believes I've done, something I'm not aware of. Who knows what's going on in his sick fucking mind? He could come after *you,* too, Frank. Best watch your back, bud," she warned, sliding into her cruiser.

Frank was silent for a moment. "We'll get the fucker," he growled, turning to check on the ME's progress.

Reluctantly, Pete got into Missy's cruiser. "I don't want to impose on you and Jake this way. Listen, Missy, if you would just give me a gun, I could protect—"

"No. Gun. You're not certified in sidearms yet," she cut in sternly.

Pete shook his head. "I don't have to be 'certified' to use a freaking shotgun, do I? I could borrow that .12-gauge semi-auto of yours and—"

She stopped him again, "And what? You think you'd be able to shoot someone in cold blood?" she asked, pulling away from the curb rapidly.

Pete simmered in his seat. "Hell, Missy, you know as well as I do that whatever raked my front door probably isn't human. This has all the earmarks of that horror-show Frank supposedly killed last year," he groused. Missy couldn't disagree.

The early morning sky was suffused with an orange glow as the sun rose over the snow-capped mountains to the east. They were quiet for the rest of the drive. As Missy parked the cruiser, Pete's cell chimed. Seeing an unfamiliar number on the screen, he let it go to voice mail, as they both got out and walked inside the house.

Jake was in the kitchen, busy making toaster waffles for breakfast. He looked up at their entry, burning his finger on a hot waffle, which he dropped on the floor—to Jinx's delight. The big feline swatted the waffle across the floor until it was cool enough to devour. It was a familiar ritual: humans' clumsiness, especially Jake's, meant treats for Jinx.

"So, what's the word?" Jake asked, sucking on his burned finger.

Missy and Pete sat down at the kitchen table. "We've got a problem. Either one of those freaking creatures has emerged, or someone is cleverly copy-catting. There's been another murder." She leaned over wearily to coo at Belinda lying in her crib.

Startled by her news, Jake dropped another waffle on the floor. Jinx pounced, carrying away his "kill," while Missy rolled her eyes.

"Who was it? Anyone we know?" Jake asked anxiously, taking a seat at the table.

Missy sighed, shaking her head. "Another of Frank's deputies, fairly new. He was savagely murdered, Jake, but he wasn't gutted like Mama or Ben. I don't think the asshole had time. I may have scared him away when I pulled up to Pete's," she told him.

"So ... you're telling me there's another one of those fucking things running around killing people?" he asked apprehensively.

Missy glanced at Pete, then back at Jake. "There were claw marks a quarter inch deep in Pete's front door, and the deputy's throat was torn out."

THE THREE OF THEM SPENT most of Saturday discussing the situation, proposing possible scenarios, and taking turns occupying Belinda between her naps.

That evening, Pete's cell chimed with another unknown number. This time he answered, putting it on speaker. "Hello, who is this?" Silence on the other end. "If you aren't gonna talk, I'm hanging up, asshole."

"You're going to die. Soon," a voice hissed from the speaker.

Pete's face paled and he stared at the phone like he was holding a snake. "Who the hell is this?" he asked heatedly. There was a pause.

"I'm the one who's going to kill you. You'll never see me coming. As we speak, I'm watching you. You all look so ... tasty," the caller continued coldly.

Pete's eyes grew wide as he cut them toward the window at Jake's back and realized the curtains were wide open. Anyone outside could see them all clearly. "Listen, shithead, I'm—" Pete began.

"No, you listen to me. I'm going to make you watch while I eat your fucking friends *alive* ... one by one. How does that grab ya'?" He howled with delight. "You'll be begging for death before I'm finished."

Before Pete could respond, the call was disconnected. He glanced anxiously from Jake to Missy. "Can we please close the freakin' curtains? That crazy bastard may be out there right now. I've got the asshole's number on my phone. Jake, better call Frank. We'll give it to him, and he can trace the prick's phone," Pete said. Jake merely looked uneasy as he closed the curtains.

Missy advised, "You know it's probably a 'burner,' Pete. He isn't likely to be stupid enough to let it be traced back to him. You should call Frank yourself and tell him about this new threat. Jake, better grab the shotgun, we may need it." She quickly took control.

Jake started for the bedroom, while Pete called the sheriff's office. Missy picked up the sleeping Belinda and took her to her crib in their bedroom.

"Nothing's going to hurt you, sweetie. Mama promises," she whispered in her sleeping daughter's ear. She placed her down gently, pulling her little blanket up over her.

"Missy, the shotgun's not in the closet. Where the hell is it?" Jake hollered.

"If it's not there, it's in your truck," she said quietly, leaning down to give Belinda a kiss.

Hopefully, Jake looked under the bed. Not there, either. *Dammit!* He'd have to go check in the truck. Outside. In the dark.

"It's not in here, Missy, better hand me my Glock. I gotta go check the truck." He glanced at her, reluctantly.

She cocked a brow. "You'd best let me cover you. Sorry, Bud, but your aim isn't that great. You couldn't hit the side of a barn with that pistol in daylight, let alone at night." She was only half-teasing.

"If I had the freakin' shotgun, I wouldn't really need to aim, would I?"

As she followed him out the front door, from the dark, a blur of fur raced straight for them, as Jinx shot between them and into the house before they could blink. Missy jumped, almost firing a round before she recognized him. She shined her flashlight out into the inky darkness surrounding the house beyond the porch light's limited scope.

Nothing unnatural was moving around. As her beam swept the surrounding forest, a pair of glowing, red eyes were reflected—a small jackrabbit searching for a meal. Still, Missy was uneasy. She could almost feel eyes on them, as Jake scurried out to the pickup. Opening the door, he spied the shotgun in the back seat.

"Jake, hurry up and get the damn gun. I have a feeling we're not the only ones out here," she commanded anxiously.

Jake grabbed the gun from the truck and turned to haul ass back inside when a deep, rumbling growl froze him in his tracks. Missy swiveled her light toward the ominous sound. A large black mama bear, with her cub, emerged from a blind spot behind the pickup. *Shit!*

"Jake, get back inside your truck. Now." Missy spoke quietly, pointing. Jake looked behind him and spotted the mother and cub in the flashlight's beam.

"Whatever you do, don't shoot her. Honk the horn, that should scare 'em away." She slowly backed up closer to the open front door.

Slowly, Jake opened the truck door and slid into the driver's seat, quietly pulling the door closed. Cracking the window so he could still hear Missy, he leaned on the horn. Its blare shattered the quiet of the forest. The startled bear let out a bawl and loped into the darkness, her small cub trundling behind.

"Okay, it's safe to come out now," Missy told him.

"*Safe* is a relative term when it comes to bears, Missy." He got back out of the truck, slammed its door, and ran into the house, with her leading the way.

They'd forgotten about Pete. He was standing near the door with a large butcher knife in one hand and a can of Bear-B-Gone in the other. Missy locked the door, turned, and looked at his weapons.

"Well, Bud, you're certainly 'loaded for bear,'" she said wryly, holstering her pistol.

Pete asked, "Is it gone?"

"I wouldn't have gotten my ass out of the truck if wasn't," Jake smirked.

They all sat back down at the kitchen table, trying to calm down from the excitement.

"I called Frank and gave him that asshole's number, but he said the same thing as you, probably a burner. He said they might have a lead, though. They found something in the deputy's throat. I—" Pete froze.

Tap-tap-tap. The sound was coming from the window behind Pete's chair. He licked chapped lips.

"Think mama bear is back?" he whispered hoarsely. His mouth was dry as a desert wind.

Jake and Missy shared a look. All three stood up, moving quickly away from the window. Jake grabbed the shotgun off the table and pulled the charging handle back to seat a shell in the chamber. No shell. He checked the magazine, it was empty.

Shit on a shingle! The bears had distracted him, and he'd forgotten to grab the shells from the back seat. He tossed the gun on the couch in disgust, narrowly missing Jinx's head. The bobcat hissed, leaping to safety.

"What's the matter, Jake? You forget the ammo?" Missy asked, checking the loads in her own weapon.

He frowned at her. "It's not my fault. You were the last one to use the damn thing. I thought you kept it loaded. The freaking bear distracted me, alright?" he added defensively. "There's extra shells in the closet."

I hope! He rushed to the bedroom closet and dug through the pile of old stuff stacked on the shelves lining three walls.

Finally, he found some shells stashed inside a box of old Christmas decorations. *Jingle bells, shotgun shells*, he rhymed nervously. These shells were loaded with birdshot. Not as lethal as buckshot or slugs, but they'd have to do. He loaded four in the magazine and one in the pipe. With the safety on, he rejoined Missy and Pete in the living area. "What's the plan?" he asked them.

Tap-tap-tap—now at the back door.

"Let's see what's out there, shall we? Shotgun leads." Missy pointed, volunteering Jake.

"Thank you very little," he grumbled. "Pete, when I say open, do it fast." He nodded toward the back door. Making sure Pete was ready, Jake took the safety off. Taking a deep breath, he flipped on the back-porch light. "Open," he said.

Pete yanked the door open, and Jake stepped out onto the covered porch. He caught a glimpse of movement at the edge of the light, as something dashed for cover in the dark.

"Flashlight, Missy," Jake hissed over his shoulder.

She turned on the powerful LED light, shining it where he aimed the shotgun. Pete followed her out the door to get a look. Jake fired a round into the air, trying to flush out whatever was there. The blast reverberated through the frigid night air, disrupting the placid silence again. They all moved out into the yard, each watching for any sign of the intruder.

Their search was interrupted by a loud crash from inside the house, as a high, piercing cry turned the blood in Missy's veins to ice. *Belinda!* Turning, she dashed back in, to find the front door standing wide open. The bastard had diverted them and broken in! Missy's heart raced as she ran to her baby's crib.

Belinda was gone ...

Chapter Forty-Four - Boulder Medical Center

Mia woke to someone calling her name. She opened sleep-encrusted eyes to find Wendy Ravenwood standing by her hospital bed.

"Oh, *now* you show up. What the hell do you want?" she asked icily.

"I see you are alright, even without the necklace I gave you. I want you to know that I never abandoned you. I would always have known if you were in danger of being seriously harmed," Wendy said coolly.

"You allowed me to be taken away by a pair of psychotic assholes who tried their best to kill me. What the fuck do you call being nearly eaten by hungry rats and carnivorous ants? Mildly alarming?" Mia asked incredulously. "On top of that, I find out my father was killed in a freak accident on his way to see me. I lost my entire family in the space of a week. Where the hell were you?" Mia accused angrily.

Wendy didn't flinch, her cold, glittery eyes contained no hint of emotion. "I am sorry for your losses. In each case, however, you were able to save yourself. You are alive and healing. That is what matters. Now you must go to your brother in Oregon. Evil besieges him and his friends as we speak," she said, in her weird, detached manner.

"Like I have a lot of freakin' choice in the matter." Mia glared at the girl, or spirit, or whatever the hell she was.

"You always have choices in life, Mia. It is what you do with those choices that ultimately defines who you are—your purpose and your destiny in this world," she remained calm.

"*Destiny*? What do you know about my destiny? Just leave me the hell alone!" Mia pointed a shaking finger to the door.

Wendy studied Mia's tear-stained face for a moment. "If that is your wish, so be it. For now. She turned and walked out.

KRIS HAD CHECKED INTO a room on the first floor of a cheap motel. Her migraine had grown worse since she'd said good night to Mia at the hospital. She went out to the ice machine and scooped out the few remaining cubes of ice from its bottom. In her room, she wrapped them in a thin washcloth to place against her throbbing temples, downing her last naratriptan.

Then she called Hendricks in Taos to tell him she'd be on extended leave for a few days.

"Did you find the Chandler girl?" he asked.

"Yeah, she's in the hospital. She's okay, but get this—her father, her grandfather and his partner are all dead," she told him. "Her father was killed in an accident on his way to Boulder. The grandfather and his partner are another story. Local PD is running the case. Depending on the evidence, she could be in serious trouble." She filled him in on what Mia had told her.

"That sucks big time. Poor girl. Sounds like you have your hands full, LT," Hendricks said.

"I should know more after the detective on the case finishes with the DBs and confirming info from the property. Oh, by the way, I spoke to the Ravenwood girl briefly. She remains a 'person of interest' in the deaths of those two girls and the mother. I'll be in touch." Kris disconnected and lay back on the lumpy bed, fully clothed.

Searching on her phone, she found the info on Pete Chandler in the town of Joseph, Oregon. She called his number and listened as it rang four times and went to voice mail. She identified herself and asked him to call her back ASAP. Then she looked at the time and groaned. It was 11:30 p.m.—10:30 in Joseph. He probably wouldn't call back that night.

She turned off the bedside lamp and laid back. She was drifting off to sleep when she heard insistent knocking at her door. She cursed, fumbling to turn the light back on. *Shit! Midnight, who the hell is this?* Startled awake, she grabbed her Glock and cautiously peered through the security peephole in the door but saw nothing. She pulled the heavy black-out curtain aside and looked out. The light over her doorway was out, making it difficult to see anyone who was close to her door.

How damn convenient, Kris thought suspiciously. "Who's out there? I'm an armed police officer, identify yourself," she shouted through the door. Only silence. *Crap!* As quietly as possible, she pulled back the cheap-shit security chain. Holding the Glock at shoulder height, she yanked the door open. The sidewalk near her room was empty.

She stepped outside, pivoting quickly left and right, but saw no movement. Sighing with relief, she turned to go back inside, and saw the note stuck to her door.

It read simply, Take Mia to Oregon. W.R.'

DET. LT. DIANNE FLOWERS disliked cats. In her view, all cats were evil, particularly those with no fur. So, when she entered the Chaney residence and found the hairless abominations wandering the halls and kitchen, she immediately called to have someone come take them into "protective custody," so to speak.

The first officer on the scene had discovered Max's grisly remains and the ants. He'd immediately run from the room and called for back-up and a pest control firm. The exterminators had sprayed the room—including the body—with strong ant poison before anyone could approach the corpse. Two burly men from the coroner's office stood around outside smoking cigarettes, waiting to collect the bodies once the forensics team finished.

Lt. Flowers met first with her "all-things-technical" guru, Danny Chen. "Think you'll be able to retrieve anything usable from the SD card, Dan?" she asked.

Danny looked hurt. "Have I ever let you down, Lt.?" He showed her a tiny camera in his hand.

"Yeah, well, do me a solid and let's not start now, shall we? How long before you have results?" she queried impatiently.

He scratched an eyebrow, thinking. "Shouldn't take long. Probably have it in half-hour, hour, tops." He winked at her confidently.

Dianne gave him a hard look. "Get it done. I want the results by the time I'm finished here," she said curtly. Danny grinned and strutted toward the front door.

Flowers walked down the hall, spotting the yellow crime tape strung across the doorway of the room where Kurt Kozer's body lay. She pulled on some booties from her equipment bag and gloved up. When she entered, the ME was talking to one of the other techs. Spotting her, he ended his conversation.

"What have you got for me, Hank?" she asked, taking in the bloody scene.

"Elderly Caucasian male, deceased. Preliminary cause of death, massive blood loss due to a punctured carotid artery. The object that caused this mess is over there. I think it's an old float-rod from a toilet." He pointed to the bloody brass rod on the floor near the body.

"Time of death?" Carefully, she scanned the blood spray pattern on the floor and bed.

"I'll say, eighteen to twenty-four hours ago, at most." He stripped off his bloody gloves.

Her gaze took in the handcuffs attached to the bedposts. *Sonofabitch!* It was starting to look like the girl was telling the truth about the old man. She stepped into the bathroom and spotted the hairdryer on the marble sink top. A toothbrush lay in the sink. Examining it, she noted that the handle appeared slightly melted and warped.

Tried to make a weapon? she wondered. She removed the toilet tank lid. Sure enough, the float rod was missing. *Looks like she made one. Smart girl!*

Chapter Forty-Five - Wallowa State Forest, Oregon

"Belinda—that fucker took her, Jake!" Missy screeched in panic.

Jake was almost as freaked out, searching in vain under the bed and then in the bathroom for the baby. *Shit! That asshole suckered us out of the house and flanked us,* Jake thought, furious at himself for leaving her unprotected.

"He can't have gotten far, I haven't heard an engine start, so we should be able to—" he stopped, as a car rumbled to life in the distance. *Damn!* He'd spoken too soon.

Pete shouted from the driver's seat of Missy's cruiser. "C'mon, hurry up, we can catch 'em before they get away."

Jake and Missy ran and jumped in the car. Pete cranked the engine, spraying gravel in a rooster tail, backing up. But when he accelerated forward, they heard a *thump-thump-thump* and the car's back end sagged to the left. Pete stopped, threw the engine into "park," and leaped out to check. The back tire on the driver's side was flat as a pancake. *Shit!* The bastard had slashed it.

"Asshole planned ahead. He didn't have time to stop and do this after he grabbed Belinda," Pete said angrily. "Looks like he got Jake's truck, too." He pointed to the truck's flat rear tire.

"Did the fucker also get my bus?" Missy asked, almost hyperventilating with worry for her baby girl.

Pete did a quick inspection around her vehicle. "Doesn't look like it. Probably didn't have time."

They all clambered hurriedly into the classic VW minibus. Missy started the engine. "Don't think we can catch 'em in this. It's not built for

249

speed," she said through gritted teeth. They all watched headlights come on as the distant car sped away down the highway, moving fast toward town. As Missy floored the gas pedal, the bus picked up speed, but no way was it going to catch up to the other car.

"Careful, Missy, you're going too fast—remember that dip," Jake barked, just as she hit the deep depression where their drive met the highway fast enough to make the bus airborne for a moment. Luckily, there was no traffic. When it met the highway, the bus bounced twice, tilting briefly up on its right two tires before righting itself.

Both guys' faces paled as the bus slid dangerously close to the deep drainage ditch on the far side of the road. Missy swerved hard left to keep them from plowing into the culvert. She swore, hitting the gas again, and the bus picked up speed. They could barely see the taillights of the other car far ahead. The speed limit was fifty mph on this stretch of road; Missy was pushing sixty-five. They came out of a tight curve in the road to find the taillights had disappeared.

"Where the hell could they go? There's no turn-off near here, is there?" she asked anxiously. With the kidnapper's car nowhere in sight, she grew more frantic. The highway was dark and empty. She drove on for about a mile before abruptly slamming the brakes, slowing to a stop. "There must be some turn-off we missed back there. They can't just disappear into thin air," she growled angrily.

She turned the bus around and headed back the way they'd come. They all craned their necks, checking both sides of the road for any break in the dense trees large enough to accommodate a car. *Please let us find an opening,* she thought, gripping the steering wheel so hard her knuckles cracked audibly.

"What's that? There on the left, between those two big pines!" she exclaimed.

Sure enough, there was a gap in the trees wide enough for an SUV to drive through, but it would be a tight squeeze for the bus. She aimed the headlights toward the opening. A weed-covered gravel road ran up a steep slope, disappearing into the dark woods.

"Do those weeds look like something ran over them recently?" she asked them.

Jake squinted. "Looks like fresh tire tracks. See, some of those taller weeds are springing back up," he noted.

Sitting in the back seat, Pete had become motion-sick from the wild ride. "I thi—I need to—open—" *urrp,* he spewed steaming chunks of vomit all over the floorboard.

As the smell hit him, Jake's face went green. "Dammit, Pete, that's disgusting! Couldn't you have held it for another damn second? Now I've got—" *urrp,* Jake stuck his head out and hurled through his hurriedly rolled-down window.

Missy gagged from the smell, barely holding down her own gorge. "Really wish you hadn't done that, Pete. Next time you feel the urge, please give me some notice if you can. *Shit Marie!*"

Even with all the windows down, the stench inside the bus was damn-near overpowering. "Sorry, guys. It hit me all the sudden, no time to open the door," Pete apologized miserably.

Clearing his throat, Jake spit out some remaining phlegm. "They must've turned in here. Missy, you think the bus can make it? That road looks pretty rough."

She ground her teeth. "Should be okay, as long as I don't poke a hole in the oil pan. She eased the bus forward along the uneven terrain. A four-wheeler would have no trouble navigating it, but the bus was low to the ground.

"Guys, look sharp. They could've pulled off this shitty excuse for a road anywhere," Missy cautioned, steering the bus slowly up the rocky slope.

The headlights illuminated the surrounding pines, throwing shadows around them as they drove past. The bus rocked back and forth over the rutted surface, making things worse for Pete in the back. Fortunately for everyone, he had nothing left to toss up. Still, he dry-heaved several times, causing Jake to glance apprehensively over his shoulder.

"This damn goat trail doesn't seem to be leading anywhere except up." Missy cursed loudly, as the bus bottomed out on the rocky road.

After twisting and climbing for what seemed like an eternity, the road finally began to level out. As the bus strained to get over a good-sized rock, a nasty grinding sound came from the undercarriage. Missy gave it more gas, and the shriek of metal against rock vibrated up through the steering wheel. Jake glanced anxiously at her while she fought to get the VW over the small boulder. With a final lurch forward, the bus finally gained traction and pulled onto level ground.

They all spotted it at the same time. Fifty yards ahead, a dark-colored Land Rover sat askew, its front tires dangling off the edge of a steep drop-off. No more road. Cautiously, Missy pulled to within ten feet of the vehicle and stopped. They couldn't see any movement inside the car.

"Jake, cover me. If that fucker's hurt my baby, I'll kill him," she snarled, pulling her Glock.

"Be careful, Missy, please don't shoot unless you have to," he warned, snatching the shotgun.

They all climbed out of the stinky bus and warily approached the rear of the Rover. The headlights of the bus reflected off the Rover's rear windshield, making it hard to see inside. Missy crept up to the driver's side, pointing her pistol shakily at the window. It was dark inside, but she could tell that the driver's seat of the precariously perched car was empty.

"Jake, the asshole's gone! I don't see Belinda anywhere." Shaking with anxiety, she yanked the front door open. Pete came from behind, shining his cell's flashlight into the dim interior.

Missy was beyond despair. She screamed into the forest, frustrated. "Where have you taken her, you fucking asshole?"

Jake handed the shotgun to Pete and wrapped his arms around her, hugging her close. "We'll find her, babe. He can't have gotten—" A small whimper from inside the Rover stopped him. The forward tilt of the car had made it difficult to see into the rear seats.

"Belinda—she's in the back! Hurry, Jake, get her out before this damn thing decides to go over the edge," Missy cried urgently.

Jake opened the door to find his daughter lying in the back seat. Scooping her up, he handed her to her mother. As she hugged her daughter tightly, behind them, a car door slammed. They turned toward the sound. Now the fucker was in her bus.

Missy growled. "You're not taking my bus, you sorry, shit-eating bastard!" Quickly handing Belinda back to Jake, she advanced on the bus with her pistol raised, taking aim. The bus started, then jerked backwards, stalling. The driver restarted and repeated the maneuver, this time with more success. The "shit-eating bastard" evidently had never driven a standard shift before.

With his daughter in his arms, Jake couldn't do anything but watch, as his wife took aim and fired at the bus.

After backing into a stand of pines, the unknown driver managed to turn the VW around. It stalled again, the driver re-started it, then drove jerkily back down the rocky hillside toward the highway.

With the bus headlights gone, they were thrust back into the night's pitch dark. Missy had aimed for its rear tires, firing two quick rounds before she lost the target in the dark.

Shit! Crap! She was almost positive she'd hit one of them before losing sight of the bus, but it continued grinding and lurching down the crappy road.

"Well, that's fucking great. What are we gonna do now?" Jake snapped angrily.

Pete turned on his phone's flashlight again. Missy joined them at the Rover. "I may have hit a tire. If so, he won't get far." She holstered her gun, taking Belinda back from Jake, and turning to Pete. "How much juice is left in your cell?"

Pete glanced down. "It's down to one bar. The flashlight eats battery juice like crazy."

"Well, turn it off to conserve power. Only use it when it's necessary." she told him. They stood around shivering in the cold mountain air. "Jake, you think he might've left the keys in the Rover? We've gotta get out of here."

Pete said, "I'll check." He turned the light back on, opened the door and looked inside. "They're here, alright," he said excitedly.

"The tricky part will be making sure the back wheels have enough traction to haul the damn thing back up over the lip," she asserted.

"You're not seriously thinking of trying to back that thing up, are you?" Jake was alarmed.

"Damn it all, Jake, how else are we going to get out of here—stumble around in the dark until we fall off the fucking cliff? We'll freeze to death out here, Bud. Let's do this." she chided. Jake was silent.

Pete volunteered to try it. "You have a family," he pointed out.

"You do, too, now, Pete," she reminded him. "Look ... Jake, you get in the back for ballast, but leave the doors open. If it starts to slide over the edge, jump the hell out," she instructed, as she eased gently into the driver's seat.

Hesitating, he handed Belinda to Pete and carefully eased into the back seat. She turned the key and ... nothing.

Crap! What now? "Jake, it won't start. I think the battery is dead."

Leaning slightly forward, Jake saw with alarm that the gearshift was in the neutral position. With any sudden movement, the Rover could roll forward over the drop-off. "Missy, you gotta put the damn thing in "park." Now!" he hissed urgently.

Instantly, she realized the danger, shifting the gear into "park."

Jake let out an audible sigh. "Okay, now try it." He edged carefully back in his seat.

Her foot firmly on the brake, she turned the key. This time the engine turned over, idling smoothly.

"Okay, let's get all four wheels back on *terra firma*," she said, turning on the Rover's headlights. She shoved the engine into reverse, applying pressure to the gas pedal. The back wheels spun, kicking up dirt and pine needles.

Helpless, since he held Belinda, Pete had his flashlight on. He watched, horrified, as the car lurched backward and forward, its back wheels smoking with the effort to pull the front of the vehicle back up over the cliff's ragged edge. Grimly, Missy acknowledged that the maneuver wasn't working.

Suddenly Jake understood. "Wait! Do you have the four-wheel drive engaged?" he asked, choking on the acrid smoke the tires were creating.

Shit! She hadn't considered that. She lifted her foot off the gas and pressed hard on the brake. Then she depressed the "all-wheel drive" button, engaging all four tires. This time, when she hit the gas, the Rover's wheels all groaned and finally gained traction, then jerked the vehicle backward to the relative safety of the skimpy road.

Despite the cold night air, Missy was sweating. Jake climbed into the front seat while Pete handed Belinda to her anxious father and scrambled into the back. Missy reversed into the small turnaround opening in the trees and steered the large SUV back down the craggy slope as fast as she dared.

"He can't have more than a ten-minute head start on us," Missy said, maneuvering carefully back down the uneven trail.

"Yeah, but which way did he turn when he reached the highway?" Pete asked.

Missy frowned. Pete had a point—there was no way to tell which direction the crazy, bus-stealing bastard had taken. They reached the highway a couple minutes later, and Missy stopped the car at the junction of the trail and the highway. *Which way now?*

She asked Pete to give her his phone. Pete shrugged and handed it to her.

"What are you doing?" Jake was puzzled.

Missy didn't reply as she got out of the car. Holding the cell's light close to the ground, she walked over to the highway a few feet ahead, first walking north, then south, paralleling the highway. Finding what she'd suspected, she hurried back to the car.

"He left a trail. Either a bullet or a rock must have punctured the oil pan on the bus. He's headed south, but he won't get far, leaking like that." With a smile, she sped onto the dark, deserted highway.

Chapter Forty-Six - Boulder PD

Det. Flowers shook her head slowly in disgust. Danny Chen was playing all of the videos he'd recovered from the Kozer video's SD card for her. Mia's scene was the most recent of several—three other girls. All were naked, showering, and obviously unaware they were being remotely observed and recorded.

One thing stood out clearly, the other girls all closely resembled Mia in appearance. *So, who were they, what had happened to them? Most important, where were they now?* Det. Flowers wondered.

While she puzzled, Danny showed her the date and time stamps on each video, pointing out that each video had been taken about a year apart from the others. "This guy was definitely whacked. But why would he do this to his only granddaughter?" Danny asked.

Good question. "Unfortunately, he isn't around to tell us." Looking up, she frowned, "Uh-oh, here comes trouble," nodding toward a tall, handsome man headed their way.

DA Howard Thornbush was a man of little patience, with large ambitions for the office of mayor. "Good afternoon, Lieutenant. What have you got for me on the Kozer case?" Howard cut right to the chase.

Chen cleared his throat. "If you'll excuse me, I, uh ... have some data to upload somewhere." He left Dianne and the DA to squabble over details of the case.

"Howard, we have hard video evidence supporting the Chandler girl's version of what happened there. Kozer apparently recorded three other girls in a three-year time span before Chandler's video. And we have these," she showed him photos of the bloody handcuffs secured to bedposts, along with the stun gun.

"So ... you're implying she's innocent?" He didn't want to hear that.

"I'm saying that girl is lucky to be alive," she snapped back. Dianne knew he'd been looking forward to prosecuting the Chandler girl. She could practically envision the headlines.

"There were three other girls; we have no idea where they are now. From what we've seen, Kurt Kozer could well have been a serial killer. Sargeant Chen is running the girls' photos through facial recognition right now. Then he'll feed them through a national database of missing persons. Maybe we'll get lucky. As far as I'm concerned, the Chandler girl is only guilty of staying alive," she finished.

Thornbush considered the information she'd revealed, disappointment writ large on his face.

"That's what all the evidence shows," she said icily. "Look, the girl's father died in an auto accident on his way to Kozer's estate. She'd lost her mother about a week before. Oh, and her house was burned to the ground. Damn it, Howard, that girl's been through hell."

Thornbush was loath to lose an opportunity to prosecute someone. Especially when it involved the murder of a rich benefactor like Kurt Kozer. "What am I supposed do? The press has already gotten wind of the story. Your own boss is out for blood. That Kozer guy contributed big bucks to help get the Chief elected—and everybody knows it. He's got to have his little 'dog and pony' show to demonstrate to the voters how diligent he is," Howard said snidely.

Dianne gave him a stern look. "Howard, I don't give a damn whether you have someone to pin the blame on. My job is to make sure innocent people are protected. The report I put on the Chief's desk is going say 'Self-Defense.' I'm not into politics. Sorry if that spoils your day, but I have work to do. Goodbye." She turned on her heel and left him seething.

Leaving the station, she drove to the hospital. All parking spots there were taken, so she double-parked, blocking in an AP&P telephone repair truck, and turned on her emergency blinkers. *Payback for all the crappy service they've provided over the years.* She smiled to herself, walking inside.

When she knocked, Mia was sitting up in bed, but she stiffened as the detective came in. Dianne gave her what she hoped was an encouraging smile. Pulling a chair close to Mia's bed, she sat, asking, "How are you feeling?"

"Okay, I guess. My nose and my feet are still sore. Am I going to need a lawyer?" Mia asked warily.

Dianne paused before answering. "Not at this time. Miss Chandler, we *were* able to retrieve the video on the SD card, and it corroborated your story. But there's a complication—three other girls had been recorded showering on that video, before you. They all appear to be about your age, and you could pass for sisters, except none of them had a birthmark like yours," she continued.

Mia blushed at the mention of her blemish. "There were others?" She was horrified to hear that.

Dianne nodded solemnly. "I'm afraid so. We don't know what happened to the other girls. We're doing facial recognition searches to find any matches. If there are, we'll see if they were reported missing and when."

Changing the subject, Mia asked, "So ... did anyone call my brother, Pete?"

Dianne frowned slightly. "I tried to contact him and had to leave a message. No word back from him yet, but I'm sure we'll hear something soon."

Mia noticed her frown and sent a silent plea into the ether, *Dammit, Pete, please be okay. You're all the family I have left!*

Chapter Forty-Seven -
Wallowa State Park Area

After switching out of the Rover's four-wheel drive, Missy pulled onto the highway and sped down the road. The tall aromatic pines lining the highway were only dark green blurs in the headlights once she picked up speed.

"He can't have gotten much farther with my poor bus leaking like a sieve," she groaned. "Pete, do you have enough juice left to call 911?" She coolly swerved around a jackrabbit in the middle of the road.

Pete's stomach lurched at her maneuver. "I can try," he replied, checking his cell. Still one bar. "The signal's fading in and out." He punched in the number.

"Nine-one-one, what is the nature of your emerg—" Silence. The phone was belly-up. *Crap!*

"Sorry, Missy, I told you the damn flashlight sucks the life out of batteries." He was kicking himself mentally, for not charging his phone earlier.

They spotted her bus up ahead, sitting haphazardly on the side of the road, the driver's door hanging open. "What if he's got a gun, Missy?" Jake nervously eyed the bus as she pulled up and parked behind it.

"Guess I'll just have to shoot first. Asshole went after our daughter. I take that as kinda personal, Bud—how 'bout you?" she snarled, opening the door to get out.

"Look, Missy, I'm as pissed at the fucker as you are, but you can't take the law into your own hands." Jake attempted to reason with her.

"He should've thought about that before he snatched our daughter," she snapped back. She exited the Rover and advanced on the bus, gun at the ready.

Jake ground his teeth, quickly handing Belinda back to Pete. "If there's any gunfire, lay the hell down over her. Keep her safe, Pete." Jake took the shotgun and scrambled out, striding through the headlights' beam to catch up to his wife.

"You—in the bus. Step out with your hands up, asshole," Missy growled, edging closer to the open door. The driver's seat was vacant. The bastard had rabbited.

Missy swore like a sailor. "We'll never find him out there in the dark. If I only had a freaking flashlight ... *ah, shit*! The smell in here is repulsive," she wrinkled her nose, reaching in to turn on the bus's dome light. In its dim illumination, she saw remnants of Pete's supper splashed over the floorboard and back seat.

Jake merely felt relief that they hadn't had to shoot anyone in a gun battle. "Let's go, Missy. In the morning I'll call Johnny Six-Fingers to tow it." He was ready to get out of the frigid air.

"He'll make a mint off me yet because of that damn bus," Missy grumbled, as she and Jake climbed back into the Rover. "I bet that kidnapping sonofabitch is sitting out there laughing at us." Jake took the sleeping baby back from Pete, cradling her close.

She drove the Rover around the bus and back onto the dark highway. "Pete, you call the Sheriff as soon as we get back—" the sputtering of the engine stopped her. *Hell's bells, now what?* she thought despairingly.

The motor coughed three times and died. The car continued its forward momentum, as Missy struggled to steer with no power steering. She glanced at the fuel gauge—sitting on empty. *Fuck a duck!* The prick hadn't bothered to keep an eye on the gas tank; now they were paying for it.

"What the hell now?" Jake asked, exasperated.

Pete leaned forward. "I think we're outta gas," he announced needlessly.

"What gave you a clue?" Missy rolled her eyes. Pumping the brakes, she managed to get the vehicle mostly off the highway and rolled to a stop, then put on the emergency blinkers.

"Okay, looks like we have two choices." Missy took charge again. "We stay here 'til someone happens by to give us a ride, in which case, we might freeze to death first—or we start walking. I think we're only a couple of miles at most from my old cabin."

"There's no choice but to walk. Belinda comes first. We've got to get her out of this cold," Jake's voice brooked no argument.

Pete spoke cautiously, "Not to ask a stupid question, but how are we going to see to walk safely in the dark? My phone's dead. So, what do we use for light?"

Shit! Pete was right, they hadn't thought that far ahead. Distant headlights appeared down the highway heading towards them.

Missy told Pete, "Let's try to flag them down."

They got out, waving their arms, as the car approached rapidly. The driver slowed down briefly to check them out but sped up again, disappearing around the curve. *Asshole!* Missy thought angrily. Shivering, they got back inside the car.

"That certainly worked well. Next time show them your tits and maybe they'll stop," Jake grumbled sarcastically, shivering from the cold air and clutching Belinda close.

"It was probably a cautious woman driver," Missy snapped.

Jake just shook his head. "Pete, look around in the back and see if there's a blanket or anything we can use to wrap Belinda in."

Pete turned and rummaged around, taking inventory. "There's a couple plastic garbage bags, a tire tool, some road flares, and—a freaking flashlight," he said excitedly. He flipped the switch, and a weak beam of light flooded the interior of the car.

Jake wrapped Belinda in the cleanest of the two plastic garbage bags Pete handed him, and they all got out of the Rover. Missy grabbed the two road flares, stuffing them in her jacket pocket. They set out walking at a fast pace in tandem, Pete in the middle with the light and shotgun.

The cold north wind gusted through the forest canopy. Branches scraped against one another like bones rattling together as the trio left the shelter of the car behind. The dark outside the flashlight's small cone of light was impenetrable.

Minutes later, the hair on Missy's nape suddenly rose. She glanced nervously over her shoulder. "You get the feeling we're being watched?" she hissed to Jake.

JAMES DOBIE

There was a long pause. "No—not until you mentioned it, thank you very little. How much farther to your cabin?" Anxiously, he picked up the pace.

"Shouldn't be too far. We've been walking at a steady pace for about fifteen minutes," she said, her long legs matching Jake's and Pete's stride.

The flashlight's glow dimmed, as the cold air quickly sucked the life from it. "This thing's about to bite the dust, Missy," Pete said.

Jake grunted. "That's about par for this fucked-up shit-show."

Making the most of the torch's fading light, they increased their speed almost to a trot. Something large and furry slipped quickly in and out of its failing beam just before the flashlight flickered twice and died. The dark swallowed them instantly, while a loud growl sounded close by.

"I think it's the same mama bear that had you 'treed' earlier, Jake. No one move," she said, as a chuffing noise quite near scared them all.

Missy reached into her jacket, grabbed one of the road flares, and pulled the igniter strip. The flare burst into life, a brilliant red flower of fire and light, which momentarily blinded them. Shielding their eyes, they watched the huge bear rear up on its hind legs, startled. It roared once at the bright, burning stick, then turned and loped into the safety of the forest.

"Well, that was unpleasant. How long you think that thing will last?" Jake gestured worriedly at the flare. He was shivering so hard that he'd woken Belinda.

"I don't know—maybe ten or fifteen minutes before it gets too hot to hold. We should be getting close to the turnoff to the cabin soon," she said hopefully, waving the flare in front of them to keep them from wandering off the road.

They heard a car approaching behind them, and as it neared, they saw it was Sheriff Blackstone's cruiser. The emergency lights came on as he pulled to a stop beside them. He rolled down the window.

"Hop in. We got a ping on your location when you called 911. Let's get you folks home and out of the cold. You can fill me in on details once you're warm." He smiled tightly.

Gratefully, they all climbed inside. The heater's air felt wonderful. Relieved to be warm again, they took turns describing the night's events to Frank. In a few minutes, they'd reached the Andersons' home.

Frank pulled to a stop and looked each of them in the eye. "Earlier, I told Pete that we might have a lead. The ME found a tooth embedded in my dead deputy's throat. Turned out to be human, not from any wild animal, according to a dentist we consulted in town," he disclosed uncomfortably.

"You're saying a person did that to him?" Missy asked incredulously.

Jake shook his head. "But what about the claw marks on Pete's door? Those couldn't have been made by a person."

Frank frowned. "It's not impossible. Maybe the perp wanted it to *look* like it was done by an animal. Regardless, we're checking dental records to see if we can get a match. In the meantime, I'll have forensics dust your bus for prints. Doubt we'll get any from the Rover, but it'll be worth a try. No use trying to search these woods at night. With any luck, maybe he'll run into that bear—save us the trouble of hunting his sorry ass down. Pete, you staying here, or can I give you a ride to your house?" Frank asked wearily.

Pete looked at Missy and Jake inquiringly. "If it's okay, I wouldn't mind getting back to my place. No offense, but my bed is a lot more comfortable than your couch," he said hesitantly.

Missy raised an eyebrow, "You really want to be by yourself with that nut-job still out there, Bud? You're welcome to stay in the baby's room. The bed in there is comfy, and she will be in the room with us. We've got ice cream ... and guns," she added, as an incentive to convince him.

Pete thought about it for about two seconds. After all they'd been through that evening, he did feel uneasy about being anywhere alone. He shrugged. "Okay, you got me. I'll stay for the night. Hopefully, Frank will catch the bastard so I can go back home tomorrow."

Frank nodded his approval. "If the guy's local, we might have a better chance of identifying him quickly. If not, well ... maybe he'll fall and break his leg or something worse, stumbling around in the dark. Get some rest. I'll contact you tomorrow soon as I know anything," he finished, as they piled out of the car. He waited until they were all inside before turning the cruiser around, heading for the highway.

Jake examined the kidnapper's damage to the front door. The lower lock keeper was stripped from the wood where the asshole had kicked it in. Luckily, though, the deadbolt still worked fine. Jake locked it and they went to their separate bedrooms tiredly, collapsing into restless sleep.

Pete woke abruptly at eight the next morning, needing to pee. He got up but saw, dismayed, that the door to his hosts' room was still closed. *Shit!* The entrance to the only bathroom in the house lay behind that door. He'd have to piss outside. He unlocked the back door and stepped out into the frigid air to relieve his bladder. As he opened the door to go back in, a blur of fur raced out, startling him. Jinx, who'd been shut inside the main bedroom, obviously needed to do his business. Pete realized that Jake and Missy must be awake.

Jake, looking disheveled in his boxers, was in the kitchen making coffee. Bleary-eyed, he glanced at Pete as he came inside, closing the back door. "Morning. I hope you slept better than we did. Between Belinda's three o'clock feeding and Jinx yowling to go out, I got maybe an hour of sleep," he grumbled, waiting for the coffee to brew.

Missy arrived with bags under her eyes, wrapped in a robe that showed pink bunnies romping joyously everywhere.

Pete smirked. "Bunnies? Really?"

Missy arched a brow. "You laugh, you can walk home, Bud," she shot back. "It was a present from Jake for Christmas. Besides, I happen to like pink rabbits."

Pete tried not to snicker. Checking his phone, he saw he had voice mail, opened it, and listened to the brief message:

'Lt. Detective Dianne Flowers with the Boulder PD calling. If this is Pete Chandler, please contact me at this number ASAP regarding your sister, Mia Chandler. It's urgent. Thank you.'

Pete looked alarmed. "*Shit*! Mia's in trouble. I should've checked my phone when it rang yesterday." He cursed, dialing the number.

It rang five times and went to voice mail, "Leave a message," the no-nonsense voice said. Damn phone tag. Pete shook his head, angry at himself.

"This is Pete Chandler, returning your call about my sister, Mia Chandler. Please call me back soon as you can. Thanks." He hung up.

Inhaling the aroma of the brewing coffee, Jake frowned. "Guess I'd better call Johnny Six-Fingers and get the bus towed to his garage. Surely, Frank's guys will have finished dusting it for prints by now."

"My poor bus. I'm gonna rip the balls off that bastard if Frank doesn't catch him first," Missy barked.

Jake wisely said nothing. Pete felt his bowels rumble. He excused himself and headed for the vacant bathroom. He'd barely sat down on the toilet when his phone rang. He dug it out of his pants and managed to answer just before it went to voice mail.

"This is Pete. Hello, who's this?" he said loudly, trying to cover the sound of his sudden, noisy expulsion of gas.

There was a pause, then, "Er, hello, this is Lt. Dt. Flowers, of the Boulder PD. Is this, Poo, uh, Pete Chandler?" she asked.

Pete turned red. *Crap!* She'd heard it. "Uh, yes, ma'am, it is. Sorry about that. Your message said it was urgent. What's happening? Is Mia okay?" he asked.

"She's fine, for the moment. But, sadly, sir, I have to inform you that your father was involved in a serious vehicle accident not far from Boulder and didn't survive. I'm sorry for your loss," the detective said solemnly.

Pete felt like he'd been sucker-punched. "D-dad? H-he's dead? How—when?" he sputtered.

"I'll give you more details when I get them, Mr. Chandler. I also need to inform you that your sister has been hospitalized here with some minor injuries. Both her grandfather and his partner were killed inside his mansion, and Mia is the only survivor.

"All the evidence so far points to self-defense in her case. The DA hasn't signed off on it yet, but from the law's viewpoint, it looks pretty cut and dried."

Pete was shocked. "I ... what the hell happened?" he asked.

Briefly, she described what police had found inside the mansion. "We're attempting to locate the three unknown girls on the video. From what we can now verify, her grandfather was certifiable. Not sure about the partner, but it looks like he wasn't quite sane, either.

"Our immediate problem is that as soon as the DA dismisses the charges against her, your sister is going to need a place to live. She's a minor. You're her only living relative," she said.

Pete got the point. He didn't hesitate. "Of course. How soon will she be ready to travel?" he asked. He hated to involve Mia in the freaking mess here, but it looked like he'd have no choice.

"I believe it should be sometime tomorrow. The DA doesn't have a case, and he knows it. A detective from Taos, New Mexico, drove up to find and assist Mia and has remained. I'm going to ask if she can work with you to get Miss Chandler legally into your care. Her name's Det. Lt. Kris Lacey. She'll be in touch soon."

"What about my father? What happens to his ... his body? Did he have a will or anything in case something happened to him?" Pete asked.

"You should talk to his lawyer—if he had one. Call the county clerk's office in Taos. Apparently, your dad was driving with a suspended license due to a recent DUI there. Again, my condolences, sir. Lt. Lacey will contact you with more information as it becomes available."

Numb with shock, Pete thanked her and disconnected. *Shit! With everything else that's happening, this is all I need.* He sighed, sending up a small prayer for his estranged father's soul. Leaving the bathroom, he joined the others at the kitchen table, filling them in on the call's grim details.

"Oh, Pete, I'm so sorry about your dad. If there's anything we can do, just name it," Missy said, giving him a hug.

Jake nodded in harmony. "Were you close?" he asked.

Pete shook his head. "Nope. Haven't heard from him once since Mom kicked him out when I was a kid. He was never a factor in my life after that. Still, it's a bit of a shock.

"Apparently, my half-sister has really been through hell these past weeks. Mia's probably going to be living with me now. Frank had better catch this nut-job soon. I don't want her to be jumping from the frying pan into the fire, so to speak." He started to pace, trying to decide what he should do next.

"If you need to take some time to sort all this out, just say the word, Pete. You'll need to make some calls, see if your father left a will or instructions about what to do in the event of his death. Hopefully, he had a lawyer." Missy's words were almost verbatim to the Lieutenant's.

"I guess I'll take you up on a brief leave of absence. I appreciate it. Can I get a ride back to my place before you go on patrol?" he asked her.

"Nope. You made fun of my 'bunnies'—it's gonna be a long-ass walk, Bud," she said with a straight face. Pete's mouth opened in dismay. She smiled quickly. "Just kidding. But you're not leaving 'til you put something in your stomach. Jake will be more than happy to make you a toaster waffle."

Pete rolled his eyes, thinking, *yes, mother hen.* Taking the hint, Jake got up and popped a couple frozen waffles into the toaster. Familiar scratching noises came from the back door. Jake opened it, and Jinx headed straight under the table to lie in wait for anything edible dropped by the clumsy humans.

Jake fed both Missy and Pete, forgoing any for himself. The frozen waffles were a terrible substitute for the real McCoy.

"You comin' home for lunch?" he asked Missy.

She nodded, swallowing a bite of waffle. "If I don't hear from Frank by then, I may start searching for that bastard myself. I refuse to keep looking over my shoulder for that asshole at every turn," she declared angrily. She finished her coffee and went to get dressed while Jake and Pete cleaned the dishes. "You ready?" she asked Pete, kissing Jake and Belinda goodbye, praying that they would stay safe.

As the morning sun peeked over the mountains to the east, the two rangers climbed into the cruiser and headed for Pete's house,

Chapter Forty-Eight - Boulder

Kris's headache was pounding so hard it made her vision blur. She hadn't brought extra migraine pills on the hastily planned trip. Her crappy insurance wouldn't pay for a refill this soon, so she was shit-out-of-luck getting any from a local pharmacy.

The pain finally got so bad the next morning that she checked herself into the ER. She told the doctor she suspected there might be something in her brain.

He glanced at her curiously. "Why would you think that?"

"Someone suggested that I get it checked out," she said evasively. "Been having severe migraines off and on for the past six months."

"I can do a CT scan. In the meantime, I'll order a shot of Sumatriptan. It should give you some relief within a few minutes." He stepped out of the room to give instructions to a nurse, who came in with the shot.

"Hopefully, this will help, hon. They'll take you back for the scan in a few." She checked Kris's vitals, entered data on a chart, then left the room.

Kris groaned. She'd never experienced so severe a headache for such a long time. Orderlies came and wheeled her into a room down the hall for the testing. By that point, the shot had kicked in, so she tolerated the scan well. As they wheeled her back to the cubicle fifteen minutes later, mercifully, the pain was almost gone. The doctor came back a half hour later, wearing a neutral expression.

"Ms. Lacey, how long have you been having these headaches?" he asked Kris.

"About a year, off and on, but the last six months have been a real bitch," she said, rubbing her sore temples.

"We don't generally process the results of these scans the same day unless the radiologist spots something … abnormal." Kris' stomach dropped like an express elevator at that word. "He spotted this and brought it to my immediate attention."

He placed her scan on a screen, showing her a small mass about the size of a walnut located near the right frontal lobe of her brain. Kris felt her bowels turn to ice water, as her worst nightmare was made real by the shadowy images on the screen. No bad guy with a gun—nothing she could possibly imagine—frightened her as badly as that malignant shadow, with its alien tendrils.

The doctor saw her reaction. "Ms. Lacey, I'll be frank. In my opinion, you should see a neurosurgeon and have an MRI done as soon as possible. He or she will probably want to perform a biopsy, as well. There's a good chance it's not malignant. However, I wouldn't wait too long before having it looked at. I'll give you a short-term prescription for your normal medication to use in the meantime. If there's anything else I can do for you, please let me know," he finished.

The doctor's advice ran together senselessly in her mind. The only words that stood out were "abnormal" and "biopsy." She shuddered at the thought of having a hole drilled into her skull.

"Thanks, Doctor, I appreciate your help," she replied. "I'll get it checked out soon as I can."

Kris climbed off the hospital bed, put her shoes on, and grabbed her purse. She left the hospital, stopping in a nearby pharmacy for the pills, then drove back to her motel in a daze, unable to shake the images in her mind. She'd known for a while something was wrong. The headaches had gotten far more frequent and much more severe. She had put off seeing a doctor for too long. *Now it might be too late*, she thought grimly.

Opening the door to her room, she flipped on the light, and froze. Wendy Ravenwood sat perched on the end of the bed, staring at the "big pharma" ads on the muted TV mounted on the wall.

"*What the hell*—how did you get in here?" Kris sputtered angrily.

The strange girl turned her head toward her. "Same way I get anywhere," she said cryptically. "Mia will not be charged with murder. The DA is informing Lt. Flowers of this as I speak."

Kris gawked at her. "Just how the hell would you know that?"

Wendy ignored her question. "She'll be free to go to her brother's today. *You* must take her to him. No more delays," she warned, dark eyes glittering.

"Listen, I don't know who or *what* you are, but I don't take orders from you, Ravenwood. You're still a person of interest in three deaths in Taos. Why should I listen to anything you say?" she asked.

Wendy gave a smile that never reached her eyes. "Did the doctor confirm the tumor?"

The blood drained from Kris's face. "That's none of your concern. You seem to have a nasty habit of popping up whenever there's trouble."

"I go where I am needed. You must take Mia to Oregon. Her brother's life is in jeopardy—and possibly, your own," Wendy said ominously. Without another word, she stood and calmly walked to the front door.

Thrown off-balance by her sudden departure, Kris turned toward the door and shouted, "Wait! Where do you think you're going? I'm not finished—"

The strange creature was gone. Kris rushed outside and scanned the parking lot for her. The only movement was the north wind blowing leaves around the mostly empty lot.

Shit! How does she freaking disappear like that? It's downright creepy. Maybe she really is some sort of "spirit, Kris thought uneasily.

She walked back inside and closed the door, engaging the security latch for good measure. When her phone rang, she jerked. The caller ID read Boulder PD, so she answered quickly. "This is Lacey."

"Lt. Lacey, this is Lt. Flowers. I just met with the DA, who informed me that no charges will be filed against the Chandler girl. It was clearly a case of self-defense," she told her.

"Yeah, I know," Kris replied.

"Excuse me?" Her statement flummoxed Flowers.

"Nothing. So, how soon will Mia be free to travel?" Kris asked.

Flowers paused, "Once the hospital releases her, that will depend on the judge. If he grants you temporary custody, you both can leave as soon as the order is given," Dianne answered.

"Okay. When can I speak to a judge? I need to to get everything expedited," Kris said.

There was a pause. "I believe Judge Timbers is on the bench today. I'll see if I can get them to squeeze you in this afternoon. That's the best I can promise," Dianne replied.

"Thanks, I appreciate your help. Mia needs to be with her brother, and it looks like I'll be taking her to him," Kris sighed.

"I contacted the brother and told him to check with the county clerk's office in Taos about his father's will. It's his responsibility to search for any legal papers left by their father. If no documents are found, the father's remains will be cremated," Flowers stated flatly.

"Don't you think Mia and her brother should have a say in all this? Shouldn't they be the ones to decide what happens to their father's remains?" she asked hesitantly.

"They do have a say. But only if they can produce a will or if the father had a burial plan. If not, the state will be forced to cremate the remains. I'm sorry, but that's the law in Colorado." Dianne was pragmatic. "I've informed the brother that you'd be contacting him with more information about the girl's situation when we know it. I'll text you when I find a time slot for the judge," Flowers finished.

Kris thanked her, disconnecting. As usual, it would be "hurry-up and wait."

Chapter Forty-Nine - Pete's house, Joseph

Missy dropped Pete off in front of his house. "If you need anything, call me. I'll let you know when I hear back from Frank. You just take care of your personal business."

Pete leaned back into the car and thanked her for the ride. "I should be done by early afternoon. If I haven't found my old man's lawyer or his will by then, they probably don't exist."

Missy put the cruiser in gear and drove away.

Staring at the claw-like marks scratched into his front door, Pete cursed. He went inside, closing and locking the door. Walking past the end table, he noticed the little wooden totem was gone. He was sure it had been there when he'd left.

He shrugged, wandered over to the kitchen table, and sat down to search the web for the Taos County Clerk's office. After being on hold for several minutes, he finally spoke to a person.

Identifying himself, he explained what he wanted. The female clerk told him to hang on for a minute and she'd check the records. The minute stretched to ten before she came back online.

"Sorry, sir, but I don't find anything filed under the name of Gary Chandler. You might try the funeral home to see if your father had a plan with them."

Pete thanked her for checking. He looked up the name of the funeral parlor she'd given him and called, thinking the name sounded more like a law firm than a funeral home.

"Bryson-Carter-Roman, how may we help you?" a man's voice said smoothly.

"I'm calling to see if my father might have bought a plan from you. His name is ... was Gary Chandler," he said.

The man said he'd check if Pete didn't mind holding. A couple minutes later he was back.

"I'm sorry, sir, no one by that name has purchased any of our services to date. Anything else I can help you with today?"

"No, thanks for your help." Pete was disappointed. *Shit!* This did not seem promising. He tried to think of another place to search. Then he thought, *what about a safety deposit box?* By that time, he was grasping at straws. *Why the hell not?*

He was "googling" the numbers for banks in Taos when a clattering noise from his bedroom startled him. He felt the hairs on the back of his neck rise. He stood, pulling the large butcher knife from the block on the countertop. The damn Bear-B-Gone was in his bedroom, where he'd left it. *Shit!*

Cautiously, he crept toward the closed bedroom door. *Did I shut that before I left?* He couldn't remember. A soft skittering sound, like claws on wood, came from inside. Clenching the knife, he turned the handle and threw open the door.

There, standing upright by his bed, eating out of a can of Prickle's potato chips he'd left by his bed, was a damn raccoon, its glimmering eyes staring back at him. Briefly, each of them stared at the other, shocked, until the crafty creature beat a hasty retreat. Dropping the can of chips, it jumped on Pete's bed, used it for a springboard, and leaped out through the partially open window.

Someone had been inside since he'd left. He knew damn well that window had been closed and locked. *So how did the animal get in? Who'd opened the window?*

Then he spotted the missing wooden totem, leaning against the wall below the windowsill. It seemed almost to be smiling at him. *Must be the light.* Shaking his head, he reached down to pick up the small figure—and swore that it moved. Pete stiffened in surprise. *That's impossible, it's just a piece of wood.* He bent down again and grabbed it. The totem twisted suddenly in his fist, and stabbing pain erupted in his palm. He screamed like a little girl, dropping the thing as if he'd been scalded. Frightened, he scrambled out of the room, slamming the door shut behind him.

With shaky hands, he speed-dialed Missy.

"Hey, Pete, what's—"

"M-Missy, it's *alive*—that fucking piece of wood is alive. It moved in my hand, and then I swear to God, it, it bit me!" He was hyperventilating.

"Slow down, Bud, what the hell are you talking about?" she said.

He described hearing the strange noise and finding the raccoon scarfing down chips in his bedroom, and how it had escaped through the open window.

"Someone's been in my house. They must have opened the damn window from the inside. I always make sure it's locked before I leave. Anyway, that creepy little piece of shit was in there, leaning against the wall near the open window. A-and when I picked it up, the damn thing twisted in my hand and bit me," he sputtered.

There was a long pause at the other end. "You're not shittin' me, are you, Pete? You're sure you didn't maybe nick yourself on a splinter?" Missy was skeptical.

Pete stared down at the two tiny punctures oozing blood from his right palm. "Believe me, it bit me, Missy. I have it trapped inside my bedroom," he said bizarrely.

"What about the window—did you close it after the raccoon split?" she asked patiently.

Shit! He hadn't thought to close the window before rushing from the room—but no way in hell was he going back in there. "No, I didn't exactly stick around long enough to think that far ahead." Now, he was defensive.

The faint scraping sound of wood on wood from inside the bedroom door had Pete glancing anxiously toward it. "Missy, I'm sorry, but I-I can't stay here. I swear to you, I can hear it moving around in there." His heart was pounding.

"Okay, Pete, get the hell out of there right now. Get in your car and lock the doors. I'm on my way. I'm calling Frank as soon as I get off with you," she snapped, disconnecting.

Pete stuffed his phone in his pocket. Before leaving, he leaned his ear warily against the closed bedroom door and listened but heard nothing. He was tempted to crack open the door and peek.

He reached for the door handle, hesitantly. *Probably just what that thing in there would expect me to do,* he decided, backing away. He rushed to the living room and grabbed his keys from the hook near the door, remotely unlocking his Honda's doors before walking outside. Locking the front door, he ran to his car, climbed in, and locked himself inside.

When Missy's cruiser screeched to a halt beside his vehicle minutes later, Pete breathed a relieved sigh. He unlocked the passenger door, and she slipped inside.

"Frank is on his way. Told me he got a match on the tooth from the deputy's throat. He'll fill us in when he gets here," she said.

"Missy, I'm not crazy. I swear that damn thing is alive. It bit me when I tried to pick it up. This wasn't caused by any splinter." He showed her his palm.

She examined it closely in the bright morning sun. "Looks like a bite mark of some kind, alright. Pete, I'm sorry, but I honestly find it hard to believe a stupid piece of wood could suddenly attack you." Missy held his gaze calmly.

"Yeah, well, a year ago, I had a hard time believing that fucking monster existed, until I saw it myself." He was indignant, hurt that she didn't believe him.

Missy's face blossomed red. "You're right. I'm sorry. It does seem crazy—but no weirder than what we all faced then, I guess," she apologized.

At that point, Frank pulled to a stop next to her cruiser. She and Pete got out and joined him.

Frank looked at Pete strangely as they approached. "Does this concern that creepy little piece of wood that mystery girl left with you?" he asked curtly.

Pete nodded. "When Missy dropped me off, I noticed that the totem, or whatever the hell it is, wasn't where I'd left it." He paused to remember. "I was making calls, trying to see if my dad had left a will, when I heard a noise in my bedroom. I opened the door and damned if there wasn't a raccoon standing by my bed, casually scarfing down the remains of a can of potato chips. Someone had to have opened my window from the inside. I always lock it before I leave. Anyway, the window was half-open, and I guess the raccoon was hungry and smelled the chips." Frank waited for Pete to continue.

"It freaked when it saw me and leaped back out the window. That's when I spotted that damn thing, leaning against the wall, right under the window frame. And when I reached down and picked it up, it squirmed in my hand, sorta like a snake and then it ... it bit me," he finished, thrusting his palm out for Frank to inspect.

The Sheriff pulled out a pair of reading glasses, squinted at the tiny wounds. "Could be bite marks, could also be splinters that got you." He was dubious.

Pete shook his head. "No, sir, it wasn't splinters."

Missy frowned. "Well, standing around out here won't solve any mysteries. Let's go inside and check it out."

Frank and Pete nodded. Quietly, the trio entered the house and trooped in to stand outside the closed bedroom door.

"Okay. I'll open it on the count of three," Pete said softly. He counted, "One ... two ... three," and threw open the door. The room was still and silent as they crept forward, Frank, then Missy, Pete bringing up the rear. The window by his bed was shut and locked.

The little wood sprite lay motionless near the same spot under the windowsill, where Pete, in his panic, had dropped it. No sign remained of the raccoon, except for some crumbs scattered across the floor and the open container of chips nearby.

With no monstrous creature lurking, Pete saw them eyeing the closed window, then him, and realized they didn't believe him. "Look, I feel like I'm being 'gas-lighted' here," he said sharply.

"You think that freaky little piece of wood somehow managed to jump up and close the window all by itself?" Frank snorted in disbelief.

"I'm telling you that window was open when I left the house and got into my car." Pete was on the defensive.

Missy could tell he was losing his cool. "I believe you, Pete, whether Frank does or not. Let me have a closer look at this thing." Warily, she picked up the wooden totem.

Picking it up in one hand, she held it at arms-length to inspect it. Sure enough, there were a couple small smears of blood on it, just below two small pointy protrusions that resembled tiny tits.

"I agree that this thing is creepy as hell, Pete, but it's just a piece of—" Suddenly her hand felt like it was on fire. She let out a yelp, dropping the totem. "What the hell? It burned me," she hissed, shaking her hand, scrambling back from the talisman.

It lay on the floor like a child's discarded doll. Frank's smirk turned into a concerned look.

"Let's see your hand, Missy," Pete said.

She showed them her palm. It was red and swollen where the skin had been in contact with the totem.

"Shit, that really hurts!" Missy exclaimed, as they moved into the living room.

Pete ran to his bathroom and came back a minute later with a tube of aloe vera gel, which he applied liberally to her palm.

"This is great stuff for burns. Supposed to help—"

"Yeah, I know, it's supposed to soothe and prevent blistering," she interrupted tersely, sucking air. Her palm still stung like crazy. "Why the hell did you let me pick that damned thing up, Pete?" she mock-accused.

He was making a sort of bandage for her hand using a folded washcloth and some duct tape from his bathroom cabinet. He frowned, "Hold still, one more piece of tape ... there, all done."

She cocked a critical eyebrow at his hastily improvised bandage. "I hope that washcloth was clean, Bud." He assured her it was.

"You need to get rid of that thing, Pete. Whatever it is, it's freaking dangerous. I think that mystery girl might be, too," Missy warned, glaring balefully at the immobile totem.

"I'm not touching that thing again without some heavy-duty gloves," Pete said.

"Don't you have some kitchen tongs or something you can use to grab it with?"

He nodded at her, traipsed to the kitchen, opened a drawer, pulled out some barbecue tongs, and returned. He grabbed the totem tightly with the tongs, holding it at arm's length. Rushing outside, he tossed it unceremoniously into a large trash container.

"That's where you belong," he addressed it, closing and locking the lid. As he turned to go back inside, a scrabbling noise came from inside the can. He froze to listen for a full minute. Nothing more. He shook his head, returning to Missy and Frank in the kitchen.

Frank scowled. "Oh, before I forget, that tooth found in the deputy's neck turned out to be human, but it had been filed to a sharp point to resemble a predator's tooth. Not only that, but it positively matched dental records of someone named Tory Morning Star, age seventeen. You wouldn't by chance have any close relatives by that name, would you, Missy?" He looked at her strangely as he asked.

She frowned, shook her head slowly. "None I'm aware of. As far as I know, my sister Elisa and I were the last children born in the tribe with that name," she replied.

"Thought I remembered you reading us that note Elisa left for you that described how she'd had a baby she was forced to give up for adoption when she was a teenager. And told you she'd held a grudge against your mother about it. Am I right?" Frank watched Missy's face, as he raised the delicate subject.

Missy mentally kicked herself; she couldn't believe she'd forgotten. *Shit! The boy would be the right age.* "Frank, you're right. It could be him. It makes a certain twisted sense. Elisa never saw the boy again after Mama forced her to give him up to be raised by the tribe. He could've found out who his real mother and father were—and how they died. If so, he might hold us all responsible for their deaths," she reasoned.

"You think he might also be a—what was it called? 'Yen-ah-lucy?'" Frank asked.

"It's '*Yenaldooshi*.' And to answer your question, I have no idea. I suppose it's possible, he'd have his father's genes." That prospect concerned Missy.

"Got your sister's, too. Her bipolar gene could've also been passed down to him," Pete reminded her.

Missy grimaced. "That would *not* be a good combination. Do you know where the boy is living, Frank?"

"We've been talking with the tribal Elders, but they haven't exactly been forthcoming. Hell, I've got Nez Perce blood in me, but if you weren't raised by the tribe, they look at you as an outsider. All we have right now is the kid's name and age. His 'juvie' records are sealed. So, we don't even know what he looks like," he said, gruffly.

Missy asked, "You've checked all the social media sites to see if his name popped up, right?"

Frank stared at her blankly. "You mean ... the internet?" He looked totally lost.

"Yeah, like Facebook, Snap-Chat, Twitter, WhatsApp."

Frank frowned at her. "I'm embarrassed to say I didn't even think about all that. *Shit*! I'll get someone on it right away," he said. "I need to go; I have an appointment in twenty minutes. I'll let you know if we can find any pics that match his name. Should have thought of that myself. Getting too old for this." He turned to leave but stopped. "Oh—and Pete? Do us all a favor, burn that damnable piece of wood." Opening the door, he started out to his cruiser. When he neared the trash can, he was startled by a frantic scratching from within. He gave it a wide berth as he passed it.

Missy was restless. "I'll go have a talk with Tommy Two-Tongues. He's an Elder in the tribe and was a friend of my mother's. Maybe he can put a face with the name. You know, Bud, you should get a dog. It's cheaper than an alarm system and a hell of a lot better deterrent, plus it would be company for you." She grabbed her purse, ready to walk out.

"I'm telling you guys, that window was open when I got home. Someone had to have been inside," he said emphatically.

Missy didn't argue. "Well, no one's here now. All I can tell you is, if you're really worried, change the locks on your front door. I'll touch base with you later. You have research to do, and I've got to go," she said. He sighed, opening the door for her. "Pete, I think you ought to take Frank's advice and burn that damn thing. You've had nothing but trouble since that girl appeared on your doorstep." She left, glancing nervously at the silent trash bin as she walked by.

"Good luck in the hunt for your dad's will. I'll swing back by to check on you after I hob-nob with Tommy for a bit," she called, getting into the cruiser.

Pete watched as she drove off. He glanced uneasily at the trash container as he closed and locked the door. *Just a piece of wood, my ass!*

Sitting down at the table, he continued to search using his cell for documents his father might have left. On his third call, he hit paydirt. The First National Bank in Taos reported that a "Gary Chandler" had rented a safety deposit box and paid for it through the remainder of the year.

Pete explained to them that his father had died unexpectedly recently, but at first, that was the only information they would give him over the phone.

"Now, if you can provide us with proper identification as his next of kin, we could proceed from there. Are you the executor of his will?" the banker asked him.

"I-I don't have a clue. The problem is, if he had a will, it would probably be in your safety deposit box," he clarified.

The bank officer sympathized. "I think we can get around that point, Mr. Chandler. Let me talk to my manager. Please hold," he said politely.

Pete set the phone down on the kitchen table and made himself a sandwich while waiting for the guy's return.

After a five-minute wait, "Mr. Chandler, can you take a snapshot of your driver's license and text it to this number?"

"Sure. Give me a minute." Pete dug his license out of his wallet. Placing it on the table, he took a picture with his cell and sent it to the bank.

"Got it. Give us a moment, please." Pete heard a muffled discussion taking place. Then the manager came on. "Ordinarily, we'd need a death certificate to proceed any further, Mr. Chandler." Pete's hopes sank. "But—I think we can at least open the box and tell you if there is a will or anything of value inside," he finished.

Pete thanked him profusely. He was asked to hold once more. Several minutes ticked by, during which he was able to eat his sandwich.

"Hello, Mr. Chandler? We've opened the box. There's an unsealed envelope with a small note inside. The name 'Mia Chandler' is written on it," the manager told him.

Pete wasn't surprised. "That would be my half-sister. She's a teenager, and she's in a Boulder hospital right now. I believe I'll be her legal guardian once she arrives here. Did you find anything else? Any burial policy or final instructions?" he asked.

"No, sir, the envelope contains only the note and what appears to be a routing number for an account that's scribbled on a scrap of paper," the banker added cautiously.

Curious, Pete asked if he could check to see if it matched an active account with their bank. Several minutes later he was back.

"Mr. Chandler? This is, indeed, a current active account with our bank. It was opened only a day ago. There is, ah, quite a large sum of money in this account, sir," he said.

"Can I ask how much?" Pete queried hesitantly.

There was a pause for more discussion at the bank. "Sir, there is a total of $999,000.38 in the account. If you or your sister prove to be the legal heir, it will be a lot of money to manage. We at First National Bank would be pleased to help with your financial management and investments."

Pete didn't hear the last part of the banker's spiel. *Holy Scrooge McDuck! My freakin' father was rich!* Then he realized the banker was waiting.

"My sister Mia is probably the only heir to that, as she should be. I'll be in touch with you after I've taken care of my father's arrangements and had a chance to talk to her. I appreciate all your help." He disconnected.

As he sat thinking for a minute about what he should do next, his cell chimed. The caller ID read TPD, and he answered, "Hello, who's calling?"

"This is Lt. Detective Kris Lacey with the Taos PD, Mr. Chandler. First off, I want to tell you Mia is alright. The DA has decided not to press charges," she said. "I'm hoping to get in to see a judge this afternoon to have her released into my care, *pro tem*. As soon as that happens, I'll be driving her to you in Joseph myself," she said.

Pete was silent as he absorbed all this.

"Have you had any luck finding any legal documents or a will?" Kris asked. "Lt. Flowers informed me that your father must be cremated if you can't quickly locate any legal papers stating otherwise," continued.

"I found out that Mia's damn near a millionaire, Det. Lacey. She won't need to worry about money anytime soon. But my father didn't leave a will, just his bank account number and a note for Mia," he told her.

"I'm sorry you haven't any other options regarding his remains. I'll bring Lt. Flowers up to speed on that. I'll call you after I've seen the judge, and we'll go from there," Kris remarked.

Pete thanked her for all her trouble, and she refused the praise. "It's part of the job, Mr. Chandler—and I've grown rather fond of your sister. No one should ever have to go through what she's experienced. I'll be in touch." She hung up.

Pete sat, thinking about the major lifestyle changes looming ahead of him with Mia's imminent arrival. He could worry about that later, though. Right now, all he wanted to do was take a hot shower and get back to work.

What should I do with that damn wood sprite? Should I burn it? he wondered anxiously. He needed to do something about the crappy thing. He assuredly was not bringing it back inside. Stripping off clothes, he got into the steaming hot shower. It felt wonderful, loosening his knotted shoulder muscles as he relaxed under the mesmerizing heat of the water. Finally, he got out, toweled off, and dressed in his uniform.

He grabbed his phone off the kitchen table, sent a text to Missy saying he was ready to get back to work, and sat on the couch to wait for her arrival. He turned on CNN to see what was happening with the daily shit-show in Washington, the sound muted.

His phone chimed as Missy texted that she was on her way. She was sure to give him shit for not destroying the damn totem, but he didn't want to think about that at the moment. For now, it was safely sealed inside the trash container.

Chapter Fifty - Boulder Hospital

"Try these on. I hope they fit, I had to guess at your sizes." Kris handed Mia a large paper bag filled with new clothes.

Opening it, Mia found a heavy zip-up jacket on top of a pair of sneakers, some socks, two bras and several pairs of panties, two flannel shirts and a pair of jeans, all neatly folded. The bag's familiar, bright red logo from a local "Mega-Mart" said it all.

Mia smiled and thanked her. "I so appreciate all you're doing for me, but I don't have any way of paying you back, and I feel terrible about it." Tears welled up and spilled.

Kris felt her heart melt. *Poor girl has suffered more pain and hardship recently than most people wade through in a lifetime.*

"I've spoken to your brother, Pete. He just discovered that your father had rented a security box in the First National Bank of Taos. He'd apparently opened the account the day before he died. There's enough money in it to tide you over for quite a while. There was also a note inside the box with your name on it," Kris informed her. When Kris told her how much Pete had said was there, Mia's jaw hung open.

"First things first. I'm trying to get in to see a judge this afternoon. If he grants me temporary legal custody, then we're outta here. If not ... well, we'll cross that bridge when we get to it," Kris said.

"So, what's going to happen to my father's body. Are they going to cremate him?" Mia asked.

Kris nodded solemnly.

"*Shit!* I just remembered—my mother's ashes are in an urn out in that hellish mansion. With everything that happened, I forgot about her. Can you get them for me, Detective? I-I can't leave her there in that awful place. She goes with me, wherever I end up. I g-guess now, Dad will, too," she said.

Kris smiled at her. "I'm sure Lt. Flowers can retrieve them for you. I'll ask her nicely. By the way, you can call me Kris."

Mia grinned at her, "Okay, Kris. I really appreciate it."

Grabbing the bag of new clothes, she walked carefully on her bandaged feet to the bathroom to change out of the hospital gown. The shirt was a bit large, but the jeans fit well. She tried on the sneakers. They were tight because of the bandages, but they would work. She left the bathroom and did an awkward pirouette for Kris.

Kris nodded her approval. "Definitely an improvement." Her cell chimed. She answered, listened for a moment, then said, "Okay, Lieutenant, thanks for the heads-up," and disconnected.

"I gotta go see a man about a horse," Kris said, with a wink.

Mia gave her a quizzical look. "You're buying a horse?"

Kris laughed. "It's a metaphor. I've got to get moving, the judge has an opening for us in fifteen minutes." She grabbed her purse. "The doc told me you were good to go. So, hang tight and keep your fingers crossed. I'll be back shortly." She gave Mia a thumbs-up. Mia sighed, returning the gesture.

Kris strode out to the hospital elevator. She squeezed into a packed elevator between a fat man whose suit smelled like a dead rat and a tall nurse wearing noxious perfume. Kris almost gagged. Everyone near her looked alarmed and tried to move away.

Thankfully, the doors opened on the ground floor, and Kris dashed out, taking in deep gulps of fresher air. Another couple of seconds in there and she would have blown her lunch. Her headache was back. *Great fucking timing!* She hurried out of the hospital to where her cruiser was once more double-parked. This time, she'd blocked in an angry intern or doctor, who shouted and flipped her off as she got into her car. *There isn't nearly enough parking in this place,* she thought, ignoring the guy's complaints.

She smiled and waved at him. "Have a nice day," she muttered, as she roared off to the courthouse. Parking, she raced upstairs and made it with two minutes to spare. Breathing hard, she reached the clerk's desk.

"HERE—TO SEE—JUDGE—ONE o'clock—'pointment," she managed between gasps.

The bored clerk took her name and ID. "Have a seat, Lieutenant. The judge will see you shortly," she said, with a yawn. *Hurry up and wait.* Impatiently, Kris took a chair. Five minutes later, the clerk looked over at her. "Judge Timbers will see you in his chambers, Lt. Lacey."

The old judge's belly would have made Santa proud. Kris introduced herself to him and brought him up to speed on her own involvement in Mia's case. As Kris continued, his caterpillar-like eyebrows drew together in a frown.

"Your honor, I'd like to take her to her brother in Oregon. He's her only living relative."

The judge tapped a pen on his desk, contemplating his answer. "Lt. Lacey, I'm going to grant you custody, *pro-tem*, until the brother petitions otherwise, but ... forgive me, may I ask you a question? Have you any children?" He'd noticed her ringless left hand.

She hesitated slightly. "No, sir, I don't. Never married. I've been working for the department since I turned twenty-one. Hard to date when you're married to the job. Why do you ask?" she asked warily.

The old judge smiled and nodded. "After reading about the girl's background, I'm of a mind that she will need someone responsible to look after her." He leaned back in his leather chair.

Kris couldn't guess where he was leading. "Yes, Your Honor, that's why I'm petitioning the court to take her to live with her half-brother in Oregon. I believe that's the best I can do for her," she replied.

He was silent for a moment, then he cleared his throat. "Have *you* ever thought about adoption?"

Kris suddenly got what he meant. She shook her head slowly. "You can't be serious, Your Honor. I-I couldn't support a teenage girl on my puny salary. The hours are crazy—and my job is dangerous. What if something happened to me, say, God forbid, I got badly injured? Who would take care of her?" She tried to reason with him.

He merely smiled patiently back at her. "How old is this brother? Is he married?" he asked.

She thought about it. "I-I don't really know. He sounded young on the phone. I'd guess he's maybe nineteen or twenty. Why?" She was curious how far he would go with this.

"Well, I looked him up, barely twenty-one. A kid raising a kid. She needs someone mature to guide her through her teenage years. Someone who can give her a moral and ethical compass to follow. Who better than a cop? Most of all, she's going to need someone with a compassionate and loving heart to be there for her. In my experience, Lieutenant, most people would not make the effort to drive someone with whom they're barely acquainted a thousand miles and four states away unless they felt something for them."

With a sigh, he looked down at his desk. "I'm hereby granting you temporary custody of the child until the brother petitions for guardianship of the girl. Now if you'll excuse me, I've another case waiting. Good day—and good luck," he finished, shuffling the papers on his desk.

Kris took the hint, thanking him for fitting her in his schedule. As she left the courthouse, her headache pounded a bass drum in her skull.

She was aware that her biological clock was ticking. *Crap! Am I that transparent? Could I really be falling for the kid? It must be more than just pity that I feel for her. Right?* She realized she wasn't getting any younger and her mating prospects were slim pickings these days. "Most people would not make the effort," the Judge had said. *Well, I'm not most people, am I!* Kris climbed into her cruiser, arguing with herself, as she drove back to the hospital.

Spotting an empty parking space, she raced into it, cutting off an Uber driver who promptly flipped her off. Ignoring him, she got out and walked inside. To avoid another claustrophobic encounter in the elevator, she took the stairs. She knocked and opened the door to Mia's room.

"You ready to go, kiddo? The judge says you're all mi—" she broke off, looking around. The room was empty. *Mia was gone!*

Chapter Fifty-One
-Wallowa State Park

He knew the ranger bitch might have figured out who he was by now. Good! Fuck her! He smiled, exposing teeth filed sharp as tiny daggers. He took the last bite of the dead girl's heart, groaning with pleasure as the warm blood squirted out the sides of his mouth while he chewed.

Parents should be a little more watchful of their children these days, he thought, as he swallowed. He'd spotted her sitting by herself at a picnic table with her earbuds in, playing some stupid game on her phone.

Her idiot parents had been twenty feet away inside a tent, fucking and moaning, with the flaps closed, oblivious to his presence. So was the child. He'd simply strolled up behind her, grabbed her by the throat, broken the little girl's neck without a sound, and thrown her limp body over his shoulder.

With little effort, he'd strolled back with his kill to the hidden cave deep in the surrounding forest. As he walked, the dead girl's head flopped around facing him. He squealed, "Stop looking at me!" as her pale blue eyes stared lifelessly, sightless accusations of her murder.

The cave's camouflaged entrance led underground to a larger opening six feet below. The dank cavern was dimly lit by an old Coleman lantern hanging from a tree root that protruded from the low rock ceiling. A filthy sleeping bag lay in the corner of the roughly ten-foot-square space. Animal skulls adorned the cavern walls like a macabre mosaic.

Having eaten his fill of her organs for the moment, he used his hunting knife to cut off her head. Brains were best eaten warm. He set the head aside, opened a large garbage bag, and carelessly stuffed the rest of her remains inside. Humming to himself, he carried the body down to the lake's edge. Placing two heavy rocks inside, he closed and knotted the bloody bag.

"Here's to swimmin' with bow-legged women. Say hi to Dora for me, okay?" he jabbered to the bag, grinning. He dropped it off the cliff into the lake below, where it landed with a muted splash, sinking quickly from sight. He wasn't worried about the remains returning to the surface—he'd eaten or removed all her organs, so there'd be no bloating gas to bring it back up. With a loud belch, he crept back to his underground home.

With a large rock, he bashed the girl's skull in, pulled the broken cranium away, scooped out the brains, and devoured them. A tiny spring filled a depression in the rock, providing ice-cold water. He drank and washed bloody brain matter from his hands, then sat down on the soiled sleeping bag.

Rocking slowly back and forth, he quietly crooned, "Itsy-bitsy spider came down the waterspout, this goblin's gonna get you, if you don't watch out." Then he lay down, sated.

WITH PETE INSIDE THE cruiser again, Missy pulled away from his house. "I don't suppose you took the advice that Frank and I gave you." She glanced at him as she drove.

He shook his head. "Sorry, but I couldn't bring myself to touch the thing again. Tongs and gloves be damned. That piece of wood—what the hell is going on with it? You think it could be, like, possessed or something?"

"With your luck, anything's possible," she said sarcastically. "I wonder what W.R.'s connection is to all this? I mean, why give you the totem in the first place?" She turned into her driveway.

Pete shrugged. "I don't know. I think she might have some sort of psychic connection to it, maybe."

Or maybe, a psychotic one! Missy glanced angrily at her bandaged palm. At a little past noon, she parked by Jake's truck. They got out and walked inside, where Jake was in the kitchen making sandwiches.

He heard them enter and wiped his hands on his hands on a towel tucked into his jeans. "I just fed Belinda, she's down for the count. I—what the hell is that wrapped around your hand?" He frowned at Missy.

"Ah ... never mind, I'll tell you later. Frank came up with the name of the probable suspect. And, Jake, I think it may be Elisa's illegitimate child—the one Mama forced her to give up seventeen years ago," she said, grabbing a sandwich from the cutting board. As she chewed, Jinx moved closer, staring expectantly up at her.

Jake asked, "How do you figure?" They all sat down at the table.

"Well, Frank got dental records matching the tooth that was embedded in the deputy's neck. It belonged to a Tory Morning Star. No picture with the dental records. Frank wasn't getting any answers from the tribe about him, so I went to visit Tommy Two-Tongues, a tribal Elder," she said, between bites. Jake waited patiently while she swallowed and continued. "Tommy said the kid is pretty much bad news. Been a loner just about all his life. Doesn't play well with others. Never joined in any reindeer games, etc. Anyway, the short of it is, now he's disappeared," she said.

"What do you mean, he's disappeared?" Jake asked, pinching off a bit of a sandwich to toss under the table to Jinx.

"According to Tommy, several people had complained to him that their pets went missing in the last few months. The boy was seen late one night carrying something in a bag, down near Bear Creek. Someone swore that it was their neighbor's dog, but no proof.

"If that's all true, I may have a psychopathic nephew somewhere out there, gunning for me. All because Birdie couldn't find someone his own age to rape," she spat vehemently. She'd lost her appetite. She gave the last piece of her sandwich to Jinx, who eagerly scarfed it down.

"Does anyone have a picture of the boy?" Jake licked mayo off his fingers.

"No. At least, not to my knowledge. The kid never hung out with anyone his own age. Very reclusive." She finished, wiping her hands on a napkin.

"Sounds like the kid's really screwed-up in the head," Pete threw in, as his phone rang. After checking the number, he answered.

"Hey, Lt. Lacey, what's up?" he asked.

"Mia is now officially placed in my care temporarily, but there's a slight delay here, Mr. Chandler," she told him.

"You-you don't sound happy. That is what we were hoping for ... right?" Pete said hesitantly.

She paused. "I—Mia is missing, Mr. Chandler. I left her at the hospital to go see the judge. I returned a few minutes ago to tell her the good news, but she's disappeared from her room. Has she contacted you?" Stress was evident in her voice.

"No, ma'am," Pete replied anxiously.

"Okay. Well, hospital security is reviewing video of the hall outside her door right now. There's no sign of a struggle in her room, so I believe she left voluntarily. Hopefully, she's somewhere nearby," Kris told him.

Pete's face turned a shade paler at the news. "You've got to find her, Lieutenant. Where the hell would she go by herself?" He was sounding agitated.

"Stay calm, Mr. Chandler, I'll find her. I don't think she's gone far." She tried to allay his fears, as well as her own. "I'll call you the minute I know anything, I promise. Okay?"

Pete didn't like it, but he really had no choice. "Yeah, thanks, Lt. Lacey. I'm sorry, I do appreciate all you're doing for her. It's just, lately, things here have also been quite ... tense, to say the least," he said tersely.

Lacey told him she had to go and disconnected. Missy and Jake both stared at him expectantly, having heard only his side of the conversation. He brought them up to speed on the changing situation in Boulder.

Missy's phone chimed with an unknown number, and she answered, "Ranger Anderson, who is this?"

"Fe-fi-fo-fum, a spider's work is never done. I'm coming for you, bitch!" With that bizarre announcement, the caller quickly hung up.

Chapter Fifty-Two - Boulder Hospital

Waiting for Lt. Lacey to return from court, Mia had grown bored and decided to walk outside for some fresh air. She left her room and got on an available elevator, still a little loopy from the pain pill she'd taken earlier. The elevator smelled like a dead rat. Wrinkling her nose, she tried not to breathe.

When the doors opened on the first floor, and she shuffled out, her tender, bandaged feet squeezed into the tight new shoes. *Ouch!* She headed for the nearest exit. No one tried to stop her as she walked outside to stand under the large canopy.

A few feet away, an old lady in a wheelchair sat smoking a cigarette, an oxygen cannula running from her nose to a tank on the back of the chair. She took a drag, nodding to Mia. "Nasty habit," she said grimly.

Mia nodded back politely, then moved upwind of her. She sat down on a cold metal bench, staring out west to the distant, snow-capped mountains. She missed Frodo something fierce. He'd been her only solace during the early days of these ongoing calamities. She sighed, longing deeply for her warm, furry friend. She wished Kris would hurry back. Her anxiety grew as she waited for the judge's answer.

An ambulance pulled to a stop in front of her, blocking her view of the front entrance. The doors opened and aides unloaded someone on a gurney, rushing them inside. Distracted by all the action, she missed seeing Lacey rush back into the hospital. She sat for another five minutes before deciding she should head back to her room. She walked gingerly past the old woman in the wheelchair, who smiled toothlessly at her.

As she limped toward her room, she saw Lt. Lacey surrounded by men in uniforms in her doorway.

Kris was speaking with them when she spotted Mia walking toward them. Rolling her eyes, she sighed with relief. "Where did you disappear to? I was ready to put out an Amber Alert on you," she chided. Mia apologized, explaining where she'd gone. "I didn't expect you to leave the room. Okay, so, the judge has granted me official temporary custody. We have a long way to go, you ready to roll?" Kris asked, impatient to get moving.

"Let's make like a banana and split," Mia replied, with a grin.

AFTER SIGNING HOSPITAL release forms, Kris finally got her discharged. Grabbing her "Mega Mart" bag, Mia climbed into the cruiser's passenger seat. Kris was talking animatedly on her phone.

"Here—I'll let you talk to her, hang on." She handed the phone to Mia, who took it, giving Kris a questioning look.

Lacey explained. "It's your brother. Time for you two to talk." She gave her a wink. Starting the engine, she pulled out of the parking lot, heading up Route Ninety-Three, and from there, on to Oregon.

"Hi, Pete, I-I don't quite know what to say. But I'm really looking forward to finally meeting you ... brother," she said with a sob.

"Same back at you, sister-o'-mine. I must say it was a bit of a surprise to learn of your existence—a pleasant one, though. I'm so sorry for all the terrible things that have happened. You must feel so alone," he said solemnly.

"Nothing in life is fair, Pete, I know that. But sometimes, it seems like the whole freaking world is against you. I feel terrible that we had to meet this way. Dad never told me about you. I ... I'm sorry all of this has all been dumped on your shoulders." She wept into the phone. There was a momentary silence but for the hum of the tires on the road.

"Listen," Pete said, "everything happens for a reason. We don't always know the why of it; maybe it's just as well we don't. It would probably drive us mad. I do know it's a blessing we found each, regardless of the circumstances. I—" The line went dead.

Mia watched the phone's bars disappear as they entered the surrounding mountains. *Shit!* The call had been dropped. Many miles lay ahead before they'd get a decent signal again. She tried 'redial' with no result.

"It'll get better once we cross the Continental Divide. Try again later," Kris told her, driving past a semi loaded with new cars stacked atop each other. Mia felt her ears pop as they climbed higher on the mountain road.

Kris said, "Sorry there's no music, Taos PD frowns on 'regular radio.' Took 'em all out. Too much of a distraction." She'd noticed Mia checking out the dash.

Mia shrugged. "Doesn't really matter. I'm tired, think I'll try to nap. Let me know when we're across the Divide," she said, yawning from the residual effects of her medication. Using her new jacket for a pillow, she laid her head against the window and was asleep within minutes.

Smiling, Kris glanced over at her for a moment, feeling a tug on her heartstrings at the sight of the sleeping girl. Turning her gaze back to the traffic, she saw she'd drifted close to oncoming traffic. Startled, she overcorrected to the right, nearly slamming into a VW Beetle, and striking the guardrail with a sickening *crunch* before she had complete control of the cruiser again.

Kris's airbag deployed, smacking her in the face. Luckily, the cruiser had slid nose-first into the guardrail, its push-bar saving both the car and them from serious damage. Kris saw that Mia's airbag hadn't deployed; only her seat belt had kept her from being thrown through the windshield. She'd banged her head on the passenger window, but otherwise seemed okay.

"What the hell happened?" Mia asked, shaken by memories of her mother's accident.

Kris gingerly touched her nose to feel if it was broken. "I took my eyes off the road for a moment, and we almost drifted into oncoming traffic. The road's a bit slippery, and I swerved back a little too hard, okay?" she replied, a bit sharply.

"Remind me to stay awake from now on while you're driving," Mia snapped.

Embarrassed, Kris had no response. Flipping on the emergency lights, she got out to inspect the damage, as traffic sped by them. The heavy-duty push-bar had taken the brunt of the impact. She saw no serious damage, except to the guardrail—and her ego.

Shivering from the cold, she got back inside the warm car, pulled out a pocketknife and cut away the remnants of the deflated airbag, tossing them into the back seat for disposal later. Slowly, she backed the cruiser up over the snow-dusted breakdown lane, then accelerated smoothly back into the flow of traffic.

She didn't bother turning off the "cop lights." Mia was impressed, as vehicles pulled over or slowed down to move out of Kris's way. As the cruiser passed a sign announcing they had just crossed the Continental Divide, Kris's migraine returned abruptly.

With the lights flashing, she made good time for a couple hours. Still, she knew she needed to find a motel as soon as possible before a predicted storm front arrived, blanketing the roads with treacherous snow and ice.

An hour later, the blue-gray sky turned ominous as the storm moved in. Blowing snow and ice made it impossible to see more than a few feet in front of her, and her fuel was getting low. They hadn't passed an open gas station in more than a hundred miles, and the cruiser's "Low Fuel" indicator flashed on and off with alarming regularity.

Finally, on the outskirts of Salt Lake City, Kris spotted a gas station that appeared to be open, and she gratefully pulled up to the pump. She zipped her coat, bracing herself, and forced the driver's door open into a howling gale of snow and sleet pellets. The wind pushed her toward the door of the station, and she entered quickly, slamming the door.

She startled an old man sitting on a bar stool behind the counter smoking a cigarette and watching porn on his iPhone. The old fart looked to be in his eighties and was sporting an obvious hard-on.

Shit! Probably takes a case of Viagra to get it up at his age, she thought. He slid off the stool, grinning like a fifteen-year-old caught jerking off. Kris gave him a tight smile while trying to avert her eyes from the obvious. She paid for the gas and asked him where the nearest motel was.

He gave her a nearly toothless grin, "That'd be the 'Salt Lick' 'bout a mile down the road," he said, rheumy eyes glued to what he could see of her chest.

"Thanks. I don't want to be out in this storm any longer than I need to. Visibility sucks," she said.

He nodded, grinned, giving her the creeps. She braced herself, fighting her way back to the car against heavy gusts of wind and snow. She filled the tank, then climbed back inside the cruiser.

Mia looked uncomfortable. "I really need to pee. Could I go in there?"

"No, it-it's ... out of order. Can you hold it? There's a motel just down the road," Kris said a little sharply, thinking of the leering old prune inside.

She nearly passed the motel before spotting the ancient neon sign, flickering faintly, "Sa t-Li k, Col r TV—WiF —V ca cy." Pulling up to the office, she ran inside to pay for a room.

Shaking, Kris tried the keycard she'd received three times before the door opened. They piled in, and Kris bolted the door against the elements raging outside. She flipped on a light switch by the door to survey the room. One queen-size bed and a TV so old, it still had a twist-dial, no remote. The décor was mid-twentieth-century kitsch, down to the ugly green shag carpet. The small lamp by the bed was bolted to a cigarette-scarred nightstand. No phone, no bible in the drawer.

Mia hurried directly to the bathroom. "Ewww, someone left a big turd in here," she exclaimed, shutting the door. A few moments later, she hurried out. "Toilet doesn't flush either." She plopped down on a dingy bed as stiff and hard as a rock. "I hope you didn't have to pay much for this room. This bed is like something out of an old 'Flintstones' cartoon," she groused. Kris grimaced with a nod. *Yabba-Dabba-Doo.*

"Well, it beats freezing our butts off sleeping in the car," Kris said.

The hair on the back of Mia's neck suddenly stood up. "Kris, did you hear that?" she hissed.

Kris frowned. "I didn't hear anything," she said, with a yawn.

They sat still, listening intently. *There it was*—a high-pitched squeal from somewhere under the bed. Mia knew that sound intimately from her agonizing time in the basement of her grandfather's mansion. *Rats! Shit!*

They leaped to their feet, scrambled for the door. Cursing a blue streak, Kris unlocked the flimsy front door and flung it open. Bitingly cold air enveloped them as they rushed back out to the snow-covered cruiser.

Freezing, they climbed back inside. The wind howled like something alive, buffeting the car with blinding flurries of snow and ice.

Chapter Fifty-Three – Highway One Eighty-Four W Near Salt Lake City

"Fucking rats. Can't seem to get away from the nasty things," Mia complained, settling back in the car.

Kris said, "We've got bigger problems than rats," speaking of the blizzard surrounding them. "We need to find a better class of lodgings fast, before this gets any worse." She started the car, revving the big engine to get it warm enough to turn on the heat.

"How are you going to drive in this shit? It's almost a complete white-out." Mia gestured outside.

"Very carefully," Kris replied.

Snow and sleet pellets swept across the highway, almost obscuring the lanes. She looked at the time: 4:30 p.m. Another hour and it would be dark. *Crap!* There had to be a better motel closer to town. At least, traffic was nearly nonexistent—anyone with a brain was sitting someplace warm, sipping hot cocoa.

Keeping the speed under twenty mph, she drove at a crawl down the rapidly disappearing highway. Snow and ice crunched beneath the tires, as Kris struggled to see more than five feet ahead in the headlights' disorienting blur.

A few miles farther, she saw the welcoming sign of a "Daze-Inn" motel. She pulled in under its canopy and stopped. A burger joint was conveniently located right next door.

"You hungry? I could eat a bear right now," Kris asked.

"I could go for a burger and fries, I guess," Mia replied, as her stomach growled.

"I'll go get us a room, then we can chow down," Kris said. She fought the wind to push inside the office. Five minutes later, she was back in the car with a keycard.

"Room 107, my lucky number." She pulled into the burger drive-thru to order. Moving into a parking space with their food, they sat in the car eating in silence, each lost in thought.

Some loud yips outside the car got Mia's attention. She looked out and spied a small black lab—still a puppy—with a dusting of snow on its coat, sitting on its haunches, staring up at her. The poor pup was shivering in the frigid cold, its brown eyes beseeching hers as it whined loudly.

Lowering the window, she tossed the remains of her burger out to the hungry pup. The pooch caught it before it hit the ground, gulping it down in one bite.

Kris gave her a look, shaking her head. "Shouldn't have done that. Now it's going to expect you to let it inside the nice warm car," she warned.

Mia gave her a hopeful look. "Please? He's freezing out there," she begged.

"How do you know it's a 'he'?"

Mia grinned. "'Cause I can see his little wiener. Please, Kris? He's shaking like a leaf out there."

Kris sighed. She wasn't much of a "dog person" but she wasn't heartless, either. "Okay, but we'll have to sneak him into the room. Can't afford to pay a pet deposit," she finally gave in.

Mia immediately opened the car door. The pup didn't hesitate, jumped inside, and promptly shook himself, lobbing a shower of snow and ice pellets over Mia and everything around her.

"Bad dog," she mock-chastised, grinning at him. The lab looked to be about six months old. He whined and licked her face until, laughing, she gently pushed him away. Kris noticed he didn't have a collar. The pup curled at Mia's feet and gazed up gratefully with his soft brown eyes. He was so painfully thin his ribs were showing.

"What are you going to call him?" Kris asked.

Mia sat thoughtfully for a moment. "Scrappy. Maybe 'Scraps' for short. That's probably all he's had to survive on, by the looks of the poor thing," Mia replied, stroking the pup's silky ears, eliciting a contented groan.

Kris raised a brow. "You're gonna call him Scraps? Whatever." She parked the car in front of their room.

"I hope we have better luck with this room; I'm not driving any more in this shit 'til the storm passes. I'll open the door, you sneak the mutt in," she told Mia. The wind lashed her face with ice pellets as she exited the car, slogging through deepening snow to reach Room 107.

Mia hopped out. Scrappy looked at her like she was crazy to leave the nice, warm car. "C'mon, Scraps. Let's go," she encouraged. As she reached in to pull him out, he growled and nipped her thumb.

"*Ouch*—you little shit! You don't bite the hand that feeds you," Mia scolded.

Scraps ignored her as he scratched an ear. She inspected her thumb, but his teeth hadn't broken the skin. She reached in again, more slowly, and Scraps let her pick him up. He glanced back wistfully one last time at the warm refuge of the car before she sat him down on the snow-covered ground.

She shut the car door and turned around to pick him up, but Scraps was gone. Blowing snow made it impossible to tell where he'd gone. The pup had vanished. She saw a few paw prints in the snow trailing off in the general direction of the burger joint next door. He'd likely gone back to the only food source he'd known.

Sadly, Mia trudged up to where Kris stood by the door. "You see that?" Mia asked.

Kris nodded. "I saw. Come on inside."

The storm passed overnight, leaving six inches of additional white stuff on the ground. Kris and Mia woke to a sunny, but cold, day.

"I'm starving, can we get something to eat?" Mia said, with a yawn.

Kris cocked a brow as she got up. "This isn't an attempt to try and win back your little pal, Skippy, with a little breakfast bribe, is it?"

"It's Scrappy—not Skippy." Mia frowned at her.

"That dog is feral, Mia. He doesn't trust humans. Can't say as I blame him. And we need to get back on the road as soon as we get the food. Skimpy's a survivor, he'll be okay," Kris said reasonably.

"It's *Scrappy*—not Skimpy. I don't have any freaking luck with animals." Mia sighed. Opening the front door, she saw Scraps shivering in the cold nearby. She smiled and bent down. He barked once, then leaned forward to lick her outstretched hand.

"Well, well, looks like Skratchy isn't quite as antisocial as he appeared—yeah, I know, it's *Scrappy*. Whatever. If he gets in the car without any coaxing, he can go. If not, you'll just have to deal, okay?" Kris said, as they walked out to the snow-covered cruiser.

The little lab followed Mia as she neared the car, but stopped short of hopping in. He whimpered, took one hesitant step, faltered, then made a decision and leaped inside to curl up at Mia's feet.

"Guess that settles that," Kris grunted, as she got in after clearing the snow and ice from the front and back windshields. They went through the drive-thru again, ordered three breakfast sandwiches to go. They were a mile away before Kris found she'd been "screwed at the drive-thru." They'd only gotten two sandwiches.

Crap! It made her mad, but she wasn't going back for it. They each gave a quarter of their food to Scraps, who scarfed it all down, farted, and fell asleep.

Due to the slushy conditions on Highway Fifteen, Kris drove twenty miles an hour below the posted speed limit. While it wasn't actively snowing, driving remained treacherous. Mia and Scraps were soon fast asleep, despite Mia's vow to stay awake. The journey was monotonous, as the passing landscape was all but obliterated by the blanket of white. There were few cars on the road.

That's because they're *smart enough not to be out driving in this shit,* Kris thought wryly, dry swallowing a couple Advil. They stopped for gas and sandwiches at a small convenience store outside of Boise, Idaho, at 2:00 p.m.

After another two and a half hours of mind-numbing driving, they reached the small town of Joseph, Oregon.

Chapter Fifty-Four - Wallowa State Park

Missy was shaking with anger at the threatening phone call she'd just received. The crazy asshole who was likely her nephew had somehow gotten her home number. She had no time to wonder how, as her phone chimed again, from a different number.

She answered, "Ranger Anderson."

A frantic sounding woman spoke through sobs. "M-my d-daughter is missing. Please, you've g-got to find her. We've looked everywhere, s-she's .." she began to cry harder.

Missy stopped her. "Ma'am, please stop and take a deep breath. Now, where are you?"

The woman exhaled shakily. "We're c-camped up on the ridge in the park, right above the lake. P-please help us. We only left her alone for ten minutes, and she's disappeared."

"How old is your daughter, ma'am?" Missy asked.

The distraught mother replied, "She's ten. She has long blonde hair and s-she—it-it's her eleventh birthday tomorrow, and now she's just gone." She was becoming belligerent.

Missy did her best to pacify the panicky woman, telling her she'd meet them at the ridge as soon as possible. "I'll be there in about ten minutes." She hung up, sighing sadly. She assumed the guys had overheard her conversation.

"Pete, come with me. Jake, please change Belinda's diaper; I smell poop. We have to go right now." She'd shifted into Ranger mode.

As the odor wafted by his nose, Jake made a face. "Seems like I get all the shit jobs lately," he grumbled. He didn't really mind, just needed to get in a small jab now and then. He plucked Belinda gently from her cradle, cooing to her, and took her to the bedroom.

"Call and let me know when to expect you. I'm making my famous chicken saltimbocca for dinner tonight," he hollered over his shoulder.

"Roger that, Bud, love you," she shouted back, rushing out.

THE TWO RANGERS DROVE up to the remote ridge in the park where the family had set up camp, spotting the couple standing a few feet from a picnic table arguing angrily. As Missy pulled to a stop, the small, skinny, blonde woman shoved the man backward and flipped him off, striding over to meet them.

"Thank God, you're finally here. If my asshole husband hadn't gotten a case of the 'hornies' after lunch, this wouldn't have happened in first damn place," she complained, before Missy and Pete were out of the cruiser.

"Oh, yeah, blame it all on me. You're the one who said Trish would be fine out here by herself for fifteen minutes," the man shouted.

"You couldn't even last for five without the help of that little blue pill," the bleach-blonde sneered back at him.

Missy had heard enough. "Stop it, now! Your little girl is lost. We need to find her before dark. You two can play the blame game later. First, what are your names?"

"I'm Ivy Griffin and that jackass is my husband."

Missy continued. "Right now, I need you to show me where you last saw your daughter," she said sternly.

The blonde's eyes shot daggers at the man. "Last time we saw her, she was sitting on that picnic table, playing on her phone," she pointed.

Missy threw Pete a look, and they walked over to the table. The girl's cell phone still sat there. Missy tried to open it, but it was encrypted, and she got nowhere.

Shit! "Do you know her password?" she asked Ivy.

The woman looked at her helplessly, shaking her head. "No—but I know she wouldn't have left that unless something bad happened to her." Anxiously, she wrung her hands.

Missy handed the cell to her. "You might give it a try. Does she have a favorite pet? Maybe the name of a song?" Missy asked hopefully.

The mother thought for a moment. "She's got a bird. A parakeet named Garfield," she told Missy.

Missy cocked a brow. "Like the cartoon cat?" Ivy nodded.

Go figure, Missy thought. She told her to try that as the password, and after three shaky tries, the lady got the phone unlocked.

"Has anyone messaged her or vice-versa in the last hour or so?" Missy asked.

Ivy quickly scanned the phone's contents. "No, there's nothing," she said despondently.

The father put his two cents in. "Shouldn't we call the cops? Obviously, she's just lost. Somebody needs to find my little girl. We don't know this park, but *you* sure as hell should," he said angrily.

Thinking about it, Missy decided he had a point, but they'd need more manpower to search the surrounding forest. It would take more than just the four of them to cover even the area nearby. She checked the time: 4:30 p.m. They had maybe an hour before sunset to find the child in the dense forest. After dark, it would be damn-near impossible.

Calling Frank, she quickly filled him in. Cursing, he said he'd gather up some of his people to help with the search. While the distraught couple continued arguing, Missy called Jake.

"It's me, Bud—listen, we're gathering people to help look for the missing girl. Just giving you a heads-up. Don't hold dinner for me, I'll call you. If we don't find her by dark ... well, it could be a whole different ballgame. Gotta go now, they're here." She watched the first of Frank's deputies arriving.

Minutes later, the sheriff's car pulled up behind them and he got out. "Okay, we've got nine people, including the parents. We're going to form a line and walk ten feet apart. Anybody sees anything, give a shout," Frank instructed, taking charge.

They spread out and started slowly searching the ridge and dense shrubbery. Twenty minutes in, someone yelled, "Over here."

AT THE R AND R DRIVE-In in Joseph, Kris finished the last tasty bite of her burger. Mia stole some of her sweet potato tots, popping them in her mouth.

"I need to call Pete and let him know we made it here okay." Mia held out her hand for Kris's phone.

Kris handed it to her. Mia scowled, wiping grease from it with a napkin. Kris rolled her eyes, got up to wash her hands in the restroom.

Pete's phone went straight to voice mail. *Dang it!* Mia left a brief message telling him they were in Joseph and asking him to call her as soon as he could.

"Let's go, kiddo, I want to find a room and lie down for like, a year," Kris said.

Mia shrugged and dumped the remains of her burger into a napkin.

Seeing Kris's look, "What?" she said, defensively. "I couldn't finish it, and this way, it won't go to waste. I'll give it to Scraps." They'd left the pup asleep in the car while they ate. Walking out of the restaurant, they heard him barking at them.

Mia opened the car door, to be met by a wet tongue to the face as she pushed the pup off her seat. Giggling, she tossed him the remains of her sandwich, which he wolfed down in a couple bites, looking up at her for more.

"Sorry, Scraps, that's all she wrote," she said, holding up empty hands. He whined, tried clumsily to circle three times in the floorboard's tight space, then gave up and curled at her feet. They found a pet-friendly motel on the outskirts of town, "pet friendly" meaning Kris had to pay extra for the dog.

"I think they overcharged me for the mutt," she groused half-joking, inspecting the receipt as they walked into the room.

"I'll pay you back as soon as I can, I promise, Kris. I can't thank you enough for all you've done for me," Mia said earnestly.

"I didn't—I wasn't complaining about paying for Scri … Scraps. I'm just really tired, and I have a freaking headache from hell," Kris tried to explain. Mia only nodded, which made Kris feel even worse.

"I'm gonna power nap for a few. Try not to let Scooby Doo chew up any furniture if you can help it," Kris said with a yawn as she plopped down on the bed.

"He doesn't look like much of a 'chewer,'" Mia huffed, watching as Scraps started to gnaw on a chair leg. Mia quickly pulled him away, whispering, "Bad dog."

He rolled on his back, with tongue lolling, giving her his best, '*Yeah, I'm a little sttinker, aren't I?*' look. She couldn't help grinning and gave him belly-rubs until he fell asleep. She lay back on the bed and closed her eyes.

She wasn't as sleepy as she was mentally exhausted, anxious, and fearful. So much had happened in such a short time. Having both parents ripped away in the space of a few days had created a huge emotional void in her life.

What if Pete doesn't like me? What if he's an asshole, like all the other men I've encountered lately? With these thoughts tumbling fitfully around in her mind, Mia slowly drifted off.

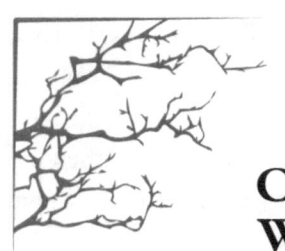

Chapter Fifty-Five - Wallowa State Park

The searchers stared down the natural looking rock stairs, toward the mouth of what seemed to be a small cave.

"Anyone think to bring a flashlight?" Missy queried the group.

"I've got one, but the battery's low. Not sure how long it'll last. Haven't charged it in a day or so." Frank pulled it from his utility belt.

"Somebody needs to get their ass down there. My daughter could be in danger. There are fucking bears out here, you know," the girl's father criticized.

No shit, Sherlock. What a prick! Missy glared at him angrily.

Frank stared daggers at the man. "We're doing what we can, mister, so back off on the attitude. I know you're scared for your little girl. Let us do our jobs and maybe we'll find her sooner." He ground his teeth, annoyed.

Turning on his flashlight, Frank cautiously worked his way down to the cave's dark entrance, motioning the other searchers to stay back. Missy and Pete followed him down. A foul odor emanated from inside the cave, making the hair on their napes rise.

Frank's light swept over the interior of the small enclosure. In the flashlight's glow, neat rows of animal skulls greeted them. The stench was worse inside. Pete gagged, feeling his gorge rise. Missy swallowed hard, while they all felt as though they'd stepped inside a charnel house.

The skulls were bad enough, but the true horror-show sat in the center of the room. A small, bloody, severed head with wispy blonde hair still attached gaped at them from its perch atop a sharpened stave of wood driven into the ground. Missy gulped and went rigid with revulsion. Pete cried, "Holy shit," before bending and tossing his cookies. Frank only grimaced disgustedly at the ghastly sight.

As they moved closer, they saw the girl's skull had been crushed like an overripe pumpkin. Her brain was missing.

"Sick motherfucker! He did this on purpose to draw us all here. She's dead because of me. He knew I'd be the first called to the scene. That poor child was just bait!" Missy was quaking with rage and disgust.

The sound of footsteps approaching from outside grew louder. "Trisha are you down here, baby?" the mother's anguished voice called from near the cave.

"No way is she seeing this," Frank growled, cutting off the light, casting them all in darkness and thus, sparing the woman the sight of her daughter's obscenely displayed head. The dim light from outside silhouetted the distraught woman at the cave's entrance.

"Ma'am, you need to turn around! Right now. Go back up to join your husband," Frank's disembodied voice spoke sharply.

"Oh, my God, what is that horrible smell? W-why are you all s-standing around in the dark, I thought you had a fucking light?" the woman asked shakily.

They moved quickly as one toward her, blocking her further advance. In the dim light, she could see the looks on their faces—in that instant, she knew in her heart Trisha would not be celebrating another birthday. She lost it.

Screaming like a wounded animal, she collapsed to her knees, sobbing. "No, no, no! Not my baa-bee! Please, please, please, God, no, not my baby girl."

Gently, Frank pulled her to her feet. "I'm so sorry, ma'am. Sh-she didn't suffer." *At least I hope not,* he thought grimly. "Miz ... I-I'm sorry, I'm afraid I didn't catch your name?" he said, supporting her as they all climbed back up the rocky crevice.

The woman stammered, "I- I'm I-Ivy, Ivy G-Griffin. Please. My baby ...?"

"What could possibly have happened to her in ten-fucking-minutes?" her husband snapped, as they neared him.

Frank hesitated, then said loudly, "We think a dangerously deranged person was responsible for her death, Mr. Griffin."

"Death? Who's dead?" the soon-to-be ex-husband repudiated.

"It's your daughter, Mr. Griffin. She's been murdered," Frank said soberly.

The man looked like he'd been pole-axed. "M-my Trisha ... d-dead? I don't believe you. You're lying—let me fucking see her!" Angrily, he shoved at Frank, who was blocking his way.

Frank stood three inches taller than Griffin and had fifty pounds on him. The Sheriff barely swayed in place, as two deputies grabbed Griffin from behind and cuffed him for his own good.

"Normally, I would arrest you for assault on an officer. Under the circumstances, I'll let it pass. But don't push your luck, Mr. Griffin," Frank told him calmly. "You have our condolences for your loss. We will catch the monster who did this. He *will* pay. My deputies will escort you and your wife back to your camp now. There's nothing more to see here."

The bereaved father started to argue, then thought better of it. "I'm fucking suing you and the State Park for criminal negligence, Ranger bitch. My daughter wouldn't be dead if you'd been here doing your fucking job," he screamed at Missy.

Missy was taken aback by the accusation. Guilt flooded over her. It was true, in part—when the girl was abducted, she had not been patrolling the park. She'd gone to speak with Tommy Two-Tongues. Not that she could likely have kept this from happening. *Shit! My freaking job,* she thought miserably.

The deputies led the bereaved couple back to their campsite to watch them pack up and ensure that they'd left. Frank called the ME and forensics and told them to get there ASAP.

"What do you think he did with her body?" Pete asked. Frank and Missy exchanged a look.

"Depends. It could be anywhere. I didn't see any blood trail leading out of the cave," Frank said.

"There was a lot of blood on the cave floor. Maybe he buried it somewhere out here. There's a shitload of hiding places in this forest, it could be anywhere," Pete speculated.

Missy frowned, "I noticed some trash bags in the cave. He could've bagged her body and dumped it in the lake. If he did, it should turn up soon enough. Maybe kept her head as a trophy, or ... maybe it's a message meant for me. Fuck it. Whoever he is, I'd like to rip his balls off and shove them up his ass." She growled that out, frustrated.

The sun was starting to set behind the snow-capped mountains to the west when the Medical Examiner and forensic guys arrived. Without its warmth, the temperature would quickly plummet. Most of the searchers wore only lightweight day jackets, inadequate to ward off the bitter cold night air in the mountains. Everyone had to keep moving to stay warm. Armed now with flashlights, they slowly walked a grid 100 yards out in each direction from the cave—except to the west, where a cliff overhung the steep drop to the lake below.

"It's gonna get colder than a rat's ass out here fast," Pete grumbled, shivering.

"How many rat's asses have you actually touched in your life, Bud?" Missy asked sarcastically, as they worked their way slowly through the brush and rough terrain.

"I had a pet rat when I was a kid. Well ... she was really a gerbil. But gerbils are kinda like small rats," he replied. Missy rolled her eyes.

After another hour of fruitless searching for the girl's body, Frank finally called a halt around 6:30 p.m. They were all tired, the temperature had dropped below freezing, and everyone was feeling the effects of the cold.

"Let's wrap it up for now. We'll have to wait for dawn tomorrow and start again fresh," Frank said wearily. Everyone looked relieved except the two deputies appointed to guard the cave overnight. No one wanted to stumble across the girl's headless corpse in the dark. They regrouped at the campsite to speculate and say goodnight.

The ME pulled Frank aside, shaking his head. "Terrible thing, Frank. I feel for the parents. The girl's head appears to have been cut off with a hunting knife. The spinal cord exhibited signs of being sawed or hacked with a serrated blade. Without a body, can't say for sure as to the COD. There was a minimal amount of blood loss. The cervical vertebra was snapped between C2 and C3," he said. "If I had to guess, I'd say he broke her neck first. She was dead before the head was removed. The skull cap was massively fractured and pulled away to expose the brain pan," the doctor droned on in monotone.

"What do you think happened to the brain?" Frank interrupted.

The doctor hesitated. "I don't like to speculate about that. It showed evidence of being ripped away from the brain stem in chunks. Like you would if you—" He stopped there, looking directly at Frank. "You've got a seriously dangerous whack-job loose out there, Frank. Catch the bastard before I run out of space to store the bodies," he said gruffly, turning to leave.

Missy and Pete wandered over to where Frank stood by his cruiser.

"What did the doc say?" Missy asked, wrapping her arms around herself for warmth.

Frank shook his head. "Not much. I don't think she suffered. Broken neck. She was dead before ... anyway, we'll pick up where we left off in the morning. In the meantime, go home and try to get some rest. And when you get there, kiss that little girl of yours for me," he said, getting in his car.

"What about the girl's parents?" she asked.

He paused before answering. "I don't think they're ever going camping again, if that's what you're asking."

"What Griffin said is true. I was not in the park when it happened. I could lose my job over this—at the very least," she told him.

"Well, if you do, you're welcome to mine. After I catch the cocksucker that did this, I'm retiring." He started the engine. He turned around and drove away as Missy and Pete got into her car.

Checking his phone, Pete saw he'd missed a call. He listened to it and let out a sigh of relief, closing it.

"That was Mia. They made town an hour and a half ago. Said they'd eaten and had checked into Nell's "No-Tell" Motel, Room 217. Her words, not mine." Pete told Missy, while calling the number back. After the fourth ring, it went to Mia's voice mail.

Pete frowned. "I really need to go and meet her, Missy. Would you mind taking me to my car?" he asked.

Missy sighed, "Let me call Jake first. He'll be upset that I didn't call him earlier with the crappy news. Well, I don't have much of an appetite right now, anyway." She could only grimace at the gruesome images replaying in her mind. Calling Jake, she filled him in on what was happening.

He was quiet for a moment. "I was afraid that would be the outcome. Frank's gotta find that fucking psycho fast. One of us could be—" the connection dropped. Damn spotty cell service. She tried calling him back. Nothing. *Shit!*

Chapter Fifty-Six - Nell's Motel, Joseph, Early Evening

Mia was dreaming deeply when something warm and wet slid across her cheek. Scraps had made it onto the bed and decided to give her an unwanted bath.

"Thanks a lot, 'Scrappy-Doo,'" she sputtered, wiping dog spit from her mouth. She pushed the pup onto the floor, where he immediately started gnawing on the table leg. Mia ignored him, noting that Kris was awake on the other bed.

She was propped up against the headboard watching TV with the sound off. "Have a good nap? You were sawing logs until Scabs there decided to play Spider-Man and scale the bed," Kris smirked.

"It's Scraps—and you're definitely not a dog person." Mia mock-pouted to her.

Kris didn't disagree. "Sorry, I wasn't raised around dogs, only cats." She got up and stretched, biting on a hangnail.

Mia got up to pour water into the small ice bucket provided by the sleezy motel, putting it down in the small bathroom for the pup. Scraps quit chewing and ran to the bowl, lapping it up sloppily.

Suddenly, he turned toward the entry door with a low growl. When someone knocked, he snarled, the hackles on the back of his neck standing straight up.

"Who is it?" Kris yelled toward the door, her hand instinctively resting on her Glock.

There was a slight pause. "It's Pete Chandler," a muffled voice answered.

Mia's heart was beating fast as she stood on tiptoe to peer through the peephole in the door before anxiously opening it. There he was—her half-brother.

Thank goodness, he didn't look much like their dad. Checking out her half-brother, Mia saw a nice-looking, young man with thick, dark blond hair and large, wide-set blue-grey eyes. A day's darker-blond stubble surrounded a narrow nose and narrow lips. Mia thought him very handsome, his grey eyes framed by thick brown lashes and brows by far his best feature, but he also had a nice smile.

Next to him stood a slim, attractive woman with curly, auburn hair pulled back with a simple scrunchie. As they walked in, Scraps barked at them twice, then ran to hide in the bathroom.

"You're ... my sister, Mia, here at last. I got your message. I'm so excited and happy to see you. Sorry we've been out of pocket. This is my boss and good friend, Melissa Anderson, who usually goes by Missy." Pete introduced her, as they stepped inside.

Giving a little cry, Mia flung herself against Pete, wrapping her arms around him in a tearful bear-hug. Out of nowhere, Kris felt a small stab of jealousy. Surprised by the strength of the emotion, she cleared her throat and introduced herself, shaking hands with Missy and Pete once he'd managed to pry Mia loose.

"It's so great to finally meet you, Sis. I'm only sorry it had to be under such terrible circumstances," Pete said somberly.

Mia wiped her eyes. "Yeah, yeah, it's been a real shit-show of a week. Losing everyone you love in the space of a few days, it's—" She broke down, weeping again.

Kris felt her heart break and started to do something to comfort her, but Pete got there first.

"Listen, Mia, you're gonna be okay. You're staying with me now. I have a spare room in my house just for you," he told her, hugging her closely for a moment.

Missy frowned at him. "I don't know if that's a good idea right now, Pete. How are you going to protect her while you're at work? As long as that freaking monster is on the loose, she won't be safe there, Bud," she pointed out.

"What are you talking about? What monster?" Kris asked, startled by this news.

As briefly as possible, Missy filled them in on the recent murders, along with her theory that her psychotic nephew was responsible—that he was killing those closest to her in retaliation for the deaths of his mother and father. The only exceptions so far were the unfortunate deputy and the little girl.

"Sounds like he's upping his game," Kris said grimly. "If he's killing indiscriminately now, you could use some help catching this kid. I'd be glad to lend a hand if you'd like."

Missy smiled tightly. "Well, I think Sheriff Frank would piss on a spark plug at this point if it would help to catch the bastard. I'm sure he'd welcome any assistance. I, for one, sure would. I have a baby girl, who was already kidnapped by that psycho piece of shit. We were lucky to get her back alive," she said angrily.

Pete nodded his agreement. Just then Scraps reluctantly came out of hiding, padding over to sit at Mia's feet and sniff Pete's shoes.

"Who's your buddy?" Pete glanced down at the rangy pup, then at Mia.

"His name is Scraps. He's a stray we found on our way here. I did have a cat named Frodo who was my best friend ... until my crazy grandfather killed him," Mia said bluntly.

"Well, from what I understand of that situation, he paid dearly for it," Pete said cautiously. He knew he wasn't aware of all the details, so he stopped there when Kris gently shook her head and mouthed the word "no."

Mia didn't seem offended by his statement. "I had to get out of there, Pete ... any way I could. Both my grandfather and Max planned to murder me. The rats they kept in the basement attacked and bit me, and Max's army ants would have eaten and killed me like they actually did to him, if I hadn't managed to escape from that plexiglass *coffin* he'd trapped me in." Impassively, she finished her brief, but shocking, account.

Pete shook his head with wonder. He'd known it was bad, but this was something out of a horror flick. "I-I think you were very brave and smart to have fought back. Your parents would have been proud of you, Mia.

You survived all those horrible things—that's what's important," Pete said encouragingly.

"I hate to be a killjoy, but I need to get home to my babies and eat some cold chicken," Missy interrupted impatiently.

"You have two children?" Mia was confused.

Missy smiled. "No—only one, but my husband acts like one if I don't eat his cooking while it's hot. I'm kidding. Jake's a great guy and a wonderful father. You'll meet him soon enough."

Kris was upset by what she'd heard. "So then, I guess Mia is staying with you tonight, Pete?" She was reluctant to relinquish her charge. Damn it, she *had* gotten emotionally attached to the girl—her dog, not so much.

Pete looked to Mia for the answer. "That's up to her. But honestly, I believe she'd be safer here with you, Det. Lacey, until Sheriff Frank has caught this maniac. I don't even have a gun yet." Pointedly, he glared at Missy, who rolled her eyes.

Mia didn't know what to do. Now that the moment had finally come, she didn't feel comfortable leaving Kris. But she realized she had to choose.

"I think I'm supposed to be with you, Pete. Well, that's what *Wendy* told me, the day before yesterday," Mia said. Lacey's face fell, with disappointment.

"Who's Wendy?" Pete asked curiously.

She hesitated before speaking. "She's this ... very strange girl—the one who told me you were in danger and needed my help," Mia replied.

Pete glanced oddly at Missy. "Mia, do you know this girl's last name?" he asked.

"It's Ravenwood. At least, that's what she calls herself."

At the mention of the last name, Pete got a knowing look from Missy. W. R. must be Wendy Ravenwood. He asked Mia to describe Wendy, and she complied. *Shit!* It was the same girl, right down to her cold, glittery eyes.

"It has to be her! Mia, that girl was here in Joseph, at my house that same day. She told me it was *you* who needed *my* help. I don't get it." Pete scratched his head, bewildered.

Perplexed, Mia looked to Kris for support. As she recalled the icy voice and feathery touch of the girl's fingers on the back of her neck, her migraine vanishing instantly, Kris shivered involuntarily, before deciding to speak.

"She's also a 'person of interest' in three suspicious deaths in Taos. Three people are dead, but so far, we have no evidence to place her at either scene. She's involved in all this somehow. She's definitely not what you'd call a 'normal' teen."

"How the hell could she get from there to here so quickly? Did she, like, magically teleport here or what?" Missy asked sarcastically.

"Actually, I'm beginning to believe that's exactly what she does," Mia said. "I don't think she's quite ... human. I know that sounds insane, but she shows up out of the blue, then disappears into thin air. I never know when or where she'll pop up. Before I even met her, she arranged to have my dad bring this weird wooden totem home to me." Hearing this, Pete's face paled. "She claimed that it would keep evil away, but that's total BS. I think somehow, she and the totem are connected, maybe even one and the same."

Now, Pete was truly shaken. "She left me one of those, too. Along with a note that said basically that same thing."

Missy tried to call Jake again. It rang only once, then went silent.

"Pete, I need to go now. I can't reach Jake, and with that asshole still on the loose, I'm getting nervous. I'll drop you at your house, but we leave now. Mia, are you coming?" Missy asked.

Mia shrugged, "Yeah, I guess so."

Missy saw the inner conflict in the girl's face. She turned to Kris, "Lt. Lacey, we have a spare bedroom at the house. You're welcome to stay with Jake and me while you're here. Beats paying for this overpriced motel, hands down," she said, with a wink at Mia.

At Missy's words, Kris felt the knot in her stomach ease. "That's awfully kind of you. Are you sure I wouldn't be intruding?"

Missy shook her head. "My husband is usually very understanding—if he knows what's good for him. Check out of this fleabag and follow me. I'll drop Mia, Skippy, and Pete off first."

Mia scowled. "His name is Scraps." She hugged the dog protectively.

Missy smirked in silence. She got Mia and the pup situated in the back seat of her cruiser while Kris checked out.

Pete climbed into his usual spot in the front passenger seat. "I hope I'm making the right decision taking her back to my place right now," he told Missy quietly.

Missy scowled with frustration. "Well, there isn't another spare bed at our place. Someone would have to sleep on the fold-out couch." Slightly embarrassed, she started the cruiser. She knew Pete was concerned about Mia's safety, as well as his own. But she and Jake only had so much space to work with.

Sighing, she surrendered to Pete's unspoken plea. "Well, If Kris doesn't mind sharing a bed with Mia, you can have the couch," she said.

Pete was visibly relieved by her words. "Thanks, Missy. I owe you."

"Yeah, yeah, whatever. Time to roll," Missy grumbled. In her rearview mirror, she watched Kris emerge from the motel office and climb into her cruiser. Kris gave her a wave as she started her engine. Getting the number from Mia, Missy called Kris and received her approval about the change in plans, then sped out of the parking lot, with Kris trailing close behind.

A few minutes later they all arrived at the house. As Missy parked, leaving the headlights on, she was alarmed to see that the porch light was not on. The house was totally dark. *Shit! What's going on now?*

Chapter Fifty-Seven – The Andersons' Home

Missy called Jake's phone again, hearing only silence. A knock at her window made her jump. Seeing it was Kris, she rolled down the window.

Kris leaned down and said quietly, "I take it this is not normal. Do you expect trouble?"

Missy shook her head, "It sure as hell isn't normal, but trouble seems to find me, expected or not." She opened the car door and got out, telling Mia to stay put.

"Grab the flashlight, Pete," Missy hissed.

Pete grabbed the light and opened his door as Mia asked anxiously, "What's going on, Pete?"

He looked at her, shrugging. "Jake always leaves a light on at night. Something's not right. Do not get out of the car, Sis." When it came out a bit more sharply than he intended, Scraps growled at him again.

Pete joined Missy and Kris as they proceeded warily. Kris's flashlight joined his as they swept the beams over the front of the house. Seeing nothing amiss outside, Missy and Kris approached the entrance with service weapons drawn.

The front door was unlocked, which was also not normal. After Belinda's birth, Jake never left the house without locking it.

Missy gently pushed the door open with her gun hand, yelled, "Jake, are you in here?" No response. *Crap! Where the hell is he?*

Kris entered behind Missy with Pete following her as they moved cautiously into the darkened living room. Missy flipped the wall light switch on and off. Nothing. They checked the kitchen—no light and no one was there. Missy was becoming panicky. They entered the hallway between the bedrooms, still with no sign of Jake.

Then she heard Belinda's cry. Flinging open her bedroom door, in the flashlight's beam, she found her daughter apparently unharmed in her crib. *Thank God!* But where was Jake?

At that point, they heard a metallic *thunk* from outside the bedroom window and the diffused glow of a flashlight showed through the blinds. *Someone* was out there.

Missy yelled toward the window, "Jake, is that you?"

She heard loud cursing, then, "Yeah, Missy, it's me. The main breaker blew. Coming back in now." His voice was muted by distance.

At the sound of his voice, Missy blew a relieved sigh. She holstered her weapon and scooped Belinda up in her arms, smothering her with kisses, as Kris and Pete looked on.

Pete abruptly said, "Shit! I forgot about Mia. She's still out in the cruiser." He turned and rushed back to the front door, nearly bumping into Jake, who was walking in.

Pete zipped past him and opened the cruiser's back door. The pup sat in the back seat, but he didn't see Mia.

"Mia, where are you?" Pete called out anxiously in the surrounding dark.

"Over here. I really needed to pee and couldn't hold it any longer," came the disembodied reply.

Pete swung the flashlight toward the sound of her voice and found her as she stepped from behind a large pine about ten feet away. "You scared the crap out of me. I asked you to stay in the car. It's dangerous to be out here by yourself," he scolded, more worried than angry.

She joined him at the car. "I'm sorry. You gotta go, you gotta go," she said defensively.

She opened the car door and Scraps jumped out to join them. He sniffed the air and growled. Then, nose to the ground, he circled three times, lifted his leg, and pissed on the cruiser's tire.

"It'll be very interesting to see Jinx's reaction when he meets Scraps. Guess we'll find out soon enough," he told Mia.

"Who's Jinx?"

"He's a big-ass bobcat that Jake raised from a kitten. He's not that friendly—temperamental as hell on his best days," Pete told her as they stepped inside.

"He sounds cool. I've never seen a real bobcat." Mia was excited to see the big cat.

Pete shut and locked the front door as they entered. Missy, Jake, and Kris hovered around the kitchen table, all staring at a small object in Jake's hand.

Pete introduced Mia to Jake, who muttered, "Nice ta meecha." Jake turned to Missy. "I'm surprised the damn thing hasn't blown before now." Disgruntled, he wiped his hands on his pants.

The fuse he held looked older than dirt. It was an ancient, round, screw-in type no longer made in the twenty-first century. Until recently, Jake hadn't had the money to upgrade the electrical panel and bring it out of the stone age. And, after Belinda's birth, he hadn't even thought about it. Now they were all paying for the neglect.

"Good luck finding a replacement for that thing at the hardware store." Pete said what everyone was thinking.

Jake grimaced, "Well, I sure don't have any spares for it. Guess we're screwed for light until tomorrow," he said dejectedly.

"Excuse me, Mr. Anderson, but I think I can fix that—at least, temporarily. May I?" Mia interrupted, holding out her hand.

Jake looked at her in surprise. "First of all, it's just Jake, and second, please, be my guest. What have you got in mind, MacGyver?" he asked, handing the fuse to the girl.

Mia finally felt useful. "I'll need a small piece of foil," she said.

Jake moved to tear a small strip from a roll sitting on the countertop. Intuiting where she was heading, he said, "Ahh, isn't that a bit dangerous?"

Bridging the open circuit with the aluminum foil, Mia handed it back to him. "It is. Basically, it defeats the purpose of the fuse. But as long as there's no overload on the circuit by an appliance like a hairdryer, I think it should be fine for a short time," she said hopefully.

Jake looked from Missy to Belinda, cradled protectively in her arms. "Famous last words," he grumbled pessimistically.

"I'd wear rubber gloves if I were you. It could arc when it makes a connection," Mia added helpfully.

"Where am I going to find rubber gloves?" he asked, rapidly losing enthusiasm for her idea.

Mia thought for a second. "Well, don't you have any dishwashing gloves ... like Playtex ones, or something?" she asked.

Since Jake looked puzzled, Missy opened a drawer by the sink, pulled out a yellow rubber glove and tossed it to him.

"You wouldn't know a Playtex glove if it snuck up and bit you in the ass, Bud. Please be careful and don't fry yourself," she told him, as he forced his hand into the undersized glove.

They all followed him out to where the old-fashioned fuse box was mounted on the wall. Kris and Pete held their flashlights trained on it.

"Well, Mia, if this doesn't work, you're fired as my electrician," Jake deadpanned.

There was a small, blue flash as the plug bridged the circuit, then the power was restored. Mia's idea had worked, for the moment, anyway.

"Okay, everyone back inside. Show's over," Jake said, closing the lid on the breaker box, and they all trooped back inside.

As Jake was closing the door, a furry blur zoomed inside. Jinx skidded to an abrupt halt, close to colliding face to face with Scraps. The two stared briefly at one another before Jinx let out a loud hiss and warning growl, his fur standing up. Scraps tilted his head, looking curiously at the big cat. The bobcat and dog were about the same size. Jinx blinked first, leaping up on the top of the couch, seeking the high ground. The pup barked and crouched down, wagging his tail, ready to play. Jinx was having none of it.

Everyone sat down around the table, waiting to see what would happen next, which would dictate whether the two pets might need to be separated. Scraps barked playfully up at Jinx, while the big cat ignored the pup as if he didn't exist. Finally losing interest, Scraps trotted over to lay down at Mia's feet. He kept one eye on the cat just in case it decided to come down and play. Jinx's disdainful look said, *'Fat chance, Fido!'*

"Looks like it's a standoff, Scraps. You're lucky your face is in one piece. Most of the time, Jinx barely tolerates us, let alone dogs," Missy observed.

She popped Jake's cold chicken dish in the microwave to nuke, asking if Mia and Kris had eaten. They told her they were good.

"Sorry to eat in front of everyone, but we worked up an appetite today," she said, juggling the hot dish to the table.

Beckoning Pete over, she cut the remains of the warmed chicken dish into two servings, plopping the larger one onto a plate for him. Between bites, she and Pete brought Mia, Kris, and Jake up to date on the day's events. As soon as Missy and Pete sat down to eat, Jinx was alert to the prospect of food—but now there was an unexpected obstacle. The pup lay between him and any stray morsels—so close and yet so far.

Missy cut a piece of chicken and tossed it to Scraps, who swallowed the bite whole. He wagged his tail and went into "mooch mode." That didn't sit well with Jinx. As Missy was about to toss another small piece to Scraps, Jinx leaped from the couch with a growl, swatting the lab lightly on the nose with a paw, sans claws. Startled, Scraps yelped and scrambled away from the big cat and the food.

"Jealous, are we?" Missy said to Jinx, tossing him the last bite of chicken. Jinx snagged it out of the air and ran into their bedroom to devour at his leisure. Thankfully, only Scraps' doggy pride was hurt. Having the huge cat steal away his treat was humbling. The humans decided the show was over for the night.

"So, what's the plan for the morning?" Kris asked.

"We're going to meet with Sheriff Frank at the cave and do another grid search in daylight. Hopefully, with better results. That Griffin guy is threatening to sue everyone in sight," Missy said.

Kris nodded sympathetically. She knew Missy was in a tough position. Leaving one's post without a damn good reason could be cause for termination in her own profession. She suspected it was the same for the forest service.

Headlights swept the blinds in the living room, as a car arrived out front. "Expecting someone?" Kris asked.

Missy got up and looked out the window. "It's Frank." She opened the front door for the Sheriff before he could knock. He seemed to have aged ten years since the previous day. Greeting her morosely, he trudged inside.

Missy introduced him to Kris and Mia and explained that Kris had volunteered to help with the search for the missing girl's remains in the morning.

He told Kris, "I could sure use another pair of eyes. Someone reported seeing a suspicious looking person walking on the side of the highway earlier, not far from here. Could be this kid. I thought I'd check it out and give you a personal heads-up." he smiled sadly.

"How long ago?" Missy asked.

"About twenty minutes," Frank replied. Missy glanced at the clock on the living room wall. It was a little after nine.

"I didn't see anyone on my way here, but that doesn't mean squat." Frank's frustration was evident. "I don't see near as well at night as I used to. For all I know, he could've hidden behind a freaking tree or a bush."

Jake frowned at him. "Shouldn't you have a deputy out here with you? That crazy bastard could be out there right now, watching our house."

Frank sighed. "Jake, I don't have the manpower to spare right now—I'm short a deputy, if you'll recall. Anyway, there's not much hope of spotting the suspect in these woods at night. He might be anywhere," he replied shortly.

Remembering the deputy's mangled throat, Jake instantly regretted what he'd said. "Sorry, Frank, I wasn't thinking," he quickly apologized.

Frank grunted. "No harm done. We're all gonna be on edge until this guy is caught and behind bars. So, I suggest everyone try to get a good night's rest. You have firearms at your disposal. If you need to use them, try to do so prudently. Call my office if there's trouble. I'll use the spot on the cruiser as I leave. Doubt I'll see anything. All right, I'll see you in the morning," he said gruffly, and walked out the door.

FRANK CLIMBED INTO his cruiser and drove slowly down the graveled lane, shining his spotlight into the densely wooded forest on the off chance that he might catch the fucker hiding behind a tree or bush.

He really needed to get his damn cataracts removed. There was a halo around every light at night now. *Too old for this shit!* he thought again, as the cruiser hit a pothole, bounced on its worn shocks.

As he reached the highway, Frank was suddenly aware of a putrid odor inside the car that raised the hackles on the back of his neck. He braked hard to a stop. *Shit! Forgot to lock the cruiser when I parked at Jake and Missy's! Too old ...*

That agitated thought was his last, before a razor-sharp knife sliced across his throat, severing both his carotid arteries with a spray of blood that drenched the steering wheel and windshield with hot gore.

Frantically, he grabbed his ruined throat with one hand. reaching for his Glock with the other but was already too weakened from shock and blood loss to pull the gun. He'd made a rookie mistake leaving the cruiser unlocked—and it had cost him his life. His head was jerked sharply back as a leering face appeared in his fading peripheral vision.

Frank Blackstone's last sight was a mouth filled with razor-sharp teeth descending on his ruined throat. As life fled the Sheriff's body, the monster was humming the chorus to Queen's "Another One Bites the Dust."

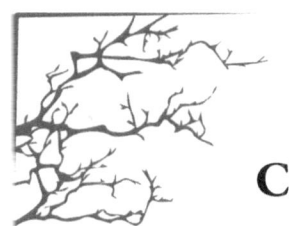

Chapter Fifty-Eight

After Frank left, a solemn group sat around the Andersons' table, eating ice cream. The kitchen and living room were of necessity open to one another in the small house, with the table easily accessible from each. A few minutes earlier, Missy had finished giving Belinda a bath and put her in her crib. She and the others were discussing the gruesome chore of locating the Griffin girl's body in the morning. Missy knew it wouldn't be pleasant if or when they found the remains.

Jake, for one, was just as happy that he'd be babysitting Belinda and would miss out on the grisly hunt.

Mia spoke to him, with a yawn. "I could watch Belinda for you tomorrow if you'd like to join the others to search for that girl's body."

He felt an instant panic at the thought of leaving his daughter with a stranger. "I appreciate the thought, Mia, but we couldn't leave you and the baby alone here with that jerk on the loose and no one to protect you. I'll be staying to make sure nothing happens to either of you," he replied.

Mia shrugged. "Just thought I'd offer."

Missy rolled her eyes. She was aware Jake wasn't the bravest bear in the woods, but she also knew he would protect Belinda with his life, after nearly losing her once to the boogeyman now hunting them.

"It's sweet of you to offer, Mia. But Jake's right, it wouldn't be safe." She smiled at the girl.

Pete readily agreed. "After all the crap you went through before we found each other, I sure don't want anything to happen to you now. Unfortunately, with that maniac loose, the timing couldn't be worse," he said.

Kris's migraine was back, reminding her that all was not well within her. She gratefully took Jake's leftover pain pill and excused herself to lie down in the spare bedroom.

"Hopefully, I'll feel better in the morning. Wake me when you get up. Mia and I appreciate the bed," she told them, leaving the table.

Mia watched Kris go with concern in her eyes. The detective had rescued her and continued to care for her far beyond the call of duty, and Mia wished she could do something meaningful for her in return. Scraps had crashed at her feet, his front legs jerking as he chased some dream squirrel in his sleep.

Everyone decided to call it a night, and Missy found spare linens to make up the couch into a bed for Pete.

Mia asked, "Is alright if Scraps sleeps on the floor by our bed?"

Missy looked at her. "If Kris doesn't mind, I don't see why not," she said.

At the same moment Jake turned off all their lights, Frank's cooling corpse was being stuffed into the trunk of his cruiser.

Chapter Fifty-Nine – The Andersons' Home

Wendy Ravenwood stood in the cold darkness, watching evil at work. She could do many things, but she could not alter destiny or the effects of free will. Mia and all those around her were now at a dangerous crossroads. The "spirit guide" had given the girl all the help she could. Mia would live or die tonight depending upon her own actions and those of others. Wendy was helpless to do more than observe.

The malevolent human had slammed the lid of the trunk containing Frank's corpse, when he suddenly stopped, snapping his head in her direction.

Wendy stood silently in the dark. *Impossible*! There was no way he could detect her presence in the pitch black of night.

He sniffed the air sharply and sang out insanely, "Fee-fi-fo-fum, I smell the blood of some ancient scum. You're not alive, but you're not dead. Whatever you are, I'll cut off your head," he cackled.

Pulling his bloody hunting knife from a scabbard on his hip, he charged straight toward Wendy. She easily evaded his attack. He might have been able to smell her peculiar scent, but his eyesight was human. He slashed empty air where she had stood an instant before. She'd *thought* herself twenty feet away—and she was there.

"Where are you, bitch? I know you're out here; I can still smell you. Come out, come out, whatever you are. You can run, but you can't hide," he hissed, shredding only the empty dark.

She saw no advantage in responding to his madness. Instead, she moved at once into the darkened house where Mia was, with the others.

Mia slept fitfully on the unfamiliar bed next to Kris, who lay beside her with a pillow over her eyes, snoring softly. Waking with a gasp, Mia glanced at the digital clock on the bedside table: 10:30 p.m. *Crap!* She'd only been asleep for about an hour.

A terrible dream had awoken her. She tried vainly to grasp what it had been about before it faded away completely. All she remembered was someone screaming, "*Run, run, run!*"

She'd gone to bed fully clothed. Now her shirt was soaked with dream-sweat, but her mouth was dry. She climbed out of bed quietly, careful not to wake Scraps. The bedroom nightlight Missy had plugged in made it easy to see her surroundings. She opened the bedroom door and walked silently toward the kitchen for a glass of water. She passed the couch where Pete lay snoring slightly, turned into the kitchen, and reached for the light switch. Flipping it on, she let out a small, shocked squeal.

Wendy sat at the kitchen table, fixing her cold, glittery eyes on Mia.

Mia's scream jolted Pete from his sleep. Alarmed, he jumped up from the couch, gawking with disbelief at the girl/creature sitting calmly at the table. Missy and Jake had heard the commotion and rushed into the living room, coming to an abrupt halt at the sight of the strange girl suddenly in their midst.

"Who are you? What the hell are you doing in my house? And how the fuck did you get in?" Jake asked angrily.

His loud, irate voice even roused Kris from the other bedroom. Both she and Missy arrived with pistols in hand, staring at the girl as if she were an apparition.

Wendy smiled coldly. "You won't be needing those. At least, not for me," she said, in her husky voice. "I have come to say goodbye." She stared directly at Mia.

Mia was confused and angry. "Goodbye? Why are you even here? You've caused me nothing but pain and misery since I met you. Because of you, everyone I ever loved or cared for is dead," she spat out vehemently, on the verge of tears.

Wendy gazed coolly back at her, silent for a moment. "I'm sorry you feel that way. I came to tell you that the first portion of your destiny has been accomplished. I can help you no more at this time. Peace be upon you, Mia Chandler." She stood slowly.

She turned to address the others. "I'm here to warn you, a monster stalks all of you tonight. Your friend, Frank, is already dead."

Missy gasped, turning pale. "Oh, my God—not Frank, too! What the hell happened?"

"He was killed by the evil one who is coming for the rest of you. Very soon, now. You must defeat him, or he will kill you," Wendy said, dispassionately.

Missy stared at her. "So, you've come to warn us, but now you're leaving Mia at this crucial moment? I thought you were here to protect her. What kind of cruel creature are you? You're definitely not human." She was grief-stricken at the news of Frank's sudden demise.

Wendy's eyes glistened with dark tears. "I am what I am. Do not judge what you cannot understand, Missy Anderson. I was sent to guide Mia to this place, this moment in time, alive. I can no longer intercede on her behalf. Heed my words—if Mia perishes tonight, so will you all." She gazed directly at each of them, solemnly. "We will meet again, Mia Chandler—providing you survive this night."

The kitchen light went out then, along with the rest of the house's illumination. "He's here!" Wendy's voice hissed softly from the dark.

Frightened by her words, Jake farted loudly.

"Eeww—something crawls up your ass and die, Bud?" Missy asked disgustedly.

"It wasn't me. It was Jinx," he replied, farting again.

"We need some freaking light," Pete said needlessly.

Kris pulled the flashlight from her utility belt and turned it on, shining it around the room. In its glare, four anxious faces squinted back at her—the Ravenwood girl's was not among them. She had vanished. *Shit!* Where had she gone?

The piercing sound of shattering glass shook them all. Kris focused her flashlight on the object that had come hurtling through the living room window.

Frank's severed head lay on the floor in front of them. His dead eyes stared up at them, a rictus of surprised horror frozen on his gore-covered face. Mia screamed, as a demented cackle came from outside the broken window.

"Mama always told me someday I'd get 'a head' in life. Guess she was right. Your dead fucking friend seems to have lost his." The mad voice jeered from the dark.

Missy was shaking with rage, her lizard brain in survival mode. She was resolved to destroy this insane creature that her psychotic sister had brought into the world, on behalf of all his victims—her mother, Ben, Frank and his slain deputy, and the innocent girl in the park—but most of all, for herself.

Until this moment, she'd been unaware of the amount of hatred bottled up inside her. Before anyone else could react, she grabbed Kris's flashlight and raced to the broken window. Shining the beam out, she saw quick movement, raised her pistol, and hastily fired three shots.

The sound was deafening in the enclosed room, shocking everyone. From her crib in the bedroom, the baby howled.

"Jake, please go and check on Belinda." Missy's voice was louder than normal because of the ringing in her ears.

Kris joined her at the window. "Did you hit him?" she asked. Her head pounded with every rapid beat of her heart.

"Not sure. I didn't have much time to line up my shots. It was pretty much just blurred motion." Missy headed for the front door.

Feeling his way in the dark, Jake found the spare flashlight they kept in a kitchen drawer. He switched it on, ran to the bedroom, and plucked Belinda up to comfort her. He looked around the room—where the hell was Jinx?

Frowning, he gently placed his daughter back down in her crib and rushed back to the living room as Missy was opening the front.

"Missy, is Jinx in here? He's not in the bedroom, and I don't remember letting him in before going to bed," he asked anxiously.

"Nope, I think he's probably still outsi—" She froze, as she thought, *the blur of movement.* She suddenly felt ill. *Oh, no, please, not Jinx!* Frantically, she swung the door open, sweeping the tree-lined yard with the light. No sign of their attacker or the big cat.

Kris joined her, and they cautiously walked out, scouring the pine needles on the ground for a blood trail. "There." Kris pointed, spotting a few drops on the pine straw.

Unfortunately, they had no way of knowing if the blood was human or not. Looking around, they found some larger drops a few feet away heading in the general direction of Jake's truck. As they got closer, they saw dark smears on the wheel-well leading up into the bed of the truck.

Missy focused the light inside the bed. *Crap!*

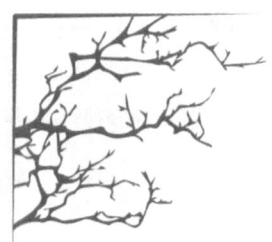

Chapter Sixty

A large raccoon lay in a growing pool of blood. The bullet had pierced its side. It didn't move as the light passed over its body.

"I-I thought it might be Jinx. Thank God, it wasn't." Relief flooded through Missy, although she felt bad for killing the animal.

"How could you mistake a raccoon for a human?" Kris questioned, as they lowered their weapons.

"I kinda lost it when I saw movement and fired without seeing a clear target. I wanted so badly to put an end to this insanity, I just didn't think before pulling the damn trigger." Missy was upset at having lost her self-control.

"We all have to make snap decisions sometimes. Good for Jinx, bad for the raccoon." Kris patted Missy's back, rubbing her throbbing temples with her other hand. Her migraine had returned with a vengeance; the loud gunfire hadn't helped.

"We'd better get back in, that asshole is likely still out here," Missy said, urgently.

"We just going to leave that there?" Kris pointed at the dead animal.

Missy shook her head as she started toward the house. "It's not going anywhere. We need to get back insi—Kris?" She stopped and turned back as she saw that Kris was not right behind her. She'd disappeared. Quickly, Missy flashed the beam of light around, finally spotting her—sprawled face-first in the pine straw, writhing on the ground as if an electric current pulsed through her. *Oh, my God!*

Missy yelled over her shoulder, "Pete, get out here fast! Something's wrong with Kris." She rushed over to kneel by the detective.

Pete ran out with a can of Bear-B-Gone in one hand and Jake's crappy flashlight in the other. Together, they carefully turned Kris over.

Trickles of blood dripped from both her nostrils. *Could have happened when she fell,* Missy thought nervously. But Kris was also breathing oddly.

"What the hell happened?" Pete asked, shining the light around anxiously, as Missy wiped the blood from Kris's nose.

"We'd found a damn raccoon that I'd shot, and we were heading back to the house. She was right behind me, then she wasn't, and finally, I found her like this. I think she's having some sort of seizure." Missy grew more alarmed, as Kris began foaming at the mouth. *Holy crap!* "What are you supposed to do for someone who's having a seizure?" she asked Pete, upset by her own lack of medical knowledge.

"I dunno, maybe you're supposed to turn 'em on their side in case they puke or something," he suggested.

"Isn't that what you do for someone that's drunk?" She was skeptical.

"I can't remember for sure, maybe try to keep 'em from biting their tongue, if you can," he added, hoping that was right.

Kris' gut-wrenching spasms gradually subsided, while they kept a watchful eye on her. Finally, she came to and looked up at them, bewildered.

"W-what the hell? What am I doing on the ground?" She wiped foamy spittle from her mouth.

Missy said hesitantly, "I ... we think you had a seizure, Kris. What do you remember?"

With their help, Kris cautiously sat up, then got shakily to her feet. "We were talking about the raccoon and my head was pounding and ... that's it."

Pete and Missy supported her as they walked back inside the house. Jake had a fire going in the potbelly stove that sat in the middle of the room. It provided a little warmth but no light. He'd found an old-fashioned kerosene lantern, lit it, and set it on the kitchen table.

"Did you hit the bastard? What happened to Kris? Did you see Jinx?" Jake rambled nervously.

"No; we think she had a seizure; and no, I didn't see Jinx." She answered all his questions.

Mia ran over to Kris to throw her arms around her, hugging her tightly. Kris smiled weakly, hugged her back, then sat on the couch while Missy got her some water.

"This ever happen before, Kris?" Missy asked, handing her a glass.

Kris shook her head, sipping the water. "I've been having bad migraines for quite some time, but at least, now, I know why. A doctor in Boulder ran some tests. I-I have a brain tumor," she said quietly.

Mia's heart went out to her. "Can they do anything for it?" she asked.

Kris gave her a tight smile "I'm not sure. I'll need to see a specialist when I get back to Taos." The seizure had left her weak and drained.

Mia didn't know what else to do, so she hugged her again. Meanwhile, Missy grabbed a towel from the bathroom to lay over Frank's grisly head.

A loud *currumph* outside caused everyone to rush toward the broken window. Flickering flames were reflected in the glass remaining in the window frame. Moving closer, Missy realized that her bus was on fire.

Shit! She raced into the kitchen to grab the fire extinguisher off the wall.

"Wait, Missy, it's probably a trap—he's just trying to draw you out. Let it go!" Jake warned.

Missy whirled around to face him. "He's not going to get away with this, Jake. The gloves are fucking off," she snapped.

Gently, Kris pushed Mia away from her and stood, slightly unsteadily. "I'll cover you, Missy, let's go kick his ass." She started toward the door.

Jake felt like he was about to throw up. "Damn it, Missy, don't go out there! He's not worth your life." He pleaded with her.

"What about all the lives he's already taken? I won't let him take another, Jake. It's me he blames for the deaths of his parents. It's me he really wants!"

She turned to Kris and nodded. Kris opened the door, and together, they ran out to the burning car.

FROM THE COVER OF TREES, he stood watching and waiting after lighting the fire. The emergency gas can in the cop's trunk had been a stroke of luck. He'd planned something a little more elaborate. But hey—when opportunity knocked ...

Sure enough, the stupid bitch went for it. He saw the front door open. She rushed out with a fire extinguisher in one hand, gun in the other, while the other woman who looked like a cop followed with a flashlight and pistol.

He grinned, quietly running around to the back of the house in the deep darkness. The peyote button he'd taken an hour ago had dilated his pupils, allowing him to see in the dark like an owl. Still, in his haste, he tripped, falling over a large tree stump with a long-handled ax embedded in it—perfect! Providence abounds tonight, *he thought, as he gripped the handle, jerking the blade free.* Ready or not, here I come!

JAKE WAS TORN BETWEEN charging out the door behind the women and staying put. He wasn't a coward, but he was not a fool, either. He knew Missy could handle herself, and he was sure the detective could, too. He had one job—to protect Belinda from danger.

Nervously, Mia joined Pete at the broken window, watching Missy frantically spray the burning bus with fluid from the extinguisher. Kris held the light, her gun at the ready. The small canister soon sputtered and quit, having barely made a dent in the flames. Missy stood there watching, helpless, as her vintage bus was consumed by the raging blaze. Sobbing with rage and frustration, she hurled the empty canister at the bus, screaming obscenities into the surrounding forest.

Kris holstered her gun to grab Missy, pulling her away from the burning bus. "Forget it, he's long gone. Now, run like hell, the tank's gonna blow!" she yelled, shoving Missy roughly toward the house.

They hadn't taken five steps when the gas tank blew. Flaming debris flew in all directions. The shock wave knocked them both off their feet, rolling them like ragdolls. Kris felt one of her ribs suddenly snap when she hit the ground. She groaned, smelling burning hair. Dimly, she realized it was hers and swatted frantically around her head.

Missy lay a few feet away, stunned, but otherwise unhurt. Seeing the explosion, Pete and Mia rushed out. He grabbed Kris under the arms to drag her farther from the burning wreckage, while Mia helped Missy to her feet.

Jake had been right. The crazy asshole had lured her away from the house. *But why?* Missy wondered, as they all got Kris upright again.

"Where's Jake?" Missy asked Pete urgently.

"He's still inside with Belinda."

As they approached the front door, a piercing scream came from inside. Missy's blood turned to ice. Drawing her weapon, she raced back inside.

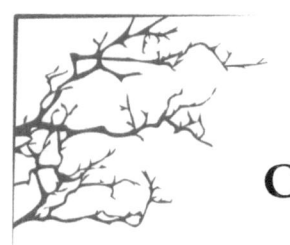

Chapter Sixty-One

As Pete and Mia ran out the front door to help Missy and Kris, Jake heard a loud noise at the back. He swiveled, shocked, as the back door exploded inward in a spray of splinters. A boy with a hideously disfigured face stood in the doorway, brandishing Jake's ax, smiling horribly, to reveal wickedly sharp teeth.

"You must be Uncle Jake, the writer. Nothing personal, but your writing sucks," he snarled. Raising the ax, he charged at Jake.

With almost no time to react, Jake grabbed Pete's can of Bear-B-Gone from the kitchen table. Backing away from the boy, he tripped over the cowering Scraps and fell—just as the demonic teen swung the ax, missing his head by less than an inch. The ax swept through empty air, its blade embedding deep in the kitchen wall with a loud *thunk*.

Jake's head struck the floor hard, and he lost his grip on the bear spray, which rolled out of reach under the kitchen table. The murderous teen growled with frustration, yanking hard to extract the ax from the wall, but it had struck a stud and buried itself in the wood.

By the time the lad finally freed the blade and turned toward him for a fatal strike, Jake had managed to reach and grab the bear spray. Depressing the button on the can, he released a potent stream of bear repellent straight into the monstrous boy's mouth and eyes. He shrieked in pain, retched, and dropped the ax. Partially blinded, he turned and stumbled out the back door into the dark, cursing Jake.

Seconds after he'd escaped, Missy charged into the living room with her gun drawn. Her eyes sweeping the room, she saw Jake lying on the floor and smelled the bear spray's pungent odor. Spotting the ax on the floor at his feet and the broken back door, she immediately thought the worst. 'Jake, Jake! Are you alright?"

He didn't answer her. Standing up, he rushed to close the back door and realized both its lock and the door frame had been shredded.

"He almost cut my freaking head off with my own ax—so, no, I'm assuredly not alright," he finally asserted testily, pushing at the damaged door.

"Jake—where's Belinda?" she asked anxiously.

"She's safe, still in the bedroom," he said, slightly chagrined that she didn't entirely trust him to keep their daughter out of danger.

She grabbed the flashlight from Kris, who'd followed her slowly in, ran to the bedroom, and shined the light at the crib. There lay Jinx, curled at the foot of her daughter's crib, both of them asleep.

"Where have you been hiding?" Missy asked the big cat, relief flooding her, finding that both were safe. Jinx glanced sleepily up at her, yawned, and curled back up. She hurried back to the kitchen, and Jake.

"I got the bastard in the face with the spray, so he may not be able to see. That shit is pretty strong," Jake said. Tears from the residual fumes ran down his cheeks. "Sorry about your bus, hon, but I did warn you it was a trap. Nothing but a diversion so he could attack from the rear. That kid is seriously fucked-up. His head and face and those teeth ... truly monstrous. If I hadn't tripped over Scabs and fallen, I would not be talking to you now."

"It's *Scraps,* not Scabs," Mia continued to correct, joining them.

Missy frowned. "We're not safe here. That back door won't lock, and I'm sure as shit not about to chase him in the dark. We need another place to stay for the night." She looked at Pete.

Pete got her meaning. "Uh, sure, we can all go to my place if you want," he said hesitantly, remembering the creepy wood sprite still locked inside his garbage can.

Kris shook her head at them. "We need—notify Sheriff's office—'bout Frank, first. Maybe state—troopers, too. Won't be able—find little asshole—on our own. Too—dangerous in—dark," she gasped out, her busted rib causing sharp pain with every breath.

"Are you hurt bad, Kris?" Mia knew it was a stupid question.

"Cracked—rib when I hit—the ground. Nothing—can do for it. I've—had worse," she grimaced.

Mia wanted to hug her but saw it would only make her pain worse. Jake offered her one of his pain pills, but Kris refused, wanting to keep a clear head.

"Jake, get Belinda. We're getting out of here, now," Missy declared.

"What about Jinx—is he coming, too?" Mia asked, grabbing up Scraps.

"Jinx can fend for himself. Jake will just put him out before we leave. He'll be safe enough, probably climb a tree and hide," Missy assured her.

Jake came out with the baby wrapped in a small coat that almost swallowed her. Handing her to Missy, he shooed Jinx out of the bedroom. The big wuss reluctantly left the safety of that room and ran into the kitchen, where he stood expectantly over his food bowl.

"Sorry, bud, can't feed you now. Go out and catch a small moose, if you're hungry," Missy told the bobcat, holding the back door open enough for him to slip through. Jinx gave her a nasty look as he zipped out. She pushed the door closed, wedging it shut.

When Pete opened the front door and stepped warily out, a gunshot rang out from the dark. A searing pain in his stomach halted him where he stood. He looked down to see a small dark hole in his coat. *Shit!* He realized he'd been shot. Clutching his stomach with a groan, he yelled, "Get back inside, go, go, go! He's got a fucking gun. Oh, God, that hurts," he moaned. He collapsed on the porch.

Missy knew instantly what had happened. Hurriedly, she placed Belinda in the crib near the kitchen table and ran out to help Jake pull Pete back inside the house. They slammed the front door just as the *thunk* of another bullet hit it and went through, barely missing Jake's left ear.

"Everybody, keep the fuck away from the windows," Jake shouted. They laid Pete down on the couch to get him as comfortable as possible.

"One down, four to go, Auntie. Bet that bullet hurts something awful," they heard from outside. "Oh, yeah, I owe you for the face-full of mace, you writer prick. Your buddy there's gonna die slow and painful. Or will he? Hard to tell. Toss of the old coin, I'd say," the boy coldly mocked.

Mia gasped, terrified by the amount of blood seeping out between Pete's clutching fingers. "Oh, no, no, no, Pete! Please ... oh God, not again. Somebody, help him. Hang on, Pete! I can't lose you, Brother, you're all the family I have left!" She sobbed fearfully.

She reached out a trembling hand to grasp his free one in hers, feeling something akin to an electric shock run down her arm. Pete jerked and spasmed as if he'd touched a live wire. An alien voice in Mia's head whispered, *Do it, now!*

Reaching over, she pulled up his blood-soaked shirt, shoving his hand away from the bullet hole. Somehow, she knew what to do. Before anyone around her could react, she covered the leaking wound with her other palm. she felt a sudden surge of energy coursing through the tendons and ligaments of her arm into her hand. She was awed by the fact that it was emanating from within her.

Pete looked down, incredulous, as steam hissed from the small space between her palm and the injury. Torn capillaries, damaged organs alike, all were healing at a highly accelerated rate. The lead slug itself was pushed up and out of the wound, rejected like some offending growth. The skin around the ragged edges of the entry wound began to miraculously mend and close.

The whole experience was surreal, like a horror movie playing in reverse. The acute pain in Pete's abdomen was dissipating. "H-holy Houdini, what did you just do, Sis?" Pete gasped, astonished.

"I—I don't know. I wanted you to live so badly ... I-I wished you healed with all my soul," Mia stuttered, equally stunned by the sight of his regenerating tissue.

Pete and the others watched in mesmerized astonishment as the wound completely sealed itself. The expelled bullet lay atop shiny, pink skin where a bloody wound had been only moments before. They stared at Mia as if she were from another planet.

"The pain—it's gone. God, I'm so thankful to be alive!" Pete hugged her gratefully.

Mia felt as though an alien entity had temporarily taken possession of her body. Whatever it was, it remained within her. She felt its power coiled as tightly as an overwound spring inside her, as if she contained a giant capacitor waiting to discharge.

"She must be—physical empath," Kris gasped out. "I've heard—people can heal—by touch. Never believed—until now." Kris shook her head.

Jake stared at Mia, bewildered. "That's definitely some strange shit! Good work, Mia. Uh, not to change the subject, but this would be a good time to call in the cavalry," he added anxiously.

Missy looked wearily at him, nodding. "We should have called them the minute that asshole threw Frank's head through the window instead of trying to catch him ourselves. Sorry," she said, apologetically. "You call them, Kris. You're a fellow cop. Tell them Frank's dead and to hurry the fu—oh, *shit*! Sorry, I forgot about your ribs. I'll call them." She walked into the hall, dialing 911.

Mia looked over at Kris, holding her gaze. "Please, Kris, I think I can help you," she said, eyes pleading.

Kris nodded and pulled up her uniform shirt, moaning as she moved. Gently, Mia placed her hands over her bruised ribcage. Kris' body went rigid, as waves of healing energy flowed from Mia's palms to the site of the injured rib. The pain rapidly abated—along with her migraine. As Mia focused her mind, she could sense some of the stored energy within drain from her and flow into Kris.

Kris shook her head, "That... that is amazing. The pain is gone. Thank you, sweetheart," she said, gratefully taking her first pain-free breath since the incident.

"You're welcome," Mia replied shyly, as Kris hugged the girl tightly to her.

Missy finished her call. "They're on the way. State troopers as well, but they said it may be a while. Most of the deputies and the only trooper in the area are working a three-car accident out on the highway. Until they can get here, we're still on our own," Missy told them.

Jake didn't like hearing that. "In the meantime, we're sitting ducks for that maniac out there. We can't just wait around until he decides to—" He sniffed the air. Smoke!

He went over to check the wood stove, but the fire inside it had been banked earlier, was nothing but a pile of glowing embers. It wasn't the source of the smoke. *Shit!* This was bad. Suddenly, a crackling sound came from the bedroom area, as bright yellow tongues of fire blossomed from their bedroom like a brilliant, poisonous flower.

Jake and Missy ran toward it, then halted. The crazy fucker had set fire to their home, and Missy had used the only fire extinguisher they'd had. No choice left but to run. "Everyone out of the house, run, run, run!" Jake yelled, pushing Missy toward the living room.

Mia felt déjà vu—those were the exact words spoken in her nightmare. Shivering with terror and a sense of foreboding, she turned to run outside with the others.

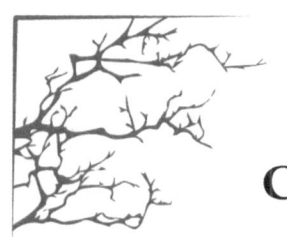

Chapter Sixty-Two

The bear spray had distorted his night vision, burning like nothing he'd ever felt. He'd make the fucker pay—make them all pay! He grabbed the gas can and stumbled his way in the dark to the back bedroom.

"Hi-Diddly-Dee, a pyro's life for me," he sang wildly, cavorted madly around, splashing gas on the window and surrounding frame. Then he pulled out a lighter and lit the gas. With a giant whoosh, *the flames spread quickly up the side of the house. He ran around to the front porch, liberally dousing the door.*

"You're gonna burn, you fuckin' witch. Payback is a bitch," he snarled, flicking his lighter. The gas caught instantly, and the flames leaped greedily up the door.

"How do ya like them apples, Auntie? Doesn't that just cook your fucking oats? Gonna turn you into a crispy critter—like you did to my folks," he cackled insanely, dancing away from the spreading flames.

JAKE REACHED FOR THE front door handle, cursed, and quickly yanked his hand away from the red-hot metal. The sorry bastard had also torched the porch. Smoke poured through cracks between the door and frame. The paint on the walls was starting to blister from the heat.

"Come on, out the back door, it's our only chance!" Jake led the group to the kitchen, coughing. As he jerked the damaged door open, Missy scooped up Belinda from her crib and hurried after Kris, who had her pistol at the ready, sweeping the yard with her flashlight.

Seeing no immediate threat, Kris shouted, "It's clear, haul ass, people!"

Mia ran out, calling Scraps. The little lab needed no encouragement, dashing through the open doorway with Pete right behind. Jake came last, was barely outside when a part of the kitchen ceiling collapsed in a shower of sparks and flaming debris.

"Fucking—asshole—almost got us," Jake yelled. He was coughing hard from the smoke.

Kris swept the flashlight's beam through the smoke-filled air for any sign of the crazy teen, as they all moved farther away from the intense heat.

The Andersons watched, stunned, as their home was consumed by the ever-hungry flames. Thankfully, they'd put Jinx out before it started. The big cat watched the inferno unfold from the relative safety of the forest's edge behind them.

"Get to my cruiser," Kris told Missy. "If he's there waiting for us, shoot to kill. Don't hesitate."

Missy nodded, giving Belinda to Jake, and they followed Kris to her cruiser. The car chirped as she unlocked the doors with her key.

"Hurry up and get inside. Missy, you've got shotgun," Kris commanded. She searched the smoke-filled air for any sign of the boy, while the rest clambered inside. Scraps leaped in, landing in Mia's lap.

Kris slid in and locked all the doors. She'd expected the violent teen to try and stop them from leaving. When he didn't appear, she grew more apprehensive. She keyed the ignition, but nothing happened. *Shit!* About what she'd expected. The sonofabitch had sabotaged the cruiser.

"Okay, folks, we've got a big problem. He's done something to the engine. Now is the time for plan B, if anyone has one," Kris announced. She slammed her palm against the steering wheel with frustration.

The fire had completely engulfed the house. If it hadn't been for their fire break and a lack of wind, the surrounding forest might have caught and a conflagration from hell unleashed.

"We could try my cruiser, but if the piece of shit tampered with yours, you can bet he jacked with it, too." Missy ground her teeth.

Suddenly, something heavy landed on the cruiser's hood with a *thump*. Missy swung the light up, illuminating a horribly deformed face leering at them through the windshield. He held Frank's pistol. His wickedly sharp teeth gleamed in a triumphant sneer as he aimed the Glock at Kris.

Both women brought their weapons up to fire through the windshield, but before either could pull the trigger, a shadowy figure slammed into the boy, knocking him off the cruiser.

The teen let out a howl of pain as twenty-five pounds of snarling bobcat sank teeth and claws into his neck and shoulders, knocking him off the cruiser's hood and making him lose his grip on the gun.

"It's Jinx! He pounced on him from behind!" Missy exclaimed, as she and Kris jumped out of the car.

The monstrous teen lay screaming on the ground, as Jinx ripped off part of his left ear, racing away with his bloody trophy.

"Freeze, asshole! Move a muscle and you die!" Kris hollered.

The deranged teen snarled back, "Fuck you, bitch cop!" Faster than a striking cobra, he leaped to his feet and seized Missy, knocking her gun away. Before Kris could pull the trigger, a wicked-looking hunting knife with a six-inch serrated blade appeared in his right hand. He whipped his other arm tightly around Missy's neck, dragging her in front of him as a shield.

"Go ahead and shoot, Colombo," he sneered at Kris. "She's dead meat, either way. Say goodbye to all of this, Auntie—and welcome to hell!" he roared, plunging his knife deep into Missy's side and twisting the blade.

Missy shrieked in agony. Inside the car, Jake and the rest watched, immobilized by shock. Kris knew she'd waited a second too long to fire. Now Missy was suffering because of her hesitation. She waited no longer.

Carefully, she aimed and fired, hitting the horrid boy twice in the head, blowing his brains out the back of his skull, killing him instantly. He dropped like a bag of stones, pulling Missy down beside him, bleeding profusely. He twitched once, then was still.

"No, no, no! God—please—no!" Jake screamed frantically, passing Belinda to Pete. He jumped out of the car and ran to Missy's side.

Mia put Scraps down on the car seat and rushed over to stand beside Jake and Kris. Pete was frustrated, wanting desperately to help Missy but knowing he must protect Belinda, he remained in the car.

Distraught, Jake knelt and pulled Missy gently into his trembling arms. "Missy, stay with me, Hon. I love you—you're gonna be okay. Look at me,

Hon, we'll get you to the hospital! Just hang on, you hear me?" he cried, hot tears rolling down his face to pool on her paler one.

Missy looked up at him, struggling to focus on his face, and coughed up small spatters of blood. "T-trying t-to—h-hurts—f-fucking b-b-bad—t-tell K-Kris—n-not—her f-fault," Missy gasped, coughing up more blood. With every beat of her heart, she grew weaker.

Tears of guilt and remorse gathered in Kris' eyes as she watched.

Missy murmured, "L-love y-you, B-Bud ... s-so c-cold—t-take c-care—B-Belinda," Then she lost consciousness.

"Don't you fucking die on me!" Jake commanded, feeling his heart was breaking. Desperately, he looked at Mia, "Please, can you help her? Please, oh God ... I'm losing her!" he begged.

"I-I can try," Mia replied, nervously. Feeling less certain this time, she knelt beside Missy's shivering body.

Pulling up her bloody shirt, Mia placed her palms over the wide, ugly wound. Missy's eyes flew open wide, her body jerking involuntarily. They both gasped as the mysterious energy bolted through Mia's arms into Missy's body.

"Holy shit!" Jake exclaimed.

"You may be right about that," Kris said reverently.

Shaking with adrenaline, Jake managed to hold Missy securely in his lap, feeling the hair on his arms stand at attention. Everyone stared, awestruck once more, as steam rose from the brutal puncture on Missy's side. She groaned, writhing in Jake's arms, as Mia fought to keep her hands linked to the injury.

Kris knelt to help Jake keep Missy from thrashing around. Her damaged tissue was again mending at an astonishing pace and the wound closed itself, as Jake and Kris watched, once more amazed at the phenomenon.

Despite the healing process, Mia felt something was still wrong. Missy's breathing had slowed, but she had not fully regained consciousness. Jake still clasped her in his arms.

"I-I don't know if she's completely healed ... you know, *inside*. She might have more damage than this ... whatever it is ... could fix. I have no way of knowing, since I don't even understand how or why this works," Mia told Jake. The intense energy within now felt thoroughly depleted.

They heard the distant wail of sirens. "Looks like help is on the way," Kris said, smiling. "We still need to get her to a hospital. Hopefully, EMS is with them. Too late for him." She glanced coldly down at the dead teen's body.

The sirens drew closer, they watched the flashing lights of multiple vehicles turning into the gravel drive. Pete climbed wearily out of the cruiser with Belinda cradled in his arms, still sound asleep. Three sheriff's deputies, a state trooper, and an ambulance all screeched to a stop in the circular drive.

The burning house had begun to collapse. Firelight and flashing lights danced across five drawn, sooty faces, making them all appear refugees from a war zone.

Warily, the troopers exited their vehicles with guns drawn as they approached the little group huddled around the two bodies on the ground.

EPILOGUE - Six Months Later, The Andersons' Home

Missy had a hell of a time opening the front door on the ancient, twenty-by-eight-foot-wide trailer. The old door handle was barely functional, not even a blast of WD-40 had helped. The small trailer was parked close to the slab of a new foundation where their old house had stood.

They were renting the timeworn trailer until the new house was built. It was small and cramped and smelled like wet cat much of the time, but it was a roof over their heads. The insurance company had finally agreed on a settlement that would fully fund the rebuilding.

Crap on a cracker! she thought, sighing deeply. Jake had promised to repair that handle more than a week earlier. Cursing, Missy yanked hard, and the door finally yielded, opening squeakily. With her armful of groceries, she clambered up three wooden steps and stepped inside to find Jake sitting at a small fold-out table in the combined kitchen/living area, tapping away on his new laptop.

Their lives and her job as a Ranger were again secure, after Kris had shot the killer and the Griffin girl's parents had dropped their lawsuit against the State Park.

"We've got an invite to dinner tonight at six, Jake. That gives us about fifteen minutes. Pete's going to barbecue pieces of some poor animal. I didn't ask what kind—don't want to know," she said, dropping the bag of groceries on the tiny table.

Jake looked up from his typing. "When are Kris and Mia due back from Boulder? I thought they'd be back yesterday," he asked, standing and bumping his head for the umpteenth time on the trailer's low ceiling.

Missy shook her head uncertainly. "Mia called and said there was more paperwork to sign. But it's official now—Mia is Kris's adopted daughter."

Jake stretched and yawned. "It all seems to have worked out well, with Kris opting to take Frank's job when they offered it," he said.

"At least until a new election, though I doubt they'll find any replacement with her qualifications. She's taking a huge cut in pay, but I think she'll be happier here," Missy was stuffing groceries into the trailer's tiny cabinets. The small, aching scar on her side reminded her frequently how close to death she'd come.

SHE'D BEEN RUSHED TO the hospital that terrible night, regaining consciousness in the ambulance, confused as to what had occurred. The EMT guys were baffled, as well. Her shirt was covered in blood, with an obvious slit in the material where the knife entered. But they could locate no wound or scar, only some dried blood. Finally guessing what had actually happened, she'd implied that the blood must have come from her dead nephew. The hospital doctor was likewise puzzled, but finding no damage, he'd released her. None of them could ever tell the truth—they'd have been locked away in a rubber room.

Jake and the others had followed the ambulance to the ER in town in his old truck. When she was released, Missy had squeezed into the overcrowded truck, and they'd driven to Pete's house to regroup.

The Sheriff's deputies had been shocked to find Frank's headless corpse stuffed in the trunk of his cruiser. During the investigation, they found that Tory Morning Star had been arrested several times for lesser crimes in the past. He'd been born with *Lionitis*, a horrific disease that caused extreme cranial enlargement and produced a gruesome physical appearance.

To spare him ridicule from cruel kids and some adults, his adopted tribal mother had isolated the two of them. No man in the tribe had been willing to father such a repugnant-looking child, but she'd tried to be a good mother until Tory reached puberty. His rare, cruel encounters with others transmuted him into a twisted loner.

Around the age of twelve, he'd killed his first animal and drunk its blood. Many more followed. At fifteen, he'd filed his teeth into razor sharp points, in order to better rip out the throats of his victims.

His mother had contrived not to notice his blood-stained mouth and hands after he'd been out late at night—afraid to discover what he had done.

When she quietly followed him one night, she had finally caught him in the act and seen the obscenity he performed on a stray cat, confirming her worst fears. With a quiet scream, she'd run. She never followed him anywhere or asked what he was doing again. Eventually, she recognized that his extreme mental illness made Tory far more dangerous than his disfiguring physical disease.

When Tory was thirteen, she'd finally told him about his real parents and how they had died—and that he had an aunt whom he'd never met. That night, he had sworn that one day he would find all those involved in his parents' deaths and make them pay—especially Missy Morning Star-Anderson.

I REALIZED HE HAD TO blame someone, and I guess I was it, Missy thought back now, sadly. If he had inherited her sister's genes ... well, dwelling on that now was useless. She went to the crib and picked up her daughter, hugging her to her chest. Belinda's powder blue eyes grinned up at her as she cooed, "Mama," drooling on Missy's arm.

Jake smiled. "She's getting big, isn't she?" He pocketed his phone. Hearing familiar scratching at the front door, he opened it and Jinx bolted inside. The bobcat stopped under the fold-out table to stare at his empty food bowl, giving them a look that said, *'feed me, or I'll crap on your pillow!'*

Missy rolled her eyes at him. "Sorry, bud, you'll have to wait 'til we get back. We'll bring you some of Pete's barbecued 'beast' when we return," she said, turning to leave. Then she stopped and went back to pull the ratty accordion door closed, just in case.

"No need to tempt him," she muttered to Jake, as they walked out of the trailer.

They arrived at Pete's place to find him outside standing by the barbecue pit, enveloped in a cloud of pungent smoke. They strolled over to where he was coughing and waving madly at the smoking pit.

"The hell kind of wood are you using there, Pete?" she asked, not getting too close, for Belinda's sake.

Pete shut the lid on the smoker, burning his fingers slightly. "Some pine limbs. Didn't think it would smoke this much, though." He sucked his singed fingers.

Missy glanced down at the small stack of wood laying near him with a grimace. It was all still green.

"Next time try using something other than fresh pine. Whatever roadkill you're cooking is going to taste like freakin' pine-scented cleaner," she advised.

He grinned. "It'll give it a good flavor. Besides, it was the only wood I had available," he said defensively.

"Speaking of barbecuing, did you ever get rid of that creepy little wood sprite?" She moved back from the thick smoke billowing out of the pit.

Pete scratched his head and grinned sheepishly. "I, ah, I decided to keep it."

Missy and Jake stared at him incredulously. "After all that happened, why in the world would you want to keep that thing?" Jake asked.

Pete explained that when he'd retrieved it from the garbage can, ready to burn it, Mia had spotted it and snatched it out of his hands. She told him she'd had an identical totem from Wendy that was lost in the fire that had destroyed her home.

"She wanted the damn thing for some reason, and I couldn't tell her no. She keeps it in her room by the window. Still creeps me out a little, just having it in the house," he said, leading them inside.

In the spare crib they kept at Pete's, Missy lay Belinda down, freshly fed and already snoozing.

Pete poured them glasses of cold sun tea he'd made earlier and got them seated around his small kitchen table. Grabbing a large serving plate, he went outside to retrieve the "mystery meat" from the grill.

He hustled back with the plate filled with the steaming *whatever*, placing it on the table. Missy had been right. It smelled a lot like pine-flavored cleaner.

"I'm afraid to ask, but what is this we're about to eat?" She did ask, anyway.

Pete grinned, forking some of the meat onto their plates.

"Try it and tell me what you think," he gave her a mischievous wink.

Missy looked at her plate, then back at Pete and hesitated. "If I find out this is possum or some other exotic critter, *you* may be an 'endangered species,' Bud," she threatened, taking a small bite and chewing.

"Not bad—but is this white meat or dark?" she asked, swallowing.

"Not sure. They're called 'Rocky Mountain Oysters.' I never had 'em before, myself," he said with a straight face.

Jake smirked, trying hard not to laugh. Seeing him, Missy stopped chewing.

"Okay, what the hell are 'Rocky Mountain Oysters?'" she demanded.

Jake cleared his throat, "Uh, they're bull testicles, Missy. They're considered a delicacy in the south." He snorted with laughter.

"Eww!" she said. Disgusted, she spit the rest into her napkin. Jake and Pete thought that was hilarious; they were laughing so hard, tears streamed down their cheeks.

"Well, *we're* not in the freakin' south. And *you're* both assholes," she shoved her plate away.

Then, they heard a car pull up outside. Pete said, "That must be Kris and Mia. Kris called earlier and said they'd be in early tonight."

"Oh—and by the way, Missy, that's just plain old yard-bird on your plate." He rose with a grin, wiping his eyes.

Missy had lost her appetite. "I'll remember this the next time I make you my 'lasagna surprise,' Bud," she smirked.

Pete's grin disappeared. He really liked her lasagna surprise. *Crap!* He realized he'd be paying for this prank. She turned her glare on Jake, who steadfastly avoided her gaze, staring down at his plate.

The front door opened, and Kris followed Mia inside, with Scraps leading the way.

Kris sniffed the air. "Pete's been burning meat again."

Mia wrinkled her nose. "Smells like 'Mr. Clean,' with piquant hints of burned feathers."

"More like 'Pine-Sol,'" Missy grumbled, as she and Jake got up to give them each a hug. "Congratulations to both of you on the official adoption," Missy beamed. They nodded their thanks.

KRIS HAD SOLD HER HOME in Taos and rented a small, one-story house in Joseph. She'd been offered the sheriff's job *pro tem*, after she terminated the 'cannibal killer,' as the papers had nicknamed the dead teen. Her decision to move had been an easy one. She'd fallen in love with the majestic beauty of the forest and the surrounding mountains—and, of course, with Mia—so, she had happily accepted the job. She wanted Mia to stay close to the brother she'd never known she had.

During their continued investigation at Kurt Kozer's mansion, Lt. Flowers and the Boulder PD had discovered the location of the three missing girls, along with Mia's own grandmother, Lily. Their skeletal remains were found floating in steel barrels of hydrochloric acid in the mansion's basement, buried under a shallow layer of concrete. Kurt Kozer had been proved a certifiable lunatic and a serial murderer, and his lover, Max Stryker, was found equally guilty.

In the settlement of Mia's grandfather's estate, the court had awarded Mia sole ownership of all his property. She was now heir and CEO of the Kozey Kitten Cat Food Company. One of the first things she'd done was transfer all the remaining money their dad had left in Taos to Pete, who had been amazed by her generosity.

Mia had started taking accelerated online classes to finish high school. She'd also begun laser treatments in Portland for the birthmark on her cheek. Although it would never disappear completely, with a little makeup, it was now barely visible. Soon, she would be going to the college of her choice to study medicine—to become a doctor, a healer. That was, after all, her calling. In the meantime, she teleconferenced with the other Kozey Kitten company execs when important decisions had to be made. She'd found she had an innate talent for managing people. She had a private helicopter and pilot on call but rarely used them. She hated flying.

Mia had not seen Wendy since that horrific night at Jake and Missy's. Nights when she couldn't sleep, she sometimes wondered just who or what the girl really was. She'd kept the little wood sprite. She didn't know why, but something about it still intrigued her.

After all, despite all the misery and heartache Wendy had instigated in her life, now, Mia recognized that the strange girl/creature had also led her to discover a new family—the gentle, goofy brother she'd never known, and a tough but caring cop who loved her enough to assume the role of her mother. Missy and Jake had become her surrogate aunt and uncle. Jinx often allowed her light strokes on his head and even tolerated—occasionally—the playful Scraps. Mia sighed contentedly. She was truly blessed. They were her tribe now.

Smiling at everyone, Mia sat and chowed down on pine-flavored yard-bird with her new family.

THANKS FOR READING this book. If you enjoyed it, I'd appreciate your leaving an honest review with the store where you bought it, through Draft2digital.com, or send it to my email, info@jamesdobiethrillers.com.

Don't miss out!

Visit the website below and you can sign up to receive emails whenever James Dobie publishes a new book. There's no charge and no obligation.

https://books2read.com/r/B-A-TZLV-GIGRC

BOOKS 2 READ

Connecting independent readers to independent writers.

About the Author

James Dobie published his first thriller/mystery novel in 2022. He has now finished his draft of the eighth, final book in his *Wallowa Lake Thrillers* series, five of which are yet unpublished. **The Wood Sprite,** published as an eBook on 10/31/2023, is thesecond of these, a standalone sequel to his first, **The Wailing,** followed in 2024 by **Angel of Oregon**. A native Texan, James lives in Austin, where he creates imaginative psychological/paranornal novels. His heroes are often defiantly different females. To relax, he plays rock guitar.

Read more at jamesdobiethrillers.com.